Las Vegas Nights

CAT SCHIELD

MILLS &
BOON

First Published in Great Britain 2016
By Mills & Boon, an imprint of HarperCollins*Publishers*
1 London Bridge Street, London, SE1 9GF

LAS VEGAS NIGHTS © 2016 Harlequin Books S. A.

At Odds with the Heiress, A Merger by Marriage and *A Taste of Temptation* were first published in Great Britain by Harlequin (UK) Limited.

At Odds with the Heiress © 2014 Catherine Schield
A Merger by Marriage © 2014 Catherine Schield
A Taste of Temptation © 2014 Catherine Schield

ISBN: 978-0-263-92093-2

05-1216

Our policy is to use papers that are natural, renewable and recyclable products and made from wood grown in sustainable forests.The logging and manufacturing processes conform to the legal environmental regulations of the country of origin.

Printed and bound in Spain
by CPI, Barcelona

Cat Schield has been reading and writing romance since high school. Although she graduated from college with a BA in business, her idea of a perfect career was writing books for Mills & Boon. And now, after winning the Romance Writers of America 2010 Golden Heart Award for series contemporary romance, that dream has come true. Cat lives in Minnesota with her daughter, Emily, and their Burmese cat. When she's not writing sexy, romantic stories for Mills & Boon Desire, she can be found sailing with friends on the St Croix river or in more exotic locales like the Caribbean and Europe. She loves to hear from readers. Find her at www.catschield.com. Follow her on Twitter, @catschield.

AT ODDS WITH
THE HEIRESS

BY
CAT SCHIELD

To Diane, Rose and Kevin.
Thanks for all your support through the years.
Researching Vegas wouldn't have been
as fun without you!

One

Logan Wolfe slowed his stride as he entered the fifth floor executive office, taking a moment to appreciate the feminine tableau silhouetted against the backdrop of the Las Vegas Strip. Although all three Fontaine sisters were brunettes of a similar height and bone structure, they could not have been less alike in attitude, style and background.

The three were half sisters who'd known nothing of each other until their common father, Ross Fontaine, died five years ago. When their grandfather, Henry Fontaine, chairman and CEO of the multibillion-dollar Fontaine Hotels and Resorts, found out that Ross had two illegitimate daughters, he tracked them down and brought them into the family fold. They'd both changed their last names to Fontaine and accepted important roles in the company in order to participate in a contest, devised by their grandfather, to see which of his three heirs would run the Fontaine empire when he retired.

"Good morning, Logan," Violet Fontaine called, waving him over. "Grandpa, Logan has joined us."

"Good morning, Logan." Henry Fontaine's deep voice sounded from the speakerphone. He was based in New York City where the company had their corporate office and kept in touch with his granddaughters through a weekly conference call.

"Good morning, Mr. Fontaine. I hope I'm not intruding."

"Not at all," the CEO said. "In fact, I have to run to another meeting. Violet, dear, once again, I'm sorry for your loss. Call me if there's anything I can do for you."

"Thank you, Grandfather."

As Harper Fontaine pushed the button that ended the call, Violet gestured to the empty chair beside her. Logan sat down and gave Violet's hand a sympathetic squeeze.

"I was sorry to hear about Tiberius. How are you holding up?"

Her eyes brimmed with unshed tears. "Even though we all knew he had heart problems, it was still such a shock. He was a live wire. His energy never seemed to stop. I figured he'd live forever."

Logan had been friends with Violet for seven years, since he and his twin brother, Lucas, had decided to expand their growing security company to Las Vegas. Violet was the grounded middle sister who had a girl-next-door charm. Her mother, Suzanne, had been a showgirl at one time, but after a brief affair with Ross Fontaine and the birth of her daughter, she'd gone to work for Tiberius Stone, owner of the Lucky Heart Hotel and Casino. Twenty years her senior, Tiberius had fallen in love with Suzanne and they'd moved in together. Growing up, Violet had shadowed Tiberius around his hotel and by the time she graduated high school she knew more about running a casino than people twice her age.

In fact, Tiberius Stone was the reason the three sisters were solemn this morning. Violet's surrogate father had been found dead of an apparent heart attack in his office at the Lucky Heart the day before.

As Violet dabbed at her eyes, Harper spoke up. "Have you had breakfast, Logan?"

The Fontaine sisters met every Wednesday morning for breakfast at one of the three luxury hotels they managed for their grandfather. Sitting side by side on the Las Vegas Strip, each property was a unique reflection of the sister who ran it. This morning, they were enjoying breakfast at Fontaine Ciel, Harper's property and the newest jewel in the Fontaine crown. Taking a cue from the French word for sky, Harper had designed her sixty-story tower to showcase panoramic views of the Strip. In the most expensive suites, high above the city, eighteen-foot walls of windows were designed to give guests a sense that they were floating just below a dome of intense blue. The signature color was echoed everywhere in the two-billion-dollar hotel.

"Thanks. I've already eaten." He'd been up for three hours already. First his morning workout. A touch-base meeting with Lucas and then the trip to Fontaine Ciel to check the progress of the team testing the security system his company had installed in the soon-to-open hotel. "But I'll take a cup of green tea if Violet doesn't mind sharing."

"There's more than enough for two." Violet's hazel eyes were warm as she filled an empty cup and nudged it over to him. "It's good to see that someone besides me appreciates the virtues of green tea." She looked pointedly at the sister to her left.

"Right," Scarlett murmured, speaking up for the first time. "Heaven forbid Logan would try anything that's bad for him."

Scarlett Fontaine, voluptuous, charismatic and just plain

sexy, had a knack for getting under Logan's skin. In his opinion, the breathtakingly beautiful former actress was the last person who should be running a billion-dollar hotel and casino. Without a college degree or business experience, she relied on her abundant charm to get things done, and it rubbed Logan the wrong way how much she'd accomplished with such techniques.

She popped a bite of sugary pastry into her mouth. Her soft murmur of enjoyment made the hair on Logan's arms stand up. He was a millisecond too slow to brace against the shock wave of awareness. Compelling and unwelcome, lust rushed through him, leaving a destructive tangle of longing and fury in its wake.

From the moment he'd entered the room, he'd done his best to ignore the once-popular child star. Being near her aggravated his composure. She exuded sexual energy the way Harper projected professionalism and Violet radiated optimism. Many times Logan had watched Scarlett shake up a roomful of men by simply appearing in a doorway. That he was similarly affected despite his best efforts to remain immune pissed him off.

He liked things that he could control. Computer systems. Fast cars. Any risks he took were carefully calculated to result in the best possible outcome. "Chance favors the prepared mind" was a motto he lived by. Scarlett would counter with "Fortune favors the bold."

"I've tried plenty of things that are bad for me," he retorted. Avoiding the allure of her witchy green eyes didn't make him immune to their impact. "I like living a healthy lifestyle. Both physically and mentally."

Scarlett gestured with her chin in Violet's direction. "You two are perfect for each other."

Logan agreed. He wanted a woman who matched him. Someone who shared his views about healthy living and maintaining a balance between work and home. Not a fiery siren who would turn his routines upside down and rock his world.

Violet shook her head, the melancholy in her eyes clearing for the moment. "We're too much alike. We'd bore each other to death. No. I think Logan needs someone who will challenge him." Violet got to her feet and aimed a wicked grin at Scarlett. "Someone like you."

There was a slight hesitation before Scarlett's dismissive laugh. Logan cursed his curiosity as he watched the exchange. What had caused the delayed reaction? His pulse spiked. He sat back with crossed arms and watched Violet exit the room. The pause didn't mean Scarlett had considered the idea. She'd never given him any reason to believe she suffered the same sexual attraction that plagued him. Quite the reverse.

In fact, Logan wasn't sure she was interested in any of the men who pursued her. She doled out flirtation like candy that her admirers gobbled up, all the while keeping them at arm's length. Which made them all the more determined to have her.

For the past five years, since she'd left her acting career behind in Los Angeles and moved to Las Vegas to run Fontaine Richesse, Logan had watched her disappoint one suitor after another. He'd decided she was a coldhearted woman who enjoyed tormenting men, and kept his own desires firmly in check. A challenge when she took great pleasure in teasing him.

Shifting his focus to what had brought him to Harper's office this morning, he gave her an accounting of what he'd found during his consultation with his team regarding her security system.

"There won't be any problem having the cameras adjusted before your soft opening," he concluded.

"Good." She'd been making notes as he spoke. "One less thing to worry about." She glanced at her watch. "If there's nothing else, I have a meeting in ten minutes." A line appeared between her brows as she muttered, "That's providing he bothers to show up this time."

"Actually, I did have one more thing," Logan said. "A favor, actually."

He caught Scarlett's sudden interest in his peripheral vision. She leaned her elbows on the table and watched intently. He would have preferred to make his request to Harper in private, but with her hotel opening only ten days away, her time was limited.

"My niece is in town for the rest of the summer and I wondered if she could shadow you for a couple weeks. Observe a businesswoman in action."

Harper, the oldest of the three women by a year, was Ross Fontaine's only legitimate child. She had the training and the ambition to take over for her grandfather when he stepped down in two years. Harper's mother came from old East Coast money and had insisted her daughter be raised in New York City and educated at an Ivy League school. Her style was elegant and professional, from her smooth chignon to her black designer pumps.

"You're the perfect role model," he finished.

"The perfect role model," Scarlett echoed, her throaty voice rich with laughter. "The ultimate professional."

Logan glared at her, realizing he'd laid it on a bit thick. But the task his sister and brother-in-law had handed him was outside of Logan's expertise.

"I'd love to help," Harper retorted. "As soon as the hotel opens."

"I was hoping you could start showing her the ropes sooner."

"I don't know how I can...." Harper sent a hopeful look in Scarlett's direction. "What about you?"

"My schedule is wide-open," Scarlett said, her gaze as steady and watchful as a psychiatrist's. "I'd be happy to help."

This was not at all what Logan had in mind. His relationship with Harper was professional and cordial. What happened between him and Scarlett could only be called acrimonious. His niece was already a troublesome seventeen-year-old. Under Scarlett's influence, the girl would become completely unmanageable.

"Unless Logan doesn't think I'm role-model material," Scarlett continued when he didn't immediately jump on her offer. Her ability to read his mind with unnerving accuracy gave her an unwelcome advantage over him.

"Don't be ridiculous." Harper appeared oblivious to her sister's subtext. "Besides, your hotel is operational. She'll get a much better sense of how things run. Now, if you two will excuse me, I have an internationally famous pain in the ass to meet with."

Logan stared after Harper, cursing his bad timing. He should never have brought up his problem within earshot of Scarlett.

"Tell me about your niece," Scarlett prompted.

"I don't need your help." Being subtle was not the way to handle Scarlett.

"No," she said in a sugarcoated tone, "you don't *want* my help." She added coffee to her cup, lifted the rim to her mouth and blew across the surface. "There's a difference."

Captivated by the small O formed by her bright red lips, he took far too long to respond to her gibe. "Very well," he agreed. "I don't want your help."

"How old is she?"

Logan took a couple seconds to grind his teeth. Despite

being trapped between frustration with his niece and the woman sitting across the table from him, he told her what she wanted to know. "Madison is seventeen. She's my sister's youngest." And in the past three months had driven Paula and her husband, Randolph, past the edge of patience.

"Madison? As in the capital of Wisconsin?"

"As in Madison Avenue." Logan winced. "Her father owns a large ad agency in New York City."

And Paula was a partner in a prestigious law firm. Madison had inherited both brains and ambition from her parents. She'd graduated second in her class and had been accepted to four prestigious universities. If she'd wanted, she could've swiftly climbed any corporate ladder she chose. Instead, to both her parents' horror, the teenager had decided to become an actress.

"And he's hoping she'll follow in his footsteps? From your sour expression I'm guessing that's not what she wants to do."

"She's refusing to go to college. She turns eighteen in two weeks and is determined to move to L.A."

Scarlett's curiosity sharpened. "What's wrong with L.A.?"

"It's not the city, it's her chosen career path."

"Instead of me dragging it out of you one question at a time, why don't you just tell me what's really going on. And why you wanted her to shadow Harper."

Sharing family troubles with outsiders went against the grain, but he desperately needed help. Anyone's help. Even Scarlett's.

"Madison ran away to Los Angeles over spring break. She's determined to become an actress."

Scarlett's full lips twitched. Over the years he'd noticed how well she could read people. Normally he concealed how easily she riled his temper and his hormones, but in this case his sarcastic tone had given too much away.

"The scandal that must have caused your family," she deadpanned.

"She's only seventeen."

"And she could've fallen into someone's evil clutches."

Logan didn't appreciate that she was having fun at his expense. "Thankfully that didn't happen."

"What did happen?"

Not a damn thing. Madison had moved in with a boy she'd met in New York City the summer before and signed up to take an acting class. She'd even gotten a callback for a commercial.

"Her father found her before she got into trouble and brought her back to New York."

"Why don't they just let her follow her dream?" Scarlett poured herself a little more coffee. "Being an actress isn't the worst job in the world."

"Paula and Ran don't think it's the proper career for a girl as bright and capable of going places as Madison," he explained. "They want her to go to college and get a degree."

Other than a brief narrowing of her eyes, Scarlett's expression remained tranquil. "I didn't go to college and I think I'm doing all right."

So said the former child actress whose exploits had kept the paparazzi awash in scandalous photographs for several years. Scarlett's support of Madison's acting dreams was exactly why he hadn't asked her for help.

"You also had a billionaire grandfather bring you to Las Vegas and hand you a hotel to run."

He didn't realize how insulting that sounded until her seductive charm vanished in a flash of annoyance. For the first time ever, Logan believed he'd been granted a glimpse of the genuine woman beneath the mask. And it heightened his already keen awareness of her desirability. He inhaled slowly and let his breath leak out as he wrestled his libido under control. As his blood continued to pulse hot and slow through his veins, he had to repeat his breathing exercise.

Damnation. Why the hell did she have to be so utterly gorgeous?

She had flawless pale skin, dramatic bone structure and a body built to drive a man insane: large firm breasts, tiny waist, lean long legs. The way she moved invited everyone to stare. And her mouth… Her lush, red lips were crafted for kissing.

"You're right," she drawled, her temper giving the words a sarcastic bite. "It's unrealistic to think I would be running Fontaine Richesse if Grandfather hadn't gotten this crazy idea that his granddaughters should compete for the CEO job. I'd still be in L.A., auditioning for roles, working when I could and waiting for the part that would reenergize my career. But I would still be a success and I would be happy."

"Look, I only meant that you never would have been considered as Fontaine Richesse's general manager if you hadn't been Ross's daughter."

For the first time in five years, she'd let him see how much he'd upset her. But all too quickly, she regained her equilibrium. "And you've made it perfectly clear you don't think I belong here."

"I'm not sure you do."

She looked astonished. "Thank you."

"For what?"

"For being honest for once. You've looked down on me from the moment we met." The directness of her gaze demanded he respond with frankness, but his mother had not raised him to insult women.

"I don't look down on you." That wasn't entirely true.

Despite the hotel's success, he didn't think she was in Violet and Harper's league when it came to running a company the size of Fontaine Hotels and Resorts.

"But you don't approve of me, either," she prompted.

"It isn't that I don't approve."

"What is it, then?" She battered him with a determined stare. "You're friendly with my sisters." She paused a beat. "You must have something against me."

"I have nothing against you."

"You believe both Violet and Harper have what it takes to be become the CEO of Fontaine Hotels." She paused for confirmation, but he gave her nothing but stony silence. "And you don't think I do." Again she'd read his mind. When he still didn't respond, her eyes warmed to soft moss. "They've both worked exceptionally hard to get to where they are. I'm a clueless actress. You feel protective of them." She regarded him with a half smile. "You are a good friend, but you don't have to worry. I don't have any business experience, which means I have no chance of besting either of my well-educated, incredibly capable siblings. Grandfather was merely playing fair when he included me in the contest." Her husky voice raked across his nerve endings. She was putting herself down to prevent him from doing so. "I'm so glad we've cleared that up."

They'd cleared up nothing. He was no more comfortable around her or capable of being friendly with her than he'd been five minutes earlier. But what more could he say? He wasn't about to tell her that she'd bewitched him.

"Getting back to your niece and her determination to avoid college," Scarlett continued, her manner becoming brisk and efficient. "What were you hoping she'd discover by shadowing Harper for a couple weeks?"

"That the business world wasn't as much of a drag as she thinks it will be."

Scarlett had a musical laugh, rich with amusement. "And you chose Harper, the workaholic, for her to shadow? She'll die of boredom before the first day is over. She'd do better with Violet." She paused and tapped a spoon on the pristine white tablecloth. "Of course, with Tiberius's death, this isn't a good time for that."

"I agree."

Which brought them back to her. The reality hung unspoken between them.

"Why don't you show her all the interesting aspects of your security business?"

She'd struck right to the heart of his troubles. "Every time I try to engage Madison, she rolls her eyes and starts texting." He made no attempt to hide his frustration. "I thought maybe someone outside the family would have better luck."

Scarlett scrutinized Logan's grim expression. Figuring she'd probably annoyed him enough for one day, she held back a smart-aleck remark about the situation requiring a feminine touch. "You're probably right to think she'll be in a better frame of mind to listen to a disinterested third party."

A disinterested third party with a master's degree in business like Harper, or ten years of hotel and casino management experience like Violet. Not a former child star who had none of the skills required to run a world-class hotel. Logan had been right about that, but his low opinion of her stung. Not that he was wrong. Or alone in his estimation of her failings. She was sure that the same thought had crossed the minds of a dozen hotel and casino owners in Las Vegas. But she hated his disdain more than all the others put together.

Uncomfortable with the direction her thoughts had taken her, Scarlett glanced around her sister's office. The room was a little over the top for her taste. It was almost as if Harper had been feeling insecure when she'd brought in the expensive furnishings and accessories. Which was ridiculous. If anyone could build and run the most successful Fontaine hotel in Las Vegas and become the next CEO, it was Henry Fontaine's only legitimate granddaughter.

"Of course, if you want someone to tell her how hard it is to make it as an actress in Hollywood, I'm your girl." Scarlett tossed her napkin onto the table. "When did you wish her reprogramming to begin?"

Logan scowled at her. It was one of several unhappy expressions he wore whenever they occupied the same space. "If you're not going to take this seriously, I'll wait until Harper or Violet is free."

"I think you're a little too desperate for that." Drawing upon a fifteen-year acting career, Scarlett slapped on a winning smile and stood. "I may not be your first choice for this project, but I'm what you're going to get."

"Fine."

Logan got to his feet and towered over her. "I'll drop Madison off this afternoon at your office. Say, around one?"

"I'll be waiting." She moved away, eager to escape his overwhelming presence, but hadn't taken more than four steps before his hand caught her wrist.

"Thank you." Logan's fingers were gentle on her skin. He'd never touched her before. The contact sizzled through her like lightning. Unnerved by the strength of her reaction, she twisted free with more vigor than necessary. "It's too late for you to start being nice to me, Logan."

His deep brown eyes developed a layer of ice. "Fine."

He scanned her from her messy updo to her hot-pink toenails, missing nothing in between. Her heart thumped like a runner's feet against the pavement and tension knotted her shoulders. Every time she got within fifty feet of the guy, she turned into an excited teenager with an enormous crush.

And he seemed completely immune.

At six feet two inches tall, the muscled hunk had a commanding presence. He wore his wavy black hair long enough to graze his collar. Bold eyebrows, a strong nose and a square jaw didn't make him classically handsome, but they combined to produce a face worth staring at. His chiseled lips lingered in her daydreams even though when she was around they were always set in a grim line.

"Can you at least wear something business-y?" he demanded, a muscle jumping in his cheek. "Madison needs to spend time with a professional career woman."

Holding perfectly still beneath his criticism was challenging as a combination of sizzling heat and disquieting tingles attacked her composure. In a flowing ankle-length dress cut low in front, and strappy gold sandals, Scarlett knew she looked more like a guest of her Las Vegas hotel than the manager.

"I don't do business-y." She turned on her four-inch heels and strode out of the office, fleeing from feelings of inadequacy.

With his long legs, Logan had little trouble keeping up. "Surely you have something in your vast wardrobe that looks professional."

"What makes you think I have a vast wardrobe?"

"In five years I've never seen you wear the same thing twice."

Stunned that he'd noticed what she wore, much less remembered, Scarlett spared him the briefest glance. "I'm flattered that you've been paying attention," she remarked, using her most flirtatious manner to hide her decidedly smitten response to his observation.

"Don't be. Part of my job as a security expert is to pay attention to details."

"Well, aren't you a silver-tongued devil," she quipped, stepping into the elevator that would take her to the second floor and the skyways that linked the sisters' three Fontaine hotels.

Logan's sleeve brushed her bare arm as he reached past her to punch the button for the lobby. As the doors closed, he lingered in her space, awakening her senses to the coiled strength lurking in his muscles.

Before she considered the imprudence of her action, she poked her finger into his firm abs. "You sure know what to say to make a girl feel special."

She expected him to back off. He'd always kept his distance before. To her shock, he shifted closer. Such proximity to his straightforward masculinity had a disturbing effect on her equilibrium. She had to fight to keep from leaning against him for support.

"Don't you ever get tired of acting?" he mused, his casual tone not matching the dangerous tension emanating from him.

Gathering a shaky breath, she forced the corners of her mouth upward. "What do you mean, acting?"

"The various women you become to fool men into accepting whatever fantasy you want them to believe."

Was he referring to the facade she used to keep Logan in the dark about the way he stirred her body and soul? He was completely mad if he believed she was going to give up her one defense against him.

"Don't you mean the one I use to manipulate them to my will?" she taunted, her breathless tone coming easily under the influence of Logan's domineering presence.

Scarlett prided herself on being able to read men. Usually it was pretty easy. Most of them enjoyed being powerful and having beautiful women available for their pleasure. Even the ones who appeared as sweet as lambs harbored a little caveman inside them.

Logan didn't fall neatly into the bucket where she lumped the rest of his gender. He seemed genuinely immune to her wiles and that's why she provoked him at every opportunity. She was challenged by his lack of physical attraction to her. And in a twisted way, because she knew he'd never step across the line, his indifference gave her the freedom to let her sensuality run free. It was quite liberating.

"One of these days someone is going to see past your flirtation to the truth," Logan warned, his voice a husky growl.

She arched her eyebrows. "Which is what?"

"That what you need isn't some tame lapdog."

"I don't?"

"No." Espresso eyes watched her with lazy confidence. "What you need is a man who will barge right past your defenses and drive you wild."

"Don't be ridiculous," she retorted, struggling to keep her eyes off his well-shaped lips and her mind from drifting into the daydream of being kissed silly by the imposing Logan Wolfe.

"You can lie to yourself all you want," he said. "But don't bother lying to me."

It wasn't until he captured her fingers that she realized she'd flattened her palm against his rib cage. She tugged to free her hand, but he tightened his grip.

The sexual tension he roused in her went from simmer to roiling boil. "Let me go."

"You started it."

She wasn't completely sure that was true. "What's gotten into you today?"

His lips kicked up at the corners. "You know, I think this is the first time I've ever seen you lose your cool. I like it."

How had he turned the tables on her in such a short time? She pressed her thighs together, but this action made the ache worse, not better.

What you need is a man who will barge right past your defenses and drive you wild. Thank goodness he'd never find out just how much she liked the sound of that.

"I'm really not interested in what you—"

She never had a chance to finish the thought. Before she guessed his intention, Logan lowered his lips to hers and cut off her denial. Slow and deliberate, his hot mouth moved across hers. Her startled murmur of surprise became a weak moan of surrender as she opened to his tongue slicking over the seam of her lips.

Canting her head to give him better access to her mouth, she slid her fingers into his hair and held on for dear life as her world shifted its orbit. If his intention had been to drive her wild, he achieved his goal in less than three seconds. Every nerve in her body cried out for his touch as he cupped the side of her neck and let his tongue duel with hers.

Scarlett wanted to cry out as she experienced the delicious pleasure of his broad chest crushing her breasts, but he'd stolen her breath. Then the sound of the doors opening reached them both at the same time. Logan broke the kiss. His chest heaved as he sucked in air. Eyes hard and unreadable, he scrutinized her face, cataloging every crack running through her composure. Scarlett felt as exposed as if she'd stepped into her casino wearing only her underwear.

Breathless, she asked, "Did that feel like acting?"

His hands slid away from her in a slow, torturous caress. He stepped back, used his foot to block the doors from closing and gestured her toward the hallway beyond the elevator.

One dark eyebrow lifted. "Needs more investigating before I can say one way or another."

Two

While his brain throbbed with questions he couldn't answer, Logan drove his black Escalade down Fontaine Ciel's parking ramp and sped toward Wolfe Security. The taste of Scarlett lingered on his tongue. The bitter bite of strong coffee. The sweetness of the sugar he'd licked off the corner of her mouth from the Danish she'd eaten.

July sunshine ricocheted off car windows and punished his vision. Despite the sunglasses perched on his nose, he squinted. Even though it was only a little after nine in the morning, it was already too damn hot. He tugged at his collar and turned the SUV's air conditioner on full blast. Sweat made his shirt cling to him beneath his suit coat. Okay, maybe not all the heat bombarding him came from the temperature outside. Beneath his skin, his blood raged, fierce and unquenchable.

Kissing Scarlett had been a huge mistake. Colossal. If he'd had it bad for her before she'd pressed that sensational body of hers against him, he was now completely obsessed. But it was never going to go any further.

Needs more investigating…

What the hell was wrong with him? Giving her a taste of her own tricks had backfired. Not only had he promised to kiss her again, he'd also revealed that he was interested in pursuing her.

He slammed on his brakes and cursed as an out-of-towner cut him off. His phone buzzed. He cued the Escalade's Bluetooth and answered.

"Got your message about Tiberius," Lucas Wolfe said. The poor connection and background noise made his brother hard to understand. "Sorry to hear the old guy's dead."

"I just left the Fontaine sisters. Violet's pretty shaken up."

"I'm sorry for Violet," Lucas muttered. "Did you get a chance to ask her about Tiberius's files?"

Impatience gusted through Logan. "Geez, Lucas. The guy just died."

"And if those files come to light a lot of people both in Vegas and beyond are at risk of having their lives ruined. She could be in danger."

Logan's twin had spent too many years in army intelligence. Lucas saw enemies around every corner. Well, he'd been right to worry on some occasions, maybe even this one. How much dirt could Tiberius Stone have collected over the course of fifty years? In a town dubbed Sin City? A lot.

Logan cursed. "Do you really think they exist?"

"I think he's the J. Edgar Hoover of Vegas."

"I never found any sign of anything in his computers." When Lucas had first gotten wind of Stone's proclivity for information gathering, Logan had hacked into the man's work and personal computers.

"He's old-school," Lucas said. "I'm pretty sure he kept paper copies of everything."

Logan pondered how much information there could be and imagined a large room lined with file cabinets. Where the hell had the old guy stored his papers? The location would have to be secure and accessible. Logan considered. If the data was digital, Wolfe Security would have been the perfect place to keep the information. They had a number of secure servers that their clients used for their most sensitive documents.

"When are you coming back to the States?" Logan asked.

Lucas was in Dubai meeting with a sheikh who had a museum's worth of treasure and art that he wanted displayed in his various homes around the world. The challenge came from his desire for the security to be unobtrusive as well as unbreakable.

"Not sure yet." Lucas's tone darkened. "This job is a lot more complex than I first thought."

"And the daughter?"

"Distracting."

Laughing, Logan hung up with his brother and dialed Violet. He wasn't surprised when the call rolled to voice mail. He left a message asking her to call him back. After that, he put in a couple hours before heading home to have lunch with his niece and break the news that her vacation was officially over.

He found Madison by the pool, her bikini-clad body soaking up the hot Las Vegas sun. She'd isolated herself with a gossip magazine and a pair of headphones and wasn't aware Logan had approached until his shadow fell across her.

"Hey, Uncle Logan, what are you doing home?"

"I thought I'd take you to lunch and then to meet a woman I know."

The resentful expression she'd had since arriving in town three days ago immediately lifted. She leaned forward eagerly. "I didn't know you were seeing someone. Way to go, Uncle Logan."

"I'm not *seeing* her." The kiss flashed through his mind. "She's just someone who has agreed to show you what running a hotel is like."

"Boring." Madison sagged back against the lounge. "When are you and my parents going to realize that I don't want to be stuck in a stupid office? I want to be an actress."

"Your parents are concerned that you haven't explored all the options available to you."

"Like they want me to explore my options. They want me to go to the college of their choice and major in business or get a law degree and become just like them. It's not what I want."

"I didn't know what I wanted at your age."

She smirked as if he'd just made her point. "That's not true. Mom said you spent all your free time messing with your computers. And you started that security software company by the time you were twenty. You were a multimillionaire before you even graduated."

"But I still graduated."

"Whatever. The point is, you were successful because you were really good with computers and it's what you loved to do, not because you have a master's in design engineering."

Logan glared at her. No wonder her parents had shipped her off to him. Bringing her into line with "because I said so" wasn't going to work on an intelligent, determined young woman like Madison.

"Fine, but I still graduated from college." He held up a hand when she started to protest. "Face it, kid, for the next month, you're stuck with me and my opinion on what's best for you. Go shower and I'll take you to my favorite restaurant."

Forty minutes later they slid into a booth at Luigi's. Madison stared around her in disgust.

"This is a pizza place."

"Not just any pizza place. They have the best Italian food outside of Italy."

"I thought you were going to take me somewhere nice."

"This is nice."

She rolled her eyes at him. Once they'd ordered, Madison leaned her arms on the table and began to grill him.

"Who is this woman you're dumping me on?"

"Scarlett Fontaine. She runs Fontaine Richesse. You'll like her. She used to be an actress."

Madison's blue eyes narrowed. "Used to be? As in she failed at it, so now she can tell me what a huge mistake I'm making if I don't go to college?"

"Used to be. As in she now she runs a billion-dollar hotel and casino."

And did a pretty good job at it. Or at least she'd hired people who knew what they were doing.

"What is she, fifty?" Madison scoffed. "There's plenty of time for me to come up with a backup plan in case acting doesn't pan out."

"She's thirty-one." It startled him to realize he knew how old she was. And that her next birthday was a month away.

"So young? Why'd she give up so fast?"

"I'm assuming because she was offered the chance of a lifetime."

"Running a hotel?"

"One of Las Vegas's premier hotels."

But Madison looked unconvinced. "She's nothing more than a quitter."

"That's not how I would characterize her."

Forty-five minutes later, they entered Scarlett's hotel and crossed to the elevators that would take them to the executive offices on the third floor. When the doors opened, Logan was startled by the man who stepped out. He and John Malcolm exchanged a quick greeting before the lawyer headed off.

Puzzling over the presence of Tiberius Stone's lawyer in Scarlett's hotel, Logan absently pointed Madison toward the restroom and told her where to find him when she was done. Seconds later, he entered Scarlett's office and caught her sitting behind her desk, full lips pursed, her attention on her computer monitor. Logan noticed immediately that she'd changed her clothes. Now she was wearing a sleeveless lime blouse with a ruffled front that drew attention to her full breasts and showed off her toned arms. She'd left her long hair down and it spilled across her shoulders in a honey-streaked brown curtain that made his fingers itch to slide through it. He sunk the treacherous digits into his pocket and strolled up to her desk.

"I didn't realize you and Tiberius shared a lawyer," he said, skipping a more traditional hello.

She stood up when he spoke. Instinctively he appreciated how the slim black skirt skimmed her lean hips. The outfit was sexy and professional, a delectable one-two punch to his gut.

"We don't." She fetched a manila envelope from her desk. "He brought me this. It's from Tiberius."

"What's in it?"

Surprise flickered in her green eyes at his sharp tone. "I haven't opened it yet. It's probably just something he wrote to say goodbye. He was a great guy. I wasn't as close to him as Violet, but we hung out a lot. He gave me the inside scoop on this town. Who I could trust. Who to watch out for." Abruptly she stopped speaking. Cocked her head. "Why are you so curious?"

"Tiberius collected information on people." Logan wasn't sure how much he wanted to tell her. Damn the wily old man and his insatiable curiosity.

"What sort of information?"

"Secrets."

Her eyes widened. "Dirt?" She turned the envelope over in her hand. When she glanced up and caught his gaze on her, her throaty laugh erupted. "And you think he had something on me." Not a question. A statement. "I'm sorry to disappoint you, but I don't have a closet filled with skeletons just waiting to be exposed." She sobered and leveled a sharp glance his way. "Are you this cynical about everyone or just me?"

"Everyone."

"Not Harper and not Violet." Her tone was mild enough, but accusations shimmered in her eyes. "You trust them."

Meaning, he didn't trust her. Well, he didn't. She was a professional actress whose talent for role play spilled into her personal life. He had a hard time reading her and that made him suspicious of everything she said or did.

"They've never given me a reason not to trust them." His mother would scold him for such a blunt statement. She'd raised both her boys to treat women with gentleness and respect. It was just that Scarlett's wicked eyes and secretive smile got under his skin.

"What have I ever done to you?"

She had him there. His prejudice against her stemmed from the way she affected him. Was it fair to blame her for the way his skin prickled when she brushed against him? Or how the scent of her, light and floral, made his heart slam against his ribs? Or the way his blood flowed hot and carnal through his veins at the sexy sway of her hips as she sauntered through her hotel.

"It's not what you've done." He bit off each word. "It's because you like to play games."

Amusement sparkled in her eyes. "Games can be fun."

Besieged by provocative images of her dressed in black lingerie and thigh-high boots, armed with a riding crop, he swallowed hard. Around the same time she'd shown up in Las Vegas, an episode of a popular crime series had aired. She'd done a guest spot where she'd played the owner of a fantasy club. Ever since he'd seen her on that show, the erotic snapshot had a habit of popping into his head at the most inopportune times.

"I don't play games." Annoyance made his voice gruff.

"Then what would you call that kiss in the elevator?" A challenge flared in her expression. "You kissed me to make a point. How is that not playing games?"

Rather than admit that he'd kissed her because he'd been unable to control his longing to do so, Logan countered with, "What point was I trying to make?"

While Logan awaited her answer with eyebrows raised, Scarlett kicked herself for letting him get to her again. Why couldn't they have a civilized conversation? Okay, she admitted, it was fun to get him all riled up. More so now that she knew that frustrating him led to impulsive kisses. Hot, passionate ones. What would happen if she really exasperated him? Anticipation quivered through her.

She blew out a breath. "That I need a man like you in my life." To her delight, she'd surprised him.

"That's not why I kissed you."

"Sure it is. And I quote—'What you need is a man who

will barge right past your defenses and drive you wild.' Isn't that what you were trying to do when you kissed me?"

Lips tight, he stared at her for a long minute. "I was demonstrating my point, not auditioning for the job."

While her heart hopped wildly in her chest, she gave what she hoped was a nonchalant shrug. "Too bad because you gave a great performance."

Stoic, Logan crossed his arms and indicated the envelope Scarlett held. "Do you know what Tiberius sent you?"

His grave question brought her back to her earlier musings.

"Not yet. Why are you so interested?"

"Lucas thinks Tiberius might have left Violet the files he gathered through the years." Logan shifted his gaze from the envelope to her eyes. "I think he might have left them to you."

"Me?" She glanced at the package in her hand, but her surprise didn't last long. "I suppose that makes sense. We shared a love of Las Vegas history. If his files go back to the fifties, there are probably all sorts of great stories that never made it into the history books." The thought excited her. "It'll make a great addition to my Mob Experience exhibit."

"It's dangerous for you to have those files."

Was that concern turning down Logan's lips and putting a dent in his forehead? She struggled to keep delight from taking over her expression. "Dangerous how?"

"A lot of powerful people have secrets they'd like to keep buried."

This was getting better and better. "I'll bet they would."

He looked none too pleased at her enthusiasm. "Up until now the existence of the files has been nothing but speculation. If anyone gets wind that you have them, someone might decide to come after them." Logan exhaled impatiently. "You might get hurt."

"You're worried about me." Nothing could have prevented her giant smile. "That's so sweet."

He actually growled. "Just because you and I don't get along doesn't mean I want anything bad to happen to you."

"We could get along just fine if you'd stop fighting your feelings for me."

"If you're referring to that kiss in the elevator—"

"That oh-so-steamy kiss in the elevator," she corrected with a smug smile. "And you never did answer my question. Was I acting?"

He regarded her without expression and said nothing.

"Maybe another demonstration would clear up your doubts." She reached out and ran her fingers down his tie.

He snatched her hand in his, eyes blazing. "Damn it, Scarlett."

Before he could complete his thought, a young woman appeared in the doorway. "Hello. I'm Madison."

"Scarlett Fontaine." It was tough taking her eyes off Logan's stormy expression, but she managed. "Nice to meet you," she said, moving out from behind her desk.

"Logan told me all about you."

Amusement twitched Scarlett's lips into a smile. "Really?" She caught his unrelenting gaze and drawled, "*All* about me?"

Logan gave her a tight nod. "I told her that you'd been an actress."

"Not just an actress," she corrected with dramatic flare sure to annoy him. "A star."

"Really?" Now Madison looked interested. "I don't recall seeing you in anything."

Scarlett's smile turned wry. "You probably wouldn't recognize me. I was fifteen when the show ended. But for five crazy years I was Hilary of *That's Our Hilary.*"

"I don't think I ever saw that. Have you been on anything since?"

"Guest appearances here and there. A short-running cable show." Scarlett glanced Logan's way and saw that he was scowling at her again. *Honestly.* What had she done now to earn his disfavor? To distract him, she gave him the envelope. "Here, maybe seeing what's inside will keep you from being so cranky."

"Tiberius left it to you." He tried to hand it back, but she shook her head.

"And not knowing what's inside is bugging you, so open it."

With a harsh exhalation, he slipped his finger beneath the envelope flap and pulled out a packet of papers. A key card slipped to the floor. Madison looked curious as she bent to retrieve it.

"It's a rental agreement for a storage unit," Logan said as he continued looking through the stack of papers. He handed a single sheet to Scarlett.

Scarlett recognized Tiberius's neat handwriting. The letter was addressed to her. As she scanned it, her throat tightened. Damn the old rascal. He had indeed passed his files on to her. She took the key from Madison and studied it.

"A storage unit?" she mused. "Do you suppose there's more than files in there?"

"Possibly. I hope you're not considering going there alone."

He might not like her, but that didn't stop him from feeling protective. She could work with that. "Why not?"

His phone chimed, indicating he'd received a text. Pulling it out of his pocket, he checked the screen. Air slipped between his teeth in an impatient exhalation.

"Something's just come up." He turned to Madison. "I'll be back for you at five."

"Five?" Scarlett echoed doubtfully. "The action doesn't get started around here until much later. You just go ahead and do whatever it is you do and I'll make sure Madison gets home."

"What time?"

"I don't know. Midnight?"

Logan's eyebrows dipped as his niece's expression lit up. "Ten," he countered.

"Seriously?" Madison piped up. "I'm seventeen years old. You don't think I've been out past ten before?"

He looked as if he were chewing glass as he countered, "Ten-thirty."

"I'm almost eighteen."

"*Almost* being the operative word."

Madison rolled her eyes at him. "My birthday's two weeks away."

"Ten-thirty."

"When I turn eighteen you can't tell me what to do."

Scarlett watched the exchange with interest, noticing the way his gaze bounced from her to Madison and back. It was good to see that she wasn't the only female who annoyed him.

"Why don't we say eleven," she offered, voice bright, smile friendly.

Her words stopped Madison's revolt in its tracks. "Perfect."

To Scarlett's surprise, Madison moved to her side and linked arms. An unstoppable female phalanx against Logan. He did not looked pleased.

"Eleven." Logan gave a tight nod. "And keep her out of trouble."

"Stop worrying. She'll be fine."

Scarlett gave Logan's authoritative shoulders and don't-mess-with-me stride one final glance as he headed out of her office. Oxygen returned to the room in a rush with his departure. The man sure knew how to dominate a room. And a woman's hormones.

"Let's start our tour in reservations," Scarlett murmured, gesturing the teenager toward the hallway.

"I thought maybe we could begin in the casino."

Scarlett shook her head, crushing Madison's hopeful expression. "We'll save the best for last."

Two hours later Scarlett had shown Madison around the entire hotel and was heading into the casino when her phone rang. Her heart gave a happy little jolt when she recognized Logan's number. *Stupid. Stupid. Stupid.* The man had given her yet another heaping helping of his bad opinion of her today and she still couldn't shake this idiotic crush she had on him.

"I'm a glutton for punishment," she muttered as she answered the call. "Hello, Logan. The tour's going great in case you're worried."

"You're still at the hotel?"

"Where else would I be?" She paused a beat. "Oh, right, the storage unit."

"You're taking this business with the files too lightly."

Scarlett's gaze followed Logan's niece as she ventured toward a display advertising the opening of the Mob Experience exhibit in a month. "I already promised not to take Madison anywhere near the storage unit."

"It's not just Madison's safety I'm talking about."

A warm glow filled her at his concern. "So, when do you want to go check it out?"

"The sooner the better."

"Tomorrow?"

"That should work."

"What time are you going to pick me up?"

She interpreted his hesitation as dismay.

"You misunderstood me," he said. "*I'm* going to check out the storage shed. Alone."

"You could. But you'll have a difficult time getting in without the key." She let her meaning settle in for a couple seconds before she finished, "So, it's a date."

"It's not a date." The vibration in his tone reminded her of an unhappy rottweiler.

"It could be if you took me to dinner first." As she plied him with her most beguiling voice, Scarlett wondered if the sound she was hearing on the other end was his teeth grinding together.

"I'll pick you up at seven."

Scarlett grinned in triumph. "I'll be counting the hours."

First a kiss, now a date. She couldn't believe her incredible luck. Too bad she didn't gamble or she'd be raking in the winnings. Practically floating across the carpet, she caught up with Madison.

"I can't believe how many people are in here," Madison said as they strolled between the tables. "It's three in the afternoon."

"Most people come to Las Vegas to gamble. Wait until later. It'll really be hopping down here then."

"I like the way the dealers are dressed up as famous movie stars."

"My friend Tiberius told me how back in the fifties it was not unusual to walk through the casino and see Lucille Ball, Debbie Reynolds or the Rat Pack. The stars loved coming here." Scarlett paused, wondering if the seventeen-year-old had any idea who she was talking about, and then saw with relief that she did. "Since I grew up in Hollywood, I thought it made sense for me to bring a little of that glamour back to Las Vegas."

"What a fun idea."

It was at that moment that Scarlett remembered Madison was an aspiring actress. "So much fun that I like getting in on the action myself." She linked her arm through Madison's and steered her toward the elevators. "Let's go up to my suite and I'll show you what I mean."

Ten minutes later, Scarlett threw open the doors to her "special" closet and waited for Madison's reaction.

"Cool."

The fifteen-by-fifteen-foot room was lined with costumes, shoes, wigs and jewelry that Scarlett used to transform herself into various starlets from the fifties and sixties.

"On the weekends I like to get dressed up and wander around the casinos. My high rollers love it and I get to pretend that I'm still an actress." A mild pang of regret came and went.

"You obviously love being one." Madison walked toward the costumes on the far wall. "Why'd you give it up?"

Scarlett watched Madison trail her fingers along a hot-pink replica of the gown worn by Marilyn Monroe when she sang "Diamonds Are a Girl's Best Friend" from the 1953 musical *Gentlemen Prefer Blondes*.

"The simple answer is that when puberty hit I went from a sweet-faced girl-next-door to a bombshell with too many curves." Scarlett stood in front of the mirror and gazed critically at her reflection. "Neither the producers of *That's Our Hilary* nor my not-so-loyal public were ready for Hilary to grow up so fast."

"What happened?"

"They spun off a few secondary characters into a new show and gave Hilary the heave-ho."

"That's terrible."

"That's showbiz." Scarlett skimmed her palms over her hips, thinking about how she'd put on the black skirt to thumb her nose at Logan's suggestion that she dress more professionally. He didn't seem to understand that unless she worked really hard to downplay her allure, her innate sexuality came through whatever she wore.

It's why the parts that came her way after her stint as Hilary were all of a kind. She'd turned down so many offers to play sexy roles that she'd lost count. Being typecast as the bitchy sexual rival of the heroine was not the part she wanted to play. She longed to be taken seriously as an actress, but her agent said none of the casting directors he spoke to could see past her looks to the talent beneath.

"I know my uncle wants you to talk me out of being an actress."

"Aren't you a smart girl." Scarlett caught Madison's gaze in the mirror. "Smart enough to have a plan for what happens if you can't make it in Hollywood?"

Madison looked away. "I'm young. I thought I'd give it a few years. If I don't make it, I can always go to school later."

Scarlett considered how many times she'd heard a fellow actor say something similar. It was hard to give up your dream of making it on the silver screen when a great part was always the next audition away.

"Or you could see if your parents would be okay with you attending college in L.A. while you take acting classes and audition." Scarlett could see that Madison hadn't considered this option. She'd probably been so focused on defying her parents and fighting for the future she wanted that she'd never considered there might be a middle ground. "It might be a lot more work than you intended, but it might also be a way to make everyone happy."

"I'll think about it."

But Scarlett could see the teenager wasn't quite ready to.

"In the meantime, do you want to be Judy Garland in *Summer Stock* or Greta Garbo from *Mata Hari?*"

"How about Marilyn?"

Scarlett laughed. "Not so fast, my young apprentice.

First you need to prove to me you've got the chops to be Marilyn."

"I've got the chops."

"Then you won't have any trouble making a casino full of people believe you're Mata Hari."

"You got that right."

Three

It was ten minutes after eleven, and Logan was pacing from one end of his thirty-foot front porch to the other. There was a pair of rocking chairs where he could sit down and enjoy the flowers cascading from long pots affixed to the railings, but he was too agitated.

Through the Bluetooth receiver in his ear, Logan half listened to his brother muse about Tiberius's files. "So, we were right."

"I'll know for sure tomorrow."

Logan squinted into the dark night as if that could help him see farther. Where the hell were they?

"I don't suppose there's any way she'd just turn the files over to you."

"Not a chance." His irritation spiked as he saw headlights appear at the end of his long driveway.

"Yeah, I forgot how well you two get along." Lucas sounded disgusted. "I don't know what the hell's the matter with you. She's gorgeous and the chemistry between you is off the charts. You'd barely have to lift a finger to charm the key from her."

"Charming people is your job," Logan retorted, stepping off the porch as Scarlett's Audi TT rolled to a stop. "You're late," he snapped as she cut the engine.

"I'm late?" Lucas said in his ear, tone rising in confusion.

Scarlett protested, "By ten minutes."

"You sound too cranky for this to be a booty call," his brother taunted, having heard the female voice. "I take it our rebellious niece wasn't home on time."

"Something like that. Later." He disconnected the call, cutting off his brother's laughter.

Logan frowned as Madison stepped from the car. "What is she wearing?"

"I'm Greta Garbo as Mata Hari," Madison announced, striking a pose, arms out, face in profile, nose lifted to the sky.

Logan surveyed the elaborate headpiece that concealed Madison's blond hair and the sparkling caftan-looking gown that covered her from chin to toes. With her dramatic makeup and solemn expression, his niece was an acceptable Greta Garbo.

But he'd asked Scarlett to steer Madison away from acting, not demonstrate how much fun it could be.

"Doesn't she look great?" Scarlett asked, coming around the front of the car. Also in costume, adorably feminine in a blond wig and pale pink ostrich-feather dress, she gave Logan the briefest of glances before settling her attention on the teenager.

The fondness in her gaze struck low and hard at Logan's gut. Unprepared for the blow, he stiffened. Scarlett genuinely liked the girl. And from Madison's broad smile and the hint of hero worship in her eyes, the feeling was mutual. When he'd agreed to let Scarlett show his niece around the hotel, he never dreamed they'd become friends. But now he understood his faulty judgment. Having an actress of Scarlett's caliber to learn from would be any fledgling actress's dream come true.

"Just great." He felt a growl building in his chest. "Madison, why don't you go in and take off the costume so Scarlett can take it back to the hotel with her."

Logan's shortness dimmed his niece's high spirits. "She said I could bring it with me when I go back tomorrow."

"I've been thinking that the hotel might not be the best place for you."

"It figures that I'd find something I enjoy and you'd take it away." Madison threw her arms out. "Do you all want me to be miserable? Is that it?"

"I thought you might spend some time with me at the office tomorrow."

"We tried that, remember?" Madison crossed her arms over her chest and dropped the enigmatic Mata Hari facade. Once again she looked like a twenty-first-century teenager playing dress-up. "You left me sitting in the lobby with the receptionist while you dealt with all the supersecret stuff for your clients. No, thanks."

Up until now, Scarlett had remained silent. Now she stepped into the fray, her manner relaxed, her voice a refreshing spring breeze. "Madison, why don't you head in. Your uncle and I will figure something out."

To his amazement, Madison did as she was told. Giving Scarlett a quick, warm hug, his niece shot him a pleading look before disappearing through the front door.

"How did you do that?" The question tumbled out of him. "She fights me on everything from breakfast to bedtime. But you tell her to do something and she agrees without so much as a frown."

"I don't know. Maybe because I've treated her like the intelligent young woman she is."

"Meaning, I haven't?"

"You're pretty bossy."

"She's seventeen."

"When I was seventeen, I had my GED, was managing my acting career and having a ball with my friends."

"She's not you."

"I'm not saying she is. But she's smart and ambitious. If she's behaving like a brat, it might be because no one is listening to her."

"So now you're an expert."

Scarlett's only reaction to his sarcasm was the warning flash in her eyes. Her tone remained neutral as she said, "I'm not an expert. I'm simply offering you my opinion."

"Noted."

"Please let her come back to the hotel tomorrow. She can shadow my general manager. Lucille's exactly what you want in a mentor. A professional career woman with a master's degree in business. Hardworking. Conservative dresser. You'll love her."

While Logan appreciated that Scarlett had taken a strong interest in Madison, he couldn't shake the concern that no matter how hard she tried to steer his niece toward college and a career that would please her parents, Madison would continue to be dazzled by Scarlett's larger-than-life persona and remain steadfast in her decision to become an actress.

"Please, Logan. Let me help." A trace of pleading had entered Scarlett's voice. "I'm worried that if everyone keeps telling her what to do, Madison will become even more determined to skip college and go to L.A."

"And you think you can change her mind."

"I'm not promising that, but I think she'll listen to what I say."

That's exactly what Logan was afraid of. She'd already half convinced him to let Madison return to the hotel. His irritation cooled and other emotions crowded in.

"And who are you supposed to be?" he asked, as he finally took in the full effect of her outfit.

She twirled gracefully. "I'm Ginger Rogers from the movie *Top Hat*."

She looked ready to be spun around the dance floor or clasped in her costar's arms for a passionate moonlit kiss. And thanks to her four-inch heels, her delectable mouth was within easy kissing distance....

Logan crossed his arms over his chest as he was flooded with the memory of her soft moan of surrender earlier that day. A low burn began in his belly. Tension built as he waited for the tiniest spark from her that would ignite him to action.

But instead of provoking him, she retreated a step. "I should be getting back to the hotel."

Did he detect the slightest hint of breathlessness in her voice? Had she sensed he was on the brink of doing something rash and impulsive? Why wasn't she inviting him to act?

"Of course."

"Will you bring Madison by tomorrow?"

"I can."

"It would be better if we formalized the internship by hiring her. That way she can take ownership of the tasks she's assigned."

Logan knew having a job she enjoyed would be good for his niece, but he worried what having her working for Scarlett was going to do to his blood pressure.

"What time do you want her?"

Only because he was so in tune with her did he note the relaxation of her muscles. The change was almost imperceptible.

"Eight."

And then, because she wasn't expecting it, he slid his hand around the back of her neck and lowered his lips to hers. For a second, shock paralyzed her, then she softened beneath the light pressure he exerted on her mouth. The moonlight and muted night sounds called for leisurely, romantic kisses. He cupped her head and focused all his attention on the texture of her plump lips and the fragrance of her skin.

Two kisses stretched into ten. Logan knew the interlude couldn't last forever. Already in the back of his mind irritation buzzed. A sizzling, sultry temptress, she was built for passion and frenzied desire, and here he was treating her like the heroine of a lighthearted romantic comedy.

But in this moment, with just a hint of coolness rushing across his hot skin, he wanted nothing more than to savor the way she yielded her lips to his mastery, to enjoy how her body trembled as he feathered kisses over her chin and cheeks.

"Thank you," she said when at long last he released her.

He noted that she kept her gaze on his shirt buttons, her thoughts hidden beneath a thick fringe of lashes. "For kissing you?"

She frowned. He'd disrupted her poise and she was slow to recover.

"For letting Madison come back to Fontaine Richesse tomorrow."

"You made a convincing argument."

Already his fingers itched to touch her again. He wished he hadn't let her go so soon, but any longer and he'd have been overwhelmed by the urge to carry her into the house and spend the rest of the night ravishing her.

As if reading his mind, Scarlett backed away. "I'd better go." She returned to the driver's side of the red convertible. With the car between them she finally met his gaze. "Are we still on for tomorrow night at seven?"

"I haven't changed my mind about how dangerous Tiberius's files are, so yes."

"Then it's a date."

"It's not a date," he grumbled, but the eager jump in his pulse made him wonder who he was trying to convince, her or himself.

"Then you won't want to kiss me goodnight."

Any response he might have made would've been drowned out by the noise of the engine as she started her car.

It wasn't until her taillights disappeared down his driveway that he realized he was smiling.

The first thing Scarlett did when she returned to her suite was crank up the air conditioning. Driving a sedate forty miles an hour back to the hotel hadn't stirred the hot June night air enough to lower her body temperature after kissing Logan.

She stripped and stepped into the shower. The cool water made her shiver, but it wasn't enough to fully banish the heat coursing through her at the memory of Logan's lips moving over hers.

Somewhat refreshed, she wrapped herself in a terry robe and sat staring out her window at the bright Vegas strip. Why the hell had he kissed her like that? Passion she could handle. That wild kiss in the elevator had knocked her for a loop, but it had been born out of conflict and chemistry. Tonight's embrace had been heartbreakingly romantic. She never imagined a straightforward guy like Logan would have had it in him to kiss her so sweetly and let her go. The explosive quality between them led her to expect him to want her hard and fast. Not slow and tender.

She felt a quiver begin in her chest and plummet downward until she was just as hot as before her shower.

A firm knock sounded on her outside door, making Scarlett's heart jump. Had Logan followed her back to the hotel intent on picking up where they'd left off in his driveway? If so his timing was terrible. Her hair was wet. She wore no makeup. The only thing sexy about her at the moment was that she was naked beneath the robe.

For several seconds she stood paralyzed with indecision. A second, urgent knock roused her. She crossed to the door and flung it open.

"About time," Violet said, holding up a bottle of Tiberius's favorite Scotch. "It's been a long, horrible day and I need a drink."

"Ditto." Harper eyed Scarlett's attire, then peered past her into the suite. "We're not interrupting anything, are we?"

Scarlett laughed, but it had a queer edge to it. "Hardly. And you're right about the day. It was crazy. I'll get some glasses."

The three sisters settled onto the comfortable couch in Scarlett's living room, each with a glass of amber liquid. Scarlett enjoyed being sandwiched between her sisters, treasured their closeness. Growing up an only child, she'd always longed for siblings. Now she had two.

"To Tiberius," Violet pronounced in solemn tones.

"To Tiberius," Harper and Scarlett echoed as they all clinked glasses.

"How did it go with Logan's niece today?" Harper asked as Scarlett refilled her glass after tossing back the first shot.

The alcohol had left a line of heat from her throat to her stomach, a different sort of burn than she'd felt when Logan had kissed her. "She's great. Wants to be an actress. Her family is horrified."

Violet frowned. "There are far worse professions."

"Not if you listen to Logan," Scarlett muttered. "He's convinced I'm going to corrupt Madison with my evil ways."

"Stop exaggerating." Harper was always the voice of order and reason. "You rub Logan the wrong way because it amuses you."

Scarlett couldn't deny it so she shrugged. "I'd rather rub him the right way, but he made it plain from the start that I wasn't his type."

"Is that why he stares at you so much?" Violet regarded her over the rim of her glass. "Because you're not his type?"

Harper patted Scarlett's hand. "I'm sorry to break it to you, but you're every man's type."

"Not every man." But few were immune. Until today she'd believed Logan was one of those. Correction—until tonight. The kiss earlier that day had been about proving a point. Tonight's kiss had been…intimate. As if the only thing on his mind was connecting with her. Scarlett shook her head and put a stop to such fancy. Turning to Violet, she said, "Something weird happened today. John Malcolm stopped by with an envelope for me from Tiberius."

"Tiberius's lawyer?" Harper sounded perplexed. "What was in it?"

"A key to a storage unit." Scarlet eyed her younger sister. "Did you know that Tiberius kept files on a whole bunch of people?"

Violet shook her head. "What sort of files?"

"From what Logan told me, they're filled with a whole

lot of secrets." Scarlett was still having a hard time taking the whole thing seriously.

"Interesting." Harper leaned forward to look at Violet. "He never mentioned this to you?"

"Not once."

"How do you know all about this?" Harper asked.

"Because Tiberius left me his files." Scarlett nodded when she saw her sisters' surprise and confusion. "Crazy, right? At least that's what Logan thinks is waiting in the storage unit. We're going to go and check it out tomorrow night."

Violet grinned. "You and Logan?"

"Apparently he thinks the files are too dangerous for me to have." Scarlett ignored her younger sister's smug look. "The files are all he's interested in."

"I'm sure." But Violet didn't look the least bit convinced.

"Is it weird that he gave them to you?" Harper asked.

"Maybe." Scarlett rolled her empty glass between her palms. She'd consumed the two drinks too fast. Her head felt light. Her blood hummed through her veins. "Tiberius and I talked a lot about Vegas history. If it wasn't for him I wouldn't be opening the Mob Experience exhibit next month. He gave me the idea, encouraged me to pursue it and most of the items on display were either things he'd collected or were donated by people he knew."

"He loved that you listened to his stories," Violet said. "I was more interested in the future than the past."

"I was fascinated." Scarlett's throat closed up. "He brought Las Vegas to life for me."

Seeing Violet struggling with her sadness, Scarlett wrapped her arm around her sister's shoulder. Five years earlier, when she'd found out she had two half sisters living in Las Vegas, Scarlett had worried they would be angry that she'd been included in Henry's contest to decide who the future CEO of Fontaine Resorts would be. After all, what did she know about running a hotel or a multibillion-dollar corporation? But to her delight, they were as excited about having her in Las Vegas as she was to be there.

"How did it go with your mom today?" Scarlett asked.

"About as you'd expect." Violet offered a wan smile. "She's taking it hard."

Tiberius might not have been Suzanne Allen's first love, but he was her longest and best. Even though she'd never married the hotel owner, she'd lived with him for twenty years.

"Was she any help with the funeral arrangements?" Harper quizzed, dropping her hand over Violet's and giving a sympathetic squeeze.

"You know my mother. She can't make decisions on the best days." Violet gave a wry smile.

"Do you have a date for the funeral?" Scarlett asked.

"Not yet."

Harper frowned. "That's strange."

"Not so strange," Violet said. She heaved a giant sigh. "There's something I haven't told you. There's something suspicious about Tiberius's death."

"Suspicious?" Scarlett echoed, goose bumps popping out on her arms as if someone had touched the back of her neck with an ice cube. Logan's earlier concerns no longer seemed amusing.

Harper looked as worried as Scarlett felt. "I thought he had a heart attack?"

"He did, but they're waiting for some toxicology results to come back from the lab. The investigating officer told Mom they think Tiberius's death might have been from an overdose of digitalis."

Four

An overdose of digitalis.

The words hung in Scarlett's mind as she dressed for her "date" with Logan. It had to be accidental. Anything else was preposterous. Who would want to kill an old man? Someone who had something to hide? She shook off the thought. Logan had put crazy ideas in her head. But she couldn't shake her nerves. And she had lots more than the ticking time bomb Tiberius had left her to worry about. She was about to embark on an entire evening alone with Logan.

Scarlett nearly jumped out of her skin when the knock sounded on her door. She set her lipstick aside and took a breath to settle her racing pulse. Would tonight be all business or would he subject her to another one of those mind-blowing embraces?

There were ways to protect herself from men who wanted to harm her. And where her heart was concerned, Logan had already proven himself a dangerous adversary.

Standing before the door to the hall, she smoothed her palms along her hips. Never had she spent so many hours trying to figure out what a man wanted her to be. In the end, she'd dressed in a pair of skinny black pants and a black blouse with a cap sleeve that bared her arms. With her hair slicked back into a severe bun and tiny pearl earrings as her only jewelry, she was as close to looking professional as she could manage.

Then, because she'd never been good at doing what was expected of her, Scarlett added a pair of heavy black-framed glasses. Now she looked like someone's sexy secretary. Wrestling her features into a bland expression, she opened the door.

Logan's eyes narrowed as he caught sight of her. "What's with the getup?"

She slid the glasses down her nose and peered at him over them. "Don't you think I look professional?"

"You look…fine."

"Fine? I spent all afternoon searching my closet for something to wear so you wouldn't be embarrassed to be seen with me." She couldn't resist the taunt.

"I thought you understood I'm not interested in your playacting."

Scarlett gave him a genuine smile. "Do you really want me to stop?"

"Why wouldn't I?" He gave her a suspicious once-over.

"What happens if you start to like the real me? Where will you be then?" It was a bold sortie, but something about the lick of heat in his eyes told her he wasn't as immune to her as he'd like her to think.

"Why would you think I'd like the real you?"

"Touché," she murmured, unfazed by his question. She intrigued him. That much was clear. He wasn't the sort of man to waste his time if he wasn't interested. For now, that was enough. "I might not be the best-educated or most suited to run a multibillion-dollar hotel business, but I've got my own talent."

"Such as?"

"I do a pretty good job reading people."

"I suppose that's your way of saying you've got me all figured out."

"Not in the least. You've always been a hard nut to crack." She gave him a wry smile. "That's why you're so interesting."

Scarlett grabbed her purse and stepped into the hall. Sharing the space with Logan's broad shoulders and powerful personality stirred up the butterflies in her stomach. Self-protection told her to give him a wide berth, but Scarlett had never been one to run from her fears. Instead, she linked her arm through his and smiled up at him.

"Where are you taking me for dinner?"

"Paul Rubin's new place."

She hummed with pleasure. Romantic and expensive. She never would have guessed Logan had it in him. "I've been dying to try it."

Without commenting, Logan escorted her down the hall. If he'd stuck to his usual pace, Scarlett would have had to trot to keep up. Was he being considerate of her footwear or was whatever weighed on his mind slowing him down?

"Did you know Tiberius's death has been ruled a homicide?" Logan asked when at last they reached the elevator.

"Last night Violet mentioned that the police thought there was something suspicious about his death."

"He overdosed on digitalis."

"Sure, but he was taking that for his heart, right? He just accidentally took too much?" She sounded way too hopeful.

"The digitalis in his system had a different chemical signature than what he was taking. Someone wanted to make it look like an accidental overdose." Logan regarded her dispassionately. "I hope this convinces you how dangerous these files are to have in your possession."

"Your concern is touching." If she gave them up would he remain concerned about her? Scarlett wasn't willing to find out. "But you have no idea why someone killed Tiberius. For all anyone knows, he might have been the victim of a random crime."

"Not random. Someone knew he had a bad heart and wanted to make his death look like natural causes."

"So maybe Tiberius was blackmailing someone. With his death, that stops."

"Unless that person thinks you are going to pick up where he left off."

"I'd never do that."

"I know that, but—"

"You do?" She'd had to interrupt him.

"Of course." He shot her an exasperated glare. "My opinion of you isn't as bad as you think."

"Thank goodness." She sighed in exaggerated relief, earning still more of his displeasure.

"Do you ever stop acting?"

"Only when you're kissing me." She wasn't sure where she found the courage to speak so boldly, but when his eyes widened with surprise, she was delighted she had.

She lifted her chin and offered him her lips but the elevator doors picked that inopportune moment to open. He growled and dragged her inside.

"If there weren't cameras in every inch of this hotel, I'd make you prove that statement," he muttered, jabbing his thumb into the down button.

"We could go back to your place after we check out the storage space," she offered, every inch of her skin tingling where his gaze touched her. Lowering her voice, she whispered, "Unless you've got cameras there for personal use."

Her innuendo was so outrageous that he laughed. "You have a smart-ass remark for everything, don't you?"

"A girl learns to stay on her toes in Hollywood. There are a lot of smart people ready to take advantage if you're not careful."

"Have you told my niece that?"

Scarlett smiled. "She knows."

"How are things going with her?"

"We spent the afternoon at the pool."

"The pool? I thought you understood she's here to learn about hotel management."

"Relax," Scarlett told him. "Every Wednesday I host a fashion show. You know, resort wear, swimsuits. The girls strut around, showing off the clothes we sell at our boutique."

"And what was Madison wearing?"

"I put her in the tiniest bikini I could find. She had men stuffing tens in the itty bit of string that held it together."

Logan drew in an enormous breath, preparing to deliver a lengthy tirade outlining all the reasons Scarlett was unsuitable as a mentor, when he noticed the glint in her eyes. She was teasing him. He shoved his hands into his pockets to keep from strangling her. Or worse. Kissing her.

Her red lips had softened into a slight smile as she watched him. That mouth of hers was going to be his undoing. Whether she was using it to taunt him or yielding to his kisses, he was completely enthralled.

"What was she really doing?"

"I considered putting her in the show, then decided you'd prefer it if I had her emcee the event. She did great. Quite a natural."

Logan knew he should thank Scarlett for demonstrating

some common sense, but anything he said would probably come out wrong.

"She's done a lot of plays and public speaking," he said instead, wondering what he could possibly do to keep this exasperating woman from creeping beneath his skin.

"It shows."

The elevator finally deposited them in the lobby, and Logan escorted Scarlett toward his Escalade parked outside the main entrance.

"You sure like your vehicles big," she commented, stepping nimbly into the front seat.

"And green. It's a hybrid."

"You and Violet." She gave her head a wry shake. "Made for each other."

He shut the passenger door harder than necessary and circled the car. She was right. He and Violet shared a like-minded philosophy about lifestyle and work. So why did it bug him that she kept pointing out the fact? It was either a subtle rejection or a defense mechanism.

Defense mechanism, he decided as he slid behind the wheel. There was nothing remotely subtle about Scarlett.

Which meant she had a reason to feel defensive around him. Interesting.

"Any chance you've talked Madison into going to college this fall?"

"I've had her for a day and a half," she reminded him. "Give me a little time to gain her trust. Then I can start steering her in the direction of school."

"How much time?"

"I don't know. How long is it going to take you to trust me?"

Her question startled him. "I don't know."

"Give me a ballpark."

"I don't know that I ever will."

"There's more of that Wolfe charm." She didn't look the least bit hurt by his reply. "You should package it and sell it on eBay. You'd make a fortune."

Her sarcasm rolled off him like water off a newly waxed car. "Don't ask the sort of questions you won't like the answer to."

"You know what I think?" She prodded his arm. "I think you're going to wake up one day and decide you really like me."

Did anything faze this woman? "What makes you believe that?"

"Call it women's intuition."

"Do you say things like that to annoy me?"

"Most of the time. I love it when you scowl at me. Which is a good thing, since that's all you ever do."

"Why would you like that I find you irritating?"

"Because every other man I meet finds me beautiful and desirable. It gets tiresome. Our relationship is completely adversarial and I appreciate knowing where I stand with you."

"You don't think I find you beautiful and desirable?"

"I guess you might." Her expression lacked its usual guile as she watched him. "But if you do it's secondary to the fact that you don't like me. I find your honesty refreshing."

Only, he wasn't being honest. With her or himself. She disturbed him in a way no other woman had. Which was unfortunate because he didn't trust her and he would never start a relationship, physical or emotional, with a woman who guarded her secrets as closely as Scarlett Fontaine.

By the time Scarlett licked the last of the chocolate from her spoon and set it down on the empty dessert plate, she was convinced she'd never enjoyed a meal so much. Part of her delight had been the delicious food, but most of her pleasure had come from her sullen dinner companion.

Logan had been in a foul mood ever since she'd confessed that she found his honesty refreshing. Why that bothered him, she had no idea. Shouldn't she be the wounded party? He was the one who'd declared he'd never trust her and called her irritating.

"If you wanted dessert," he growled, "you should have ordered your own."

"I just wanted a bite."

"You ate almost all of it." And she knew he'd enjoyed watching her devour the rich treat.

In fact, she wondered if he'd ordered it for just such a reason. From their dinner conversation, she'd learned that he wasn't usually one to indulge his sweet tooth. No dairy. Steamed vegetables. Lean meats. Whole grains. His body was both a fortress and a temple.

"Shall we order another one? This time I won't steal a bite. I promise."

"It's getting late. We need to get to the storage unit." He signaled for the check.

Scarlett was torn. On one hand, she'd love to linger over a cup of coffee and enjoy the thrust and parry of their banter a little longer. On the other, she was tired of having the barrier of the table between them.

Unfortunately, now that dinner was through, the glint faded from Logan's eye and his features hardened into a professional mask. Sighing in resignation, she let him guide her out of the restaurant and into his SUV. With his focus so far away from her, Scarlett knew the only way to reengage with him was to discuss the purpose behind their dinner tonight. "What sort of secrets to you suppose Tiberius had locked up?" she asked, hoping to jostle him out of his thoughts.

"Dangerous ones."

His dark tone gave her the shivers. She studied him as the lights of the Strip faded behind them and they entered an area of town where tourists never ventured. Another man might have played up the seriousness of their outing for effect. That wasn't Logan's style. He was genuinely troubled and Scarlett was less confident with each mile they drove.

"What do you think I should do?"

"Shred the whole mess."

Honestly, did the man not watch TV? "That's not going to help. The killer will assume that I made copies of everything. Or at the very least that I went through all the files and know what Tiberius knew." Whatever that was.

Logan grunted but didn't comment.

By the time they arrived at the storage facility, Scarlett had run the murdered-blackmailer plot from a dozen detective shows through her mind. If Tiberius had been killed because of these files, was she in danger? Her stomach churned, making her regret muscling in on Logan's dessert.

He stopped the SUV in front of Tiberius's storage unit. "Are you okay?" he asked, noting her expression.

"I've played a dead escort and a drowned party girl. I'm not sure I'm ready to play murdered hotel executive."

"This isn't television."

"My point exactly."

Logan took her hands in his and gave them a squeeze. "No one knows you got the files. You're going to be fine."

"This is Las Vegas." She drew courage from his strength and let the heat of his skin warm away her sudden chill. "There are no secrets in this town."

"There are thousands of secrets buried here."

"Did you have to use the word *buried*?"

With one last squeeze, he set her free. "I'll make sure nothing happens to you."

"That's a charming promise, but you're not around 24/7," she reminded him. A smile flirted with her lips. "Unless that's your way of telling me you want to step up our relationship."

His growl helped restore her sense of humor. She slipped out of the passenger seat and waited in front of the storage unit until Logan joined her. With great ceremony she handed him the key to the lock and stood, barely breathing, while he opened the door and raised it. The musty smell that greeted them was similar to that of a used bookstore.

Logan stepped to the wall and switched on the light. "Damn."

The stark overhead bulb revealed two walls lined with four-drawer file cabinets, stretching back fifteen feet. Bankers Boxes sat atop the file cabinets and were clustered on pallets on the floor.

Scarlett whistled. "There are eighty-eight drawers of secrets in there, not to mention what's in the boxes. That's a lot of dirt." She glanced Logan's way and noticed a muscle jumping in his jaw. He hadn't seemed to hear her, so she nudged him. "Were you expecting this much?"

"No. This is worse than I imagined."

"It's going to take us a year to get through all of it."

Logan turned and blocked her view of the files. "Not us. You need to let me deal with this. It's too dangerous for you."

"Tiberius left this to me." His dictatorial manner was a double-edged sword. She liked his concern for her welfare, but she'd left L.A. because she was tired of being told what to do. "You wouldn't even be here if you hadn't shown up just as Tiberius's lawyer was leaving my office." She wasn't trying to make him mad, but he had a knack for bringing out her worst side.

For a second he looked irritated enough to manhandle

her into his SUV and dump her back at the hotel. He still had the key and she doubted her ability to get it back either through manipulation or force. Her best bet was to convince him they needed to work together.

"Two of us will make the search go faster." She took a half step forward, expecting him to back up to maintain his personal space. When he didn't, she splayed her fingers over his rib cage and moved even closer. "Please, can't we work together?"

Beneath her hands, his abs tightened perceptibly, but he stood as if frozen. "There's really no way I can stop you, is there?"

It wasn't exactly an enthusiastic confirmation of their partnership, but she'd take whatever she could get from Logan.

"No, you can't." She gave him a smug smile and pushed back, but his hands came up to cup her arms, just above the elbow, keeping her in place.

"I swear, if anything happens to you because of this..." His mouth settled on hers. Hard. Stealing her gasp and replacing it with the demanding thrust of his tongue. The kiss wasn't calculated or romantic. It was hot, hungry and frantic. Confusion paralyzed her. By the time she recovered enough to react, he'd slid his lips across her cheek. "I would never forgive myself," he murmured in her ear.

He released her so abruptly she wobbled on her four-inch heels. To her immense relief he spun with military precision and marched into the storage unit without a backward glance. The time required to restore her composure was longer than it should have been. But no man had ever kissed her with such hungry desperation. Or rocked her world so fast.

Smoothing her hands down her hips, Scarlett strode toward the files lining the wall opposite from where Logan was searching. The drawers were unmarked, but when she opened the first one, a quick scan of the folders revealed that they were filled with newspaper clippings, handwritten notes, copies of documents and an assortment of photos. A more thorough review indicated each bit of information came from individuals associated with the long-demolished Sands casino.

It seemed as if Tiberius had something on every employee going back to when the casino opened. Not all of it was incriminating. Some of the information merely consisted of impressions he'd recorded upon meeting the person. But there were thick folders on several others, including some legendary performers.

"This is amazing." She turned with a file in her hand. "Tiberius has enough stuff in these files to keep Grady busy for decades."

Grady Daniels was the man Scarlett had hired to help create the Mob Experience exhibit. He lived and breathed the history of Las Vegas. His doctoral thesis had been on the Chicago mobs, but during his research, he'd learned quite a bit about Las Vegas because of the natural migration of mobsters in the forties and fifties.

"Lucas was right," he muttered, either not hearing her or ignoring her enthusiasm. "Tiberius was the J. Edgar Hoover of Vegas."

"You told your brother about the files?"

Logan shook his head. "He told me. We've suspected what Tiberius has been up to for a while." From his guarded expression, there was more he wasn't sharing with her.

Scarlett decided a subtle push was called for. "Finding anything is going to be impossible unless we have some idea what we're looking for. Or a notion of who might have something to hide."

"And we're not going to find anything tonight."

"Give me half an hour to indulge my curiosity, then I'll let you take me back to my suite and have your way with me."

His unfathomable stare told her he wouldn't dignify her flirtation by responding. So with a sigh, Scarlett continued to work her way around the storage unit. She wasn't surprised to find a whole lot of information on the mob, but resisted the urge to take any of the files with her. Some of Tiberius's notes read like pages from an old-time detective novel. The stories were fascinating. Scarlett could easily have spent days in here poring over the metal cabinets, but Logan was showing signs of impatience.

At last she found the file drawer she was looking for. Sure enough, there was a thick file on her father. His antics were well-known around town. Her grandfather's file was not as full as his son's, but it still contained a lot of newspaper articles as well as a history of the company and background on Henry. It took her less than a minute to unearth two other files. One for her mother. One for Violet's. To her surprise, Tiberius had a file on Harper's mother, as well. What could he possibly find of interest about a New York City socialite?

Scarlett shut the final cabinet door and carried her booty to an unmarked Bankers Box near the front of the unit. She thought it was empty until she lifted off the top, but it was a third full of files. From the look of them, these files must have been some of the last Tiberius was working on. She dropped the files on her family into the box and picked it up.

Logan stood outside, radiating impatience as she emerged. "What are those?"

"Files on my family."

"Are you sure taking those is a good idea?"

"Have you met Harper's and Violet's mothers? I'm sure

there's nothing scandalous in their pasts besides our father. As for my mother…" She handed him the box and dug out a photo to show Logan. It was a full-color eight-by-ten photo. "Wasn't she gorgeous?"

"You inherited her legs."

Her pulse stuttered. "You've noticed my legs?"

"It's hard not to."

Unsure whether he meant the comment as praise or mere observation, Scarlett headed toward his SUV without replying. Logan was an enigma. Most of the time he acted as if every second in her company taxed his patience, then suddenly he'd behave as if he was actually worried about her. To further confuse her, he had developed a distracting fondness for kissing her whenever the mood struck him.

He didn't like her. He certainly didn't respect her as a businesswoman. On the other hand, she wasn't his responsibility, so he didn't have to worry about her safety as much as he did. And his kisses…his amazing, confusing, contrary kisses. They certainly weren't the sort a man planted on a woman he was trying to seduce. What was his angle?

Scarlett studied him as he drove back to the hotel. He wasn't classically handsome. More the rough-and-rugged type. Brawny. Take-charge. The guy everyone else in the room deferred to because he had all the answers.

Nor was he a good choice for a woman who only felt safe with men she could wrap around her finger. Was she attracted to the danger he represented? He would break her heart in a millisecond if she gave him the chance. Damn it. It would be so easy if only she didn't like him so much.

Logan glanced her way and caught her staring at him. "What?"

"I was just thinking what a heartbreaker you are."

He snorted. "I think you have us confused."

"I flirt, but I never commit. No one's heart actually gets

engaged. You are completely sincere. You could make a woman fall in love with you without even trying." She angled her body toward him. "Why haven't you gotten married?"

"If this is another one of your games…"

"No game. I'm insatiably curious. I think that's why Tiberius left his files to me." "Knowledge is power," he'd been fond of saying. "Did the right girl never come along?"

"I was engaged once."

Rather than prompt him to continue, she let silence hang between them.

Logan scowled. "She broke it off."

Scarlett shifted her gaze away from his stony expression, wishing she'd left well enough alone. No wonder he was such a hard man to get to know. He'd been hurt by the person who should have loved him best. That wasn't something Logan would let go of easily. Scarlett pitied the women who tried to get close to him. They would find his defenses as impenetrable as the security systems his company was famous for.

"I'm sorry."

"It was ten years ago." He said it as though the pain was a distant memory, but she suspected his wound wasn't all that well healed.

"That doesn't mean it stops hurting."

He greeted her attempt at sympathy with cold silence. At the hotel, per her request he stopped the SUV outside the employee entrance. When he tried to hand the key to her, she shook her head. "Find whatever it is you're looking for."

"Why do you think I'm after something?"

"You don't really expect me to believe you came along tonight because you enjoy my company." Managing a light-hearted smile despite the heaviness in her chest, Scarlett exited the vehicle and lifted the box containing her family's files from the backseat.

"Scarlett…"

"Keep in touch, Logan."

Then, before she could make the mistake of asking him up to her suite, she shut the car door and headed toward the hotel's employee entrance.

Five

A week went by before Logan admitted defeat regarding Tiberius's files. Scarlett had been right. Someone could spend decades going through the fragments of data. The hotel and casino owner had accumulated thousands of interesting tidbits throughout the years, some of it newspaper articles, some rumors, many firsthand accounts of events that had never become public knowledge.

The problem was, there was so much information, most of it random, that connecting the dots would take forever. Logan had neither the time nor the patience to locate the needle in the haystack. If he'd had some idea what he was looking for, he might have been able to ferret out Tiberius's killer. But although the files held a lot of smoking guns, many of the people who'd once held them were long dead.

Nor were the cops interested in looking through the files. They were looking at the wife of a local businessman. Apparently the woman had been having an affair and after finding a file on her at his office, the police had a theory that Tiberius was blackmailing her. Logan didn't believe it. Tiberius collected information on people, but he didn't appear to use it. If he had, the casino owner wouldn't have been nearly bankrupt when he died.

Despite having no luck, giving up the hunt was the last thing he wanted to do, but Scarlett was eager to have her historian comb through the files in search of material they could use in her Mob Experience exhibit, which was due to open in a few weeks. He could have given the key to one of his guys to return. In fact, that would have made a lot more sense. He was hip-deep in the data Lucas had sent to him from Dubai. They needed to have a proposal done in the next couple days and he'd lost a lot of time in his search through the storage unit.

Instead of leaving the key with Scarlett's assistant, a stunning blonde woman with an MBA from Harvard, he tracked Scarlett herself down on the casino floor. He found her chatting with one of the pit bosses. With her hair cascading down the back of her sleeveless bronze sheath, she looked every inch a successful hotel executive. His chest tightened as he watched her smile. Seven days away from her should have diminished his troublesome attraction. Instead, he'd found his thoughts filled with her at the most inopportune times.

Desiring her had been his Achilles' heel for some time now, but he'd been able to keep his head in the game by remembering that she was first and foremost an actress and a woman who enjoyed manipulating men. Until last week, however, he'd never spent an extended time alone with her. He'd been working off assumptions he'd made from their infrequent encounters.

He now knew she was more than the manipulative man-eater he'd first dubbed her as. Not that this made her any less dangerous. Quite the contrary. His fascination with her had ratcheted up significantly. And not all of it was sexual. He'd enjoyed her company at dinner. She was provocative and took great pleasure in testing his boundaries, but she was also very well-read and had surprised him with her knowledge of Las Vegas past and present.

She was more clever and insightful than he'd thus far given her credit for. She knew her limitations and had a knack for hiring people who were experts in their field. It's why her hotel was so well run, he'd decided after eight days of listening to Madison go on and on about how smart Scarlett was. For the first couple of days his niece's hero worship had worried him. But Madison hadn't mentioned L.A. once in the past several days, and he was happy to let her praise Scarlett's virtues if it meant his niece was going to give college a try.

"Hello, Logan." Scarlett had finished her business with the pit boss and caught sight of him. "Are you looking for Madison?"

"No." He held his ground against the onslaught of sensation that battered him as she drew close enough for him to smell her perfume and see the gold shards sparking in her green eyes. "I came to return this." He handed her an envelope containing the storage key.

"You're done with it, then?" She slid the envelope into the black leather folder that contained her daily notes. "Did you find what you needed?"

"I looked through our client's files and removed anything of interest." He paused before saying more. Lucas would be angry with him for spilling even that much. "I also found a number of secrets that should never see the light of day."

"Then they won't."

"You can't guarantee that."

"Some of those files have been hidden for over fifty years," she reminded him. "What makes you think they can't stay that way for another fifty?"

"Because Tiberius was killed for something he knew."

"That hasn't yet been determined. Besides, no one but you and I know I have the files."

"You forget about John Malcolm."

"Attorney-client privilege. He's not going to say anything."

"I'd feel better if the files were destroyed."

"I can't do that. Grady can't wait to get started on them."

Logan could hear the determination in her tone and knew he was wasting his breath. He could only hope he and Lucas were wrong about the connection between the files and Tiberius's death. Yet Logan couldn't shake the sense that something bad was going to happen.

"Do you have time for a cup of tea?" Her offer came at him out of the blue. "I got some of that green stuff you and Violet drink."

He opened his mouth to refuse, thinking she was flirting with him as always, but then saw her expression was serious. "Sure."

"Can I invite you up to my suite without you getting the wrong impression?"

"Unlikely."

"What a naughty mind you have." Amusement flared in her eyes and was gone just as fast. "I really could use your advice." She looped her arm through his and turned him in the direction of the elevators.

A week ago he might have assumed she had a nefarious purpose for luring him upstairs. That was before Tiberius's files had come to light. And Scarlett was radiating an apprehensive vibe, not a seductive one.

"My advice on what?"

"I discovered something in the files I took from the storage unit, and I'm not sure how to handle it."

Logan felt his anxiety kick in. Had she possessed the answer to Tiberius's murder all along?

"Which ones?"

She frowned. "The ones on my family."

So her concern was for Violet or Harper. His agitation diminished slightly.

"I took my father's file because I was curious about a man my mother rarely talked about," she continued. "It was a pretty thick file and took me three days to get through it all. He had affairs with a lot of women. I don't know how Harper's mother stood it."

"The way I understand it, she split all her time between New York City, the Hamptons and their winter place in Boca Raton. I don't know how often she came to Las Vegas."

"That's what I gathered from her file." Scarlett paused as they neared the elevator. Other people were waiting within earshot and she obviously didn't want them to overhear her, so she changed the subject. "How was your week? Successful?"

He knew she was referring to his search of the storage unit and shook his head. "Not at all. Your friend is going to have his work cut out for him. There's a lot of history."

"He'll be delighted."

"I'm sorry I didn't call this week." The apology came out before he knew what he was saying. "It was a hectic few days."

Surprise fogged her expression for a moment. "It's okay. I had a lot on my plate, as well."

"Lucas and I are developing a security system for a sheikh in Dubai. He has an extensive art collection that he wants to display and the logistics are proving quite complex."

She watched him with lively interest as he spoke. "Sounds fascinating," she murmured.

When the couple riding in the elevator with them got off on the twelfth floor, the snug space seemed to shrink.

"I don't know about that, but it is challenging." It wasn't like him to fill the silence with chitchat, but her open and sincere manner made him long to draw her into his arms and capture her lips with his. This frequent and increasing urge to kiss her was becoming troublesome. To his relief, the elevator door slid open on fifteen before he could act.

"I'd love to learn more about what it is Wolfe Security does besides casino security." And to her credit, she seemed to mean it.

"Perhaps another time." And there would be another time, he realized. She'd found a way beneath his skin and he feared it was only a matter of time before she took up permanent residence there and started redecorating. "Right now, I'd like to hear about what you found in Ross's file."

She waved her leather portfolio near her door's lock. All the rooms in Fontaine Richesse used proximity cards to open rather than ones with magnetic strips. The radio frequency in the cards was a harder technology to copy. Logan had been suggesting it for use in Fontaine hotels for three years as a more effective security measure, but none of the executives wanted to upgrade. Until Scarlett came along and decided it was the system she wanted in Fontaine Richesse. Now, all of the new Fontaine hotels had this system and as the older hotels were being remodeled, proximity card systems were being added.

Before she entered her suite, she gripped his arm. "Logan, I'm really afraid of what this is going to do to my family."

He stared at her, a bad feeling churning in his gut. This wasn't Scarlett being dramatic or overreacting. Genuine fear clouded her expression and thickened her voice. What could possibly have upset her to this extent?

"Tell me."

She entered her suite and headed for the kitchen. "I'll get the water started. The files are on the table." Scarlett indicated a stack of neatly arranged folders on the coffee table. "I noticed something odd about my father's business travel."

Logan sat on the pale green couch, noting its decadent softness, and leaned forward to view the contents of the open file. Tiberius had jotted some notes about Fontaine Hotels and Resorts's trouble with their Macao casinos. Ross had gone to investigate.

"What am I looking at?"

"See when he left? July 1980. He was gone for four months."

Logan shook his head, not understanding what Scarlett was getting at. "What's the significance of that?"

"Harper was born in June 1981." She raised her voice over the scream of the teakettle. "Now look at Penelope's file."

Penelope was Harper's mother. The only daughter of billionaire Merle Sutton, whose fortune revolved around chemicals and refining, her marriage to Ross Fontaine had brought an influx of cash to Fontaine Hotels and Resorts at a time when, unbeknownst to his father, Ross had bought some land without the proper environmental surveys. Ultimately, they'd been unable to develop the property and lost several million on the project.

Logan opened the file and scanned a private investigator's report on Harper's mother. Below it were several black-and-white photos that left little to the imagination.

"She had an affair." He stared at the pictures and felt

a stab of sympathy for the woman who'd been part of her father's business arrangement with Ross Fontaine. "Given the man she was married to, I can't say I blame her."

"At first I thought Ross had ordered the investigation." Scarlett carried two steaming cups over to the couch and set them down on the coffee table before sitting beside him. "I thought it was a little hypocritical of him to have Harper's mom investigated when he went after anything in a skirt. But it wasn't him."

"You sure?" Logan glanced sideways in time to see her lips close over the edge of the cup. "How's the tea?"

The face she made at him caused her nose to wrinkle in a charming manner. "It tastes like dead grass." But she gamely tried a second sip. "I checked on the private investigator." Scarlett pointed to the man's name on the report. "He's been dead for ten years, but his partner didn't find Ross's name in their list of former clients."

"Was it Tiberius?"

Scarlett shook her head. "Of course, Ross could have been considering divorce and gone to a lawyer who contacted a PI to get evidence of Penelope's infidelity. But once he got proof, why not start divorce proceedings? Then there's this." Scarlett opened a second file and showed Logan a document. "Harper's parents were not in the same hemisphere when she was conceived."

"She might have been conceived during a brief visit either in Macao or here in the States."

"I agree, but coupled with the fact that Harper's mother was having an affair during that time, it seems much more likely that this guy—" she tapped the photo "—is Harper's father."

Scarlett scrutinized Logan's impassive expression while she waited for him to process her conclusion. When she'd found the damning evidence last night, she'd longed to pick up the phone and share the burden with him, but it had been three in the morning and she hadn't wanted to wake him up.

Loneliness had never been an issue for her. In L.A. when she wasn't busy with friends, she'd enjoyed spending time alone. It was one of the benefits of growing up an only child. But lately she'd been dreading her own company. Sharing the secret of Tiberius's files with Logan had turned their animosity into camaraderie and their temporary break in hostility was something she wanted to make permanent.

"Which brings me back to why I invited you up here," she said, breaking the silence when it began nibbling on her nerves. "What should I do?"

"What do you want to do?"

She decided not to answer his question directly. "If I do nothing, Harper will become the next CEO of Fontaine Hotels and Resorts."

Logan sat back and stretched his arm across the back of the sofa. The move put his fingers very close to her bare upper arm and made her skin tingle.

"After your father died and before your grandfather came up with his contest to run the company, she was the obvious choice."

Scarlett pondered his words. "She has the education and the training to be Grandfather's successor. But Violet has the marketing savvy and the experience of running a Las Vegas hotel to give Harper a run for her money."

"If you share what you know, Harper would likely be kicked out of the running and the contest would be down to you and Violet."

"That's not what I want."

"You don't want to run Fontaine Hotels?"

Could she convince Logan that having two sisters who

loved her was more important than becoming CEO of a multibillion-dollar corporation?

"You and I both know I'm a distant third in the running. And even if I wasn't, I would never want to win if it meant hurting either Harper or Violet."

"Then you have your answer."

"But I keep asking myself, if I was Harper would I want to know I was living a lie? When I was first contacted by Grandfather, I was angry with my mother for evading the truth about my biological father. I don't know that it's fair to put Harper through the same thing."

"On the other hand, if you'd never found out, you would still be in L.A."

"Finding out I was a Fontaine was a wonderful thing. I gained an entire family that I'd previously known nothing about." Having two sisters was such a blessing. For the first time in her life she felt safe and content. "If I tell Harper the truth, she loses her entire family. And I know her well enough to be certain she would withdraw from the contest and give up Fontaine Ciel. And if that happened it would be my fault."

"What if her dream isn't running Fontaine Hotels?"

Scarlett couldn't imagine such a thing. "It's what she's spent her whole life training for."

"Just because you think your life is going to go a certain way doesn't always mean that it's the best thing for you."

What was Logan trying to tell her? She'd invited him up here for advice. Was he being impartial, trying to get her to look at both sides, or was he couching his opinion as questions?

"Do you think I should tell her?"

"What do you want to do?"

"Give the problem to someone else." She arched her eyebrows. "Feel like being the bearer of bad news?"

"I'm not going to get involved. Tiberius left the files to you."

"And I asked you to help me make a decision."

"You asked for my advice," he corrected.

"Same thing."

"Not really, but since you asked so nicely, I'll tell you that I think being honest with Harper is the way to go. Give her the file, don't tell her what's in it and let her make up her own mind about what she finds."

His advice didn't make the weight slide off her shoulders. "I don't want to keep anything important from Harper. And I could be jumping to conclusions. It's completely possible that Harper is Ross's daughter." But deep in her heart she believed she was right and that telling her sister what she suspected would do more harm than good. "You've given me a lot to think about." She set her hand on his. "Thank you."

For a few seconds he went still beneath her touch. Before she had time to register the way his mouth tightened, he was on his feet.

"I've got a bunch of work waiting for me back at the office," he said. "Thanks for the tea."

"You didn't drink any of it." He'd almost reached her front door by the time she'd regained her wits and chased after him. "Logan." She didn't reach him in time to stop him from walking out the door, but her breathless voice made him pause. "Would you have dinner with me tomorrow night?"

His refusal came through loud and clear before the words left his lips. "I don't think that's a good idea."

She was ready for his rebuff. "Oh, not like that." She plastered on a lively grin and laughed. "You certainly have a high opinion of yourself, don't you?" To her relief, he looked surprised by her reaction. Conceited man. He really expected her to take his rejection hard. "I thought we could discuss what to do for Madison's birthday party. She's only going to turn eighteen once and without her parents here to celebrate with her, I thought we should do something special to mark the occasion."

"What did you have in mind?"

"Have dinner with me tomorrow and I'll lay it all out for you."

"Can't you tell me now?"

"I don't have my notes and I need to get ready for a conference call in half an hour. How about eight o'clock tomorrow? I'll get us a table at Chez Roberto."

"Eight."

He nodded curtly, but when she expected him to walk away, he didn't. She stopped breathing while she waited for him to move or speak. His intense gaze trailed over her features before locking on her mouth.

A thousand times this past week she'd relived his kisses. Like some silly teenager she'd tried to guess how he felt about her when logic counseled it was nothing but simple lust. Hadn't his absence this week demonstrated his lack of interest? When men wanted her, she received flowers, offers of dinner or, at the very least, phone calls. From Logan: nothing.

And it was driving her crazy.

Which is why she'd concocted the excuse for tomorrow's dinner. She was perfectly capable of arranging a fabulous birthday party for Madison by herself. In fact, everything was already handled. She just wanted to spend more time with Logan. And she'd take him any way she could get him.

To her surprise, he cupped her head in his palm and dragged his thumb across her cheek. Mesmerized by the contact, she grabbed the door frame to steady herself as he leaned down and captured her lips in a demanding kiss. Before her shock faded, he lifted his mouth from hers.

"Eight," he repeated, voice and expression impassive. A heartbeat later he strode off down the hall, leaving a weak-kneed, much-bemused Scarlett in his wake.

He'd done it again. Logan strode into his house and threw his car keys on the counter. He was utterly incapable of a clean getaway. He'd nearly made it out of Scarlett's suite when she'd stopped him. He should have given her some excuse and gotten out of there. Instead he'd lingered and agreed to have dinner with her again. And why? So they could discuss plans for Madison's birthday party. He suspected she had the whole thing planned already. This was just an excuse to torment him over another rich chocolate dessert.

And he'd agreed. As if he hadn't guessed what she was up to. Worse, he'd then succumbed to the urge to kiss her again. Demonstrating once more that she'd completely mesmerized him. She no longer had to stir him up with her sharp wit and sexy smiles. Now he just took any excuse to seize her delectable lips for his own.

Madison was seated on the couch in the family room as Logan walked past. Beside her was the boy she'd been seeing a great deal of, Trent something, the son of one of Scarlett's restaurant managers. She'd been instrumental in introducing the teenagers, which had naturally made Logan suspicious of the boy. But a phone call to one of his employees had provided the sort of information on Trent that kept Logan from getting overprotective.

Currently they were joined at the hip and shoulder, both peering at the laptop balanced on the boy's lap. Madison's happy smile was the first he'd seen in this house. It lifted his spirits.

"Hi, Uncle Logan."

"Hello, Madison. Trent." Logan gave the boy a friendly nod. "Madison, are you planning on sticking around for dinner?"

"Yes. Is it okay if Trent joins us?"

"The more the merrier."

Logan left them and headed to the master bedroom. As badly as he wanted to know what they were looking at on the computer, he left his question unasked. The boy was a good kid. Spending time with him improved Madison's attitude.

And all the credit belonged to Scarlett. Instead of lecturing the eighteen-year-old about what would be the best thing for her to do, Scarlett had talked with her. Let Madison express her dreams and ambitions and found a way to broach the topic of college in a positive fashion. By introducing her to kids her own age who were college-bound and excited about it, Madison had started talking about college again. Granted, with little enthusiasm, but he shouldn't expect miracles.

If Scarlett actually pulled this off, he would owe her a favor. The thought of it made him shudder. What would she ask in return? Something difficult for him to deliver, no doubt.

After a half hour of energetic laps in the pool, he showered and headed back toward the kitchen. To his amusement, Madison had chosen to host her new friend in the dining room. She'd had his housekeeper, Mrs. Sanchez, set the table with all the crystal and fine china. Usually, Logan grabbed a plate and headed into his study to work on whatever he'd left hanging throughout the day. When Madison was home, he made an effort to give her a stable family experience and ate in the kitchen. He couldn't remember the last time he'd used his dining room.

Logan sat down at the head of the table and waited only until the teenagers had joined him before launching into his interrogation.

"Madison tells me you are going to be a sophomore next fall," he said to Trent, determined to get his money's worth out of his housekeeper's roast beef with garlic mashed potatoes and steamed asparagus. "What college do you attend?"

"I'm at Duke."

Logan turned to Madison. "Didn't your mother tell me you'd gotten into Duke?" Maybe she liked this boy well enough to follow him to college in North Carolina. Her parents would be thrilled.

"Yes." She leveled a warning stare at him. "I also got into Brown University, Cornell and Mother's alma mater, Amherst." All prestigious East Coast schools.

"Wow." Trent gaped at her in astonishment. Apparently she hadn't shared her academic triumphs with him. "That's impressive."

"I guess." She was so obviously glum about it that for the first time Logan felt sorry for her.

"You guess?" Trent asked. "I applied to Brown and Cornell and couldn't get in."

She had the grace to look a little ashamed of her attitude. "All I mean is that none of those were schools I wanted to get into. I didn't get into my top choice."

This was the first he'd heard of a college she hadn't been able to get into. Was that why she'd been acting out all spring? Paula and Ran had pushed hard to get her to apply to schools they considered suitable. Madison's two older brothers were at Harvard and Yale, respectively. Could she have felt too much pressure?

"What school could possibly have turned you down?"

Logan held very still, hoping that Madison would forget he was sitting across from her and keep talking. He might be able to get her back on track if he understood why she derailed.

Madison waved one slender hand. Her expression had gone mulish again. "It doesn't matter. I didn't get in and I have no interest in going to any school my parents badgered me into applying to."

Trent was smart enough to realize he'd hit a nerve and rather than continue to pursue what was obviously a touchy subject, he stuffed a forkful of Mrs. Sanchez's excellent food into his mouth and chewed with relish. Madison pushed beef around her plate and seemed preoccupied with her thoughts.

Logan applied himself to his own dinner and pondered what he'd learned tonight. Madison wasn't opposed to going to college, she just didn't want to go to any of the ones her parents had encouraged her to apply for. And she'd been disappointed after putting all her hopes in one basket and losing out.

Perhaps if Paula and Ran could let Madison make her own choice about where she went, she could be college-bound in the fall. He would call Paula and talk it over with her in the morning.

Scarlett sat on the overstuffed chair in her bedroom, her feet tucked beneath her, and stared out the window. While Harper and Violet had chosen to occupy suites that overlooked the Strip, Scarlett preferred a view of the mountains that circled Las Vegas. During the cooler months, she enjoyed hiking the trails in nearby Red Rock Park. The peace and quiet was a nice change from the constant activity around the hotel.

It was an hour before she was supposed to meet Logan for dinner, and she still needed to jump in the shower and get ready. She'd finished her day at six so she could get back to her suite and have plenty of time to prepare, but she'd spent the past hour sitting and daydreaming.

No. That wasn't true. She was waiting. Waiting for Logan to call and cancel their date.

She glanced at the clock on her nightstand and frowned. Surely he wasn't the sort of man to stand a girl up at the last minute. He was far too honorable for that. Her stomach gave a queer lurch. Was it possible he wasn't going to cancel on her? Scarlett jumped to her feet. She only had an hour to get ready. What had she been thinking to wait so long?

Her cell rang as she reached the bathroom door. If she didn't answer Logan's call, was their date officially canceled? She shuffled back to the dresser she'd passed and scooped up the phone. To her relief, it wasn't Logan.

"Bobby," she exclaimed. She hadn't spoken with the television producer in over six months. "What a lovely surprise."

"Scarlett, L.A. misses you." Over the phone Bobby McDermott came across as staccato and abrupt, but in person, he was a warmhearted teddy bear. "You must come home."

Her heart twisted in fond melancholy, but she kept her voice light. "Las Vegas is home these days."

"Bah. You're an actress, not a hotel manager."

"I used to be an actress." She thought back over yesterday's conversation with Logan. "At least when I got work, which wasn't often."

"You are a wonderful actress. You just weren't getting offered the right parts."

She couldn't argue with him there. What she wouldn't have given for a role with some meat. Something that scared her a little and forced her to stretch. She'd never been a fame hound, although with her sex appeal and early success, she was well-known to the gossip magazines and paparazzi.

"That's why I'm calling," Bobby continued. "I have something you'd be perfect for."

Scarlett sighed. She'd heard that before. Bobby had brought her numerous opportunities, but his opinion of her talent always seemed to clash with those of his directors. Still, it was nice having someone of his stature in her corner even if she never did get the part.

"I'm really happy here, Bobby."

"Nonsense. You're an actress. You need to act." The producer switched tacks. "At least come to L.A. and take a meeting."

"There's no point. I'm committed to staying here and managing the hotel." She didn't explain about her grandfather's contest or the pride she felt for all she'd accomplished in the past five years. "You're a darling for thinking of me, though."

"I'm going to send you the script," Bobby continued, ignoring her refusal. When he had his mind set on something, it took an act of God for him to change direction. "Don't make any decisions until you've read it through."

Knowing it was dangerous to open the door even a crack, she nevertheless heard herself say, "I'd be happy to give it a read. But I can't promise anything."

"You will once you've finished. Gotta run. Love you."

She barely had a chance to say goodbye before Bobby hung up. Stewing in a disorderly mash of dread and excitement, Scarlett quickly showered and dressed. At seven forty-five, a knock sounded on her door. Her hair was still up in hot rollers and she hadn't finished applying her makeup. Cursing Logan's early arrival, Scarlett quickly stripped out the rollers and shook out her hair. A second knock sounded on her door, this one more insistent, and she raced to answer it.

"You're early," she declared as she threw open the door.

But instead of Logan, a man in a ski mask stood at her door. "Who—?"

Before she could finish, his fist connected with her jaw. She saw stars. Then darkness.

Six

With each hour that passed, Logan found himself growing more impatient for the evening ahead. By the time six-thirty rolled around he was positively surly, or at least that's what his executive assistant had called him. Then Madison had complained about his bad temper when he'd arrived home.

Now, as he negotiated the eastbound traffic back to Fontaine Richesse, his mood perked up alarmingly. Damn it. He was looking forward to spending the evening with her. To seeing what sort of delectable outfit she'd prepared for him. To letting her steal food off his plate and wheedle out of him intimate details about his life. Why had he agreed to have dinner with her? He should have insisted on meeting her at her office during the regular workday when he wouldn't be tempted to linger for a nightcap in her suite.

A nightcap that might lead him to forget how quickly she turned on the charm. He would find himself seducing her and believing it was his idea. He'd have her naked and writhing beneath him before he realized she'd orchestrated the entire event. He simply couldn't let her manipulate him that way.

By the time he arrived at Fontaine Richesse, he was running five minutes late. He dialed Scarlett's cell, but she didn't pick up. That was odd. She was rarely beyond arm's reach of her phone. Driven by an irresistible sense of urgency, Logan's pace quickened as he made his way through the casino. By the time the elevator deposited him on Scarlett's floor, he was deeply concerned at her lack of response.

Rounding the corner to her suite, he noticed the door was wide-open. When he spied her on the floor, he ran the rest of the way down the hall. He entered her suite just as she lifted a hand to her jaw and opened her eyes. He knelt at her side as she groaned in discomfort.

"What happened?" he demanded, his throat constricting as he surveyed her for damage.

"I answered the door and a man hit me." She sounded bewildered and weak.

"What did he look like?"

"He was wearing a ski mask." She blinked in disbelief. "All I remember is that his hand shot out. Then everything went black."

"How long ago?" Logan dialed the Fontaine Richesse's security office.

"It was quarter to eight. Someone knocked. I thought it was you at the door." Her gaze found his. "I was mad at you for showing up early. My hair wasn't done and I hadn't finished putting on my makeup."

"You look beautiful," he told her brusquely.

A voice came on the line and Logan quickly outlined what had happened. Security would call the police and get working on tracking the guy who'd broken in. A man in a black windbreaker and jeans would be a challenge to find in a hotel as large as Richesse.

As soon as he hung up, he scooped Scarlett into his arms and headed toward her bedroom.

"No!" She tugged at his suit coat to get his attention. "Not in there…"

"I'm not planning on taking advantage of you."

"I had trouble deciding what to wear tonight, so…" She stared at him, her green eyes dazed. "Logan Wolfe, did you just make a joke?"

He raised his eyebrows in answer. "Where would you like me to put you down?"

"The couch would be fine. And then if you wouldn't mind getting me the package of lima beans that's in the freezer."

"Lima beans?" He eased her down on the sofa and settled a pillow behind her head.

"I happen to like lima beans."

"No one likes lima beans."

"Not even someone as health-conscious as you?"

"Not even me." He brought her the package of frozen beans and gently applied it to her bruised jaw. "Where's your ibuprofen?"

"In the kitchen cabinet to the right of the sink."

He fetched the pills and brought her a glass of water. Her gaze tracked his movements as warily as a cat watching a large dog who'd invaded her territory. Snatching a throw off a nearby chair, he spread it over her legs. A part of him realized he was fussing over her, but he needed to act. And since charging out into the night in search of her assailant wasn't an option, seeing to her comfort made him feel as if he was accomplishing something.

"Nothing in here looks disturbed. Do you keep your valuables locked away?"

"I have a safe for my jewelry. There really isn't much else of value here." She glanced toward the dining room table. "The files."

He followed her gaze. "The ones you took from the storage unit?" From where he stood he could see that the box was still on the table, but the number of files looked smaller. "Some are missing."

"Which ones?"

She swung her feet off the sofa and started getting to her feet. Before she'd fully straightened, her body swayed. Logan caught her around the waist and drew her against him. Her head found his shoulder as she leaned more fully into him.

"Slow down." He should have immediately deposited her back on the couch, but the feel of her, soft and yielding against him, was too appealing. His palm rode her strong spine up and down.

"I have to know which ones are missing. What if the information about Harper gets out? I need to tell her what I discovered."

"Nothing can be done about that at this second. You were hit hard enough to black out. I think you should go to the hospital."

"There's no need for that."

Before Logan could argue further, a hard knock sounded on her door.

"Sit. We'll discuss the hospital as soon as you make a report to security and the police."

"I'm not going."

Grinding his teeth at her stubbornness, Logan resettled Scarlett on the sofa and went to let in Security.

By the time she'd given her statement and her suite had been dusted for prints, Scarlett's agitation had reached an acute stage. Logan's presence calmed her anxiety at having her privacy so roughly violated. The package of frozen lima beans had helped numb her jaw, but nothing could ease her worry over the missing files.

The thief had taken the files for Harper and her mother, Scarlett and their grandfather. In addition, although she hadn't yet looked through the files that had originally been in the box, Scarlett thought two of those might be missing, as well.

"I really couldn't have gotten through this without you," she told Logan after he'd walked the uniformed officers to the door.

"You needed me. I was here."

And now she sensed he wished he were elsewhere. Whether to chase down the man who'd stolen the files or just to be on his way, Scarlett wasn't sure.

"I suppose you need to get home."

Inwardly she cringed at the obvious reluctance in her voice. Sure, he'd been acting solicitous and protective, but that was how he'd treat any damsel in distress. She shouldn't take it personally. No matter how wonderful it felt to have him hold her in his arms and treat her as if she were made of the finest porcelain.

"I called Madison to let her know where I was and sent one of my guys over to keep an eye on her."

"I'm sure she'll love that," Scarlett retorted, her skeptical tone masking her need to snuggle against his powerful chest and take comfort from the strength of his arms around her. For such a hard, unyielding man, he'd demonstrated he could also be gentle. She found the combination both calmed and excited her.

"He'll watch the house from the road. She'll never know."

His somber words caused her uneasiness to spike. "Do you think she's in danger?"

"No." The single word came out too fast and too sharp.

Scarlett didn't find his frown reassuring. "I don't believe you."

"Until we know what's going on, I prefer not to take chances."

"We should probably let Violet and Harper know what happened."

"Already done." He'd been busy while she'd been telling her story to the police. "They will call you tomorrow."

"I guess there's nothing left for me to do, then." Her statement hung in the air between them. She needed him to stay but couldn't bring herself to admit it. Huddling deeper into the throw wrapped around her shoulders, she waited for him to leave.

"I don't think it's a good idea for you to remain here alone tonight."

Her stomach flipped. Usually he was no more willing to offer his help than she was likely to ask for it. The change in his attitude made him more dangerous than a hundred ski-mask-wearing intruders.

"I'm sure I'll be fine if I don't invite anyone in." She tried to compel her lips into a reassuring smile but couldn't.

Logan assessed her and his expression grew more determined. "Nevertheless, I'm going to stay."

She'd already let him take control of the situation. In fact, she'd enjoyed having him in charge. But letting him know how desperate she was for his company could give him the advantage in the future.

"Fine," she said, her manner grudging. "I don't have the energy to kick you out anyway."

His lips quirked. "You're welcome."

"The guest room is made up if you want to use that for what's left of the night."

"The couch will be fine."

"Because you don't want to get too comfortable in my suite?"

"Because if anyone is getting back in, they're coming through that door." He gestured over his shoulder toward the door to the hallway.

Scarlett shivered. The idea that the robber might come back was unnerving. Suddenly it was hard for her to breathe. She began to feel dizzy and set her forehead against her knees. A quiver passed through her as the anxiety she'd bottled up these past couple of hours refused to stay contained a second longer.

"Scarlett." Logan knelt beside her. His large hand was warm and reassuring against her shoulder. "Are you okay?"

"I'm fine." She sat up straight and dashed away the wetness on her cheek.

He exhaled impatiently. "Will you stop trying to act like nothing is wrong when it's obvious you're upset?"

"Of course I'm upset." She let her temper flare. It terrified her to let down her guard around him. "Shouldn't I be? I was attacked and whatever the thief took tonight might have damaging consequences for my family."

"Right now what you need is sleep." He held out his hand.

His suggestion made sense, but she didn't move. It was far nicer to be in the same room where she could be comforted by his reassuring strength. But telling him that would give him too much insight into how she thought.

"You're sending me to bed?" She let him pull her up and forced a mocking smile. "Most men would be escorting me there."

"Then most men are jerks for taking advantage of you in such a vulnerable state."

Vulnerable? If that's how he saw her, she'd given far too much away tonight. "Most men can't help themselves. They find me irresistible."

"That's a pretty powerful feeling for you, isn't it?"

She set her hand on her hip, a trace of spunk returning. "What's wrong with feeling powerful?"

"Not a thing. Unless you have to be that way all the time."

"I don't." But she was lying. Being strong was how she'd survived being a child star and how she'd struggled back from the dark years of partying too much and falling once too often for the wrong guy. "There's nothing that I can do right in your eyes, is there?"

She turned away before the longing to throw herself at him grew too strong to resist. Her feet felt heavy and sluggish as she crossed the living room. With each step she took, her heartbeat slowed. She hoped he'd come after her, sweep her into his arms and carry her the rest of the way to her bed. When that didn't happen, she closed her bedroom door and left a trail of clothes to mark her passage. Naked, she fell into bed.

But the weariness that dragged on her limbs didn't reach her mind. Scarlett lay on her back, staring at the ceiling, and turned the theft of the files over and over in her head. Had the thief taken them without seeing what they were because he was in a hurry? Or had he broken in specifically because he wanted something that was in them?

She'd gone through her family's files a dozen times. The only damaging item was the fact that Harper's father wasn't Ross Fontaine, and Scarlett couldn't imagine Penelope hiring someone to steal the files. It had to be something else. What had she missed?

Closing her eyes, Scarlett sifted through the contents of her father's file, but all she got for her efforts was an increased throbbing in her head. Ross had been a rotten husband, but that wasn't exactly a huge secret. He'd preferred his women young and single so there weren't any jealous husbands. And he'd been more ham-fisted than ruthless in running Fontaine Hotels and Resorts to have made any enemies among the other hotel owners in Las Vegas.

Scarlett just couldn't see why the guy had wanted the files. And then she recalled the rest of what was in the box. Caught up in the drama surrounding her family, she'd only glanced through the other files once.

Most of the material had been about Tiberius's brother-in-law, Preston Rhodes, the current chairman of the board and CEO of Stone Properties, which was headquartered in Miami, Florida. Like Fontaine Hotels and Resorts, Stone Properties owned hotel and resort properties all over the world.

Scarlett had once asked Tiberius why he didn't work for the company his father had founded and learned how his brother-in-law had schemed to get Tiberius kicked out of the family business so he could take over.

No surprise, then, that Preston had never set foot in Las Vegas. Stone Properties had one hotel on the Strip: Titanium. Run by JT Stone, Tiberius's nephew and namesake, the five-star hotel sat several blocks north of the trio of Fontaine hotels.

An hour ticked by, bringing her no closer to sleep. Logan's presence in the living room was far too distracting. At last she got up and slipped into a hot-pink cotton lounge set. She stood with her hand on the doorknob for a few minutes, debating what excuse she'd use for wanting his company. In the end it didn't matter because when she reached the living room, Logan was nowhere to be found.

Her disappointment was difficult to ignore as she headed into the kitchen for a bottle of water. Instead of drinking it, she set the cool bottle against her still-aching jaw. The coolness washed through her and without warning, tears sprang to her eyes. Normally she'd blink them away and shove down her unhappiness. *Never show weakness.* She'd learned that early in Hollywood. But being abandoned by Logan was too much on top of everything else she'd gone through tonight.

As the tears began working their way down her cheeks, the door to her suite opened. Heart pounding in sudden alarm, Scarlett was too overcome by panic to move. When Logan stepped into view, she was awash in relief.

"You came back."

His gaze swung in her direction. "I never left."

"You weren't here when I came to get water."

"I stepped outside to talk to Lucas." He gestured with his cell phone. "I didn't want to disturb you." As he spoke, he narrowed the distance between them. "Is your jaw still sore?"

He'd moved within reach and before she could question the wisdom of her actions, Scarlett pressed herself against his strong body. She wrapped her arms around his waist and felt him tense. But when his hands touched her shoulders, it wasn't to push her away but to gather her still closer.

"Don't worry," he said. "You're safe."

And for the first time in a long time, she knew she was. Letting someone take care of her wasn't comfortable for Scarlett. She'd developed a deep and wide streak of distrust not long after reaching puberty. The older brother of one of her fellow actors had cornered her in a dressing room and stuck his tongue down her throat. Afterward he'd threatened to say she'd come on to him if she told anyone what had happened. She'd been twelve years old at the time and was just beginning to understand what it meant to be a woman.

"I'm not always strong," she told him, her voice muffled against his shoulder. "Usually I'm terrified that what I'm doing is completely wrong."

Logan stroked her hair. "You've sure fooled me."

"That was the idea."

Logan drew Scarlett toward the couch. They sat together in the middle with little space between them. Scarlett snuggled against his side and her lips curved into a dreamy smile when his arm came around her shoulder. It was a serene, domestic moment, unlike their normally tempestuous encounters. The invasion of her home had cracked her shell, knocking her off her game.

For the first time he didn't question whether this was honest fear or just a performance to make him sympathetic toward her. He'd seen her acting range. She could transform herself into whatever played into a man's fantasy. Since he'd criticized the way she dressed, he'd noticed her wardrobe had become more professional. Was she donning another costume, one designed to win him over? Did she even comprehend what she was doing? Or was it second nature to her?

"You're a hard woman to read, Scarlett Fontaine."

Tonight, she'd been as rattled as he'd ever seen her. So much so she couldn't bring herself to tell him she was afraid.

Her sigh brushed his neck. "I hate to admit it, but you bring out the worst in me."

He was silent a long moment. "Why is that?" He asked the question, not expecting she'd tell him the truth.

"I guess I want too much for you to like me."

Her declaration caught him off guard. Had she recovered her equilibrium? Was this an act? She'd been prickly when he'd told her he wasn't going to take advantage of her. She hadn't appreciated his chivalry. And she'd been right to say that few men would've let her go to bed alone. Sitting alone out here with nothing but an unlocked door between them was a harsh test of his willpower.

"Why do you care what I think?"

"Because I like you and I know you don't approve of me."

He couldn't believe what he was hearing. "Why do you care what I think?"

"There aren't a lot of people who don't like me." She huffed out a small laugh. "I know how that sounds, but I've always had a knack for winning people over."

"I've seen you in action many times."

"I can hear it in your voice. You don't approve of how I behave." She sounded grumpy.

Against his better judgment, Logan found her dismay charming. "Does it occur to you how ridiculous it sounds to say you want me to like you when you've been provocative and difficult at every turn?"

"I'm simply responding to your scorn." She flashed him a baleful glance. "Call it self-preservation."

Hadn't he been just as guilty of provoking her? "Should we call a truce?"

"And have you lose interest in me because things become boring between us?" Her green eyes had regained some of their wicked sparkle. "Half the reason you find me so attractive is because I keep you guessing."

"You're sure I find you attractive?"

He'd no sooner uttered the challenge when her hand curved across his thigh. His muscles twitched in response and her lips arced impishly. That she was touching him to prove a point was the only thing that kept him from flipping her onto her back.

"If you knew all my secrets," she said, "you'd find me deadly dull."

"I can't imagine that's possible."

To hell with his earlier stance on not taking advantage of her in a vulnerable state. There was only so much temptation a man could take. And the pressure behind his zipper demanded that he give up the fight.

He bent down and captured her mouth in a slow kiss meant to satisfy his need for deeper intimacy with her. She moaned beneath his lips and twisted her body until she was sliding backward. Unwilling to be parted from her even for a second, Logan broke off the kiss and scooped his hands beneath her ass, repositioning her with her spine flat on the couch, his weight crushing her into its soft cushions.

"Are you okay?" he asked noticing her slight wince. He pushed a hair away from her face and eyed the spot where the intruder had hit her. "If your jaw is hurting, we should stop."

"Don't worry about it."

Logan wasn't convinced. "You've swelled up a bit where he hit you."

"I'm fine."

"Really?"

"Just shut up and kiss me."

As fierce as his desire was for her, Logan wasn't about to rush the moment he'd been fantasizing about for weeks. No matter how deeply lust sank its talons into his groin, he intended to explore every inch of her skin, taste each sigh, absorb the entirety of her surrender.

He applied gentle kisses to her parted lips, causing her to murmur in encouragement. With his weight pinning her, she had little hope of wiggling and driving him mad with provocative movements, but her hands were free and she used them to her advantage.

After ruffling his hair and tracing his spine, she tightened her grasp on his shirt and pulled it free of his pants. Braced against the first touch of her skin against his, he kept up the slow seduction with his lips and tongue. She sighed as her palms connected with his lower back. Logan couldn't prevent the instinctive twitch his body gave as she raked her long nails up his sides.

Ignoring the heat blazing between them, he cupped her cheek and licked at her lips, running his tongue along her teeth before flicking her tongue. Beneath his palm he felt her facial muscles shift and knew she was smiling. He kissed her nose, a grin of his own blooming at her heartfelt sigh.

"Why so impatient?" he teased, taking her plump lower lip between his teeth and sucking ever so lightly.

Her nails bit into his back. "Because five years of foreplay is too long."

"Five years?" Carefully avoiding her bruised jaw, he nuzzled the soft skin below her ear, inhaling her smooth, fresh perfume and the sharper tang of her earlier stress. If nothing else reinforced his need to take his time, this reminder of what she'd been through tonight did. "Is that what we've been doing all this time?"

"Of course." She adjusted the angle of her head to grant him better access to her neck.

"How do you figure?"

"You don't seriously think all that animosity between us was anything other than frustrated sexual energy, do you?"

He knew what it had been on his part, but was surprised she admitted to being similarly afflicted. "Are you saying you've wanted me this whole time?"

He tried to make his voice sound shocked, but ended up

fighting a groan as she found a way to free her left leg from beneath him. By bending her knee, she was able to shift his hips into the perfect V between her thighs. Her intimate heat pressed against his hip even through the layers of fabric between them. Breath rasping in and out of his lungs, he held perfectly still to savor the sensation.

"Of course."

He believed her because whenever they touched, the walls tumbled down between them. And in this place where they communicated truth as easily with words as they did with their bodies, he was in serious danger of falling hard.

Was that why he'd doubted and taunted her all these years? Because he suspected that if they had a civil conversation he might have to face just how crazy he was about her? All her flaws became insignificant. All his misgivings seemed to be paranoia.

"Make love to me, Logan," she pleaded when the silence dragged on too long. "Don't make me wait any longer."

"I want nothing more," he admitted. "But let's take it slow."

"Slow?" She didn't look happy.

"Slow," he confirmed. "You're worth savoring. Relax." He reclaimed her lips and soothed her with soft, romantic kisses. "We have all night."

Scarlett put her impatience aside and let Logan set the pace. The ache between her thighs didn't abate, but neither did it intensify as they exchanged a series of slow, sweet kisses. The give-and-take of his lips against hers was comforting and the fog of desire dissipated from her mind, offering her a chance to enjoy the feel of his strong body where it pressed against hers and the subtle cologne he'd applied for their date tonight. She concentrated on relaxing her muscles, ignoring the hunger needling her. Logan was right. They'd waited this long. Why rush it?

His kisses did unexpected things to her emotions. Lighter than soap bubbles, joy pushed outward from her center. Logan made her feel like no other man ever had. Cherished. Appreciated. Understood. The excitement she'd expected to feel as his body mastered hers was tempered by the need to relish every second of their time together.

"Why are you smiling?" Logan asked, drifting his lips across her eyelids and down her nose.

"I've never necked on the couch like this."

"Never?" Surprise peppered Logan's question. "I find that hard to believe."

"It's true. Necking is something you do with your boyfriend on your parents' couch or in the back of your boyfriend's car."

"Seems to me you had both a boyfriend and access to a couch and car."

"I wasn't a normal teenager. For one thing, I didn't go to regular school. I had tutors and studied between scenes. For another, my boyfriend at the time liked partying with friends and hitting the club." Not kicking back and hanging out alone with his girlfriend.

"Oh, right, you were dating that boy-band reject back then."

Hearing Logan's derision, Scarlett wished she'd kept her mouth shut, but now that the door was open, she might as well step through.

"We started dating when we were fifteen." Lost in girlish, idealistic fantasies about love, she'd relished their role as America's sweethearts, but their private interaction wasn't nearly as romantic as their public one. "After being fired from *That's Our Hilary* because my image was becoming too sexy and getting offered nothing but vampy bad-girl parts, I tried to clean up my image by trotting out this vow of chastity until I got married." The armies of paparazzi following them had eaten it up. Reacting the way any normal eighteen-year-old boy would, Will had dumped her.

"You're a virgin?" Logan did a lousy job hiding his amusement behind mock surprise.

"Don't be absurd." To punish him, she rotated her hips and rubbed her pelvis against his erection. His eyes glazed with satisfying swiftness. "After Will and I broke up, I discovered celibacy wasn't all it was cracked up to be."

"So, you've never necked on a couch before," he prompted. "Anything else I should know about?"

Too much. But those things would have to wait until she had a better handle on what was happening between them. "One revelation per day is all you're going to get."

"At this rate, it'll take the rest of my life getting to know you."

His offhand remark created a vacuum between them. Scarlett kept her eyes lidded and her breath even as she said, "It never occurred to me that you'd let it take that long. You're so impatient when it comes to getting answers."

"Some things are worth waiting for."

It wasn't like Logan to be cryptic, but Scarlett had no chance to question him further. His lips returned to hers with more intensity, and she knew the time had come for serious play between them.

When she'd dressed in the lounge suit, she hadn't planned on Logan's strong, sure hands smoothing over her curves, but now she was glad she hadn't slipped into her underwear first. As bare beneath the hot-pink fabric as the day she was born, Scarlett knew the instant Logan's fingers discovered her secret.

"Scarlett," he groaned her name as her nipple tightened against his palm. "What you do to me."

She arched her back and bared her throat for his lips and tongue. After working her into an unsteady mess, he glided his mouth across her collarbone and deposited gentle kisses in the hollow of her shoulder. His chin nudged along the edge of the fabric as he dusted his lips across her breastbone and worked his way toward her cleavage.

The zipper of her lounge suit surrendered beneath the downward pressure of Logan's fingers. She gasped as cool air washed across her bare skin, but his lips skimmed over her ribs, warming her once more. Desire rushed through her as Logan finished unfastening the jacket and laved her quivering stomach. Sensation lanced straight to her hot core, leaving her head spinning.

Impatience clawed at her, but the man refused to move at the speed she so desperately craved. Now, instead of kissing her lips and neck, he was paying entirely too much attention to her abdomen, rib cage and the ticklish spot just above her hipbone.

"Logan, there are other parts of me that are hungry for your attention." She tugged on his shirt, urging him to stop ignoring her breasts.

"Are there, now?" He kissed his way upward. "And what might those be?"

"My breasts are feeling very lonely." She gathered them in her hands and offered him their aching fullness.

With a smile he licked around one nipple. "They are so beautiful, I was saving them for later."

She was half-mad with the anticipation of having his mouth so close but just out of reach. "Not later," she insisted as his tongue flicked one sensitive button. "Now."

"Whatever you say."

She had never imagined that ordering him to do what

she wanted would be so thrilling. A moan ripped from her throat as he pulled her nipple into his mouth and sucked. Scarlett sank her fingers into his thick black hair and held on tight as an ocean swell of pleasure pushed her out of her depths.

"More," she ordered as he switched to her other breast. "I need more."

He soothed her with a single word. "Soon."

But her need for him was escalating too fast and they both had too many clothes on. She grabbed ahold of his belt and tugged to get his attention. "This has to go."

Unable to budge him, she hooked her fingers in the waistband of her own pants and eased them downward, knowing she couldn't get them off but hoping he'd get the hint and help her.

"Not yet."

But as he reached down to tug her hand away, she turned the tables on him and pulled his fingers across her mound.

"Yes," she purred, parting her thighs still farther to encourage him to explore. She was rewarded by the slide of his finger against her moist heat. "Right there."

Throwing her head back, she closed her eyes and centered every bit of concentration on the swirl of Logan's tongue around her breast and the drag of his fingers at her core. She could feel tension invade his muscles and knew what he'd hoped to prolong was moving forward at its own speed, gaining momentum as it swept them toward their ultimate destination.

Her own body was tightening pleasurably. A smile curved her lips as she once again felt the downward drift of Logan's mouth on her body. This time he didn't linger at her stomach, but continued to move at a torturously slow pace to the place where she burned.

* * *

Logan eased her pants down her thighs. Blood pumped vigorously through his veins, clouding his vision. He blinked, needing desperately to focus on the exquisite body he was slowly baring—the large, full breasts, tiny waist and flat stomach. The jut of her hipbones and those long, toned legs. Absolutely gorgeous. And all his.

Tossing her pants aside, he settled between her thighs and cupped her round butt in his palms. Her eyes flew open as he set his tongue against her and drank in her essence. As demanding as she'd been a moment earlier, she melted like butter beneath his intimate kisses now. Her fingers clutched at his shirt, gripping hard enough to tear the seams.

He opened his eyes and watched her come apart. As she surged toward completion he experienced a rush of gratitude that he was here, giving her this pleasure. Her mouth opened as her entire body stiffened. His name escaped her in a keening cry.

As she drifted back to earth, he sat up and stripped off his clothes. He pulled a condom out of his wallet and sheathed himself. Any hope of taking his time was smashed by her parted thighs and welcoming arms. He lay back down, and angled his hips until the tip of his erection sat at her entrance. Her arms closed about his neck, her fingers playing with his hair.

"I need to feel you inside me," she murmured, kissing his chin.

He dipped his head and kissed her soft lips, the contact tender and slow. When her tongue stole out to mate with his, he slipped into her in one smooth stroke and groaned. She clasped him in a snug embrace and the sensation was too much for words. But one stood out in his mind.

"Amazing."

"Absolutely."

Moving inside her was the single most incredible thing he'd ever experienced. Somehow she knew exactly how to shift her hips to achieve the ideal friction. Making love on the couch wasn't ideal, but their shared laughter as they jostled for leverage and strained to pleasure each other with lips, hands and movements made the moment completely perfect and totally theirs.

He'd never imagined feeling such a strong connection with any woman, much less the one who'd been a thorn in his side for five years. Maybe she was right. It had been simple sexual frustration. Once they satisfied their itch for each other, they could go politely on their way, never to take jabs at each other again.

Somehow the idea that he might never get another night with Scarlett filled him with anguish. He kissed her hard, grappling with the notion that his desire for her could ever be fully slaked. But if she continued to drive him crazy, what did that mean for the future?

He quickened his pace as control abandoned him. Scarlett matched his intensity, her expression tight with concentration as they drove together toward completion. As she began to peak, her eyes opened and locked on his. The smile that emerged on her passion-bruised lips speared straight into his heart. It wasn't carnal or greedy in nature. It was heartbreakingly open. She'd offered him a glimpse into her soul and it was brimming with optimism and hope.

Logan buried his face in her neck to escape what he'd seen, but the image haunted him as he felt her body begin to vibrate. The bite of Scarlett's nails against his back triggered his own orgasm. Muscles quivering, nerves pulsing with frantic energy, he thrust hard into her and let himself go. Together they crested, voices blending in perfect harmony.

Bodies trembling in the aftermath, they clung to each

other. Logan's chest pumped, drawing much-needed air into his lungs. Scarlett's fingertips moved languidly up and down his spine, her touch soothing.

Damn. What the hell had just happened?

"Give me a second and I'll move," he muttered, his voice raw and shaken. He hoped she would credit the workout they'd just had for causing him to sound so unsteady. She couldn't find out how his feelings for her had deepened until he could sort out what to do about it.

"Take your time." Scarlett's voice was maddeningly relaxed and calm. "I'm enjoying the feel of all this brawn."

While his heart thumped hard enough to break a rib, Logan kissed her cheek and the corner of her mouth. "Why are you smiling?"

"Are you kidding?" She laughed. "When was the last time you tore someone's clothes off and had sex on a couch?" Her finger dug into his ribs. "And don't you dare tell me last week."

"I did not tear your clothes off."

"No," she agreed. "You took way too much time removing them." She framed his face with her hands and forced his gaze to hers. "Are you okay?"

"I'm the guy," he reminded her, turning his head so he could kiss her palm. "I'm the one who's supposed to ask that."

She twitched her shoulders. "So ask."

"Are you okay?"

"Never better."

Logan kissed her lips. "You know, we really should get off this couch."

"Don't you dare." Her arm wrapped around his neck, holding him in a tight vise. "I like it right here."

"At least let me…" He shifted his weight off her and lay on his back, pinning her on her side between him and the back of the couch. "That's better," he said, pulling the conveniently placed throw over their naked, cooling bodies.

"It's nice."

With her cheek resting on his shoulder and her body a curvy miracle half-draped over him, Logan closed his eyes and wondered when he'd enjoyed such contentment. Usually he was a burn-the-candle-at-both-ends kind of guy. He spent most of his days overseeing his company's massive operations here in Las Vegas and his evenings dreaming up better technology to keep his clients' assets safe.

Taking time for a personal life had been a low priority. Sure, he dated. A guy had needs. But he wasn't one to linger after a nice dinner and some satisfying sex. He never exactly bolted for the door, but he certainly didn't stick around long enough to snuggle.

This experience with Scarlett was much different. He was at peace. Delighted to hold her in his arms until the sun came up, watching her sleep or talking. Was it crazy that they argued about everything but blended seamlessly the instant they kissed? Would their differing points of view eventually taint their lovemaking?

It was no surprise that Logan was already thinking in terms of endings. Didn't he enter every relationship with an eye on how and when it would end? Perhaps it wasn't fair to the women he saw that he perceived their time together as finite, but his perspective was realistic. Even nine-year relationships ended. That his fiancée could choose her career over him had struck a devastating blow. One he wasn't going to let happen again.

And he needed to be more wary than ever because slipping into sleep beside him was the first woman since Elle who had the potential to catch him off guard.

Seven

Humming happily, Scarlett dived into the clear, cool water of the private pool located on the same floor as her private suite. She loved to swim, and tried to spend at least thirty minutes in the morning doing laps. If she had a little more time, she floated across the dappled surface and enjoyed the lush vegetation planted around the pool deck.

She ached in all sorts of muscles this morning. Making love on a couch was just the sort of thing she might have expected from Logan. Waking up to his soft kisses and hard erection had been a nice surprise. If she'd been asked to bet how he'd behave in the cold light of a Las Vegas dawn, she would have put her money on him returning to his impatient, bad-tempered self. And she would have lost every cent.

Not only did he wake up aroused. He was playful in the morning. And unexpectedly romantic. For a woman who was used to being treated like some sort of trophy, Logan's willingness to make her coffee and feed her orange slices had given her hope that she wasn't simply a conquest.

Her happy glow persisted through the rest of the morning. At noon she headed to her office, where reality intruded. The script Bobby had promised to send sat in the middle of her desk. She tore open the package and scanned the short note he'd included. Even though she'd already decided against auditioning, there was no stopping the excitement that rushed through her. New scripts meant new opportunities and so few had come her way in the past few years.

Although she had no intention of returning to Hollywood and told herself it was foolish to get worked up about the project, she cleared her afternoon schedule and read the entire script twice. The writing was really good. The story fresh and daring. It was the exact thing she'd longed to do, but no one would give her a chance.

Almost as if on cue, as soon as she completed her second pass, her cell rang. It was Bobby. She set the pages aside.

"Well?" He sounded confident and smug as if he already knew what her reaction would be. "Aren't you perfect?"

"I don't know if I'm perfect," she hedged, struggling to keep enthusiasm out of her voice. "But it's a wonderful script and it's going to be a great show."

"Then you'll come and test?"

Here was where she had to face reality. "I really can't. I live in Las Vegas now. I'm responsible for this hotel. I can't just abandon everything and run off to L.A. because of a great part." Besides, there was no guarantee that she'd get the role, and being rejected for something so perfect for her would be a devastating blow.

"The director's an old friend of yours."

"Who'd you get?"

"Chase Reynolds."

Damn. As fabulous as Chase was in front of the camera, the former actor had proven himself to be even more worthy behind it. "He'll do a great job."

"So will you."

"Bobby…" Her tone had taken on a desperate note.

"Gotta run, Scarlett. I'll be in touch later this week."

The call ended before she could protest further. Scarlett's head fell back. The ceiling became a blank canvas for her thoughts. She wouldn't be the first actor to live outside of Hollywood and practice her trade. But how many of those had a demanding position as executive manager of a hotel? Not that she was all that hands-on. She'd hired the right people for key jobs and was little more than a figurehead. Wasn't that how Logan perceived her?

Logan.

Now that they'd taken things to the next level, this was a terrible time for her to be away from him. But she'd never let a man stand in the way of her career before. Of course, she'd never had a man like Logan Wolfe either. And keeping him there was worth a little sacrifice. A little sacrifice, maybe, but this was a fabulous part in a groundbreaking new show. A show that could give her career an enormous boost.

If she still wanted a career as an actress. Did she?

Scarlett surged to her feet and exited her office. In the excitement of getting the script, she'd almost forgotten the other pressing problem facing her. That of telling Violet and Harper that Tiberius had accumulated files on them. And that those files had been stolen. She'd start with Violet. See how that encounter went. Perhaps she'd even pick her half sister's brain about the best way to approach Harper. As well as how much to tell her.

After letting her assistant know where she'd be, Scarlett headed to the walkway that would take her to Fontaine

Chic. She sent Violet a quick text to find out where they could meet up and followed that with a call to Madison.

"I'm sorry to make this so last-minute," Scarlett said to the young actress wannabe, "but I'm going to have to cancel dinner tonight. In fact, why don't you take the rest of the night off."

"Are you sure?"

"Weren't you telling me something about a party one of your friends was having?"

Concerned that Madison wasn't spending enough time with kids her own age, Scarlett had arranged for her to meet some college-bound teenagers that Logan couldn't help but approve of. Sensible kids from good families, they were keen to start at their various schools in the fall, and Madison had caught some of their enthusiasm. Another couple weeks with them and Logan's niece would be ready to resume an academic path.

"Trent is having a few friends over."

"Then you should go. You've worked hard all week. Time to have a little fun."

"I'll tell Uncle Logan that you said that."

Scarlett winced. As amazing as last night had been, she wasn't sure Logan would appreciate hearing her make suggestions about his niece's social life. "Oh, please don't."

"Why not? He really likes you."

"He does?" Scarlett had reached Fontaine Chic and her steps slowed.

"Sure. Just like you have a thing for him."

Why fight it? "I have a huge thing for your uncle. And we're just starting to get along. I don't want to risk annoying him."

Madison laughed. "After the way he was smiling this morning, I don't think you have to worry about it. See you tomorrow."

Left to muse over Logan's good humor, Scarlett didn't even notice she'd passed by Violet until her sister grabbed her arm and gave her a shake.

"You were certainly miles away," Violet said with a curious smile. "Thinking of anyone in particular?"

Scarlett felt the jolt all the way to her toes. Was Violet fishing? There was no way she could know what Scarlett and Logan had been up to the night before. Nevertheless, a guilty flush crept up her chest.

"Nothing like that."

"Look at your poor jaw." Violet murmured, abruptly sober. "How bad is it?"

"I'll survive." Scarlett brushed off her sister's concern. "But the incident last night is why I need to talk to you."

"Sounds serious."

"Let's go to your office so we won't be disturbed."

"That's the worst place we could go. How about we head to Lalique?"

The centerpiece of Violet's hotel was an enormous three-story crystal chandelier that enclosed an elegant two-story bar in dazzling, sparkling ropes. It was three million dollars' worth of *oh, wow* and set the tone for her decor. Like the sky-blue in Harper's Fontaine Ciel, crystal was Violet's signature. Multifaceted and ever-changing, clear crystals sparkled above the gaming tables and from the fixtures that lined the walkways. Pillars sparkled with embedded lights made to resemble crystals and all the waitstaff and dealers wore rhinestone-accented black uniforms.

Settling into a quiet corner table, Violet ordered two glasses of sparkling water with lime and an olive pâté appetizer to share. She then turned to her sister.

"Something is obviously bothering you," Violet commented.

Scarlett gathered a large breath and began. "I told you how Tiberius had left me his files."

"Yes. Have you had a chance to dig into any of them?" Violet's eyes were bright with interest. "What kind of dirt did he have on people?"

"I haven't had time to look at more than a couple." This was the part that was tough. "There were files on our father and you, Harper and me."

Violet didn't look surprised. "I can only imagine what he dug up about Ross." Unlike Scarlett, Violet had known from an early age that she was Ross Fontaine's illegitimate daughter. She'd never had any contact with him, but was pretty sure he knew he was her father. That he'd refused to acknowledge her had been hard on Violet.

"Quite a lot. But none of it was that damning. I mean, we all know he was a philandering jerk, but mostly Tiberius was interested in keeping an eye on his running of Fontaine Hotels and Resorts."

"So the reason you're upset has nothing to do with Ross?"

"Not directly."

"Spill it."

"The files were stolen last night."

"That's what the thief was after?"

"I don't know for sure. He took other files as well. Ones that had nothing to do with us. Tiberius was keeping an eye on his brother-in-law. Almost half the box was filled with stuff on Stone Properties. Financials. Their employees. I just glanced at it."

Violet nodded. "Tiberius hated Preston for the way he treated his sister. Blamed him for her death."

Scarlett's pulse jerked. "Why is that?"

"Preston's priority was the company he took over after his father-in-law died. He wasn't much of a father or a husband. Unfortunately, Fiona Stone adored her husband and couldn't handle his neglect. She turned to drugs and alcohol to cope and died of an overdose when JT was about twelve."

JT Stone ran the family's operations in Las Vegas. A handsome, enigmatic businessman, he didn't socialize with the Fontaine sisters, but Violet had gotten to know him a little because he was Tiberius's nephew.

"How awful to lose his mom so young," Scarlett said, thinking of all the substance abuse she'd seen ruin lives during her years in Hollywood. "Anyway, in addition to those files, the guy grabbed the files Tiberius had on all of us." Scarlett noticed Violet wasn't at all surprised. "You knew?"

"I suspected." She grinned. "Anything interesting?"

Scarlett felt a little of her dread ease. "There was a great deal on my time in L.A. Nothing too shocking there. I kept the paparazzi busy for several years during my dark period. Your file was the thinnest of the bunch."

Violet sighed. "I'm deadly dull."

"You should do something to fix that," Scarlett teased before growing serious once more. "But getting back to the problem. Last night the thief stole all our files. Including one I pulled on Harper's mother." She paused, still unsure how much to share what she knew with Violet.

"If there's nothing much in the files, why would he risk getting caught stealing them?"

"He might have been fishing. I don't know if he went there looking for other files and just grabbed up whatever he could get or if he came specifically to take our family's files."

"But you said there was nothing of interest in them."

Again Scarlett hesitated. She knew she could trust Violet, but didn't want to anger Harper by spilling her secret. If it even was a secret. Maybe Harper knew. Maybe Grandfather knew. Maybe Scarlett and Violet were the only two in the dark.

But she didn't think that scenario was likely. Family meant too much to Henry Fontaine. It's why he'd given his illegitimate granddaughters the same shot at running Fontaine Hotels and Resorts as he'd given his legitimate one. Scarlett wasn't sure how he'd react if he found out Harper wasn't his granddaughter.

"Scarlett," Violet prompted, her tone tinged with alarm. "What aren't you telling me?"

"It's not about you. It's about Harper."

Violet laughed. "Harper? If anyone doesn't have skeletons in their closet it's her."

"It actually has to do with her mother. And what I discovered in the files has the potential of turning Harper's world upside down."

"If it's that bad," Violet said, dismay clouding her expression, "I don't want to ask what you unearthed."

Scarlett was relieved that Violet was letting her off the hook. The secret wasn't hers to share. If she told Harper, and if she in turn wanted Violet to know, that was different.

"Do I tell her?" Scarlett would love it if Violet told her what to do. "Would you want to know?"

Violet took a long time pondering Scarlett's questions. "I can't answer for Harper, but I don't think I'd want to know. Maybe it's awfully naive of me to think that anything that's been buried this long should stay hidden."

"Which is the way I was leaning before the files were stolen. But what happens if the guy figures out the same thing I did and the information gets out? She'll be blindsided. At least if I tell her, she can prepare."

"It's something she needs to prepare for?" Violet frowned. "In that case I don't think I can tell you what to do. On one hand, she deserves to know the truth."

So did other people. Like Grandfather. But Scarlett couldn't bear to be the one who damaged Harper's relationship with the man she looked up to and adored.

"On the other hand, the truth might ruin everything."

Logan entered his house and left his briefcase on the table in the foyer. Tugging at his tie, he strode into the kitchen to fetch a cold beer. He'd spent the better part of the afternoon in a meeting with a new client discussing a proposal that would be worth several million dollars over the next year or so.

Most of the new business Wolfe Security generated was handled by his sales staff. But every now and then a project came along where the client demanded to meet with Logan or Lucas. Considering this was the sort of deal that would strengthen their global-market position, Logan was willing to meet with the guy, no matter how much of a pain in the ass he was.

Beer in hand, he headed toward the master bedroom, intent on grabbing a shower and changing. He was heading back to Tiberius's storage unit next. Something about last night's theft had been nagging at him. Maybe another journey through the files would spark inspiration.

A tiny part of him recognized that visiting the storage unit was an excuse to avoid what he really wanted to do—spend time with Scarlett. All day long he'd caught himself reaching for the phone to call her. He'd known making love with her would aggravate his fascination with her. It was the reason that he'd resisted crossing that line for as long as he had.

He slowed as he neared Madison's room. "You're home early," he remarked, spying her facedown on her bed, feet kicking the air in slow sweeps.

She looked up from her reading, her gaze slow to focus

on him. "Scarlett gave me the night off. Said she needed to take care of something." Madison's smile grew sly. "Are you planning on staying out all night again?"

He ignored her question and asked one of his own. "What are you reading?"

"A script for a brand-new TV show. It's terrific. There's a part in here I'd be perfect for."

"Where did you get it?"

Madison's expression settled into worried lines. "I took it from Scarlett's office. I'll get it back before she even notices it's missing."

So Scarlett was reading scripts. And not just any scripts but ones featuring teenage girls. Surely she didn't think tempting the seventeen-year-old with juicy acting jobs that would never materialize was a good way to convince Madison to go to college? Did Scarlett think that once he'd given her his trust, she could go and do what she thought was right where Madison was concerned?

He prowled into the room. "Give me the script." His tone brooked no argument and he received none.

Madison sat up and handed him the bound pages. "I know I should have told her I wanted to read it, but she sounded so distracted when we spoke I didn't think she'd even notice."

To her credit, his niece sounded more apprehensive than argumentative. That was a change from the sullen teenager who'd appeared on his doorstep two weeks ago. Ten minutes ago he'd have been happy to give Scarlett credit for the transformation. That was before he found out she was looking at television projects.

"I'm sure if you'd asked her, she'd have let you read the script."

"You're right. I should have asked." Madison crossed

her legs and gave him her most solemn expression. "When you give it back to her tell her I'm sorry."

Giving Madison's repentant attitude a distracted nod, Logan continued toward his room. He finished showering and dressing in record time and was back on the road before his hair had a chance to dry. The script on the passenger seat beside him kept his irritation fueled. Scarlett had assured him she was done with Hollywood. So why was she bothering with a script?

Before leaving the house, he'd texted her and found out she was heading back to her office after meeting with Violet. He had twenty minutes to ponder what had passed between the sisters as he navigated the traffic between his house and the Strip.

The floor containing the executive offices at Fontaine Richesse was still active at seven o'clock. He nodded brusquely at the employees he passed as he strode the hall to Scarlett's large corner office. She was behind her desk, attention focused on the computer, when he entered. In the split second it took her to notice him, his heart bumped powerfully in his chest.

She was as beautiful in her gold silk blouse as she'd been last night wrapped in nothing but his arms. With her hair scraped back in a low ponytail and simple gold jewelry at her ears and throat, she looked every inch the successful executive. And nothing at all like the passionate temptress who'd unraveled his control.

"Logan." Her smile drew him across the room to her. "I didn't expect to see you tonight."

Instead of circling the desk and snatching her into his arms, he sat down in her guest chair and dropped the script onto the uncluttered surface between them. Her fingers slid off the keyboard and onto her lap.

She frowned. "Where'd you get that?"

"Madison had it."

"Madison?" Acting as if it was of little importance, Scarlett picked up the pages and dropped them into the trash. "She must have come by while I was meeting with Violet."

"Why do you have a script, Scarlett?"

She got up from her desk and circled around to lean against the front. "A producer friend of mine sent it to me."

"Let me guess, you know a teenager who would be perfect for his new TV show."

"What?" Her eyes went wide as his accusation sunk in. "No. Of course not. Is that what you think?"

"What else should I think?"

"That maybe I was offered a part. A good part. Something I would be perfect for." Her tone was insistent, defensive.

"I thought you were done with Hollywood."

She hesitated slightly before saying, "I am." But it was a telling pause.

What happened to all her protestations about how difficult her life as an actor had been? Was all of that merely a defense mechanism to keep disappointment at bay? When the opportunity came along to resume her acting career, would she jump at it?

"Of course I am," she insisted, her voice gaining conviction. "I have a life here in Las Vegas."

"But if this opportunity had come along five years ago and you had to choose, which life would you have picked?"

"That's not a fair question."

Her protest told him her answer was not to his liking. "You'd have chosen to stay in L.A."

"Probably. But only because acting was all I knew. Moving to Las Vegas and taking over the running of this hotel wasn't an easy decision for me to make. I had no experience. Frankly, I was terrified of making a mistake."

"Everyone makes mistakes."

"Yes, but do everyone's mistakes mean millions of dollars are at risk?" With a deep breath she clamped down on her escalating aggravation until her composure returned. "All this speculation is a waste of time. What I might have chosen to do five years ago has no bearing on what I do today."

Relief washed over him. She wasn't going to leave Las Vegas. Leave him. "I guess I jumped to the wrong conclusion."

She widened her eyes dramatically. "Was that an apology?"

"No." He pulled her onto his lap. "This is."

His kiss let her feel all his frustration and longing. The emotions she aroused troubled him. How could he mistrust her and still want her this much? Saying it was simple lust didn't ring true. She'd become his last thought at night and his first one in the morning. He was mesmerized by her beauty and intrigued by the layers she kept hidden.

"Feel like ordering room service in my suite?" she asked him once he'd let her come up for air.

"Maybe later. I want to check out the files in the storage unit."

"They're not there."

"Where are they?"

"I had them moved to a secure records storage unit this morning."

"I wish you'd told me that's what you were doing."

"Why? They're perfectly safe. Grady was eager to get to work and I feel better with them someplace secure."

"I'm not convinced keeping the files is a good idea."

"I can't part with them until someone I trust goes through everything. Plus, their historic value can't be measured until we know what's there."

"Wasn't last night proof of how dangerous they could be for you? Tiberius lived awfully well for a man whose casino was barely staying out of the red."

"What are you saying?"

"If it was a plot for a TV series, what would you deduce?"

"That Tiberius was blackmailing people?"

"That may have been what got him killed."

"Even if I had a clue what to look for, I'm not planning on blackmailing anyone."

"Maybe not—"

"Maybe not?" She interrupted in mock outrage. "Definitely not."

"Very well, then. Definitely not. But just because you and I know that doesn't mean Tiberius's victims know that."

Nonplussed, she stared at him for several seconds. "Then I guess the smartest thing for me to do is get with a lawyer and make certain that if anything happens to me, the files go public."

Her calm determination impressed the hell out of him. This was no scared female in need of rescue. She was a woman who survived by her wits as well as her beauty.

Logan tightened his hold around her waist. "Then I guess until you meet with an attorney, I should plan on sticking with you."

"Twenty-four/seven?"

"Whatever it takes."

Eight

Scarlett had chosen to have Madison's birthday party at Fontaine Chic's poolside nightclub, Caprice. During the day, the pool offered a sexy Mediterranean beach-lounge vibe. At night when the well-dressed young crowd showed up, it became an extension of the club.

With all of Madison's Las Vegas friends too young to drink, Logan had voiced concerns that the eight teenagers would get into trouble, but Scarlett had met the kids and knew that even if they partied on a regular basis, they understood that abusing her trust would lead to all sorts of misfortune in their future.

Everything would go smoothly. It had to. She'd given Logan her word that Madison's party would be as safe as it was fun. Nothing could get in the way of that. It was the reason she was double-checking her arrangements prior to showtime. She wanted to make sure all the waitstaff knew the kids were underage and shouldn't be served alcohol no matter what sort of identification they produced.

After an afternoon at the pool, Scarlett had arranged for them to enjoy a suite at Fontaine Richesse. There would be fabulous food, a birthday cake at ten, and later the boys would be escorted home in a limo while the girls enjoyed a slumber party.

Madison had been over the moon with the arrangements, cementing Scarlett's status as the coolest boss ever. Logan had accused her of buying Madison's good favor, but his street cred had risen significantly when he'd agreed to Scarlett's plans.

Scarlett was standing at the entrance to the club when the first of Madison's guests arrived. Two girls and the boy Madison had been dating for the past couple of weeks. Trent was tall and lean with serious eyes. He had been captain of the basketball team in high school and third in his class. Under his influence, Madison had begun talking more and more about going to college in the fall.

"You all look like you're ready to have fun," she said, nodding to the doorman to let them through the velvet rope. "I booked you into cabana four."

"Is Madison here?" Trent asked.

"She's having lunch with her uncle," Scarlett answered. "I expect her any minute."

"She thinks you're the best to do all this for her birthday."

The teenager's earnest declaration made Scarlett's heart bump. "I'm happy to do it. You only turn eighteen once."

As her gaze followed Trent and his two companions across the pool deck, Scarlett thought about her own eighteenth birthday. She'd been doing some pretty hard partying in the year leading up to it. The crowd she ran with in Hollywood had been wealthy and wild, hitting clubs, doing whatever they felt like. She stood watching Madison's friends and tried to remember when she'd last known such innocuous delight.

"Don't worry, Scarlett," the bouncer told her, misinterpreting her melancholy as concern. Dave had biceps the size of full-grown trees and a nose that looked as if it had been broken a few times. "We'll keep an eye on the kids. Everyone knows that Madison is Logan's niece."

"Thanks, Dave." She touched his arm to show her appreciation. "I can't have anything go wrong today."

Four more kids showed up before the birthday girl made an appearance. Scarlett directed them to their friends and wondered what could be keeping Madison. Logan had to know his niece was super excited about her birthday party. Why would he delay her? Knowing Logan, he was probably lecturing Madison on all the things she wasn't supposed to do for the next twelve hours.

Scarlett unlocked her phone's screen, preparing to call Logan, when it began to ring. It was her assistant calling.

Sandy's voice was an octave higher than normal as she explained the reason for her call. "Chase Reynolds was here." Although the words were professional enough, Sandy sounded more like an infatuated teenager than her usual unflappable self.

Scarlett couldn't stop herself from smiling. The six-foot-three-inch action hero turned director could electrify the most jaded starlets in Hollywood. Sandy wouldn't have a chance. Then her assistant's words sank in.

"He *was* there? You mean he left? Where did he go?"

"Logan and Madison stopped by to find you and he left with them."

Her stomach clenched. "Was anyone else with Chase?

"An older man. Balding. Bobby something."

Chase must have really turned on the charm. This was not the efficient way Sandy normally functioned.

"Bobby McDermott." Scarlett didn't wait for Sandy to confirm. "Did Chase and Bobby say where they were heading?"

"To find you."

Several unladylike curses raced through Scarlett's mind. She should have known that dodging Bobby's calls was a bad idea, but she thought he'd realize she was serious about her disinterest in the project and move on. Sure, she was perfect for the part, but there were a dozen other actresses that would fit the bill just as well.

Anxiety rushed to fill the space where contentment had been only minutes earlier. Bobby and Chase couldn't have appeared at a worse time. In the past two weeks, she and Logan had begun to form a connection, but he still didn't fully trust her. If he thought she'd been lying about returning to acting, it might damage the tentative rapport growing between them.

"Thanks for the heads-up," she told Sandy before disconnecting the phone.

She imagined Bobby filling in Logan on the reason for his visit and the TV series they wanted her to do. Her muscles tensed as she contemplated how disappointed Logan would be in her. Of course he would assume the worst— that she'd lied when she'd told him she wasn't interested in the part.

She'd worked herself into quite a panic by the time Madison stepped off the elevator, her gaze glued on Chase Reynolds's handsome face. Despite her grim, chaotic emotions, Scarlett's amusement flared. Chase's good looks and charisma were a forceful thing. What made him completely irresistible, however, was that beneath the larger-than-life movie star lurked a genuinely nice guy.

Scarlett's focus shifted from the movie hero to the real-life hero and her mood plummeted. Logan looked like an advancing army intent on total annihilation. When he caught sight of her standing at the entrance to the club, she decided she'd seen attacking pit bulls that looked friendlier.

Tearing her gaze from Logan's stony expression, she greeted Bobby. "Hi. What are you doing here?" Twenty years of acting wasn't enough to keep the tension from her voice, but only Logan seemed to notice.

"Well, if Mohammed won't come to the mountain…" Bobby boomed, his eyes crinkling as he left the rest of the idiom hanging. "You look fabulous as always." He leaned in to kiss her cheek.

From the corner of her eye, Scarlett caught Logan's expression shift into a glower. She ignored the hollow in her stomach and pulled back to smile at Chase. "Hello, Chase. Nice to see you again."

Chase nodded, sweeping her into a very tight, very friendly hug. "Been a while. And Bobby's right, you look great."

"Vegas agrees with me." She meant the remark for Logan, but when her eyes met his, they were hard and flat. His disapproval wasn't a surprise, but her anxious reaction to it was. Feeling this vulnerable with a man was a miserable sensation, but if she raised her defenses she might push Logan away. And that would be so much worse. "I see you've met Logan Wolfe and his niece, Madison."

"Yes," Bobby said. "She's been telling us that it's her eighteenth birthday today and you've planned a fun-filled day for her and her friends."

"Yes, and they're all waiting for her in the club." Scarlett wasn't sure if Madison heard her because the birthday girl's attention remained fixed on Chase. His blinding white smile and the glint in his light brown eyes had mesmerized her. "You shouldn't keep them waiting."

"Oh, I'm sure they won't mind."

"But you're the guest of honor." Scarlett's speaking glance was wasted on Madison, but Chase noticed. "Logan, why don't you escort Madison to cabana four and make sure you're happy with all the arrangements."

She put a slight emphasis on the final word, hoping he'd understand her message. To appease Logan she'd agreed to let four of his security people—two men and two women—hang out with the party. To keep them unobtrusive, Logan had caved to them guarding in bathing suits. The kids would be kept under observation and never know it.

"But…" Madison looked as if she'd rather die than have her uncle show up at her party, but before she could protest, Chase spoke up.

"I'll come, too," the actor said. "I've heard that Caprice is a terrific club."

"It's fabulous," Madison agreed, catching him by the arm and turning him toward the pool.

While the teenager practically floated into the club between Logan and Chase, Bobby said, "Beautiful girl. She told me she's an actress."

Scarlett recognized the look in Bobby's eye. "It's not what her parents want for her."

"She seems pretty headstrong."

"You don't know the half of it."

Bobby laughed at her tone. "You know, she might work as our main character's daughter."

Seeing that the producer wasn't kidding, Scarlett grabbed his arm. "Oh, please don't put that idea in her head. I'm supposed to be spending the summer convincing her to go to college. If she heads off to Hollywood instead and her uncle thinks I had anything to do with it, he'll kill me."

Her vehemence made Bobby's eyebrows go up. "Well, if it's that important to you, of course I won't say a word."

"Thank you."

Her gaze shot across the pool deck to where the four teenage girls had clustered around Chase. As handsome and perfect as he was, her attention was drawn to where Logan stood, conversing with one of his employees. He possessed a charismatic pull as potent as the movie star's, but was too serious-minded to let it shine. Scarlett experienced a delicious thrill as he caught her watching him. He looked powerful and dangerous as his eyes promised her they were going to have a long and intense conversation.

"Looks like you have your hands full at the moment," Bobby said. "And I'm feeling lucky. Perhaps we should catch up over drinks later."

She shifted her attention to the producer and smiled in relief. "That would be great. I'll have my assistant get you and Chase set up in a suite." As she called Sandy, Scarlett spotted Logan and Chase heading her way. Whatever they were talking about wasn't improving Logan's mood.

He practically vibrated with annoyance as he stopped beside her. "Chase here tells me that you two are doing a TV series together."

"Ah…" Scarlett felt off balance, as if she'd been struck by a rogue wave. This was not the time or place for this conversation. "That's not exactly true."

"No?" Logan demanded, his hard voice low. "So what is exactly true?"

"I told Bobby no." She shot the producer an apologetic look.

"If that's true, then why are they here?"

"To talk her into changing her mind," Chase explained. "The part could have been written specifically for her and she knows it."

"Then maybe she should move back to Hollywood and take it." His congenial tone didn't match the tightness around his mouth.

Stung by Logan's negative assumption about her, Scarlett hastened to correct him. "I'm not going anywhere. My life is here. I love what I'm doing." Why wouldn't he give her the benefit of the doubt?

"But you're an actress," Bobby insisted. "And a damn good one."

"Will you all stop ganging up on me?" Scarlett took Bobby and Chase by the arms and turned them toward the door. "You two run along and win some money. I'll see you in a couple hours."

With those two taken care of for the moment, Scarlett turned to her next problem, but before she could defend herself against the recriminations in Logan's eyes, a pair of slim arms slipped around her neck in a gleeful chokehold.

"You are the best. I can't believe Chase Reynolds came to meet my friends. He's so amazing."

"That's Chase for you. Always ready to make new friends." Released from the exuberant hug, Scarlett turned to smile at Madison.

"I can't believe you two used to date."

Scarlett's gaze shot to Logan. He had his phone out and was texting someone. She could only pray he hadn't heard. "Yes, well. It was a long time ago. Now, I hope the rest of the day isn't a letdown. I don't have anything to top that."

"No worries. Everything is fabulous. I'm so glad Uncle Logan let me hang with you this summer." She winked at Logan.

Scarlett patted Madison's arm. "You can show your gratitude by going to college this fall."

Madison rolled her eyes, but her smile was bright as she blew Logan a flirty kiss and returned to her guests.

"I'll be back around five to escort you to Richesse," Scarlett called after her. Then she turned her attention back to Logan. "You can stop looking all annoyed with me. No matter how perfect the part is, I'm not taking it."

Logan hated to feel her slip away from him bit by bit, but he didn't want to invest his heart only to have it crushed when she went back to her life in L.A. "Are you sure that's a good idea? If those two came all this way to meet with you in person, they must really want to work with you. Perhaps you're making a mistake by turning them down."

"You seem pretty eager to get rid of me," Scarlett pointed out. "What's the matter, Logan? Are you afraid you'll get used to having me around?"

Her remark hit way too close to home, but Logan had spent enough time with her these past few days to recognize the uncertainty she was trying to hide. Glimpsing her vulnerability took the edge off his irritation.

He took her hand and began pulling her out of the club. "I'm already used to having you around," he told her, his voice rough and unhappy.

"Then why...?"

"What do you want me to tell you?" he demanded. "That I don't want you to go?"

"That would be nice."

She looked resolute and yet hopeful at the same time. Was she really that clueless about how strongly she moved him? After the past few evenings they'd spent together, how was that possible? Making love with her had turned him inside out. He wanted her with a fierceness he'd never known before.

"I can't tell you that."

He didn't want to care one way or another what she did with her life. What they were doing wasn't serious or life-changing. They were simply indulging in some good old-fashioned lust. So what if he couldn't stop thinking about her? Or that he missed her whenever she wasn't around? When she returned to L.A., he'd have no further need to make up reasons to visit Fontaine Richesse. He could stop acting like a smitten fool and recommit his attention to the business.

"Why not?"

"Because you need to make up your own mind about what you're going to do with your future." Even as he said the words he wished them back. Hadn't he already lost one woman because his pride had kept him from asking her to stay?

"Maybe I want a little input from you. I thought something was happening here. Am I wrong?"

When he didn't immediately respond, she tossed her head and strode off, not once looking back to see if he would follow. Which, of course, he did. His long strides brought him even with her in seconds.

"I'm sorry I can't give you what you need." After seeing the hurt that lanced through her eyes, he opted to explain himself further. "If you decide to stay here because of something you think is happening between us, what are your expectations for down the road?"

"I don't know." She narrowed her eyes and regarded him warily. "What are you trying to say?"

"We're very different. We argue all the time. Do you see this thing between us going anywhere?"

"Obviously you don't."

From the sharpness of her tone, he realized she wasn't thinking in terms of a few weeks or even a few months. It shifted his perception. But no matter what either of them wanted, the fact remained that their personalities had a knack for rubbing each other raw. How long before passion faded and all that was left between them was a long list of grievances?

He liked her too much to end up with animosity between them.

"Tell me about the part those Hollywood guys came out to discuss with you."

"I don't know why they're so determined to have me." If any other woman had uttered those words, she might have been fishing for a compliment, but Scarlett wasn't reticent about her talent or her beauty. "I can think of a dozen other actresses who would be just as good or better."

"Maybe they all turned the part down."

She bestowed a droll smile on him. "Amazingly enough, I'm the first person they've offered the part to."

Logan hadn't meant his remark the way she took it. "I didn't mean to imply that you were a last choice. Based on what you've been saying about being committed to Fontaine Richesse, I thought you wanted me to believe you'd left your career behind in Hollywood."

"I did leave it behind." She sighed. "Mostly."

It was her equivocating that renewed his frustration. "But it followed you here."

"Bobby is a hard man to say no to."

"I suppose it depends on how sincere you were." Why couldn't she just admit that the offer intrigued her?

"You can't seriously believe that I would give up my life here?" She scrutinized his expression. "My family's here. I have a career I love, and things…have gotten very exciting."

He gripped her arm and stopped her. "What sort of things?" He hadn't meant to sound so intense. But he needed to hear her admit how she felt about him.

Her lips parted, but no words emerged. Finally, she shrugged. "Tiberius's unsolved murder. His files. My attack."

All of which meant she was in danger. Maybe returning to Hollywood wasn't such a bad idea. "All good reasons for you to leave Las Vegas and take the part."

Scarlett shook her head, then regarded him. "Why is it so damn important to you that I take Bobby's offer?"

Because he needed to prepare himself if she was going to leave.

"You have a knack for finding trouble. I just want to know when my life is going to get back to normal."

Irritation with Logan burned in Scarlett's chest during the hours after they parted until she returned to collect Madison and her friends and bring them back to Fontaine Richesse. She tried not to let his willingness to be rid of her dent her ego, but his "support" of her career had leveled a crushing blow to her heart. How had she so misread the situation between them? Granted, it wasn't easy getting past his hard exterior to the caring, passionate man beneath. But in the past two weeks, she'd thought she was starting to make inroads.

He'd never be a tender romantic, but she'd eat that sort of guy up in two bites. Logan was difficult and fascinating. She could spend a lifetime with him and never get bored. The tail end of the impulsive thought snagged her full attention.

When had she starting thinking in terms of a lifetime with Logan? Her immediate reaction was to shy away from her heart's answer. She reminded herself that her first description of the man was that he was difficult. Did she really want to spend the rest of her life with such an intractable male?

The answer was yes if the man was Logan Wolfe.

He was the only man she'd never been able to manipulate. This meant that she had to be her genuine self around him or he'd call her on it. That was both liberating and terrifying. Letting him glimpse her faults and vulnerabilities meant at any moment he could use her weaknesses against her. Would he?

A breathy laugh puffed out of her. And she'd accused *him* of having trust issues. She was not much better. She could count on one hand all the people she trusted in the world. The first was her mother. The next two, her sisters, Harper and Violet. The fourth, she was on her way to meet for a drink. Scarlett contemplated her thumb. Did she count Logan among her allies?

"Hello, Bobby," she said, sitting down beside the producer. "Is Chase joining us?"

"No. He's on a winning streak at the craps table and didn't want to leave."

Scarlett smiled. "What about you? Any luck at the tables?"

"A little." He grinned at her. "Now, let's get down to business. I know you, Scarlett. You want this part."

"It's a fabulous opportunity."

"So come to L.A. and test for it."

Agreeing would set her foot on a path that might not lead back to Las Vegas. She shook her head. "I really appreciate what you're trying to do for me," she told the producer. "But I'm not interested."

"You're an actress, not a hotel manager."

He made it sound as if she was dealing drugs for a living. "I'm not turning you down because of my position with Fontaine Richesse," she explained. "I have a life here. A life I really love."

"What if we could shoot all your scenes in one day? You wouldn't have to move back to Hollywood. Just commute. You still own your house, don't you?"

She had a place on the beach in Malibu that she'd bought

shortly after turning eighteen. She'd told herself she'd kept the house because market values had dropped, but the truth was she loved the California coast and kept it as a getaway when she needed to escape the glitter and rush that was Vegas.

Or as a backup plan?

Was Logan right? Deep in her heart, was she thinking of Las Vegas as something to fill the time during the lull in her acting career? With the way her heart was skipping at the thought of going back to work in front of the camera, she had to consider if she'd been kidding herself all this time.

"It's been seven years since I've done more than a guest spot here and there. What if I'm terrible?"

"Not possible."

She covered Bobby's hand and gave it an affectionate squeeze. "No one was beating down my door five years ago," she reminded him. "There had to be a good reason for that."

"You were turning down the parts offered."

"Because I wanted to do something that called for me to do more than look pretty and act sexy."

"Here's your chance."

"No wonder you're the most successful producer in Hollywood."

"I know what I want."

"And you don't stop until you get it."

"Then you'll come do the test?"

If Logan had asked her to stay, would she be at all tempted by Bobby's faith in her? Scarlett sighed. She'd never let a man sway her decision about anything. Why was she doing so now?

"Let me talk it over with my sisters. I'll let you know before you leave tomorrow."

Bobby's smile broadened with triumph. "Perfect."

Maybe Logan had been right about the message she was sending the producer. She'd gone from a definite no to agreeing to consider a screen test.

"If you'll excuse me," Scarlett said, getting to her feet, "I have some party arrangements to check on. Sandy secured you an eight-thirty reservation at Le Taillevent this evening. Dinner's on me."

"As always you're the perfect host." Bobby rose to his feet and leaned forward to kiss her cheek. "Chase and I are leaving at one tomorrow. Can you join us for lunch before we go?"

"Why don't I come to your suite at eleven-thirty."

"I'll see you then."

After getting Madison and her friends settled into the hotel suite with pizza and a warning to keep the music at a reasonable volume, Scarlett organized a quick dinner with her sisters in her suite at Fontaine Richesse. As the three sat down to salads topped with salmon and glasses of white wine, Scarlett quickly broached what was on her mind.

"I've had an offer to do a television series," she said, sipping her wine.

As usual, Harper was the first to react. "I thought you were done with acting."

"I was." Scarlett heard the uncertainty in her tone and qualified her response. "I mean, I thought I was."

"Is it an interesting part?" Violet quizzed.

"The best I've ever been offered."

"A lead?" Harper was the sort who set her eyes on the top prize and wouldn't consider anything less worth her time.

"No. It's a small supporting role, but the character is complex and interesting." Scarlett looked at each of her sisters. "Five years ago, even two years ago, I wouldn't have hesitated to race back to L.A. and take the part."

"But now?" Violet prompted. "Something's changed?"

"I really feel as if I've hit my stride with the hotel. Then there are you guys. I love being your sister and don't want to live so far away from you."

"That's awfully sweet of you to say." Harper's lips curved in a dry smile. "But are you forgetting that we're your chief competition in our grandfather's contest?"

Scarlett laughed at Harper's question, despite her lingering uneasiness over her decision to conceal what she knew about her sister's true parentage. "You don't seriously think I have a shot at running Fontaine Hotels and Resorts, because I'm convinced I don't."

"You don't know that," Violet insisted, always the peacemaker. "Fontaine Richesse has done really well under your management. Grandfather could choose you."

"I don't have the experience or the education required to run the company." Scarlett pointed her fork first at Harper, then at Violet. "You two are the only ones in the running. I'm just happy to have been given the chance to be considered."

"Have you told Logan that you're thinking about heading back to L.A.?" Violet asked.

"Logan?" Harper interjected before Scarlett could answer. "Why would she tell him?"

"Because they've been seeing each other," Violet said, her tone exasperated. "Don't you notice anything that happens outside your hotel?"

"Not in the past three weeks." She turned to Scarlett. "How serious is it?"

Scarlett lifted her hand to bat away the question, but the concern laced with curiosity in her sisters' eyes was a powerful thing. "It could be anything from casual to involved. I can't really tell. He's pretty cagey about his emotions."

"Cagey?" Harper echoed, her tone doubtful. "He's positively Alcatraz. I've gotta say, I didn't see that coming. You two are like oil and water."

"More like gasoline and matches," Violet put in. "All that animosity between you had to be hiding a raging passion."

Scarlett didn't comment on her sister's observation, but couldn't prevent heat from rising in her cheeks. As an actress she could control her body language and facial expressions, but stopping a blush was something she'd never mastered.

"Raging passion?" Harper echoed, her eyes widening. "What exactly have I been missing?"

"A lot." Violet looked smug. "How many nights has he stayed at your place in the past two weeks?"

"Not one." He liked to be home when Madison got up in the morning.

"Then how many nights has he gone home in the wee hours of the morning?"

"Several." Scarlett couldn't believe how giddy she felt at the admission.

"Then it's serious?" Harper asked.

"He's encouraging me to head back to L.A. and take the part. That tells me it's pretty casual."

"But hot," Violet piped up.

Both Harper and Scarlett ignored her.

"Maybe he knows how important acting is to you and wants you to be happy," Harper suggested with a pragmatic nod.

"But I told him I was done with acting."

"But you're telling us that you're not."

"I really thought I was. It's been a year since I've been

offered a guest spot. And that's been fine. I've been completely content here. I put L.A. and acting behind me." Scarlett sorted through her conflicting emotions. "I've already turned down Bobby three times, but he won't take no for an answer and after Logan told me to go, I'm wondering why I'm hesitating."

"Why *are* you hesitating?" Harper asked.

"You're going to think I'm an idiot."

Violet said, "I promise we won't."

"Logan is so against my past acting career and I didn't want to do anything to jeopardize our relationship. But today he was behaving like there's nothing going on with us. I'm starting to think I made up our connection because I'm crazy about him." Admitting her deep feelings wasn't something that came easily to Scarlett, but time spent with her sisters had eroded the walls she kept up to guard against disappointment and hurt.

"You are?" Violet looked surprised. "How crazy?"

"The kind that's going to end up with my heart broken." Being able to share her concerns with Harper and Violet gave Scarlett a sense of relief. "Maybe I should go back to L.A. and take up my career again."

"We'd miss you," Violet told her.

"We would."

Scarlett's eyes burned. "Thanks."

"I'll bet Logan would miss you, too," Violet said, her hazel eyes sparkling. "Maybe he's pushing you away because he's afraid it will hurt too much to lose you."

That sounded sweet to Scarlett's ears, but she wasn't susceptible to romance the way Violet was. In fact, until Logan came along, she'd interacted with men with an eye toward what they could do for her.

"Logan Wolfe isn't afraid of anything," Scarlett declared. "Least of all losing me."

"Everyone's afraid of something," Harper said in an un-usual display of insight. "You'll just have to figure out if he's more afraid of keeping you around or letting you go."

Nine

Logan paced his living room, aware that he resembled a grumpy, caged bear. He squinted against the sunlight streaming in his large picture window, but Scarlett's flashy red convertible was not streaking up his driveway. For the tenth time in half an hour he glanced at his watch. Not surprisingly, the hands hadn't crept forward more than a couple minutes. It was 12:23 p.m. and Madison should have been home from her birthday party almost two hours ago.

If something happened to her…

A car was moving through the vegetation that lined the driveway, but it wasn't Scarlett's. As the vehicle drew closer, Logan spied his niece in the passenger seat and recognized Scarlett's assistant as the driver. Annoyed by the change in plans, Logan strode through the front door and went to meet the car.

"Hey, Uncle Logan." Madison exited the car, her overnight bag slung over her shoulder, and waved at the driver.

She stretched and yawned with dramatic flair as she neared him. "What a birthday party. That was the most fun I've ever had." Lifting up on tiptoe, she kissed his cheek. "Thanks again for letting Scarlett plan the party."

"Where is she? She was supposed to drive you home."

His sharp tone caused Madison's eyes to widen. "She had a meeting with Bobby and Chase, so she had Sandy bring me home. You can't disapprove of Sandy, Uncle Logan. She's thirty-five, never had a ticket. She drove the speed limit the whole way here."

Ignoring Madison's sass, Logan focused on what was really bothering him.

"So it's Bobby and Chase, now, is it?" he demanded, his temper getting the better of him. "When did you get so cozy with them?"

He knew better than to take his frustration out on his niece. It was Scarlett who'd stirred up his ire. Scarlett who was hell-bent on returning to L.A. and her acting career.

Or maybe he was mad at himself for encouraging her to do so.

"I'm not cozy with them," Madison retorted. "They were just being nice. Bobby gave me his card and Chase told me to look him up when I get to L.A."

Logan's focus sharpened. "What do you mean, when you get to L.A.? You're heading to college this fall."

Madison tossed her hair in a perfect imitation of Scarlett at her most exasperating. In fact, now that he thought about it, Madison had adopted several mannerisms from the actress. How had he not noticed the metamorphosis before this? His niece admired everything about Scarlett, why wouldn't she think it was a good idea to behave like her?

"I know my parents sent me here so you could work on me about college, and heaven knows that's a drum Scarlett has beaten to death, but I really think my path lies in

Hollywood." She rested her hand on her hip and tilted her chin. "And I'm eighteen now. I can do whatever I want."

Logan ground his teeth and regarded Madison in silence. This wasn't the tune she'd been singing yesterday morning. She'd been debating two of the schools she'd gotten into, trying to decide which way to go.

"You might be eighteen, but you've never been on your own without your parents' money before."

"I'll get a job waiting tables or something and support myself until I get an acting job."

Logan was beset by visions of his niece all alone and at the mercy of a string of people with bad intentions who would use Madison up and spit her out. "Do you really think it will be that easy?" How had weeks of good advice been erased in one short night? "And where are you going to live?"

"I can stay with Scarlett."

Icy fingers danced up Logan's spine. So Scarlett had decided to return to L.A., after all. And why not? Hadn't he told her to go?

"She's definitely moving back to L.A.?" he asked, trying to keep his voice neutral.

Madison looked surprised that he even had to ask. "Of course. Why would she turn down a part that will kick-start her career once more?"

The thought of losing her swung a wrecking ball at his gut. He'd been a fool to let her think he would be unaffected by her departure. Had he really thought this was a good time to test her? To see if she meant all her passionate kisses and romantic gestures? Sheer stubbornness had made him complacent that she'd choose Las Vegas and him over her acting career and stardom.

"Did she invite you to stay with her?"

"Not in so many words, but I know she will do whatever she can to help me get started."

Hadn't she already done enough? Logan fished his car keys out of his pocket. He and Scarlett needed to have a face-to-face chat.

"We'll talk more about this when I get back."

"Where are you going?" She sounded less like a confident woman and more like a teenager who was worried she'd pushed her luck too far.

"To talk with Scarlett."

"What are you going to say?"

"That you are not going to L.A., so she can forget about having you as a roommate."

"It won't do any good. She was thrilled that Bobby was willing to help me."

Two weeks ago Logan might have believed Madison's claim. Since then, Scarlett had stuck to his wishes and encouraged the teenager to finish college before she made any career choices. He also knew just how headstrong Madison could be. She'd proven that when she'd run off to L.A. on her own last spring.

"Why don't you give your parents a call and tell them how the party went yesterday. I'm sure they're eager to hear how you spent your birthday."

He was heading his Escalade down the driveway when his phone rang. He cued the car's Bluetooth. "Wolfe."

"Boss, it's Evan. You wanted me to let you know when the Schaefer assessment was done. Jeb and I finished half an hour ago. The report is on your desk."

"Thanks."

Preoccupied with the troublesome women in his life, he'd forgotten all about the multimillion-dollar proposal they were working on to overhaul Schaefer Industries's security system. The deadline for the bid was four this afternoon. He needed to look over the final numbers and make sure there were no holes in the strategy they'd created. Scarlett would have to wait.

The big closet full of costumes wasn't having its usual soothing effect on Scarlett. She grazed her fingertips along sequined sleeves and plucked at organza skirts but couldn't summon up the charisma to wear Marilyn Monroe's white dress from *The Seven Year Itch* or the slinky green number Cyd Charisse wore to dance with Gene Kelly in *Singin' in the Rain*. Her heart was too heavy to play her namesake, Scarlett O'Hara, and she'd never be able to pull off Cleopatra's sexy strength.

Her confidence had been dipping lower and lower ever since she'd told Bobby her decision about the television series. Logic told her she'd chosen correctly, but she couldn't shake the worry that she'd irrevocably closed the door because she was afraid of putting herself out there and being rejected.

She came across Holly Golightly's long black dress from the opening scene of *Breakfast at Tiffany's,* pulled it off the rack and held it against herself. Perfect. Holly's mixture of innocence and street savvy had always struck a chord in Scarlett. Many days she felt that way. Tough on the outside because acting was a rough business to be in. Fragile as dandelion fluff on the inside. Some weeks she'd go for a dozen auditions and not have a single callback. It had been hard on her, a change from the days when she'd basked in the studio's love and appreciation.

Running Fontaine Richesse had brought her defenses and her longing into balance. She'd gained confidence in her abilities and no longer faced daily rejection. Dropping her guard had taken a while, but eventually she'd stopped expecting to hear what she was doing wrong. She'd begun to thrive.

Scarlett put on the iconic black dress, zipped it up and fastened on a collar of pearls. She regarded her reflection in the mirror. This costume was a head turner. With the sixties-style wig, black gloves and long cigarette holder, she bore an uncanny resemblance to Audrey Hepburn. And becoming Holly Golightly gave her a much-needed break from her current worries.

It's what she loved about acting. Becoming another person was like taking a vacation without going anywhere. For twelve or fourteen hours at a time she was transported to a simple house in the suburbs where her parents laughed at misunderstandings about fixing dinner and her siblings got into trouble at school. Simple complications that resolved themselves in twenty-two minutes. Where lessons were learned and everyone hugged and smiled in the end.

The pleasure such memories gave Scarlett reaffirmed that she was an actress at heart. It was something that would always come between her and Logan. He preferred everything straightforward and realistic. She was pretty sure he wasn't the sort of man who wanted his woman to dress up like a naughty schoolgirl, a cheerleader or even Princess Leia. Which was too bad because she had a copy of Leia's slave girl costume tucked away in her closet.

As she tugged on the elbow-high black gloves, she heard a knock on her door. Her heart jumped into her throat as she raced across the living room. More cautious after her attack, she checked the peephole and saw Logan standing in the hall. They hadn't spoken all day. She'd been both hoping and dreading that he'd call. She was terrified to tell him about her decision. Although he'd encouraged her to take the part, it was such an about-face from his earlier stance on her career, she didn't understand his motives.

Breath uneven, she threw open the door, uncertain about what to expect. His tight mouth and fierce gaze stopped her forward momentum. A muscle jumped in his jaw as he stepped into her suite, compelling her to shift to one side or be trampled.

"Hello, Logan."

He strode past her without responding and began pacing in the middle of the room.

"Don't go."

His brusque tone matched the tension vibrating off him. She was used to his demanding ways, actually enjoyed surrendering to his desires. Not that she would ever admit it. Ninety-nine percent of the time she preferred being in complete control. It was a throwback to her days in Hollywood when she'd had very little power. But she had learned she could trust Logan and it was nice to hand over the reins once in a while.

"Sure. It won't matter if I don't make an appearance in the casino tonight." Her body tightened with hunger as she moved toward him. "What did you have in mind?"

He spun to face her. "I don't mean tonight. I mean at all."

Scarlett stretched out her arm and set her palm against his shoulder, treating him like a skittish dog, trying to gentle his mood with her touch. "Logan, I'm in charge of this hotel. I don't see how I can stay away from my own casino."

His arm snaked around her waist and brought her tight against his body. "Not the casino, you simple-minded darling. Don't go to Los Angeles."

"But you said—" She broke off when he stroked his hand up the side of her neck and wrapped his fingers around the back of her head.

"I know what I said." He leaned down and seized her mouth with his, short-circuiting her brain.

The kiss was so like him. Commanding, skillful, hungry. He claimed her breath, stole her willpower and insisted on her complete surrender. Whether he'd admit it or not, he found her strength attractive. What if her weakness disgusted him? One way or another, she needed him to see the real her. Only by letting him glimpse her fear of rejection could she be free.

Terror and joy washed over her as she unraveled in his arms. Immediately, the kiss softened. Passion became play as his tongue and teeth toyed with and tantalized her.

How had she ever dreamed she could leave him? Only with Logan did she feel this alive and complete. She broke off the kiss and arched her back as his lips trailed fire down her neck. Gasping as his teeth nipped at her throat, she struggled to clear her thoughts from the drugging fog of desire.

"I'm not going to take the part," she murmured, kissing his temple and the bold stroke of his dark eyebrow. "I'm not going to L.A."

He straightened and peered into her eyes. "Madison said you were going to accept the role."

"I never told her that." If the teenager's misunderstanding had caused Logan to admit how he truly felt, Scarlett would make certain she would do something extra nice for the girl. Maybe a day at the spa. "I don't know where she got such an idea."

"She said you were having breakfast with that producer fellow."

"I did. I told Bobby once and for all that I wasn't going to take the part."

"But you wanted to." Logan took her left hand and began peeling the black glove down her arm.

The drag of the fabric against her sensitized skin made Scarlett shiver. "For seventeen years my identity was caught up in being an actress."

He hooked his finger beneath her pearl necklace and stroked her feverish skin. "I don't see where anything has changed in that respect."

She smiled as Logan set to work on the other glove. Being undressed by him was always such a treat. Occasionally their hunger for each other grew too feverish for preliminaries, but most of the time he took such pleasure in every aspect of making love, from removing her clothes to cuddling with her in the aftermath of passion.

"I think I'll always be an actress in my heart," she assured him. "But that's no longer all I am. Managing this hotel has shown me that I'm also a darned good business-woman." She tunneled her now-naked fingers into his hair and pulled his head toward her. "I'm glad you didn't want me to go, because I didn't want to leave you."

This time when they kissed, he let her lead. She understood why as her dress's zipper yielded beneath his strong fingers. He stroked the material off her shoulders and left her standing before him in her pearls, a strapless black bra and panties and black pumps. His gaze burned across her skin as he took in the picture she made.

Divesting herself of the necklace and casting aside her wig, Scarlett stripped away the final trappings of Holly Golightly. The character was a woman with many lovers, but no burning love. She was a wild thing who craved freedom even as, deep in her heart, she longed for a place to belong.

Scarlett had no such conflicts. She knew exactly what she wanted, just as she knew where she belonged. In Logan's arms. Pretending to be someone else, even for a while, couldn't compare to the reality of being herself, in love with him. Her throat contracted as she realized why she'd turned down the part. It wasn't just because she loved her new life as the manager of Fontaine Richesse. It was because she loved Logan Wolfe and all the heartache and joys that went along with being the woman in his life.

Lifting onto her tiptoes, she wrapped her arms around his neck and kissed him firmly on the mouth. "Take me to bed, you big bad hunk."

"Your wish is my command."

Logan scooped Scarlett into his arms and headed for her bedroom, glad he'd followed his instincts and sought her out tonight. Those six hours between learning she'd decided to return to L.A. and showing up at her suite had been hell and he had no interest in reliving them anytime soon. His unhappiness at her leaving had forced him to assess just how reluctant he was to be without her.

How far would he have gone if she'd been determined to leave Las Vegas? Once upon a time he'd let Elle go and had never really stopped regretting it. What was happening between him and Scarlett claimed neither the duration nor the depth of what he'd shared with his ex-fiancée, but he felt as invested as if they'd been together for years.

Laying Scarlett on her bed, he began unfastening his shirt buttons. She made no attempt to remove her bra or panties, knowing he preferred to strip her bare himself. All she did was shake her hair free of the pins that held it in place and kick off her shoes.

She lifted herself onto one elbow and twirled a lock of her hair as she watched him shuck off his shirt and send his pants to the floor. She gave him a sultry, heavy-lidded look as she waited for him to join her.

He trailed his fingertips up her thigh and felt her shudder as his thumb whisked along the edge of her panties. With a half smile, he used his hands to memorize each rise and dip of her body. No matter how many times he touched her, he found something new to fascinate him. With her full breasts and hourglass shape, she was built for seduction, but as he'd discovered the first time he'd made love with her, she had a romantic's soul.

Taking her hand, he kissed the inside of her wrist, lips lingering over her madly beating pulse. He'd cataloged about a hundred ultrasensitive areas on her body and enjoyed revisiting them each time they made love. The inside of her elbow was mildly ticklish and she loved being lightly caressed on her arms. He did so now and was rewarded when she uttered a little hum of delight, her version of a purr.

It had taken her a bit to realize he wasn't going to rush the sex between them. Even when they were both too caught up in their passion to enjoy extended foreplay, he made certain to arouse her with words as well as hands and mouth.

He leaned forward to kiss her mouth, pressing her back against the pillows. She melted against him, soft curves yielding to all his hard planes. They kissed long and slow, enjoying the blending of their breath, the feint and retreat of tongues. Logan slipped his hands beneath her and rolled them a half turn so she sat astride him.

She lifted her hair off her shoulders, arching her back and tilting her breasts toward the ceiling. Her movements were measured and graceful like a cat indulging in a languid stretch after rising. The flow of muscle beneath her soft skin mesmerized him. He ran his hands over her rib cage, riding their waves upward until he reached the lower curve of her breasts. Through half-closed eyes she watched him cup her breasts through the black lace and gently massage.

Reaching behind her, she popped the bra clasp and the fabric sagged into his hands. He tossed it aside and traced the shape of her breasts with his fingertips. He circled the tight nipples, noticing that she rocked her hips in time with his caresses, easing the ache he inflicted on her.

His erection bobbed with her movements, the sensitive head scraping against her lace-covered backside and aggravating his already ravenous hunger. As much as he yearned to seat himself inside her, the pleasure he received from watching her desire build made the wait worthwhile.

Noticing his eyes upon her, Scarlett shook her head, her hair cascading about her shoulders in riotous waves. Some of it fell forward over her face and she peeked at him from between the strands, her eyes beckoning. Setting her hand on his chest, she bent forward and planted a lusty, open-mouthed kiss on him, showing her delight in the moment with a deep thrust of her tongue.

Logan filled his hands with her firm backside.

"Let's get these off you, shall we?"

"Please do."

Working together, they slid her panties down her thighs. As he tossed them aside, she produced a condom and used her teeth to tear open the package. Logan braced for the wonderful pain of what would come next and locked his jaw as she fitted the protection over the head of his erection, and with a thoroughness that was both a torment and a treat, rolled it down his shaft. A groan ripped from his throat as she finished, but she gave him no chance to recover before settling herself onto him.

The shock of being encased in so much heat so suddenly made his hips buck. She rode his movement with a faraway smile and a rotation of her pelvis.

"Geez, Scarlett," he muttered, wiping sweat from his brow. "Warn a guy."

"What's the fun in that?"

And fun is what she was having. Letting her do whatever she wanted with him was almost as entertaining as making her squirm. Half his delight came from watching her explore his chest and abs while maintaining that delightful rhythm with her hips. She was a living, breathing goddess and Logan couldn't take his eyes off her.

But the chemistry between them had a mind of its own and soon they were both swept into a frenzy of movement where each surge pushed them closer to the edge. Wanting to watch her come, Logan slipped his hands between them and touched the button of nerves that would send her spinning into the abyss. Her eyes shot wide, signaling the beginning of her orgasm. She clenched him tight, increasing the friction, and he pitched into the black, spinning in a vortex of pleasure so intense it hurt.

With a whoosh of air from her lungs, she collapsed forward and buried her face in his neck. Logan didn't have enough breath to voice his appreciation of what had just happened, so he settled for a firm hug and a clumsy kiss on her shoulder.

His heart rate took a long time returning to normal. The way she affected him, Logan wasn't surprised. Since that first kiss in the elevator, she'd shattered his serenity and caused him to reevaluate what made him happy. For a long time he'd resisted accepting how much he needed her. Today, he stopped fighting.

And now she was all his.

"I'm going to make damn sure you don't regret turning down the part," he told her, gliding his fingertips along her soft skin.

She laughed breathlessly. "I like the sound of that. Can we start now?"

He snagged her questing fingers and returned them to his chest. "I can't stay. I promised Madison that when I got back we'd talk about her moving to L.A."

"What?" Scarlett made the leap from languid to outraged in an eye blink. She pushed herself up so she could meet his gaze. "But yesterday she was talking about college."

Logan approved of her irritation. It matched his own. "Apparently that changed after she met your producer friend and Chase Reynolds."

Her face shuttered. "Bobby is a man who makes things happen and Chase is larger than life. I can see how they could've reawakened her dreams of going to L.A., but she and I talked about how important college was to your family. She agreed to get her degree and afterward, if she was still determined to be an actress, to then go to L.A."

"Apparently Bobby gave her his card and told her to look him up." Logan recalled the rest of what his niece had said. "She believed since you were returning to your acting career that you would offer her a place to stay."

A pained expression twisted Scarlett's features. "I'm sorry she got the wrong impression of what I intended to do. As for Bobby, I know he really liked her," she admitted in a low voice. "Even told me he might have a part for her in an upcoming TV series. I told him not to mention anything about it to her. I guess I should have been clearer and told him not to give her any encouragement at all."

"That might have been a good idea."

Scarlett tried to stay calm as she was caught in the riptide of Logan's growing annoyance. "I told him she was going to college this fall. I'm sure he didn't expect her to change her plans because he told her to look him up."

"There must have been more to it."

"I'll call her tomorrow and get her back on the path to college."

"I'd really appreciate that."

"My pleasure.

"Maybe she's just impatient to start living her dream," Scarlett suggested. "I certainly don't blame the girl for going after what she wants."

Placing her palm on Logan's chest, she set her chin on

her hand and scrutinized him. What was it about this often difficult, sometimes surprising and always sexy man that turned her insides into mush? They were at odds as much as they were in accord, but whether they were arguing or making love, he always made her feel as if being with her was exactly where he wanted to be.

And for that matter, what did he find appealing about her? He was scornful of her lack of a college education. Disparaging about her former occupation. Critical of her wardrobe, her abilities as a businesswoman and the way she used her sexuality to her advantage.

Granted, the chemistry between them was off the charts, but she was pretty sure she wasn't just a conquest. No, there was something more between them than fantastic sex, but she had no idea what.

"I'll tell you what," she said into the silence. "I'll talk to her tomorrow and get her back on the college track. Will that make you happy?"

"Are you sure you can do that?"

She had absolutely no clue. "Haven't I been doing a great job so far?" She acknowledged his skepticism with a wry smile. "Up until yesterday, I mean?"

"You have."

"Grudging praise from Logan Wolfe? I'm thrilled."

With a humph, he deposited a brief kiss on her mouth and began rolling toward the side of the bed where he'd left his clothes.

"Do you have to go?" Scarlett flopped onto her stomach and kicked her legs slowly in the air. As if drawn by a force too powerful to resist, his gaze swept over her disheveled hair and toured her naked backside. She knew exactly how appetizing she looked lying there and thrust out her lower lip in a provocative pout. "If you stay the night I'll make it worth your while."

Logan paused with his boxers in one hand, his shirt in the other. "How?"

"Let's see." She tapped her chin with a finger. "I can cook you breakfast."

"You mean order room service."

"I'll listen with interest as you tell me all about your work."

"You'd be snoring in five minutes."

"I don't snore." She pursed her lips and frowned as if in deep thought. "There's always morning sex." At last she'd found something to pique his interest. "I'm very energetic after a good night's sleep."

He dropped his clothes and rolled her onto her back. "How are you after no sleep at all?"

"Try me," she dared, wrapping her arms around his neck to pull him down for a kiss. "And find out."

Ten

"See," Scarlett murmured, sounding sleepy and smug. "I told you morning sex was worth sticking around for."

Logan slipped a hand along her delicate spine as she set her cheek against his heaving chest. He soothed a strand of dark hair off her damp forehead and deposited a kiss just above her brow.

"I never doubted you for a second." Logan rolled her onto her back and kissed her slow and long.

The sky visible through Scarlett's bedroom window was a bright blue. Not wishing to set a bad example for Madison, he'd never stayed the whole night with Scarlett. She'd said she understood his reasons.

But last night he'd let her see how much she meant to him, and sharing his emotions with her had increased the intimacy between them. Leaving had been impossible, so he'd called the guy keeping an eye on Madison and told him to stay until morning.

Tangled in sheets and warm, naked woman, he pushed all thought to the back of his mind and concentrated on the contour of her lips, the way she moaned when he licked at her nipples and the unsteady beat of her heart as he nibbled on her earlobe.

"Last night was amazing." She burrowed her face into his neck so he couldn't see her expression. "I'm really glad you came by."

"I'm glad you decided to stay in Las Vegas."

"You were pretty sure I needed to go."

"I wanted my life to get back to normal."

She put her hand on his chest and pushed him back so she could look into his eyes. "Has that changed?"

"No." He flopped onto his back beside her and set his hands behind his head. Staring at the ceiling, he debated how much to tell her. "But I'm not sure I recognize what's normal anymore."

She rolled onto her side and rested her head on her palm. "What does that mean?"

"You've bothered me from the first moment we met." The words came out of him slowly. "Whenever we're in the same room it seems as if my senses sharpen. I can discern your voice amongst a dozen others. Your perfume seems to get on my clothes and infiltrate my lungs. And when I close my eyes it's your face, your eyes, your body I see." From her wide eyes and open mouth, he gathered his romantic blathering had surprised her. Logan let a smile creep over his lips. "In short, I've been obsessed with you for five years."

"Were you one of those little boys that shoved and shouted at the girl he liked because he didn't want to be teased for liking her?"

"I don't remember." He did recall in junior high that he'd been a lot more comfortable with computers than the girls in his class. While his buddies were serial-dating, he'd been modifying motherboards and hacking into the school's database. "Lucas was the one who excelled with the opposite sex ever since he was six years old. Always dating someone. Most of the relationships didn't last more than a couple of months before he was on to someone new."

"You are never going to get me to believe that you were a monk."

"Not a monk. I had a steady girlfriend from the time I turned fourteen. We dated all through high school and college."

"Fourteen?" She gave him a wry grin. "What happened after school?"

This was the part he didn't like talking about. After ten years, it still stung. "She chose her career over me and moved to London."

"Why didn't you go with her?"

Because he'd been too stubborn and arrogant to realize he was losing the best thing that had ever happened to him. "My life was here. I'd started a computer security company and I wasn't about to give it all up."

"Then it couldn't have been that serious."

Resentment burned at her easy dismissal of what had been the most important relationship of his life. "We'd been dating almost nine years. Been engaged for three."

"But neither one of you had pulled the trigger. Maybe it was more about how comfortable and easy it was than that you were in love."

His temper continued to heat. She was the furthest thing from an expert on how he felt.

"You weren't there." He'd devoted years to loving Elle. Giving up a future with her hadn't been easy. "You can't possibly know how it was between us."

"Of course not," she soothed. "I'm simply pointing out

that if she'd been your everything you'd have figured out a way to stay together."

It cut like glass that he considered the merits of her argument for even a second. He and Elle had been devoted to each other for nine years, and he had let her go without much of a fight. Just like he'd been ready to let Scarlett move to L.A. Only this time, he'd come to his senses and asked her to stay. He hadn't done the same with Elle. She'd been determined to go, asked him to join her, but he'd never requested she turn down the job offer. Had she been waiting for him to?

"From your expression, I'm going to guess something new has crossed your mind," Scarlett said. "Care to tell me what?"

"You might be right. Maybe what kept us together all through school was that we were traveling the same path."

"Sometimes that's the only thing that does keep people together. Giving up your dream so another can live theirs isn't a sacrifice many are willing to make."

"When I came in tonight you were dressed up. No matter how dedicated you are to managing this hotel and competing against your sisters to run Fontaine Hotels and Resorts, you are at heart an actress." He noted the way her lashes flickered at his statement. "Are you sacrificing what you truly want to stay here?"

"I made a choice between two heart's desires," she said, her smile cryptic. "And I'm never going to second-guess myself about it." With a languid stretch she swung her feet to the floor and stood. "I'm going to grab a shower. Want to join me?"

After an early lunch in her suite, Logan headed to Wolfe Security, leaving Scarlett to wander downstairs to her office in a happy daze. She sat down behind her desk and stared out over the Las Vegas skyline, hoping no big emergencies came up while she was in this state of bliss because she couldn't count on her problem-solving abilities.

Her cell phone rang at a little after two o'clock, rousing her out of a pleasant memory of the night before. It was Grady.

"Scarlett, I think you are going to want to come down here and see what I found in Tiberius's files."

After the theft of documents in her suite, they'd agreed nothing was to leave the secure-documents facility.

"Can you tell me what it is?"

"I'd rather not. You will want to see it for yourself."

Disturbed by Grady's caginess, Scarlett grabbed her car keys and headed for the door. "I'm going to MyVault Storage," she told Sandy as she left. "I'll be back by four for the senior staff meeting."

Through most of the half-hour drive she wondered what Grady might have found. The fact that he'd been reluctant to share the information over the phone had been odd. What, was he thinking that someone could be listening in? For an instant all she could see was the man in the ski mask. How easy it would have been to plant listening devices in her suite while she was unconscious. Almost as soon as the thought occurred, she brushed it away. Logan's paranoia was beginning to rub off on her.

She used her key card and entered the facility. The security guard in the lobby nodded in recognition as she signed in. Cameras watched her from three directions. The security had seemed a little much when she'd first visited the place, but right now she was glad she'd listened to her gut.

Halfway down a long corridor, she stopped in front of a door marked 23. Again she used her key card to gain access. Grady spun around as she entered. She noted his pale complexion and startled gaze and decided he needed to spend a little less time here.

"Have you eaten lunch?" She held up a bag of Chinese food and a six-pack of Diet Mountain Dew, his favorite.

"No. I was going to go grab something before I found this." He nudged a file toward her and accepted the bag of takeout.

What he showed her was an old photo of a group of teenagers. One of them looked familiar, but she couldn't place why.

"This is a photo of someone named George Barnes and his buddies." Grady turned the photo over and showed her the names jotted down on the back. "There's an old police report from 1969 that mentions George Barnes as well as a few other guys in this photo in connection with some neighborhood burglaries, but nothing was ever solid enough to arrest any of them."

"So Barnes was a bad kid." Despite her confusion, Scarlett felt a jolt of excitement at the old documents and what they meant to Grady.

"In another file, I found this newspaper clipping about an accidental drowning during a storm. A local boy by the name of George Barnes had been killed. An eighteen-year-old kid from California had tried to save him. A wealthy, orphaned kid by the name of Preston Rhodes."

"Preston Rhodes?" Scarlett looked from the article to the photo. "As in Tiberius's brother-in-law, the current CEO of Stone Properties? That explains why Tiberius had collected information on George Barnes. But what does it mean?"

"The article says Preston was traveling cross-country on his way to attend college on the East Coast. Thought he'd go out and do a little hiking."

Despite the weird sensation crawling up her spine, Scarlett couldn't discern anything in either the article or the photo that had prompted Grady's call. "I'm not sure I understand what's so important about this information."

"Look more closely at George Barnes." Grady was buzzing with excitement. "Does he remind you of anyone?"

"No. Yes. I'm not really sure."

"He looks like JT Stone."

"What?" Scarlett looked closer and the pieces slipped into place. "You're right. What are you thinking, that this George Barnes guy and the Stone family are related somehow?"

"No." Grady grew serious. "I'm thinking that Barnes and Preston Rhodes are the same guy."

"How is that possible?" Then a door in her mind opened and a hundred detective-show plots raced through her brain. "You think George Barnes stole Preston Rhodes's identity?"

"Why not? Barnes's file paints a picture of a kid with no future. Mom's a hooker. Dad's probably one of her clients. He'd been in and out of the foster care system. Spent some time in juvy. Three of his buddies in the photo are in prison. Then he meets Preston Rhodes, a kid his own age who has money and no family, and who's moving clear across the country to go to college. Who would know if George Barnes put his wallet in the dead kid's pocket and assumed Preston's identity?"

"And when Tiberius found out…" Scarlett stopped breathing as she absorbed the implication. "You think that's why he was killed."

"Makes a good motive."

It certainly did. Perhaps it was time to let the police know what they'd discovered.

As Logan was turning into his driveway, his cell rang. It was Scarlett.

"Logan, you won't believe what Grady and I found in

Tiberius's files." She sounded both exhilarated and anxious. "We might have figured out who killed him."

Logan entered his house and made a beeline for Madison's room. Earlier that afternoon his sister had called. Madison hadn't done as he'd asked and called her parents. Nor was she answering her phone. Giving her the summer to change her mind about college wasn't working. It was time for her to go home.

"The police already have a suspect in custody. A detective buddy of mine has been keeping me updated on the case and he called to tell me that a little after noon today."

Madison's bedroom had an empty, unlived-in feel. No clothes cluttered the chair by the window. The dresser wasn't littered with jewelry and cosmetics. Even as he crossed to the closet, his instinct told him what he'd find. Nothing. His niece was gone.

"Are they sure they have the right guy?" Scarlett's doubt came through loud and clear.

"Positive." Cursing, he retraced his steps down the hall and found a folded piece of paper on the breakfast bar. "He confessed that he was hired by Councilman Scott Worth to silence Tiberius and get a hold of some documents that proved he was embezzling campaign contributions."

"That's what he stole from my suite?"

"And grabbed some other random files to hide his true purpose."

Madison had taken off for L.A. again. No wonder she wasn't answering her cell. What the hell was she thinking?

"Oh, well, good." Scarlett sounded less enthusiastic than she should.

"Did you ever talk to Madison?" he asked.

"No. I was going to and then Grady called." Scarlett sounded subdued. "Have you tried her cell?"

"She's not answering. She took off for L.A."

"No," Scarlett assured him. "She wouldn't do that. Not without talking to me first."

"Well, she did."

"Damn." Worry vibrated through Scarlett's tone. "I really thought I'd gotten through to her."

"I think you did," Logan said. "Only not about college. Ever since that producer friend of yours came into town, Madison has had nothing but stars in her eyes. And you didn't do anything to dissuade her." Even as he took his frustration out on her, Logan recognized it was unfair to blame Scarlett when he had a truckload of regrets at how he'd handled Madison yesterday. "Can you try her cell? Her mother and I aren't having any luck getting her to pick up. Maybe she'll answer for you."

"Sure." Her voice was neutral and polite. "And then I'll call Bobby to see if he's heard from her."

"Is he trustworthy?"

"Absolutely. She won't get into trouble with him."

"What about the rest of the people she's bound to meet?" His concern came out sounding like accusation.

Scarlett's answer was slower in coming. "She's a smart girl, Logan. She'll be careful."

"She's ambitious and overly optimistic."

"I told her in no uncertain terms how hard the business is," Scarlett countered. "She isn't as naive as you think."

"She's only eighteen."

"I get that you're worried about her, Logan."

"Do you? She was hoping to stay with you in L.A." He knew Madison had enough money from her birthday and from what she'd earned working for Scarlett to put herself up in a decent hotel for a week or so. Longer if she chose something on the seedier side. "Where is she going to go if you aren't there?"

"This isn't her first trip to L.A. I know she has friends

there she kept in touch with. She'll probably crash with one of them. Let me try calling her. I'll let you know in a couple minutes if I get ahold of her."

While he waited for Scarlett to call back, Logan stared out the sliding glass door at the pool where Madison loved to hang out. The sun sparkling off the water was blinding, but he stared at the turquoise rectangle until his eyes burned. Although part of him agreed with Scarlett that Madison was capable of taking care of herself, the other part recognized that he'd been tasked with a job and had failed miserably at it. Paula was going to kill him when she found out he'd lost her baby.

His cell rang after what seemed like forever, but the clock on the microwave revealed it had only been ten minutes.

"Her phone must be off. It's rolling straight to voice mail," Scarlett said. "So I called Bobby. He hasn't heard from her, but he promised to call me as soon as he does."

"Thanks." He sounded grim.

"She was determined to go to L.A., Logan. We all may have been kidding ourselves that she intended to go to college this fall. When there's something Madison wants, she goes after it. You should all be proud of her. I wish I'd had half her confidence at her age."

"You expect me to be proud?" he demanded, his voice an impatient whip. "She ran off without letting anyone know her plans."

"Maybe it was the only way she could do what she wanted."

Logan didn't want to hear what Scarlett was trying to tell him. "What happens when this acting thing doesn't pan out?"

"She can always go to college."

"Like you did?"

An uncomfortable silence filled the phone's speaker before Scarlett replied. "Madison and I grew up very differently. I started acting when I was nine. That's all I knew. I didn't have the opportunity to choose what I wanted to do at eighteen. By then I'd been a star with all that came with it and was on my way to becoming a has-been. Maybe if I'd grown up around normal kids, gone to school, and the only expectations put on me were to go to college and get a regular job, I might have ended up a savvy businesswoman like Violet or Harper." Her voice took on a husky throb. "Or maybe I'd have ended up just like Madison, feeling trapped by what everyone else wanted me to be."

"You think Madison felt trapped by her parents' expectations?"

"And yours. You are a hard man to please, Logan."

"Is that what you've been trying to do?" he questioned, infuriated by her reproach. "Please me? Because if that's the case, you haven't been doing a very good job."

"It figures you'd see it that way. For a few days I thought our differences were behind us, but now I see they'll never be." She sounded immeasurably sad. "I knew this thing between us would be short, but it was way more fun than I could have hoped."

Logan's anger vanished at her declaration. He'd never imagined this phone call would lead here. "Scarlett—" Was she really ready to call it quits? Was he? "This is not the conversation we should be having right now."

"Why not? No reason to draw things out when it's so obvious that you blame me for Madison heading to L.A. I realize now that I'm always going to be doing something you disapprove of. And I need someone who has faith in me." She was trying to sound calm, but he could hear the emotion in her tone.

She stopped speaking and offered him a chance to respond. The violent rush of blood through his veins made his ears ring. She was giving him an opportunity to take back his accusations and abandon his disapproval of her past. Her silence pulled at him, but he couldn't form the words she wanted to hear.

"I have to go," Scarlett said. "I've got something important waiting for me. I'll call you if I hear from Bobby or Madison. Goodbye, Logan."

And then she was gone, leaving him to curse that he'd treated her badly when all she wanted to do was help. And thanks to his stubbornness, he'd lost her.

Overwhelmed by a whole new set of worries, Logan sat down at his kitchen table and tried to push his conversation with Scarlett out of his mind. First things first. He had to find Madison before she got into trouble.

Once that was accomplished, he could figure out what to do about Scarlett.

Unsure how she'd gone from walking on clouds this morning to trudging through mud this evening, Scarlett turned back to the photos Grady had uncovered. She'd sent the man home to shower, eat and sleep an hour ago. He hadn't gone without protest. Grady's passion for Las Vegas history was boundless. It's why she'd hired him to develop her Mob Experience exhibit. Days of sifting through Tiberius's files had yielded many things of interest, but little that Grady didn't already know. This recent discovery was something completely new and not wholly related to Las Vegas.

She should drop it. Preston Rhodes was not the sort of man you accused of criminal activities without a whole lot of solid evidence. And she had none.

Scarlett slipped everything into the folder marked George Barnes. A business card had been stapled to the manila file. It belonged to an L.A. reporter by the name of Charity Rimes. On a whim, Scarlett pocketed the card. Just because Tiberius's killer had been caught didn't mean she had to drop the mystery of Preston Rhodes and George Barnes.

After that, Scarlett left the storage room. Her fight with Logan moved to the forefront of her mind as she walked to her car. What was she thinking to push him away like she had? Sure, he'd taken his frustration out on her, but it wasn't the first time. Now, thanks to her impulsiveness, it would probably be the last. What had she done?

But she couldn't just blame herself. It stung that he continued to throw her lack of a formal education in her face. Granted, a business degree would have helped her when she'd first taken over Fontaine Richesse, but she'd always been a quick study and had mastered her responsibilities faster than anyone expected.

Why couldn't he appreciate that she was better at thinking outside the box than either of her sisters? Street smarts had to count for something. She understood how people's greedy nature could get the best of them and made sure her marketing appealed to their desire for fun and profit. Granted, she might not pull in Violet's younger sophisticated crowd or Harper's überwealthy clientele, but her casino was always packed and always bringing in huge profits.

On her way back to the hotel, she worried over the fact that she had too few answers and too many questions. Madison. Logan. Tiberius's files. Her thoughts spun like a hamster on a wheel, going faster and faster but getting nowhere.

Instead of heading straight for Fontaine Richesse, she drove to Violet's hotel for a liberal dose of her sister's optimism.

She found Violet in the middle of Fontaine Chic's casino,

with her long dark hair pulled back into a smooth ponytail. Violet's evening style was like her hotel, elegant, sleek and cosmopolitan. Dark eye shadow made her eyes pop in her pale face. Crystal chandelier earrings swung from her earlobes. Her form-hugging black dress showed off her lean lines and toned legs.

"Got a second?" Scarlett asked as she approached. "I need to talk to you. I really blew it with Logan and I don't know how to fix it."

"Come with me while I check on things at Baccarat." She was referring to the stylish lobby bar that overlooked the strip. "We can sit down and you can tell me what happened."

Scarlett settled in a quiet corner of the bar while Violet went to speak with her bartender. He seemed more animated than usual and their conversation stretched out for longer than Scarlett expected. While she waited for Violet's return, her gaze drifted over the crowd. As usual, the young and beautiful occupied the sofas and chairs. Violet's hotel attracted a twenty-something clientele from L.A., New York and Miami. They liked to party more than gamble, but when they did hit the casino, they spent more than a dozen of Scarlett's customers combined.

One man stood out from the other bar patrons. With a jolt, Scarlett recognized him. JT Stone, Tiberius's nephew. What was he doing here? Scarlett followed the direction of his gaze. Staring at Violet is what he was doing here.

"That's JT Stone," Scarlett said as Violet sat down on the sofa beside her. "I'm surprised he's here."

"He comes by most nights around this time."

"You know he's staring at you, right?"

"It's just his way of telling me he's angry because I stole Rick away." Violet nodded toward the bartender who was whipping up one of his legendary cocktails.

"He doesn't look angry. He looks hungry." Scarlett paused for effect. "For you."

Violet waved her hand dismissively. "Why don't you tell me what happened with you and Logan."

Despite Baccarat's dim lighting, Scarlett spied bright color in Violet's cheeks. But rather than torment her sister with more questions, Scarlett decided to let the matter drop. For now.

"Madison took off for L.A. and Logan blames me." Scarlett paused as the waitress brought their drinks. Eager to see what Rick had made for them, she took a sip. It was a spicy blend of jalapeño and lime with just a hint of sweetness. "Delicious."

Violet coughed, probably caught off guard by the punch of heat. "I'm not sure this is one of my favorites."

"It's definitely not for everyone." Scarlett tasted the cocktail again.

"You two have fought before," Violet reminded her.

"Not like this. He said things. I said things." Scarlett felt hot tears fill her eyes. "I think I told him that I was done."

"You think you told him?"

"I didn't actually come right out and say that I never wanted to speak to him again."

"What did you say exactly?"

"I think I told him I need someone who has faith in me." She'd been so hurt that words had just poured out of her. "He makes me feel as if everything I do is wrong."

"You two have very different ways of approaching things." Violet patted her hand. "What did he say?"

"Nothing. I gave him a chance to tell me that he believed in me, or to tell me that not everything I do is wrong, but he didn't say anything. So I ended the call."

"It doesn't sound like you two are done."

"It sure feels that way. I can't imagine a future with a man who can't love me, faults and all."

"Give him a little time to calm down. From everything you've said, being in charge of Madison has been really stressful for him. I'm sure he simply overreacted to her going to L.A. without warning."

Scarlet wanted very much for Violet to be right, but wasn't sure she could make herself believe that she was.

"Thanks for listening to me," Scarlett said, forcing herself to smile past the ache in her throat. "Now let me give you a piece of advice. Take JT one of these." Scarlett lifted her glass and smirked at her sister over the rim. "Unless, of course, you think he's already hot enough."

Violet scowled at her, but the burst of color was back in her cheeks. With a laugh, Scarlett finished her cocktail and bid her sister goodbye.

On her way back to Fontaine Richesse, Scarlett's fingers itched to dial Logan's number. She was desperate to find out if he'd heard from Madison, but decided to heed Violet's advice to give him some space.

Scarlett returned to her office. Normally she would go down and make sure everything was running smoothly in the casino, but tonight she needed some uninterrupted time to sort through the day's revelations.

The message light on her office phone made her heart leap. Maybe Madison had returned her call. But it was Logan who had left the message. He was heading to L.A. to find his niece. Why hadn't he called her cell? The most obvious answer was he hadn't wanted to talk to her.

She dropped into her desk chair with a frustrated exhale, her thoughts coming full circle. Maybe she'd been right to end things. Logan showed no sign that he'd stop treating her like a friendly enemy and start regarding her as his partner. On the other hand, the chemistry between them was explosive enough to make it worth their while to find some middle ground.

Of course, Logan's steely determination wasn't conducive to compromising any more than her stubborn streak made her easy to get along with. But she'd sacrificed a fabulous part in a television series in order to stay in Las Vegas and be with Logan. And he'd tracked her down at her suite to ask that she not leave town. Surely that spoke to change for both of them.

Scarlett couldn't stop thinking that if she'd called Madison today the teenager might not have headed to L.A. Nor was she happy with the idea of sitting around and waiting for the situation to resolve itself. What she needed to do was head to L.A. and track Madison down. She'd convince the eighteen-year-old to give up acting and choose college. Logan would then see that she might make mistakes, but she could fix them, as well.

Decision made, Scarlett booked a plane ticket for the next morning and called Sandy to let her know she was going to L.A. Next, she called her second in command and put him in charge of the hotel with instructions to contact her if anything serious arose. She doubted he'd have any problems. The hotel had been running smoothly for months with only the occasional blip.

In a cab on the way to the airport, Scarlett debated calling Logan and letting him know she was coming. In the end, she decided not to give him the opportunity to say no to her help. On the other hand, he wasn't a man who appreciated being surprised. If she found Madison and he didn't know she was in L.A. looking, he would be angry. Her earlier reflection on their relationship determined her course of action. If she wanted Logan to consider her a partner, she needed to be open and up-front with him. Even if it went against her normal operating procedure to do so.

Not surprisingly, her call ended up in voice mail. Once she'd delivered the news that she was on her way to join him, she sat back and waited for the explosion. But when her phone rang it was Chase.

"Madison decided to take off and go to L.A.," she explained. "I'm on my way there now. I hoped maybe you'd heard from her."

"And here I was thinking you wanted to get together and relive old times."

Scarlett forced her voice to relax. "I'm sure you have better things to do than that. Has Madison called you?"

"I gave her my number, but haven't heard from her."

"If she does call, would you let me know? We're all worried about her."

"Sure enough. And give me a call later if you want to get a drink."

"Thanks for the offer, but I've got my hands full at the moment."

"That Wolfe guy?"

"As a matter of fact, yes."

"I figured the way he was mooning over you and glaring at me." He sounded amused. "If he doesn't treat you like you deserve, let me know. I'll kick his ass."

Scarlett grinned. "Thanks, Chase. You're a pal." She hung up just as the flight attendant announced that all electronic devices needed to be shut off and stowed. Logan hadn't called. Anxiety stretched her nerves thin. It was going to be an agonizing hour or so until the plane landed in L.A.

Eleven

As he sat behind the wheel of his rental car glaring at the traffic clogging the 110 Freeway, Logan decided that coming to L.A. had been an impulsive, rash idea. Nothing that he'd accomplished today couldn't have been done from the comfort of his air-conditioned office at Wolfe Security. Randolph had put him in touch with the private investigator they'd used the last time they'd tracked Madison down and he'd met with the guy an hour after touching down in L.A.

Now, he was heading back to LAX. Not to return to Las Vegas, but to meet Scarlett's flight. When he'd left her a message last night, he'd half expected, half hoped she'd jump on a plane and come to L.A. He was damned glad she was on her way.

It was hard on a stubborn bachelor like him to realize that Scarlett's absence hit him physically as well as psychologically. He had an ache in his gut that hadn't subsided since she'd hung up on him yesterday afternoon. She'd only been trying to help and he'd criticized the choices she'd made in her youth. The same choices that had created the strong, sexy, sometimes vulnerable woman who gave herself to him completely in bed and kept him guessing the rest of the time.

In the past twelve hours he'd come to the realization that what had bloomed between them wasn't just sexual. His heart ached with emotions too strong to contain and too new to voice. But he had to try.

Standing near the gate exit, Logan couldn't ignore the churning in his stomach. He was anxious to see her. Eager to apologize for taking his frustration with Madison out on her.

And then she was sauntering in his direction. Accustomed to her vibrant energy, he wasn't prepared for how pale and subdued she looked and hated the worry lines etched between her eyebrows. His heart thundered against his ribs as she spotted him waiting for her. Before his lips formed a hello, she held up her hand to forestall whatever he'd been about to say.

"Don't be mad at me for coming," she said. "I'm just as worried about Madison as you are and I know it's my fault she's here."

"I was wrong to blame you. Madison is strong-willed and once she sets her mind to something, there's no swaying her." The need to find his niece weighed on him, but so did the damage he'd done to his relationship with Scarlett. "About our last conversation…"

She shook her head, but wouldn't meet his gaze. "Not until we find Madison." When he began to protest, she cut him off. "Promise me. We need to keep the focus on her."

"Fine," he told her, cupping her face and staring into her beautiful eyes. "But I'm not happy about it."

"I didn't expect you to be." The throb in her voice gave

away more than her expression. She was wary of him in a way she'd never been before.

The end to their last conversation sprang to mind and his joy in her arrival dimmed. Why did he feel as if she was only here to tie up the loose ends of their relationship so she could have a clean break with him?

Logan relieved her of the overnight bag she carried and took her free hand, gratified that she didn't try to pull away. "The car's parked this way."

"Have you had any luck locating Madison?"

"No. I've called the boy she followed out here last spring and made contact with the private detective my brother-in-law hired once before, but no luck."

"You should never have let me near her," Scarlett said. "If she'd worked with either Violet or Harper she never would've met Bobby and been encouraged to pursue acting."

"Maybe." Logan drew her into the warm Los Angeles evening. "Or maybe she was playing all of us this summer and never intended to go to college in the fall."

"But she said…" Scarlett trailed off and frowned. "If you're right, she's a better actress than I ever was."

"I know that's not true."

Scarlett laughed. "You've never seen me act."

"I've seen everything you've ever done."

"That's impossible."

He felt the weight of her disbelief as he unlocked the doors on his rental car and ushered her inside. Before he closed the door, he took ahold of her gaze. "What can I say? I'm a fan."

Shutting the door on her stunned expression offered him a moment of amusement. She had shifted sideways on the seat and was poised to get answers as soon as he slid behind the wheel.

"Since when?" she demanded as he started the car.

"I think I saw you for the first time when you starred on *That's Our Hilary.*"

"Don't tell me you watched that."

"Not me. My sister, Paula. Her, Lucas and I used to fight over who got to watch what. We outnumbered her, but she was older by a year and always got first choice. I really learned to hate that show." He flashed her a wicked grin. "Lucas thought you were hot."

Her eyes narrowed. "I thought you said you were a fan."

"You were really amazing in *Sometimes Forever.*"

"Do you really expect me to believe that you watched that show? It really isn't your thing." Her self-assurance began to slip a little, exposing her quieter, fragile core. "And there weren't more than eight episodes. It never even made it to DVD."

"When you first came to Las Vegas, as much as we rubbed each other the wrong way, I couldn't stop thinking about you. I found and watched everything you'd done because I had you pegged as just some woman who read lines someone else had written." He took her hand in his and lifted her fingers to his lips. "It really bugged me that not only were you beautiful and fascinating in whatever role you played, you also brought great depth to your characters."

"But ever since I've known you, you've been nothing but critical of my career." Her green eyes went soft with confused hurt. "Why, when you felt like that?"

Admitting that he was wrong was like swallowing foul-tasting medicine. He knew it was good for him, but hated the punishment on his senses. "Because I might be able to step outside the box and see all the possibilities in a computer program or security system, but when it comes to people, I take a narrow view."

She cocked her head. "Is that your way of telling me you're sorry for being such a judgmental ass?"

"Sorry?" He winced dramatically and watched her outrage grow. "I'm not sure I'd go that far." When her lips popped open to chastise him, he cupped her cheek in his palm and leaned closer so she couldn't miss the sincerity in his gaze. "You make me want to be a better man."

"I think you're pretty terrific already."

"You must be in love with me," he declared, kissing her on the nose.

"Why would you say that?" She tried for a light tone, but it came out sounding a little too anxious.

"Because only a woman in love would think I'm terrific after I took my anxiety and exasperation out on her earlier."

"Oh, that." She waved her hand in dismissal. "I'm just used to your bad-tempered ways."

She took his hand. The feel of her fingers meshed with his lowered his blood pressure and calmed the agitation he'd been feeling since she'd hung up on him yesterday.

She, too, looked more at ease as they exited the parking ramp. Silence reigned as he got them onto the freeway and heading north.

"I'm all out of ideas where we should look for Madison next," he said, prodding her out of her thoughts.

"I called Chase before the plane left Las Vegas, but he hadn't heard from her."

"I can't believe she'd call him."

"Why not?" Scarlett smiled. "Chase might be a mega star, but he's also a great guy. He's never forgotten the help he had on the way up and donates a ton of his time to charities. He likes to give back. And he really hit it off with Madison."

"He seems to hit it off with you, as well." Logan made no attempt to conceal his irritation.

"We've worked together."

"It seemed more familiar than I would expect between two colleagues."

"We might have dated briefly."

That piece of information didn't surprise Logan, but it made his heart feel like a cumbersome weight in his chest. "Was it serious?"

Scarlett stared out the side window. "We were young." Her phone began to ring before Logan could press further. "It's Madison."

Logan saw his niece's smiling face on Scarlett's phone screen. Relief rushed through him.

Scarlett keyed the speaker. "Madison, oh, thank heavens. I left you three messages. Are you all right?"

"Fine. I forgot my charger when I packed for L.A. and my phone died. I finally got around to buying a new one."

"Well, I'm glad you did. Logan's here with me. We've been frantic. Why didn't you tell us you were headed to L.A.?"

"I left a note for Logan."

"I wish you'd talked with me instead," Logan said.

"You don't talk," Madison complained. "You command."

"I can't argue with you there." Scarlett spared Logan a brief glance and saw his lips tighten. "But didn't you think you could tell me what was going on?"

"I should have, but I was so mad at Uncle Logan and you two are so tight these days...."

But not so tight anymore. The thought tempered her joy in finding out Madison was okay.

"Besides, I wanted to surprise you once everything was finalized," the teenager continued.

"Once what was finalized?" Logan asked.

"I'm going to attend UCLA in the fall."

"UCLA?" Scarlett silently demanded answers from

Logan, but he shook his head. "That's wonderful. How come you didn't mention that you'd been accepted there?"

"Because I didn't know. I never got an acceptance letter and assumed that they'd rejected me."

"But they didn't?"

"No. Turns out my parents intercepted the letter and didn't tell me I'd gotten in. It was my top choice because it's in L.A. and they've got a fantastic school of theater, film and television. I was devastated when the letters went out last March and I didn't get one."

Is that what had accounted for her running off to L.A. last spring? Scarlet exchanged a glance with Logan. "So how did you find out you were accepted?"

"They also posted the acceptances online. I was so bummed about the letter, I completely forgot that I could find out from their website until I was clearing out old emails yesterday and found the ID and password."

"I'm thrilled for you," Scarlett said, giddy with relief and delight. "So you came to L.A. to…?"

"Tour the campus and check out the dorms."

"Of course." Weak with relief, she grinned at Logan. "Where are you? We'll come pick you up and take you out for a celebratory dinner."

"You're in L.A.?"

"Logan and I came here looking for you."

"You really were worried." Madison sounded as if she finally realized the impact of what she'd done. "I'm sorry, but I can't do dinner. I already have plans with some of the people I met last time I was out here."

"Where are you staying?"

"With them. They're going to drop me off at the terminal after breakfast tomorrow so I can catch the bus back to Las Vegas."

"We could come get you. Fly you back to Las Vegas with us."

"Why don't you and Logan hang out in L.A. for a few days? I'll be fine."

And Scarlett knew she would be. "We'll catch up tomorrow and let you know our plans. Have fun." She didn't bother to add "be safe."

After disconnecting the call, Scarlett said, "I'm guessing her parents are not going to be happy she got into UCLA."

"To hell with them," Logan growled. "They're getting what they want. She's going to college. The least they can do is let her attend the school of her choice."

Nothing could have demonstrated what a tough month it had been for Logan better than those words. Scarlett kissed her fingertips and pressed them against his cheek.

"You're going to make a fabulous father someday," she declared, grinning broadly. "As much as you grumble and complain about her, you've been behind her all along. She might not tell you so, but I know she appreciates that you haven't dictated to her like her parents did and that you were willing to support her choice of whatever college she went to. She's lucky to have you."

"Thanks." Logan captured her hand and pressed a sizzling kiss into her palm. "Now that we've accomplished our mission, where should go to celebrate?"

"Why don't we head up to Malibu? I have a house on the beach."

"You keep a house here?"

"It was the first thing I bought when I turned eighteen. I know it doesn't make sense to keep a three-million-dollar piece of property sitting around empty, but I love it too much to sell."

If he'd found out about this a week ago he would have been utterly convinced that Scarlett perceived her stay in

Vegas as a temporary one, but he was coming to accept that L.A. would always be a part of who she was.

"I can understand that. I have a place in Aspen that I don't get to often enough anymore, but I can't bear the thought of giving up the skiing."

"Oh, hot tubbing after a day on the slopes. Sounds heavenly."

"We'll have to go there this winter."

"I'd like that," she began, her voice sounding peculiar. "But…"

He shot her a glance and was surprised at how concerned she looked. "Time to talk?"

She directed him onto Interstate 10 before answering, "Let's wait until we get to my house."

Little more passed between them until they reached the Pacific Coast Highway. Scarlett could tell Logan had a lot on his mind, but for once she wasn't interested in knowing what it was. As they drew closer to her house, she warned him so he wouldn't miss her driveway.

"I hope you like it," she said, unlocking the front door and leading the way into a spacious white living room with tiled floors, a turquoise-blue couch and panoramic views of the Pacific. "I called ahead and had the property management company stock the fridge. I thought we could have dinner and take a walk on the beach."

"That sounds nice," he said, regarding her intently. "Where do you want me to put the bags?"

The question hung in the air between them.

"It would be easy to tell you the master bedroom," she responded. "So many things are wrong between us, but sexual chemistry isn't one of them."

Scarlett threw open the sliding glass doors that opened onto the oceanside terrace and let in the breeze.

"Yesterday you said you needed someone who had faith in you," Logan said, coming up behind her.

Even though he didn't touch her, Scarlett felt his presence like a caress, and it was hard not to lean back against him. "And I gave you ample opportunity to say you did."

Logan put his hand on her upper arm and spun her to face him. "I've given you no reason to grant me another chance, but I wish you would."

Scarlett couldn't believe what she was hearing. "I don't know why you're asking. No matter how hard I try not to irritate you, I'm eventually going to do something and you're going to get mad."

"Would you believe me if I told you that I like being upset by you?"

"No." But her eyes sparkled with amusement.

"How about if I told you that you've made me happier than I've ever been?"

She grew somber. "Then I consider my work here finished."

"You can't mean that."

"I don't, but the way things are between us, I can't see our future being anything but one long argument."

"If this is about your accusation that I don't believe in you, that's not true."

Logan's scowl made hope flare in Scarlett's heart, but could she trust his declaration?

"I'm only speaking from what you've said and how you've behaved."

"Including the night I showed up at your place demanding you stay in Las Vegas?"

"Yes." She would forever cherish the memory of that night. "And how, less than twenty-four hours later, you were furious at me. And that the day before you couldn't wait to find out when your life was going to get back to normal."

Logan looked chastened by her words, but he continued to argue. "That's when I thought you were leaving. I didn't want you to go, but couldn't bring myself to ask you to stay."

"So you pushed me away?"

"It's how I react when I'm feeling vulnerable. I did the same thing to Elle all those years ago. I wanted her to choose me, but I was too proud to ask her to. I was bullheaded and wrong, and I almost made the same mistake with you."

"But you were in love with Elle."

"I'm in love with you."

For a second Scarlett gaped at him. "No wa—"

Logan silenced the flow of her words with a kiss. Startled by the abruptness of his lips against her, she nevertheless surrendered to the flood of heat and emotion his touch inspired. Any thoughts of dinner or a walk on the beach fled. She was flushed and dizzy by the time he lifted his lips from hers.

"Marry me."

Fearing wishful thinking had made her mishear him, Scarlett didn't answer. Her heart was pounding so hard she thought her chest would explode.

"I'm sorry," she said at last. "I don't think I heard you correctly."

"I asked you to marry me."

"Now I'm certain I'm not hearing you correctly."

He scowled at her. "Stop turning this romantic moment into a comedy."

"Well, excuse me if I'm caught a little off guard." Despite her tone, she couldn't stop grinning. "Of course, I'll marry you."

"That's great," he told her, an edge of impatience to

his voice. "Because I love you and I don't think I can live without you."

"You don't think?" she prompted, nuzzling his neck and nipping at his earlobe. "Or you know you can't?"

"I'm pretty damned sure that I am going to be very happy spending the rest of my life being aggravated by you in the best and worst possible way."

"That's my guy," she murmured, kissing him with all the love in her heart and glorying in the love she got back. "I'm pretty smitten with you myself."

"Smitten enough to test for the project Bobby came down to talk to you about?"

She pulled back far enough to scrutinize his expression. "I thought you understood that I'd decided to pass."

"I understand that you love to act. And I understand that the part is perfect for you. What I don't understand is why you decided to pass when Bobby was willing to bend over backwards to accommodate your schedule."

How could she make him see what she couldn't quite grasp herself? "I'm afraid."

"Of what?"

Where did she start? "Not being good enough. That if I don't give my full attention to the hotel, something bad will happen." And in a smaller voice, "Losing you."

"You'll be wonderful. You have the best-run hotel on the Strip." He kissed her slow and deep. "As for losing me, that will never happen. You're the most amazing thing that's ever happened to me."

Her throat tightened almost painfully. His faith bolstered her courage. Snug in his arms, Scarlett dared to consider whether she could have the two things in the world she loved most.

"I suppose I could call Bobby in the morning and see if we could meet with him to talk about schedules." She framed Logan's face with her hands and peered deep into his eyes. "As long as you understand that you'll always be my first priority. I can live without acting. I can't live without you."

"That's the one thing you don't have to worry about," he promised, espresso eyes soft and warm as they toured her face. "I'm never going to let you go."

* * * * *

A MERGER BY MARRIAGE

BY
CAT SCHIELD

For Kevan Lyon, my fabulous agent.

One

With his arm stretched across the back of the black leather couch, JT Stone sipped one of Rick's signature cocktails and brooded over a woman.

Tonight Violet Fontaine wore a black, skin-tight mini with long sleeves and a neckline that concealed her delicate collarbones. Despite the snug fit, the dress looked modest when viewed from the front. But the back of the dress. Oh, the back. A wide V bared an expanse of golden skin, crisscrossed by spaghetti thin straps from her nape to the indent of her waist. As he suspected the design intended, his gaze was drawn to the curve of her tight, round backside.

His fingers twitched as he imagined holding those luscious curves in his hands. Before he'd met Violet six years ago he'd been a diehard breast and thigh man. These days he was on a mission to find a butt better than hers. To date he hadn't found one. Good thing she had no idea what she did to him or he might lose something more irreplaceable than his favorite bartender.

The resident mixologist of Fontaine Chic's lobby bar Baccarat, Rick was a genius when it came to creating

unique cocktails. Tonight JT was having Rick's version
of a dirty martini in the lounge. His excuse for showing
up six nights a week was that he was wooing Rick back
to Titanium where he belonged.

JT finished the last of his drink. Who was he kidding?
In the year since Rick had switched employers, JT was
here most nights because Violet swung through on her
rounds at exactly eleven-fifteen and lingered to chat with
the clientele. As the proprietor of the Fontaine Chic, she
was very hands-on.

"Another drink, JT?" The waitress cocked her head and
smiled warmly at him.

"Sure." Why not? He nodded toward Violet. "And whatever she's drinking."

Charlene followed his gaze. "You know she doesn't
drink when she's working."

"Maybe tonight she'll make an exception for me."

"Maybe." But Charlene's tone said something completely different.

"Would you send her over?"

The nightly ritual made the waitress's lips curve in wry
humor. "Sure."

Violet herself brought his drink over, setting it before
him with practiced ease. "Rick said this is what you're
drinking tonight."

"Will you join me?"

When she shook her head, the diamond drops dangling
from her earlobes swayed seductively. "I'm working."

"And I'm your best customer."

"You're a fan of Rick's, not Fontaine Chic."

"I'm a fan of you," he murmured and her eyes widened
briefly as if startled by his admission. Was it possible she
was oblivious to his interest? Not one of the waitresses
thought he came here every night just to drink.

It did no good to remind himself that he liked his women

curvy, blonde and agreeable. That with her long lean frame inherited from her showgirl mother and her father's wavy brown hair, she was not his type. Or that her strong-willed personality had been cultivated by his estranged uncle, Tiberius Stone, her surrogate father. A man who blamed JT's father for orchestrating his disinheritance.

"You can take a couple minutes," he said, gesturing to the empty space beside him.

Her eyebrow arched at his implied command, but she settled sideways on the couch and crossed her long legs. She'd fastened her waist-length hair into a high, sleek ponytail. The look was both modern and retro and showed off her large brown eyes and bold cheekbones to great advantage.

With the toe of her black stiletto a mere inch from his pant leg, she propped her elbow on the back of the couch, rested her cheek on her palm and waited for him to speak. Quick to smile, she was the most upbeat, optimistic person he'd ever met. She was sunlight to his shadow. Forever close, always untouchable.

He sipped his drink and surveyed her over the rim. The dark circles beneath her eyes told him she was working harder than ever since Tiberius had been murdered several weeks ago.

"You should take some time off," he said, aware that what she did was none of his business.

"And do what? Sit around and grieve?" She must have heard the edge in her tone because after a long sigh, she continued on a milder note. "I know it's what most people do when they lose a parent, but I can't think of a better way to honor Tiberius's memory than to work."

JT nodded in understanding. "I'm sure he'd approve."

Although he'd been given the middle name, Tiberius, after his mother's younger brother, until the last few months JT had never had the chance to know his uncle by anything other than reputation. JT had been raised in Miami where Stone Properties had their headquarters. Tiberius rarely left Vegas. And the bad blood between Tiberius and his brother-in-law and JT's father, Preston Rhodes, made any chance of a relationship between JT and his uncle impossible.

The hard feelings between Tiberius and Preston went back twenty-five years. According to what JT had gleaned from family friends, Preston had accused Tiberius of embezzling from Stone Properties and had convinced James Stone to fire his son. Then, five years later, James had died and JT's father had used his influence over his wife, Fiona Stone—bowing to pressure from her father, she'd never taken her husband's last name—to get the board of directors to vote in favor of making him chairman and CEO.

"Thanks for coming to the memorial service this morning," Violet said. "I know you and Tiberius weren't close, but lately he'd talked a lot about how he regretted all the years he kept you out of his life and how he wished he'd gotten to know you."

Regret tightened in his chest. "I had no idea Tiberius felt that way." JT sucked in a deep breath and let it out slowly.

When he'd arrived in Las Vegas to run the local family operations, his opinion of his uncle had been formed by what he knew about Tiberius from his father and grandfather. Although relations between him and his uncle stayed tense for many years, after seeing how much Violet admired Tiberius, plus all the positive things said about his uncle by other Las Vegas businessmen, JT had begun to suspect that if Tiberius had done what his father had accused him of, there'd been a good reason.

"When it came to your family, he could be hardheaded," Violet said with a faint smile. "And he really hated your dad."

"The feeling was definitely mutual."

Violet remained lost in thought for a moment. "Lately he'd mentioned quite a few times that he thought you'd do a terrific job running Stone Properties."

The compliment landed a direct hit in his gut. He wished he'd had a chance to get to know his uncle the way Violet did. Now it was too late. "I'm leaving the company."

JT heard himself say the words and wondered at his impromptu disclosure. He hadn't divulged his inner thoughts to anyone. Not even his cousin, Brent, and they were as close as brothers. JT peered into his drink. Had Rick infused some sort of truth serum into the cocktail? JT set the glass down. When he looked up, he caught Violet staring at him in surprise.

"Why would you do that?"

"When I turned thirty two months ago, I gained control of my trust fund and the thirty percent of Stone Properties shares my mother left to me when she died. This enabled me to dig into the finances and see what my father has been doing lately."

"And?"

"The properties are overleveraged. My father's been borrowing too much trying to expand and with each property that gets built, our resources are stretched closer to their breaking point." In his gut was a ball of frustration that had been growing steadily these last sixty days.

"I had no idea." Sympathy made her voice soft. She felt sorry for him and he hated it. "Have you shared your concerns with your father?"

It wasn't like him to disclose his difficulties to anyone, least of all someone as tightly connected to the competition as Violet. But then, she wasn't just anyone. She was special. Through her he was linked to a part of his family he'd never known and just being around her made him feel less alone.

JT picked up his drink once more. "He won't listen and

since he controls the majority of the shares, I don't have leverage to affect current policy."

"If you leave Stone Properties, what are you planning to do?"

He'd never been one to show his cards, but Violet's attentiveness made her easy to confide in. She acted as if she had all the time in the world to listen to what ailed him and offer sensible feedback. He'd be a fool not to listen to her opinion as a businesswoman. But it was her friendship he craved. And if he was honest with himself, her body he longed to devour.

"I've been cultivating some investors," he said. "I'm going out on my own. My uncle didn't need the family business to be successful and neither do I."

"Are you sure that's the best idea? Tiberius let your father drive him out of the business and never stopped regretting it."

"No one drove him out," JT corrected her. "Tiberius was caught stealing from the company and was fired."

Her disappointment in him was like clouds passing in front of the sun. "He was framed." She truly believed that. "By your father."

JT sat perfectly still beneath the weight of her accusation while his thought raced. A normal person would rush to defend their father against such slander, but JT had seen the company's financials for himself and knew his father was not telling the stockholders everything. That made him a liar in JT's books. Nor would he ever champion his father after the way Preston had treated JT's mother.

But he wasn't ready to jump on the bash-Preston bandwagon either. As conflicted as JT was about his father, he put a high value on loyalty.

"If that's true," he said, his tone neutral, "all the more reason to break with the company and my father."

Determination flared in her eyes. "Or you could stay and fight for what's yours."

While JT appreciated her spirited defense of his inheritance, he'd been contemplating the wisdom of staying with Stone Properties for a couple years. It was worse now that he had seen the company's financials.

"I hate being powerless to stop him from taking apart all that my grandfather built."

"I can understand that." Without warning her gaze sharpened. "These plans of yours, do they mean you're leaving Las Vegas?"

Was she hoping he wouldn't? The thought of not seeing her every day made him grim. Did it bother her as well?

JT searched her eyes for answers, but saw only curiosity. With Violet, what you saw was what you got. Her openness fascinated him. She never seemed to worry about guarding herself against hurt or disappointment.

It was a major factor in why he'd never pursued her.

Not long after he'd arrived in Las Vegas, he'd run into his uncle and Violet at a charity event. Despite his instant attraction to the twenty-three-year-old, he knew better than to act on his interest. The bad blood between her adopted father and his biological one was a significant barrier. So was JT's playboy lifestyle.

Before he'd moved to Las Vegas, JT had made quite a name for himself in Miami's social scene. Going at life at a reckless pace whether it was fast boats, expensive cars or unavailable women, he hadn't cared whom he hurt as long as he displeased his father.

He liked Violet too much to subject her to his unhealthy family dynamic. Besides, she wasn't a good choice for him. Unlike the women he usually pursued, she would expect things from him. Things he couldn't give her. Openness. Joy. Trust. In order to be with her he'd have to surrender the defenses that muffled his emotions and protected him from pain and disillusionment. She'd lure him out of his comfortable dark cave and require him to find happiness.

How was he supposed to do that when his childhood hadn't given him the tools?

His father believed anything that got in the way of business was bad. As a kid, JT had had that philosophy hammered into his head. His mother had been weakened by her hunger for love. Being ignored by the domineering husband she adored had made her life hell, and she'd started retreating into drugs and alcohol around the time that Tiberius left town. By the time he turned twelve, JT was used to being ignored by his parents, forgotten by his grandfather and alienated from his uncle. Nor was there any family on his father's side. The only person who'd showed any interest in him was his grandmother and she split her time between Miami, Virginia and Kentucky.

Traditional family. Love. JT had never grown up with these things.

Being around Violet gave him a glimpse of what a normal personal life could be. The love she had for her sisters, her mother and Tiberius made him long to be included in her circle. But he couldn't take the steps needed to put himself there. Nor could he leave well enough alone either. The need to connect remained. A tantalizing temptation. One of his deep, dark secrets.

So he visited Fontaine Chic night after night and sat in the bar. He craved a relationship with Violet, but had no idea how to go about having one. In casino terms, he was betting the minimum. He'd never win big, but he wasn't going to lose everything either. Playing without risk was not how he lived. He got a rush from flinging his body into danger, but gambling with his heart was something else entirely.

"I don't know what the future holds," he responded at last. "Will you miss me if I go?"

The question caught her off guard. Her eyes widened and her lips parted, but no words came out. Usually their exchanges hovered on the verge of personal without either of them crossing that line. Tonight, he'd changed the game by giving her a glimpse into what was bothering him, by trusting her with his plans for the future.

"I'll miss your business," she retorted with a wry smile that didn't quite reach her eyes. She uncrossed her legs, signaling their conversation was at an end.

"Violet." He caught her hand before she could rise. The casual contact created a complex chain reaction in JT's gut. He wanted her. That had never been in doubt. But what lay below the lust was dangerous beyond belief. "I'm really sorry about Tiberius."

He gave her hand a gentle squeeze and released her. It rattled him how hard it was to relax his fingers and set her free. What he wanted to do was draw her into his arms and let her soak the shoulder of his suit coat with her tears. He knew it was impossible. They didn't share that level of intimacy. The fact both relieved and frustrated him.

"Thank you." Two polite words, but her tone carried a wealth of emotion. She dabbed at the corner of her eye, catching teardrops on her knuckles. "I'm such a mess."

"I think you're beautiful."

Such a simple statement from such a complicated man. Unvarnished and without subtext, the words shook her. Needing a second to compose herself, Violet made quick apologies and headed for the bar to snag a couple of drink napkins to soak up her tears. Feeling steady once more, she returned to where JT now stood.

"Are you okay?"

The hard, unyielding businessman was back. As Violet nodded in response to his question, she breathed a sigh of relief. Whatever glimpse she'd had behind the curtain, however brief, made JT that much more interesting. And that was problematic.

Long ago she'd accepted that one look from him set her hormones off like Roman candles. Lust she could handle. She was a modern girl with a healthy appetite for sex. Maybe she didn't indulge often, but that didn't mean she wasn't interested. Just cautious.

It was the way her heart sped up whenever she spotted JT that concerned her. Getting romantic notions about a man as emotionally unavailable as JT would only lead to heartbreak. And she'd seen the effects of that sort of misery up close. Violet's mother had been abandoned by her married lover and left with a baby to support. Ross Fontaine had taken everything Lucille Allen had to give and moved on without a backward glance. Yet despite her heart being a shattered mess, Violet's mother still loved Ross and would to her dying day.

No. Violet was way too smart to end up like her mother. The instant the uncharitable thought surfaced, Violet regretted it. She loved her mom like crazy. It was just that being Lucille's daughter had forced Violet to grow up too fast. If not for Tiberius, she'd have had no childhood at all.

He'd adored Lucille. Taken on the responsibility for her and her daughter. They'd been his family. Not legally, of course, because even though he loved Lucille and wanted to marry her, she refused to give up on the hope that one day Ross Fontaine would return to her.

When Violet gave her heart, it would be to someone available, emotionally as well as legally. His reputation as a smart, fair businessman impressed the hell out of her, but when it came to personal relationships, he never went all in.

Not that he'd given her any reason to believe he thought of her as anything other than a competitor who'd stolen his favorite bartender. Tonight that had changed. Tonight he'd asked if she'd miss him if he left Las Vegas and made her believe his next heartbeat hinged on her saying that she would.

Violet brushed away her fanciful thoughts, but she couldn't ignore how her pulse had hitched at the gentle strength of his hand on hers. This was just simple desire. Nothing more. The man was six-feet, one-inch of rock solid male. Handsome with his black hair and bold eyebrows. The slight downturn of his chiseled lips. The fathomless ocean blue of his eyes.

Her instincts said he was a man who could use some help and she was a girl who loved cheering on her teammates. Only he wasn't on her team or even part of her circle. She would be wise to mind her own business where he was concerned. If she became too invested in offering him help that he did not want, she'd end up getting burned.

"I'd better get going or I'll be completely off schedule," she said, but couldn't bring her feet to move. Something had changed between them tonight and walking away from JT was proving difficult.

"I'd better get going as well," he told her, glancing at his watch. "If you need anything I hope you'll call."

More surprises. "Sure." She couldn't imagine what sort of help she'd turn to him for. Most of the time she was pretty self-sufficient. She'd had to be. Her mother was too easily overwhelmed by the least difficulty. Violet had learned to take care of herself from an early age, even when life had grown less challenging after they'd moved in with Tiberius when Violet was six. "That's nice of you."

For a brief moment his eyes softened. Before she could draw an unsteady breath he'd retreated behind his reserve once more.

"It's not being nice," he said, neutral and polite. "We're family."

His declaration was the cherry on top of a triple scoop sundae of surprises. "How do you figure?"

"It might not be the most traditional connection, but you were my uncle's daughter."

"Not legally." Violet wasn't sure how to cope with a connection of this sort with JT. If things became affectionate between them she might just step out of the neutral zone and into treacherous territory.

"Do you really think that mattered to Tiberius?"

"No." Violet cocked her head and regarded him. "But I would have thought it mattered to you."

"Why?"

Violet floundered. Confronting people didn't come naturally to her. It was a skill she'd worked hard to develop during her years in management positions and when she did speak her mind, it was after careful preparation.

But JT had flustered her tonight and she'd spoken without thought.

"The truth is I really don't know."

"But you had a reason to say it," he persisted, his interest laser-sharp.

Admitting her flaws wasn't something she did often, but Violet felt she owed JT an explanation after he'd been so kind to her tonight. "I didn't like growing up the bastard daughter of Ross Fontaine," she explained. "Being treated as if I didn't exist by the entire Fontaine family gave me a huge chip on my shoulder."

"That's changed now. Henry Fontaine not only welcomed you as his granddaughter, he gave you a hotel to run and a shot at becoming CEO of the family business."

Violet nodded. "And most days that amazes me. But sometimes I regress to that eleven-year-old girl who was ridiculed by her classmates for bragging that I was Ross Fontaine's daughter when everyone could tell he wanted nothing to do with me."

"I can see where that would be hard."

She had a difficult time believing JT could sympathize

with her situation. The sole heir to Stone Properties, he'd grown up knowing who he was and where he belonged. Maybe things hadn't been perfect with his parents and maybe the company was struggling with his father at the helm, but that could be turned around with the right moves.

"So, you think we're family," she said, aiming for a warm smile. She could tell by JT's expression that she missed the mark.

"I didn't have a chance to know my uncle," he explained. "I think I missed a lot. You knew him better than anyone. I feel connected to him through you."

It took a second for Violet to register that JT was reaching out to her. All of a sudden she felt a little giddy. "Your uncle was my father in all ways but legally." She sounded a tad breathless as she finished, "I suppose that makes us cousins."

JT cocked his head and regarded her. "I suppose it does. Good night, Violet."

He departed Baccarat without touching her again and Violet was dismayed by her disappointment. She could get used to having his hands on her. Was that creepy now that they'd agreed to consider each other cousins?

Violet continued on her rounds, and contemplated what her sisters would make of her conversation with JT. With her traditional upbringing and ambitious professional goals, Harper would give her sensible and conservative advice. Younger than Violet by a few months, Harper was nonetheless the voice of pragmatism. She would encourage Violet to keep her distance from a complicated man in a tricky family situation. Violet's relationship with Tiberius had made her by extension an enemy of Preston Rhodes, JT's father. If she and JT became friendly, it would only complicate what she sensed was a strained relationship with his father.

While Harper's rational arguments would appeal to Violet's head, Scarlett's opinion would go to work on her heart. A few weeks ago Scarlet had pointed out that there was more to JT's nightly appearance at Baccarat than simply that he missed Rick's mixology expertise. Scarlett would encourage Violet to get to know JT better; she was convinced that something would ignite between them. Shock waves pummeled Violet's midsection as her thoughts ventured down that path.

Sex with JT would be explosive. Tonight when he'd squeezed her hand, she'd been hard-pressed not to lean over and plant a very uncousinly kiss on his well-shaped lips. Her skin tingled at the thought and she gave her head a vigorous shake. She couldn't go there. Shouldn't even think about going there. Trouble was when she was around JT, she had a hard time thinking clearly.

Angst and passion simmered beneath his expensive suits and professional demeanor. During the six years she'd known him she'd occasionally caught glimpses of deep pain, and her instinct had been to offer comfort or help. But JT was a man who stubbornly resisted admitting to any vulnerability or weakness. From Tiberius, Violet knew JT's childhood hadn't been ideal. His father was a ruthless businessman who'd manipulated his father-in-law into disowning his only son. His drive for power had caused him to neglect his wife.

JT's mother had not taken the banishment of her brother well. She'd retreated into alcohol and pills. Tiberius had kept tabs on her through friends, but he'd been unable to do more than stand by and watch her fade away. What Violet had never understood is why she'd never divorced Preston. She might have had a chance at happiness if she had.

Violet finished her rounds and returned to her large executive office. Even though it was three in the morning, she didn't expect to sleep. Reports awaited her attention.

The hotel's management offices occupied a small chunk

of the third floor. She spent little time here, preferring to be on the floor, eyes on the action taking place in her hotel.

It's what she'd learned from shadowing Tiberius around the Lucky Heart. Her throat closed as she stared down the Las Vegas strip to where the small hotel and casino sat. Built in the sixties, it lacked the amenities of the modern hotels and casinos: five-star restaurants, extravagant décor and luxury suites. The ceilings were low. The carpet needed replacing. And the clientele came in for the cheap bar drinks and stayed for the loose slots. But for Violet it would always be home.

Which is why she'd been surprised how Tiberius had reacted when Henry Fontaine approached her about coming to work for him. She'd expected Tiberius to discourage her from joining the family business. Quite the opposite. Tiberius knew how hard it had been for her to be Ross Fontaine's bastard daughter. Unlike Scarlett, Ross's other illegitimate daughter, Violet had grown up in Las Vegas within the long shadow of the gorgeous hotels and casinos that were owned by the Fontaine dynasty.

The older she got, the more being an outsider frustrated her. Without Tiberius as her champion, constantly making as if she was the smartest, most capable person he'd ever known, she might never have accepted that she didn't need approval from the Fontaines to make her happy.

Maybe that's why she sympathized with JT. If his grandfather hadn't died when JT was ten, Preston would never have taken over Stone Properties and ousted his brother-in-law. The company would have stayed in Stone hands. First Tiberius's, then JT's.

Attending his uncle's memorial service today must have really upset him. She had no other explanation for why he'd shared with her his concerns regarding Stone Properties. They'd known each other for six years and as much as he made her pulse dance, he'd always just treated her like a business acquaintance. Was it any wonder his behavior to-night had thrown her off balance? Did he regret telling her about his worries for his family's company? It just wasn't like him to be so…forthcoming.

She smirked as she imagined him kicking himself the entire way back to Titanium.

It was a spectacular property. He'd spent his first two years in Vegas rebuilding the hotel and casino. It was larger than both Fontaine Chic and Richesse combined, with a huge convention facility and an eighteen-hole golf course in the back. Admiring the hotel's style, she'd used the same design company to bring to life her vision for Fontaine Chic.

What would happen to Stone Properties if JT left? As hurt as Tiberius had been that his father believed Preston's lies and disinherited him, Tiberius's biggest concern had always been for the company beneath Preston's steward-ship. He would be worried that JT was quitting.

"Not my problem," she muttered, but already the wheels were turning in her mind.

Tiberius would have wanted her to help JT. Despite all the years they'd been estranged, right before his death, Ti-berius had started reaching out to his nephew.

And Violet was confident she could keep her head screwed on straight and her hormones in check long enough to figure out a way to help JT save Stone Proper-ties. With the decision made, Violet headed to her suite for a hot shower and a good night's sleep.

Two

Violet stared at the shelves of law books that covered the walls of the lawyer's office, her eyes gritty and dry. In contrast, her mother sat beside her, weeping softly. In the weeks since Tiberius's death, Lucille had gone through a dozen boxes of tissues.

A part of Violet was ashamed that she'd moved swiftly through the five stages of grief while her mother had gone straight to stage four—depression—and stayed there.

"That takes us to the Lucky Heart," John Malcolm, Tiberius's lawyer continued. "As you probably know, the casino is deep in debt."

Violet nodded, absently squeezing her mother's hand in comfort, relieved that Tiberius had invested his personal fortune wisely and set aside enough for Lucille to never have to worry about money. "I don't understand why. The entire time I worked there, it always operated in the black. Nor has business fallen off in the last five years. Tiberius was too savvy to let that happen. So where did the debt come from?"

"He was mortgaging the Lucky Heart in order to buy stock."

"Stock?" That didn't sound like Tiberius at all. "Why would he do that? He didn't trust Wall Street. Said it was a sucker's bet."

"He was buying private stock."

Even more curious. A rhythmic ache had manifested in Violet's temples. She rubbed to ease the pain. "So can we sell the stock and get the Lucky Heart out of debt?"

"Unfortunately, you're not going to be able to do that."

"Why not?" Making bad business decisions was something Tiberius had never done. "What sort of stock was he buying?"

"Stone Properties stock."

Violet leaned forward. Had she heard the gray-haired lawyer correctly? "Why would he do that?"

John's solemn blue eyes were the gatekeepers of a thousand clients' secrets. "He had his reasons."

Her thoughts rushed through a dozen scenarios as to why Tiberius had kept something this huge from her. Then she contemplated her conversation with JT a few days earlier. "How much stock did he have?"

"In the three months before his death he'd managed to get eighteen percent."

Violet's curiosity spiked. Did his purchase of Stone Properties stock have anything to do with why he'd been reestablishing his relationship with JT? Together they would've controlled forty-eight percent of Stone Properties, not enough to take over and force Preston out, but if they could secure another three percent…

Is that what Tiberius had been up to?

"Did he leave the stock to JT?"

John Malcolm looked surprised. "No. He left it to you."

Any normal person who'd just inherited eighteen percent of a multi-billion dollar company might be dancing around the lawyer's office or at the very least grinning. Violet had no desire to celebrate. The price tag for her windfall was too high. She'd lost the man who'd been her father in heart and soul if not by blood or marriage.

"Why me and not my mom?"

"Because he trusted you'd know what to do with it."

"First Scarlett inherits a warehouse full of secret files and now this," she muttered, thinking about all the private information Tiberius had gathered over the years on acquaintances and family. "What other surprises does Tiberius plan to unleash on the Fontaine sisters?"

"Now, as to the conditions of the inheritance."

"And there it is," Violet grumbled. She loved Tiberius, but he was a cagey bastard.

John Malcolm ignored her outburst. "You can't sell the stock, donate it or give it away." The lawyer smiled ironically as he said this last bit, if he couldn't understand why anyone could part with that much money and expect nothing in return. "Until the death of Preston Rhodes."

Obviously Tiberius wanted to make sure his brother-in-law never got his hands on the stock.

"Chances are it won't be worth anything by the time that happens," she murmured.

"And there's one other issue," John Malcolm continued as if she hadn't spoken. "You can't vote the shares because you're not family."

Violet sat back in her chair and regarded the lawyer in utter bafflement. Why hadn't Tiberius just left the shares to JT? The answer occurred to her an instant after the question had formed. Because his relationship with JT hadn't reached that level of trust yet. Tiberius probably thought he had months to get to know his nephew. It wasn't like he was planning on getting murdered.

"Thank you for all your help," Violet said, standing to shake hands with the lawyer.

"Yes," Lucille echoed. "Thank you. I know you were a good friend to Tiberius all these years."

"Sometimes I felt more like a co-conspirator," John Malcolm with a wry smile. "But it was my pleasure to call him both friend and client."

Violet and her mother left the lawyer's office and headed to the parking lot.

"I can't believe Tiberius left you all that stock," Lucille said, "without there being anything you can do with it."

"Did he talk to you about what he was up to?"

Lucille's beautiful smile was always a little bit sad, but since Tiberius's death it had become downright melancholy. "You know he didn't talk business with me."

No. Tiberius had always made it his mission to bring all things joyful and fun to his conversations with Lucille. He'd loved when her eyes sparkled. Discussing something as upsetting as staging a coup against Preston Rhodes would never have happened.

"Maybe I'll check his office when I drop you off," Violet said.

"There might be something in his files."

When they arrived at the house Lucille had shared with Tiberius for years, Violet discovered that her mother was right. There were ten files pertaining to the stock acquisition. Two contained the paperwork for the stock Tiberius had purchased. The other eight contained information on family members he hadn't yet contacted. Her interest rose as she read through Tiberius's notes. Gaining another three percent wouldn't be easy, but she had a notion of how it could be done. Not that it did her any good. She owned eighteen percent of a stock she could neither get rid of nor vote.

So, what the hell was she supposed to do with it? Better to ask, what would Tiberius want her to do with it?

The thought of becoming embroiled in the intrigue surrounding Stone Properties gave Violet a bad taste in her mouth. She was quite content with her own piece of the

Las Vegas strip. From the second she'd been put in charge of Fontaine Chic, she'd known complete happiness. It was all she needed. She didn't care if she won the contest their grandfather had created to decide which of the three Fontaine sisters would succeed him as CEO. Violet was realistic about her chances. With Harper's education and hotel training, it was her contest hands down. Besides, it was her birthright. Just like Stone Properties was JT's.

If only there was something Violet could do to make it so he could claim his rightful place. Not that he wanted her help. She dismissed that as insignificant. She needed to focus on keeping alive Tiberius's plan to reclaim his family's company. But how?

When the answer came, she was stunned by its simplicity and foolhardiness. She couldn't. The idea was crazy. On the other hand, maybe crazy was what the situation called for.

And there was only one way she was going to know for sure.

JT was about to leave his usual spot in Baccarat and head back to his hotel when he spotted Violet approaching the bar. Tension he'd not been aware of released its grip on his muscles. He relaxed his clenched teeth and felt a scowl melt from his forehead.

Since finding out what his father had been up to with Stone Properties, he'd been frustrated and in great need of a confidante he could trust. He trusted Violet. Sharing his problems with her had eased his mind.

For the last five days she'd been absent from the lounge. Either she'd been detained by hotel business or she'd been avoiding him. Thinking she might be avoiding him had been a bitter pill to swallow.

He'd stepped across the line at their last meeting. Claiming her as family had pushed their association past the boundaries of casual acquaintances. But no matter how much it worried him that he might become dependent on her, he couldn't stop craving her support.

To his unreasonable delight, the instant she entered the bar, her gaze sought his and she immediately headed his way. As she drew near, the spicy scent of her perfume preceded her and he had just enough time to draw a heady lungful before she sat beside him. Tonight's black dress was a knee-length sheath with a deep scoop neckline that showed off the upper curves of her breasts. Keeping his attention on her face proved challenging as she gathered a deep breath before speaking.

"I'm glad you're here tonight," she said, her voice brisk, expression resolute.

He resisted the urge to remind her that he was here every night. She already had him eating out of the palm of her hand. Why give her more power?

"You look beautiful," he told her, letting his gaze drift over her.

His compliment caused her to blink. "Thank you." For a moment she looked as if she'd lost her train of thought.

Despite the bar's low light, he spied a rush of color in her cheeks and noticed an uneven hitch to her breath. In that instant he realized she'd felt the impact of his attraction for her, even if she wasn't ready to admit it.

The revelation inspired a rush of longing to touch her smooth skin, to pull her body tight to his and hear her sigh beneath his lips. He imagined sweeping his tongue across her breasts and hearing her cry out. Not seeing her these last few days had fueled his hunger for her. He'd spent far too much time pondering exactly how he would make love to her.

"JT, are you listening to me?"

He shook his head and dispelled the evocative images

lingering there. "Sorry. I was distracted. Is that a new perfume you're wearing?"

"It's something Tiberius gave to my mother last Christmas. Since his death she can't bear to wear it, but I love the scent so she gave me the bottle."

"It's nice," he murmured.

"Thank you." She paused and regarded him through narrowed eyes. "We went to Tiberius's lawyer for the reading of his will a couple days ago."

JT wrestled his libido back under control as her words registered. "And he left everything to you and your mother."

"Yes." She scowled at him as if he was supposed to comprehend a deeper meaning to what she'd said. "But it's *what* he left that caught me by surprise."

"His house, bank accounts, the hotel." JT ticked the items off on his fingers. "What else?"

A smug grin bloomed on her full lips. "How about eighteen percent of Stone Properties stock."

The news dealt him a sturdy blow. "How did he get it?"

"He mortgaged the Lucky Heart and bought every share he could."

"But why?"

"To take on your father?"

"Eighteen percent wouldn't do him any good. When my mother died she left my father thirty percent of the company. Combined with the rest of what my family owns, he has enough votes to control the company."

"Until two months ago when you turned thirty. Your father controlled your trust fund until then, didn't he?"

"Yes." JT didn't know what to make of what he was hearing. "You think my uncle wanted us to join forces?" He recalled the dinners Tiberius had invited him to. "He never said anything of the sort."

"I think he wanted to get to know you before he committed to anything."

For the first time in years JT felt a flutter of excitement. Combining what he'd inherited with Violet's shares left him three percent away from taking the company back from his father and repairing all the damage that had been done.

"How much do you want for your stock?"

Violet had been watching him closely, grinning at his reaction to her news, but now delight drained from her expression. "That's where things get a little tricky."

Suspicion flared before JT remembered that this was Violet he was dealing with. She was loyal and a team player. She wasn't here to get something from him. She honestly wanted to help. But none of his trust reflected in his tone as he asked, "Tricky how?"

"The terms of Tiberius's will don't allow me to sell, trade or donate the shares in any way." She looked as if she expected him to explode in frustration. "Otherwise you have to know, I'd let you have them."

Although disappointed by his uncle's unorthodox terms, JT knew there was a way he could work this to his advantage. "But you can give me your proxy vote." Of course, he only had eighteen percent, but if Tiberius had convinced several of their family members to part with the stock, surely that meant JT could do the same. He only needed three percent more.

"That's the other problem," she said, apology in her tone. "The way your grandfather set up the stock, only family members by blood or by marriage can vote. Since I'm not family, my votes can't count."

JT exhaled in exasperation. "So we're back to square one. With your votes voided, my father remains in control of the majority of the stock."

But Tiberius's plan was still a viable option. JT and

his father each had thirty percent of the shares. With Violet's eighteen percent excluded, that left twenty-two percent up for grabs. If he could buy twelve percent of the shares belonging to the rest of the family or failing that, convince them to swing their votes his way, he could take the company back.

"Not back to square one," Violet said, interrupting his train of thought. "If I was family, I could vote the shares."

"If you were family, yes," JT agreed, his gaze fixed on the lights racing around above the bar. "But you're not."

"I could be."

Something in her tone caught his attention. A tentative smile trembled at the corners of her lips. She was trying to tell him something, but his mind was darting in too many directions to grasp the nuances of her meaning.

"How?"

"We could get married."

If she'd nailed him with a cattle prod he couldn't have been more stunned. "Married?"

"In name only, of course." She offered him a cheeky grin that didn't reach her eyes. "There's nothing in my uncle's will that prevents me from marrying the shares away."

"Since he knew we'd never get married, it probably never crossed his mind."

She cocked her head and regarded him solemnly. "And how did he know something like that?"

"I told him I had no intention of starting anything up with you."

Violet sat up very straight. Her eyes narrowed. "You two talked about me?"

JT nodded. "When I first arrived in town. Tiberius had heard about my activities in Miami and was worried that if I pursued you, you might get hurt. I agreed to keep my distance."

"How noble." Her tone dripped with scorn.

"Not that noble," he retorted, deciding if they were going to consider her wild scheme, she might as well hear the whole truth. "It was an easy promise to make. You really aren't my type."

Mouth tight, she stared at him for several seconds. But then her hand stole across his leg, mid-thigh, and lingered.

"You aren't my type either." But her husky tone and the come-get-me-big-boy look in her eyes said the exact opposite. "So that should make a marriage in-name-only a snap."

JT kept his expression bland. No need for her to learn the truth. He'd promised himself that nothing would happen between them. He needed her in his corner far more than he needed her naked in his bed. He wasn't about to ruin their fledgling connection over something as fleeting as lust.

"It should." But he didn't feel as confident as he sounded. "And it isn't forever."

"Right. We only need to be married long enough for me to vote my shares at the annual meeting. It's at the end of August, right?"

"August twenty-fifth."

"That's only six weeks away."

JT had another thought. "Your family isn't going to be happy if you marry me without some sort of a prenup."

"At the moment I'm not worth more than the stock I inherited from Tiberius and what I've saved towards retirement. We can sign a simple agreement that states we leave the marriage with what we arrived with."

She made everything sound so reasonable. So why was he resisting?

Sure, marriage wasn't on his to-do list. He enjoyed playing the part of confirmed bachelor. Las Vegas was the perfect place to find attractive, single women looking for a little fun. They came in for a weekend and he gave them the royal treatment. Then they were gone. No fuss. No muss.

Violet was a whole different package. She was in Vegas to stay. Getting involved with her would be complicated and undoubtedly end in heartbreak. His.

But it wasn't as if they were getting married for real. He just needed to remember that.

"So are we going to do this?" She'd plucked her palm from his thigh, leaving behind a distracting tingle.

"You're sure you want to marry me?" His heart thumped hard against his ribs as he reminded himself this was a business deal.

"Want to marry you? Absolutely not." Her lighthearted laugh had a slightly wicked edge. "But I feel like I owe it to Tiberius to finish what he started. And I'd like to see you take back your family's company."

He scrutinized her lovely features, finding only altruism in her expression. Her self-sacrifice made him uncomfortable.

"I get that you feel an obligation to Tiberius, but I'm not sure this is the best idea."

"I don't feel obligated."

From her earnest expression he could tell she didn't. And that's what worried JT the most.

"Okay, but you're also looking for a way to make your shares pay off too, right?"

She cocked her head and regarded him in silence for several seconds. "You yourself said the company isn't doing well with your father at the helm. If he continues, the shares will lose value. Maybe even become worthless. I know you'll make a much better CEO. I'm protecting myself the best way I can."

Her answer rang with conviction. JT's resistance eased minutely. Still, he should refuse. The only way this wasn't going to backfire on them both was if he turned down her help. But the idea of getting that much closer to Violet was a temptation of the hard-to-resist variety.

But marriage? Was the opportunity to rescue Stone Properties from his father's clutches worth the danger of getting too attached to Violet? He already liked her far too much for his own good. Watching her walk into the lounge was enough to make his day. What if he started to rely on spending lots of time with her? He knew himself well enough to know that just being friends wouldn't cut it. He wanted her. Badly. It was only a matter of time before he did something about it.

After a fast and furious debate, JT kicked self-preservation to the curb.

"Then I'm in." He was on the verge of getting on one knee and proposing to her properly when she spoke up.

"I think we should do this sooner rather than later. Before either one of us comes to our senses."

"How soon?" She'd saved him from going all romantic—even if it was just for show—and making an ass out of himself. "Like Saturday?"

"What about now?" Seeing his shock, she rushed on. "Too fast?"

"A little." But what the hell. If they waited, the anticipation might prompt him to do something stupid. Like let her see how badly he needed her. "But it's doable. Your chapel or mine?"

"How about someplace neutral. The Tunnel of Love Chapel?"

Some of JT's tension faded. She really was approaching this as a business arrangement and he needed to do so as well. But ignoring her effect on him was easier said than done.

"Positively romantic," he said, his tone dry.

"Good." She glanced at her phone. "I booked it for midnight."

"You were feeling pretty confident I'd say yes."

She shrugged. "It made perfect business sense that you would."

But business was the furthest thing from his thoughts at the moment. He was contemplating all the delightful things a husband did with his brand-new wife. "Are you going to leave the booking of the honeymoon suite to me?"

She looked positively horrified. "Perhaps I wasn't very clear. A marriage in name only means no sex."

"Not even on our wedding night?" he couldn't resist asking. She was so delightfully earnest. It made teasing her a pleasure.

"I thought I wasn't your type." Her voice lacked any trace of amusement.

"Since you're going to be my wife," he said, "I figured I should make an exception just this once."

"It's a lovely thought but we should really keep this all business between us."

"Whatever you say."

"It will make things easier."

She was oh so wrong about that. Nothing about being married to Violet was going to be easy. In fact, he'd better brace himself because things were about to get a whole lot harder.

Three

On her way across Fontaine Chic's lobby, Violet decided it was okay if a bride felt excited and slightly terrified on her wedding day. Especially if the groom was sexy and enigmatic and the decision to marry was somewhere between logically conceived and wildly impulsive.

Wearing an off-white lace dress she'd bought on impulse that morning from one of the hotel's shops, Violet's heart double-timed to each click of her heels on the black marble floor. She clutched an overnight bag and a briefcase filled with Tiberius's files on the holders of Stone Properties stock. Against her better judgment, she'd let JT talk her into spending their wedding night together at his house. In separate bedrooms, of course.

She wasn't worried that he'd take advantage of her. He'd already pointed out that she wasn't his type. That declaration still stung. With his reputation as a player, she hadn't suspected he had a type beyond female, single and young. She was all those. So what about her didn't appeal to him?

Was she the wrong height? Too thin? Too fat? Not pretty enough? Not sexy?

Violet slammed the door on curiosity. It didn't matter if she was his type or not. Their marriage was a business arrangement. She needed to remember that. And to guard against demonstrating the way her body came alive whenever he drew near.

A bright blue BMW convertible stood at the ready in the hotel's circular driveway. JT leaned against the car's hood, wearing a dark gray, almost black suit and white shirt with a blush-colored tie that emphasized his potent charisma. He hadn't spotted her yet so she had a private moment to observe his relaxed posture and utter gorgeousness as he joked with one of her bellhops. Thanks to anxiety, her muscles hadn't been responding properly to the signals from her brain for the last hour; now they were positively spastic.

He was still laughing when their gazes met. The power of his smile knocked the breath from her lungs. Wanting his eyes to light up with pleasure at seeing her, she was crushed at how fast he sobered.

"Right on time, I see." He stepped forward to take her bags.

Was he used to waiting for the women he dated? They probably took longer to primp and fuss than she had. In truth, her nerves had prevented her from applying eyeliner with a steady hand so she'd just dusted her lids with neutral eye shadow, buffed her cheekbones with blush and used a little powder to keep down the shine. It didn't occur to her that she hadn't applied lipstick until his gaze locked on her mouth.

A bride shouldn't attend her wedding in such a state. She dug in her purse, but all she found was some lip balm. "Damn," she muttered. "I don't have any lipstick."

"You don't need any." He opened the passenger door for her and gave her plenty of room to get by him. It was almost as if he was avoiding her. But why would he need to do that?

"I'm not sure I feel completely dressed without it."

"I assure you, you're completely dressed."

Was that humor she saw in his expression? Oh how she wished she could read his mind. It would be nice to know how the man she was about to marry thought, but it wasn't likely to happen now, or ever. He would make certain of that.

"I wonder what else I forgot to pack," she mused, her brain on autopilot. "I had some last-minute things to take care of with my assistant. I was afraid I was going to be late."

"And that I might change my mind?"

"The thought occurred to me." She slid into her seat and watched him circle the car. "What about you? Did you think I might chicken out?"

"No. I think you are the most dependable person I know." His statement made it sound as if he knew more about her than their limited association had led her to believe. He slipped behind the wheel and started the engine.

Violet regarded his strong profile, admiring the precise cut of his jaw and his ridiculously long eyelashes. "What makes you say that?"

"From your reputation around town. Whenever you make a commitment to a cause or a promise to a friend you come through. No matter what."

As the car rolled toward South Las Vegas Boulevard, Violet put her hands to her cheeks and found them hot with embarrassment. "I don't do more than anyone else."

"And then you rarely take credit for all the good things you do." The light turned green as they approached it and JT was able to turn onto the strip without stopping. "It causes people to take advantage of your generosity."

Was he trying to warn her that this is what he was

doing? If he was, it was too late. She was already committed to their goal.

"You make me sound like a sap."

"I was trying to pay you a compliment."

"A backhanded one, maybe. *You're a dependable doormat*." She made a face. "That's a fine way to talk about your bride-to-be."

An impatient sound erupted from him. "In the future I'll remember that flattery makes you prickly."

"See that you do. I prefer honesty to sweet talk." She stared at him in silence until he'd stopped at a light and looked her way. "Are you going to have a problem with that?"

"Not at all."

"Good. Just think of me as a fellow businessperson and we'll get along just fine."

JT merely nodded his agreement.

Ten minutes later, they swung into the Tunnel of Love Chapel. It wasn't Violet's first trip through the tunnel. Her best friend from high school had tied the knot here the day after graduation and two short months before baby Cory was born. JT, however, looked like he'd never seen anything like the blue ceiling adorned with cupids and stars.

He stopped the car before a booth with a sign that read "The Little White Wedding Chapel Drive Thru Window," and they filled out the paperwork for the marriage license. Getting married in Las Vegas was a simple matter. Maybe too simple? Time for second thoughts came and went in the blink of an eye. As the opening words of the wedding ceremony began, a strange buzzing filled her ears.

Was she really marrying JT Stone? Violet glanced from the man framed by the booth window to JT. Her lips twitched uncontrollably. As first JT then she repeated the vows spoken by the minister, Violet was overwhelmed by the dreamlike aspect of her wedding. She didn't feel attached to the body sitting in the car beside JT. And she didn't recognize her voice promising to love and honor him. It wasn't until JT pulled out two platinum rings and she felt the cold metal slide onto her finger that she crashed back to earth.

She had only a second to scrutinize her ring's antique setting. The setting was square, the diamond round, the corners filled in with ornate filigree. Violet guessed the stone to be over two and a half carats. Smaller round diamonds flanked the center stone. He slipped the ring on her left hand. The instant she realized it fit, all her agitation disappeared and she was struck by the rightness of what she was doing.

The minister interrupted her thoughts. "Now the bride."

JT handed her the other ring, this one embossed with waves and swirls. Repeating the vows that symbolized love and commitment, Violet slipped the ring onto JT's finger. She couldn't look him in the eye. Her wild idea to marry JT so she could use her stock to put him in charge of his family's company was on the verge of becoming legally and morally binding.

"I now pronounce you man and wife," the minister proclaimed.

Violet's heart had been erratic since JT had agreed to marry her. Now it was positively aflutter. They'd done it. For good or for bad, there was no going back.

"You may kiss the bride."

Mouth dry, Violet waited for her first kiss from JT. Her stomach had been in knots for the last several hours since they'd agreed to get married. How would he kiss her? Would it be passionate? Romantic? Would he sweep her into his arms and steal her breath or would he woo her with slow, sensual kisses? Either way, she knew it would be perfect.

She'd never dreamed he'd catch her chin in his fingers and plant a quick kiss at the corner of her lips. Lost in a fog of disappointment, she automatically went through the formalities that followed and accepted the congratulations of the witnesses with a heavy heart.

And then the car was rolling out of the Tunnel of Love Chapel and emerging into the noise and lights of Las Vegas once more. While JT negotiated the traffic on his way to the freeway, Violet stared at the ring on her hand. How had he gotten a set of wedding rings on such short notice? And such unique ones at that.

"It's my grandmother's," JT said as if reading her mind. "And this is my grandfather's." He held up his left hand. "I drove to the ranch before picking you up."

Rendered speechless at the significance of wearing a family heirloom, Violet gaped at him. Harper would laugh at her for believing that jewelry held the energy of the wearer, but what else could explain the tranquility that came over her the instant she'd put on his grandmother's ring? They'd married without love. She didn't deserve to be wearing something so dear.

"Is something wrong?" he prompted.

"We could have bought rings at the chapel."

"Why, when these were collecting dust in my safe?"

"But it's your grandmother's ring."

He eyed her. "And I trust that as soon as it's no longer necessary, you'll return it."

"Of course." It was beginning to annoy her that he wasn't getting the significance of the jewelry he'd just pledged his troth with. Heaving a sigh, Violet decided to let it drop. In a few months it would be back in his safe where it belonged.

As the car streaked through the Nevada night, the adrenaline rush she'd been riding for the last two days began to fade. Her confidence waned as well. She was now married to a man who was for all intents and purposes a virtual stranger. And with the strength of his deflector shields, he was likely to stay that way no matter how delicately she probed. Which she really shouldn't do.

What she had to remember was that despite the marriage vows they'd just exchanged, theirs was a union of expediency. Mutual benefit. JT got the chance to reclaim his family's business. She would finish what Tiberius had started and preserve the stock's value.

It was a business arrangement. He would resist her efforts to dig around in his private thoughts in an attempt to get to know him better.

"Now what's bothering you?" JT quizzed.

"Nothing, why?"

For the last half hour they'd been heading north out of town on I-25. His sixty-acre ranch sat just beyond the outskirts of the city. At first she'd resisted being away from the hotel on such short notice, but since Tiberius's death, she'd been working herself hard and could really use a night off.

"You haven't said a word in fifteen minutes," JT said. "It's not like you."

"Was it crazy, what we just did?"

"Completely." He exited the freeway and turned left onto a two-lane highway. "Have you changed your mind?"

"No." And she was surprised at how strongly she felt about staying the course. "It's all going to work out. We just need to get the last three percent Tiberius had been working on before the next stockholders' meeting."

JT nodded. "One way or another, we can be divorced before fall."

Her stomach fell at his eagerness to be rid of her and she chided herself for reacting so foolishly. That was the deal they'd made. She had no right to wish for something else.

"Then we'd better get to work immediately," she said. "I brought all the files from his desk at the house. He was about to approach eight more shareholders. Four of the leads look promising."

"I'll look at them first thing in the morning."

His use of first person singular wasn't lost on her. Before she returned to Fontaine Chic tomorrow, she was determined to make him understand that this undertaking was going to be a team effort. She'd married him and was determined he would not do battle with his father alone.

"This is going to work, you know."

He shot her a dour look. "Are you always this optimistic?"

"You make it sound like a bad thing."

"It's not bad, but I'm not sure it's realistic. Don't you ever worry?"

"Not about the future." She lifted her face to the wind streaming off the windshield. "Why bother? It's a blank slate, full of possibilities."

He didn't reply and she tried to be comfortable in the silence that filled the space between them once more. But the unfinished conversation itched like a case of hives.

"All the brooding you do in the bar every night. Tell me what good it does you to worry about things that haven't happened?"

"It's not the future that concerns me, but the past. Things I'd like to take back, do differently, but can't."

Delighted that JT was on the verge of a revelation, she prompted, "Such as?"

"Nothing I feel like talking about."

And just like that she was shut down. Violet heaved a sigh and lapsed into silence. What a puzzle he was. She knew his childhood hadn't been one to brag about. His father's ambition. His mother's retreat into alcohol and drugs. Emotional injuries he'd suffered at a fragile age had turned him into a wild teenager. When JT had first arrived in Las Vegas, Tiberius had warned her to stay away from him. He was not a bird with a broken wing or a kitten who'd been struck by a car. He was a grown man who only knew how to use people and cast them aside.

Tiberius's initial opinion of his nephew had been right on, but Violet suspected it wasn't the whole picture. Curious about the Stone family, she'd conducted an internet search and discovered what sorts of trouble a party boy from Miami could get into. Although her contact with him had been limited these last six years, she didn't think he was the type to act out without cause. But whatever motivated him was locked deep inside and given the firm set of his jaw, likely to remain so.

"So you have a hard time letting go," she said. "How can you think that's good for you?"

"Reliving past events helps me avoid similar situations in my future."

When Violet considered her life, she decided she could probably spend a little time learning from her experiences. How many men had she dated who'd needed her to be their cheerleader or their psychologist or their financial advisor or their life coach? Too many. And here she was doing it again. Only this time she'd gone too far and had actually married someone.

JT turned down a long driveway bordered by landscape lighting and stopped the car in front of a massive stucco-and-stone prairie-style house. Curved planting beds held desert plants and tropical flowers. Their round lines softened the home's square architecture.

"This is definitely worth the commute," Violet said as she exited the car. The covered walkway to the front door was flanked by pillars covered in square stone and lighted by sconces. The effect was elegant and welcoming. "I can't get over how quiet it is." For a girl who'd practically grown up on the strip, the silence was a bit unnerving.

"Wait until morning. The view from the living room is what sold me on the property." He collected her bag from the trunk and gestured for her to precede him toward the front door.

The house continued to impress Violet as JT gave her a quick tour. From the expansive two-story foyer he led her into the combination living room-dining room. Such large spaces could seem cold and uninviting, but the coved ceilings, inset lighting and desert tones made it very homey. In the living room, sliding glass walls opened out onto a wide patio. The gourmet kitchen was almost as large as her suite at the hotel and contained all restaurant-quality appliances as well as a large wine chiller.

"I wish I knew how to cook," Violet said, gliding her palm along the center island's cool granite.

"You don't?" JT had fetched a bottle of champagne and a couple of glasses. He popped the cork and filled both flutes.

Violet accepted the champagne he handed her. "Just the basics. Not well enough to do justice to all this." She was proud of herself for standing her ground as JT stepped into her space and held up his glass.

Finding out that Tiberius had left her the stock. Her wild proposition to JT. The quick drive-through wedding that followed. And now, being alone with JT in his house. So much had happened. She was feeling a little exposed and emotional. Primed to do something stupid like demand a far better kiss than the one he'd deposited on her in the Tunnel of Love.

"To our successful merger," JT declared, touching his flute to hers. Crystal chimed in the large room.

"To getting Stone Properties away from your father." Violet drank sparingly. The man before her was a heady concoction. She didn't need to add alcohol to the mix.

"It's after one. Do you want me to show you to your room?"

"So I can do what?" Violet quizzed, walking toward the breakfast nook's bay windows. "Pace for hours? I don't know about you, but I rarely get to bed before three." She spied a turquoise pool behind the house. "Can I use that?"

"As of twelve-fifteen the house became half yours. You don't need to ask."

Violet gasped, all thoughts of a moonlit swim forgotten. "Oh, no. That's not what we agreed to. And when we get divorced, we'll just go our separate ways—I don't want half of your house."

"Maybe we should renegotiate our deal. I might need to demand alimony in the divorce settlement."

"Why would you need alimony?"

"Because if our plan fails my father will surely kick me out of the family business and the way he's running things, the stock won't be worth much." He leaned back against the counter and crossed his arms over his chest. "While you will be worth millions as Fontaine's CEO."

Because she couldn't tell if he was poking fun at her or not, Violet refrained from commenting on her chances of winning her grandfather's contest. "I never imagined that I would end up supporting you," she replied. "Perhaps we should get an annulment—"

"While we still can?" JT interrupted, his silky voice spreading shivers along her skin.

"Stop kidding around." She tried for lightness, but a hint of anxiety crept into her tone. "Just because we're married and alone in this house on our wedding night…" Violet trailed off. What point was she trying to make?

"Doesn't mean that we'll fall prey to our basic urges," JT finished.

"Exactly."

"Even if those urges are fueled by champagne and curiosity?"

Violet set her glass down and dismay sparked when she realized it was empty. "I think it's time you show me the bedroom. My bedroom," she corrected, feeling her cheeks heat. "Where I'm going to sleep. Alone."

JT picked up her bag and gestured back the way they'd come. "It's upstairs."

Violet attributed her lightheadedness to the champagne, refusing to believe that she was overwhelmed by the thought of spending the night alone with JT in his house. Was his room way down the hall from hers or a convenient few steps away?

Get a grip. You're not a virgin at your first frat party. You're a successful businesswoman and this man is a colleague. Keep your head and everything will be fine.

"Here you are." JT opened a door and gestured her inside. The large room contained a queen-size bed with matching cherry nightstands, a triple dresser, and a small seating area in front of a gas fireplace. He set her overnight bag on the bed and returned to where she stood just inside the bedroom door.

"This is nice. Thank you."

"I'm the one who should be thanking you. If this wild idea of yours works, I'll be able to save my family's company. And that's a debt I can't repay." JT leaned down and kissed her gently on the cheek. "Good night, Violet. I'll make sure I have green tea ready for you in the morning."

He knew that she didn't drink coffee? She vaguely recalled having a tea versus coffee discussion with him long ago. And he'd remembered.

"That's nice of you. And one more thing." Before she considered the wisdom of her actions, Violet lifted on tiptoe and coasted her palms along JT's massive shoulders. Shoving aside rational thought, she tunneled her fingers into his hair and murmured, "You didn't give me a proper kiss at our wedding."

"Then let me rectify that right now." He lowered his lips to hers.

Her breath stopped. Every nerve in her body screamed to life. Newly sensitized, her skin prickled at the slide of his cotton shirt against her bare arm as he cupped the side of her head to hold her in place. His lips were firm, but softer than she'd expected. The friction of his mouth on hers dragged a moan from her chest.

The sound spurred him to intensify the pressure of his kiss, but he retreated before she could act on her rising passion. His teeth caught at her tender flesh and gently tugged. She arched her back, seeking closer contact. This was so much better than she'd ever imagined.

He flattened his palm against her back, locking her in place before treating her to the first delicious lick of his tongue. A slow thrust followed. Warm. Wet. Skilled. He claimed her mouth as if he'd done it a thousand times. Taking his time, he explored every corner of her mouth, tantalizing her with his leashed passion. What happened if his control snapped? Violet was fast losing her wits. Much longer and her stance on a sexless marriage would topple.

Anticipation built as his hands coasted over her ribs, thumbs whisking provocatively over the outside curves of her breasts. She pulsed with need, craving his possession, and shifted restlessly against him to ease the ache.

JT tore his lips from hers and gulped air into his lungs. "Better?"

Better? Glorious was more like it.

Chest heaving, knees like pudding, she blinked to clear her vision and was startled to see they hadn't moved from the doorway. How was that possible when he'd turned her entire world upside down?

"Now I feel married," she said.

"You'd feel even more so after a proper wedding night," he murmured, letting his lips graze temptingly close to hers once more.

Unsure whether he was serious or merely taunting her, Violet clutched at his strong shoulders and leaned back in order to survey his expression. With eyes that glittered, JT probed her gaze. His compelling curiosity alarmed her. What was he looking for? Proof that his kisses rendered her insensible?

He swept his hands down her spine, fanned his fingers against the small of her back. Ever so slowly he pressed her hips forward, easing her against the hard length of him. Violet's legs trembled. She wanted nothing more than to be filled by him. To lose herself in his evocative touch.

Damn. She never should have asked for that kiss. If she'd just ignored the tension building between them, her body wouldn't be throbbing with unfulfilled longing nor would she be fighting temptation at the idea of one night with him. One incredible, mind-blowing night.

"JT, I…"

Before she figured out what she intended to say, shutters dropped over his gaze and she was left staring at an insurmountable wall. The speed with which he'd shut her out acted like a bucket of ice water on her overheated hormones.

"You don't need to explain." He relaxed his hold on her and stepped away. A sardonic smile tugged at his lips. "I know our marriage is only for show."

And she'd been seconds away from forgetting that fact. Humiliation chased away any lingering traces of desire. No question, she'd just dodged a bullet. So why was she so miserable about it?

"It's not that," she began and then frowned. "Well, it's mostly that, but the truth is, I don't know you very well and I'm not in the habit of falling into bed with a man this quickly."

"You know more about me than most of the women I date."

Really? Did that somehow elevate her above the numerous women that passed through his life? She bit her lip, disturbed by the yearning to be more than just another of his conquests. That was a dangerous road to travel. Better that they keep things all business between them.

"It'll just be easier if we keep everything strictly hands off." Who was she trying to convince, herself or him?

"Then I suggest you refrain from asking me to kiss you in the future." His icy tone was meant as a reproach, but Violet had tasted more than passion in his kiss. Or was she merely hoping that was the case?

"It was one kiss." She heard the defensive ring of her voice and dug her nails into her palms. "What's the big deal?"

"The big deal—" a muscle jumped in his jaw "—is that when I start something like what just happened between us, I like to finish it."

Why was he so exasperated? Not because she'd turned him down. Surely women had said no before. Hadn't they? "Haven't you ever kissed a woman without expecting to sleep with her?"

"Not since high school."

If he was trying to annoy her with his self-satisfied smirk, he was doing a fine job. "So, are you saying you don't bother to kiss a woman unless you're going to have sex with her?"

"I'm saying after I kiss a woman, she rarely says no to having sex with me."

This was so obviously a declaration of JT's reality that Violet crossed her arms over her chest and scowled. "Then I'm thrilled to be included in that minority of your female acquaintances."

"You forget that you are not one of my acquaintances. You are my wife."

JT took possession of her left hand and lifted it to eye level. His grandmother's ring caught the overhead light and sparkled. He couldn't explain why he was so angry with her at this moment. Could it be the unrelenting desire rumbling through him? Going to bed alone and horny was not how he'd expected to spend his wedding night—or it wouldn't have been if he'd ever considered getting married before now.

But the odd hollowness in his gut had begun the instant she'd dismissed the earth-moving kiss as *no big deal*. When he'd pulled her into his arms, he'd expected the urgent need to get her clothes off and have his way with her. It was the other sensation he'd experienced, the one not tied to anything corporeal, that would require privacy and time to sort out.

"I'm your business partner," she retorted, snatching her hand back.

Damn. She was beautiful with her brown eyes shooting sparks and outrage painting her high cheekbones with rosy patches. As quickly as it had flared, his temper dissipated. She wasn't someone he could afford to alienate even if it would make keeping his distance that much easier.

"And you're doing me a huge favor." He inclined his head. "I'm starting to understand why you took sex off the table. Things between us are a little too volatile, aren't they?"

Violet nodded in obvious relief. "I think we will be fine as long as we stick to the plan."

"A plan we can start to flesh out after a good night's sleep."

"I'll see you in the morning."

JT walked out the door and heard the click of the latch behind him. He strode down the hall to the master bedroom and without turning on a light, crossed the room to the double French doors that led out onto the terrace. Throwing them open, he stepped into the night. His nerves were a tangle, too raw to allow him to enjoy the desert air or the crescent moon that hung low in the clear sky.

Did Violet have any idea how close she'd come to being ravished tonight? First she'd shown up for their wedding in that romantic lace dress. Then she'd flirted with him over a glass of champagne. The final straw was complaining that he hadn't given her a proper kiss at their wedding. Was she trying to drive him mad or did she honestly not have a clue what she did to him?

It was the latter, JT suspected, gripping the terrace railing hard. And where she was concerned, he was his own worst enemy. When she'd stared at him with her big soulful eyes all soft and earnest, the consequent firing of all his nerve endings had short-circuited his self-preservation.

So now what was he supposed to do with all this pent-up hunger for her?

It had been one thing when he sat in her bar night after night, driving himself crazy with lurid fantasies he'd never act on. He could enjoy tangling with her verbally, knowing that her open, sunny nature would eventually grow tired of his talent for closing himself off. She'd said it herself. She knew nothing about him. He hadn't let her in. He never let anyone in.

And yet, she knew things about his past few others did. His uncle had told her about his mother's addiction so Violet had some idea how miserable his childhood had been. She would want to talk about all the things that had happened when he was young. He would resent her questions. Withdraw even further. When it came to intimacy and love, he lacked the skills to find happiness.

She wouldn't want to be with him until she'd solved all his problems. Made him see the silver lining in everything that had happened in his past. She'd expect him to come around to her positive way of thinking and would grow frustrated when he didn't.

A splash from the pool below drew his attention. Violet swam through the turquoise water, her stroke powerful and elegant. JT watched her as she came up for air at the far end of the pool. Once again she dove under. She used her feet and legs to push away from the wall with great power. When she surfaced, she headed for the opposite wall in a strong freestyle.

He watched her lap the pool for fifteen minutes. Her focus and determination amazed him. It was how she approached everything, he decided. Once she set her mind to something, she wasn't going to be deterred.

At long last her energy seemed to burn itself out. She lazed in the middle of the pool and her stillness roused JT to the uncomfortable realization that she was naked. Cursing, he pushed away from the railing and headed for the stairs that led down from his terrace to the pool house and lounge area.

He enjoyed throwing parties and often his guests forgot to bring a suit along so he kept a stock of bathing suits in the pool house for their use. By the time he found a bikini he thought might fit Violet, she had gotten out of the pool and had wrapped herself in a towel. She looked up in surprise as he approached.

"Next time you decide to go swimming," he began, holding up the bikini he'd selected, "I'd appreciate it if you didn't skinny-dip."

"I'm sorry," she murmured, taking the bathing suit from him. Water streamed from her long dark hair, dampening the towel. "I didn't realize you'd still be up."

It eased his irritation a little that she looked so utterly mortified to have been caught. "Like you, I'm often still working at this hour."

"Thanks for the suit. I won't bother you any further tonight."

Was she kidding? He'd never get to sleep with the tantalizing glimpses he'd had of her naked body parading through his thoughts. JT ground his teeth as she retreated toward the house. Only when her towel-clad form had disappeared from view did he return to the master suite.

At least one positive thing about this marriage in name only was that they didn't have to live under the same roof. After less than an hour alone in his house with her, he was a finger snap away from tossing her over his shoulder and spiriting her off to his bed.

Thank goodness he wasn't going to share his living space with her day and night. His control would snap like a dry twig if he had to put up with her sassy humor and artless sensuality. Before she could remind him of their agreement, he'd have her in his bed, her beautiful body writhing in pleasure.

Making love to her would only be the beginning. Soon she'd be ferreting out all his ugly childhood secrets and he'd be living in fear that something she discovered would be so awful she'd cut him out of her life.

And then he'd be alone again, turned inside out, his raw emotions exposed for all the world to see. No. That was something that could never happen. And if he kept her at arms' length, it wouldn't.

Four

At eight the next morning, Violet found JT in the room he'd dubbed his playroom. She paused just outside the door, needing a second to collect her wits before approaching him.

Clad in worn jeans and a black cotton button-down shirt, he was bent over what looked to be an antique pool table. With his left hand, he rolled the eight ball toward the far bumper and caught it as it returned, all the while studying the papers scattered over the table's beige felt. The briefcase she'd filled with Tiberius's files sat empty on the floor beside his bare feet.

Being confronted by so much casual masculinity first thing in the morning wasn't fair. Especially not after she'd lain awake staring at the ceiling until the sun starting lightening the horizon, regretting that she'd kissed him, wishing she'd dropped her towel when he confronted her on the pool deck. Her conflicting desires were tearing her apart. She'd have to choose one path and commit to it.

"Did you get some tea?" he asked without glancing her way.

His question made her realize she'd been silently staring at him for far too long. "Your housekeeper made me a cup. It's delicious." She didn't need to ask why his kitchen was stocked with four different blends of green tea. She already suspected the house saw a lot of guests. While in Miami, JT had been known for his parties. She doubted much had changed in the last six years. "Find anything that might help us?"

"My uncle accumulated copious amounts of information and enjoyed making detailed notes on all his business dealings. Every share he bought is documented. What I'm missing is the information on the family members who turned him down."

She drew close enough to the table to see that he'd created two lists of names. From past experience she knew how much Tiberius loved to collect information. The files from his home office overflowed with details—some of them helpful, most of them too trivial to waste time on.

"Let me help. Maybe I can speed things up."

She waited for him to acknowledge her offer, but he remained lost in thought. Had he not heard her, or did he want to handle everything himself? If it was the latter, too bad. She'd come up with this plan and intended to be involved at every stage. Running her gaze down JT's list of relatives who still owned their stock, she saw he'd notated which ones were definitely in Preston's pocket.

"You should know Paul and Tiberius had a huge argument three years ago," she said, indicating his mother's cousin. "Something about a rare comic book that Tiberius and Paul supposedly bought together using Tiberius's money when they were eight. Paul kept the comic book, but never paid Tiberius for his half and now it's worth like ten grand."

She shook her head. No matter what the comic's worth, it was silly to still be feuding about it all these years later, but Tiberius wasn't one to forgive a slight. She glanced at JT's strong profile. It was a characteristic Tiberius shared with his nephew.

"Thanks." JT made a note next to Paul's name and returned to the file he'd been reading.

"You've gotten a lot done." She assessed how he'd organized the files, and then pulled five out to make a third pile. As she finished, she noticed JT's glare. "What?"

"I had a system."

"And now it's better." She flipped open the top file and pointed to a gossip article about his third cousin. "Casey is in the middle of a nasty divorce. He has a mistress with very expensive taste tucked away and I believe she sees herself as the next Mrs. Casey Stone. Then there's the problems he's been having with his investment firm. He'd probably be receptive to an influx of cash."

JT looked no less displeased. "My father has done several favors for Casey. He has no interest in selling his stock to me, nor would he throw his votes in my direction."

Violet opened her mouth to argue, but decided from JT's set expression that she'd be wasting her breath. Instead, she set Casey's folder aside and opened the next one. She sifted through several documents before arriving at the one she wanted. "Your great aunt Harriet has recently come under the influence of a rather clever con man who has convinced her to fund his charity in New Orleans." Seeing the flicker of interest in JT's gaze, she sidled closer. "I can be a big help. No one knew the way Tiberius's mind worked better than me. Did you know that over the past thirty years Tiberius had collected a storage unit full of Las Vegas history? Some of it was significant. Most of it was trivial nonsense. He left the entire collection to Scarlett for her *Mob Experience* exhibit."

"I'm sure that's fascinating, but you've done enough." He pushed away from the pool table and nodded toward the open door. "Have Pauline fix you some breakfast. I'll take you back to Fontaine Chic when you're finished."

She repressed a protest. Assuming he'd accept her as his business partner just because she'd come up with the idea of getting married was shortsighted. A man as closed off as JT wasn't going to jump at the chance to work with her. If she didn't accept that, frustration was going to make her crazy.

"Before we head back to town, there are a few things we should talk about."

"Such as?" He crossed his arms over his chest.

"How would you like me to explain this?" She held up her left hand and indicated the ring with her right pointer finger.

For a moment he didn't speak, just stared at the ring. "However you'd like."

Violet gnashed her teeth and tried a different approach. "What are you planning to say about our impulsive wedding last night?"

"If it comes up, I will say we've been involved for almost a year, but we've been keeping it quiet."

"And that's it?"

"I do not expect anyone will press me for details."

"Truly?" How could he not comprehend people's curiosity? "You don't think someone will ask where we met? How long we've been seeing each other?"

"They won't."

"Isn't there anyone in your life you share things with?"

His isolation continued to baffle her. Did he choose to keep everyone out of his life or was he such a pain in the ass that no one was interested?

"My staff knows better than to show an interest in my personal life and those I see socially aren't interested in my business dealings. Since our arrangement falls in neither of those categories, I won't have to explain our marriage to anyone."

"That's great for you," she retorted sarcastically. "But I have two sisters and a mother, who when they hear I got married, are going to expect me to share every juicy detail of what we're doing and why."

At last he gave her his full attention. "There are no juicy details."

She shoved her hands into the back pocket of her jeans to keep from acting on the desire to jolt him out of his stoic calm. "Can I tell them what we're really doing?"

"Do you trust them to keep the truth to themselves?"

Given his tendency to play his cards close to the vest, the question shouldn't have shocked her as much as it did. "I trust them completely."

She bared her teeth in a spiteful grin. "But if you don't think I should, I could tell them that you've pined over me for years, but were too afraid that Tiberius would ruin you if you made your feelings known."

Irritation tightened his mouth into a thin line. "They won't believe something so ridiculous."

"Scarlett will." Violet gave free rein to the demon riding her shoulder. Being reasonable hadn't worked, and she badly wanted a peek at the hand he held. Time to play dirty. Maybe if she antagonized him, he'd let something slip. "She already has it in her head that you show up in Baccarat every night because you want me."

If he denied it, she wouldn't be surprised.

"And she bases that on what exactly?" His even tone gave nothing away.

Violet found herself in deeper water than she expected. Nothing for her to do but swim hard for shore and hope she wasn't eaten by sharks. "The way you look at me."

"And how exactly do I look at you?"

Violet frowned, trying to remember exactly how her sister had phrased it. "She said you look hungry."

JT might be a master at hiding his thoughts, but Violet swore she saw a slight widening of his eyes. To her delight, she'd scored if not a direct hit, then one fairly close to the mark. Fascinating. She was pondering the possibility that he wasn't as disinterested in her as he'd claimed when he spoke up.

"Your sister has a flare for the drama," he said. "She's fallen in love and sees nothing but potential love matches all around her."

"You're probably right."

But he hadn't actually come out and denied it. Violet decided she'd pushed enough for one day. Much more and she'd run the risk that he'd become even more enigmatic. By allowing herself this tiny win, she now had something she could build on. It was like gaining the trust of a wild creature. Better to use short positive sessions to get them to drop their guard than to try and rush things and make it more skittish.

"Have you eaten?" she asked.

"An hour ago."

She masked her disappointment. "I'll eat something quick and be ready to go back to town in half an hour if that works for you."

"I think I'm in a place where I can take a break and I could use another cup of coffee." He scooped an empty mug off the edge of the pool table and followed her out of his playroom.

Violet's pulse kicked into high gear. Maybe she'd learned the secret to dealing with JT: she'd pretend she didn't care if he spent time with her or included her in his plans to take over his family business and wait for him to come to her. It wasn't the way she was accustomed to dealing with the men she got involved with. Most of the time they liked her to take the lead.

That would never be the case with JT.

"You were right about the view," she remarked a half hour later. She and JT were sitting in the breakfast nook just off the kitchen. The wall-to-wall windows offered a panoramic view of the desert and the mountains to the north that speared an impossibly blue sky. "Do you miss the ocean? Growing up in Miami, I would think the desert would be hard to get used to."

"At first I was worried that I'd hate the dust and the heat, but the mountains make it all worthwhile. And if I need to get on the water, I have a boat on Lake Mead."

Something about the view or sharing a meal—he'd sampled her eggs and stolen half the fruit off her plate—had worked some sort of magic on him. For the last half hour he'd been almost…charming. And Violet was loath to break the spell. So she sipped tea and nibbled on toast, delaying the end of the meal so she could prolong her time with this more accessible version of her new husband.

"Sounds like the best of both worlds." She popped a grape into her mouth. "I am curious though, why are you living on a horse ranch out here instead of closer to Titanium?"

"My grandmother grew up on a horse farm in Kentucky." He took Violet's left hand and regarded the ring he'd put on her hand to seal his wedding vows. "Even after she married my grandfather and moved to Miami, she kept several show jumpers. Starting when I was five, my mother used to take me to watch her. I'd sit in the stands and marvel at how she and her horse flew over six-foot-high jumps."

As he spoke, his gaze grew less focused. He'd stopped seeing his grandmother's ring and was revisiting a happy moment from his past. The muscles of his face relaxed into a fond half smile. Violet watched him with dawning wonder. This wasn't the first time he'd opened up to her—after all, he'd shared his decision to quit his family's company. But it was the first time he'd shared a happy memory from his childhood.

Based on their interaction to this point, she'd labeled him as guarded and brooding. She'd assumed his unhappy childhood had left him emotionally shut down and incapable of letting joy in. But maybe it wasn't that he didn't feel but that he felt too much? If he was a powder keg ready to explode, what happened when someone lit a match?

"She insisted I learn to ride," JT continued, oblivious to the thoughts churning inside Violet's head. "During the summer, she would take me to her family's horse farm in Kentucky and we would spend hours riding. When I was good enough to compete, she took me to horse shows. It all stopped when she died."

JT had lost his grandmother when he was ten. Hearing him speak so warmly of her, Violet suspected he'd been devastated to lose the one person who'd showered him with love and attention. She remembered what a tough time Tiberius had gone through when his mother had died. He'd taken Lucille and Violet to the funeral and she remembered how unwelcome they'd been.

"I never had any grandparents around when I was a kid," she told him. "My mom left Cincinnati when she was seventeen and never looked back." She smiled wryly. "And you know the situation on my father's side."

"I've never met any of my father's relatives. His parents died when he was very young."

"I remember Tiberius saying something about that. I guess I didn't realize Preston didn't keep in touch with his family. Wasn't he from California? Have you ever thought about looking some of them up?"

The shutters were back over JT's eyes. As soon as he'd

mentioned his father, his expression became as remote as the mountaintops that made his view so extraordinary.

"No."

His abrupt answer discouraged further conversation on that topic. Violet sighed as she realized JT was done sharing.

"If you don't mind," she began, setting her napkin on the table beside her plate. "I think it's time I headed back to Fontaine Chic."

"I'll get my keys."

While JT waited in the foyer for Violet to collect her overnight bag, he replayed their conversation in his mind and revisited every expression on her lovely face. He'd enjoyed sharing breakfast with her. So much so that instead of giving her a brief, dry explanation of why he'd chosen ranch life over a house in the city, he'd gone all sentimental on her and let her see how his grandmother had influenced him.

Nor did it surprise him how tempted he was to trust her. Her earnest curiosity and upbeat outlook weren't a clever cover for ulterior motives. She honestly wanted to help. Her impulsive suggestion that they get married so he could get control of Tiberius's Stone Properties stock had demonstrated she was far too quick to believe in people.

Take him for example. She expected him to stick to their understanding that this wasn't a real marriage. Which meant hands off. And the best—no, only—way he could think of to honor their agreement was to stay as far away from her as possible.

"Ready when you are," she said, as descended the stairs. She was a feminine marvel in a pastel floral dress with thin straps that bared her delicate shoulders and a full skirt that flirted with her knees. Pink sandals with three-inch heels drew attention to her spectacular calves and her hair was swept up into a loose top-knot. She made his mouth water.

With a slight bounce, she stepped from the stairs onto the foyer's marble floor and crossed to where he stood by the front door, tongue-tied, his hormones in an uproar. As she neared, he snagged her luggage and opened the door.

"I don't think we should live together," he stated, his voice short and clipped.

"How are people going to believe we are married if we don't?"

"We both work a lot. No one will notice."

Her lips thinned. "That's not going to work."

"We'll talk about it when I return to town."

She eyed the second overnight bag he held. "Where are you going?"

"As soon as I drop you off, I'm heading to North Carolina." The sooner he secured the necessary shares of Stone Properties, the sooner he could replace his father as CEO. And the sooner he could be free of this marriage-in-name-only before he did something to change their relationship forever.

"Who's there?"

"My cousin Brent. His dad's Alzheimer's has made it necessary for him to take charge of the finances in the last few months. He has several thousand shares. It's not all that I need, but every bit helps."

"I don't recall seeing him in Tiberius's files."

JT held the passenger door open and gritted his teeth against the sweet seduction of her perfume as she brushed past him and slid into the car. Damn, but she was a tempting armful. Resisting the impulse to reprise last night's kiss actually caused a dull ache in his gut. When he'd agreed to marry her, he'd underestimated just how challenging it would be to keep his hands to himself.

"He's not." After depositing their bags in the trunk, JT

got behind the wheel and started the BMW. "I don't know why Tiberius didn't include him."

The car picked up speed as he drove down his long driveway toward the highway and JT noticed that the air-flow in the open convertible whipped Violet's skirt into a frenzy of dancing flowers and bared a whole lot of lean, toned thigh. He daydreamed about sliding his hands along the soft, smooth length of her leg and finding her hot and wet and eager for him. It wasn't until a truck flashed past on a perpendicular course that he realized they'd reached the end of his driveway. JT slammed on his brakes and the BMW skidded to a halt.

"Are you okay?" he asked, glancing her way.

She regarded him curiously. "I'm fine. Are you?"

Not even close. "I think we'll be more comfortable with the top up." He hit the button that raised the convertible top and while it was closing, stared at his grandfather's ring on his left hand.

Yeah, staying as far from her as possible for the next couple months was the only way he was going to survive this marriage with his heart intact.

On the thirty-minute ride to Las Vegas, he kept his eyes to himself and his thoughts on the trip ahead. Violet seemed to understand his need to plan because she kept her gaze on the passing landscape, only occasionally glancing down at her ever-vibrating smartphone.

Finally, JT had to ask, "Is it always this way for you?"

"I'm sorry?" She blinked as if she had a hard time re-focusing her attention on him.

"Your phone. It's been going off non-stop since we got in the car."

A wry smile curved her lips. "It's my sisters. I'm not usually off the grid for twelve hours."

Envy stabbed at JT. What would it be like to have someone fret about your wellbeing? Nice? Smothering? "They must be worried about you. Why don't you answer them?"

"I sent them a text last night. They know I'm safe." Her smile developed sharp edges. "I told them I was with you."

JT ignored the way his pulse leapt at the challenge in her manner. She would take any opening he gave her to provoke him; what she didn't realize was that once unleashed, his emotions would overwhelm them both.

"Did you explain that we got married?"

"I didn't want to do that in a text."

"Then what do they think you are doing with me?" His body tensed, but the sensation was pleasurable rather than distressing.

"Probably what most of the women do when they spend the night at your house."

Damn her sass. "Why would you want your sisters to think we slept together?"

She didn't answer him immediately, and when she did speak, all amusement had fled her voice. "I suppose that's something else we should discuss."

"Aren't we already discussing it?" Her change of topic made him feel as if he was spinning in place.

"Do you intend to bring women home while we're married?"

Her question sparked a ridiculous urge to snatch her into his arms and kiss her silly. He wasn't allowed to make love to her, but she didn't want him having sex with anyone else? "I hadn't really thought about it."

"I know our marriage isn't real, but I'd appreciate it if you could refrain from dating other women until we can get divorced."

"I think I can last a couple months."

"What if you can't get the shares or the votes you need in time for the annual stockholders' meeting?"

"What are you asking?"

"Our goal was to make you CEO," she said, her manner matter-of-fact. "If that doesn't happen in the next few months it's because we didn't have enough time. You aren't horrible to be married to. I could see sticking it out for another year."

A year of being married to Violet with the temptation of making love to her eating him alive? JT recoiled from the thought. "We'll get divorced in the fall regardless."

Her expression was inscrutable as she nodded. "Then we'll get divorced."

Conversation dried up after their exchange. Fortunately they'd reached the city limits and traffic wasn't as backed up as usual, so their journey to her hotel was accomplished quickly. He swung the BMW into Fontaine Chic's circular driveway and stopped the car by the lobby doors. Before he could shut off the car, Violet put a hand on his arm.

"If you just open the trunk, I'll grab my bag."

In that instant, JT realized the last thing he wanted to do was fly off and leave his brand-new wife to her own devices. What an idiotic notion. They weren't really married. It wasn't as if they'd shared a grand night of passion he couldn't wait to duplicate. But she was already far more important to him than a casual acquaintance, which—their connection to Tiberius aside—was all they were.

"I'll call you and let you know how things went in North Carolina." He slipped the garage remote off the visor and extended it to her. "Here."

Her brows came together briefly. "Why would you give me that?"

Because he liked the idea of her sleeping—and skinny-dipping—in his home.

"Our house," he corrected her. "I might need some information from Tiberius's files. It would be useful if you could get to them."

"Let me get this straight." A playful light glinted in her eyes. "You're going to let me help and you're going to trust me alone in *our* house?"

"Are you planning on digging through my underwear drawer?"

She leaned close and whispered, "Is that where you keep your secrets?"

No, those were all locked up in his head. "Please feel free to investigate and see."

"It doesn't bother you to have me snooping?"

To his surprise, it didn't. "What do you think you'll find?"

"I don't know." She plucked the opener from his grasp. "But everything about you is such a closed book I'm sure I'll find the most mundane of things utterly fascinating."

With a sassy wink she slipped from the car and collected her bag. JT watched until she'd sashayed through the lobby door before shifting into drive. He'd been married to her for less than twenty-four hours and already he was noticing cracks in his defenses. Sunshine was seeping in, illuminating emotions that hadn't seen the light of day in over eighteen years. He felt lighter, more optimistic as if her positive outlook was contagious.

It took all his determination to put aside thoughts of his new wife and her unsettling effect on him, but by the time JT reached long-term parking, he'd managed to focus his attention on the trip ahead. Earlier that morning he'd had his assistant book a flight from Vegas to Charlotte. He'd decided to fly commercial instead of borrowing the company jet. He didn't want his father to start questioning why he was traveling all over the East Coast.

After parking his car, he headed to the terminal. An email message arrived on his phone as he exited security. His secretary had forwarded his itinerary for the coming week. He was booked from Charlotte to Atlanta to Louisville and finally up to New York City. Four cities in six days. He hoped like hell it would be a profitable trip.

Five

As soon as Violet entered Fontaine Chic, she headed straight for her office. Since no one had called her in a panic, she assumed nothing earthshaking had happened in the last twelve hours, but she wanted to touch base with her assistant. Patty brought Violet a cup of tea and the previous day's report. Violet crossed to the seating area near the window and sat down on the couch. A quick scan assured Violet that her hotel continued to run smoothly in her absence. Now to address the problem of convincing her sisters that marrying JT didn't mean she'd lost her marbles.

I'm back.

She sent the text to both Scarlett and Harper and wasn't surprised how fast the responses came.

I'm on my way. From Scarlett.

Give me twenty minutes and don't tell Scarlett a thing until I get there. From Harper.

With a fatalistic sigh, Violet set the phone down on the coffee table. Exhaustion washed over her as her night of little sleep caught up to her. She let her muscles relax. Her head fell back against the comfortable leather couch. Almost immediately she was besieged by hysterical amusement. Had she seriously just married JT? Demanded that he give her a proper kiss? Not that there was anything proper in the way his tongue had coasted against hers. She shivered as the memory swept over her.

"I demand to hear every last detail immediately," Scarlett proclaimed from the doorway.

Violet's eyes flew open. She hadn't even realized she'd closed them. "Harper said to wait."

"You don't seriously think I'm going to sit here in suspense for twenty minutes, do you?" Scarlett flopped onto the couch beside Violet and pinned her with a steely glare. "Spill."

Now that the moment had arrived, Violet decided it was harder to justify her actions than she'd imagined. "I really think we should wait. I don't want to explain myself twice."

She wasn't sure she wanted to explain herself *once*.

Scarlett waved Violet's objection away. "What's there to explain? You finally gave in to the chemistry between you and JT. Was it fabulous? Is he an intense lover? He has such great hands and those lips…"

Violet choked back a laugh. "Scarlett!"

"What? Harper will want to lecture you on moving too fast. I won't get to hear any of the hot stuff once she shows up."

"There is no hot stuff."

"Really?" Scarlett's face reflected disappointment. "I would have thought there'd be major fireworks between you."

"It wasn't like that."

"Then why are you blushing?"

Violet put her hands to her cheeks and found them on fire. "He caught me skinny-dipping in his pool."

"And…?" Scarlett leaned forward, her eyes wide and encouraging.

"He handed me a bikini and told me to wear it next time I wanted to take a swim."

Scarlett sat back and regarded her sister in absolute confusion. Violet had never seen her so utterly baffled.

"I thought your text said you spent the night with JT."

"I did. Only not the way your naughty mind thinks. I slept at his house."

Before Scarlett could reply, Harper breezed into the room. She was slightly out of breath as she demanded, "What did I miss?"

"Not a darned thing," Scarlett muttered in disgust. "Apparently there's nothing for her to tell."

"What about that?" Harper settled next to Scarlett and reached across her to point at Violet's left hand.

Scarlett snatched up the hand and stared at the ring. "You're engaged?"

"Not exactly," Violet murmured.

"That looks like an engagement ring."

"Actually it's a wedding ring. JT and I got married last night at the Tunnel of Love Chapel."

"Married?" Scarlett gaped at her sister.

"JT Stone?" Harper shook her head. "Have you told Grandfather? Are you at all worried how he'll react when he finds out you're married to the competition?"

"I'm going to call him in a little while." Violet was all prepared with a rational explanation for her actions. "He'll understand when I explain what happened."

"What did happen?" Scarlett asked. "The last time I mentioned him being interested in you, I got the distinct impression you had no intention of letting anything develop."

"It hasn't exactly developed the way you think," Violet said.

"You're married," Harper pointed out. "Something had to happen between you."

"It's all a little complicated."

"Did Rick slip something special into one of his signature cocktails?" Scarlett narrowed her eyes. "By that I mean, were you drunk?"

"I was perfectly sober." Violet rushed to answer the question in Harper's eyes. "So was he."

"So, you didn't just spend the night at JT's house," Harper clarified. "You spent the night with JT?"

"No. It's not that kind of marriage."

Harper regarded her gravely. "What sort of marriage is it?"

"It's strictly a business arrangement."

"But not funny business obviously," Scarlett groused.

Violet ignored her. "Mom and I went to the lawyer a few days ago and it turns out Tiberius had been purchasing Stone Properties stock from other family members."

"I thought he didn't want anything to do with the company after what Preston did to him," Scarlett said.

"I think it was more a matter of not being able to do anything to get his brother-in-law removed as CEO. Preston controlled the shares he inherited on his wife's death as well as the ones that were in JT's trust. Shares that JT took control of on his thirtieth birthday two months ago."

"How much stock had Tiberius managed to buy?" Harper asked, her keen business mind catching on quickly.

"Eighteen percent."

"And how much was in JT's trust?"

"Thirty percent. Preston owns thirty and the other twenty-two percent is split up among the family."

"So what does this have to do with why you and JT got married?" Scarlett asked, returning the conversation to what she was interested in.

"Obviously Tiberius left her his shares," Harper said.

Scarlett shot her sister a pained look. "I get that, but why marry JT when she could sell him the shares?"

"Because according to Tiberius's will, I have to keep the stock until Preston dies."

"You know you didn't have to marry JT," Harper pointed out. "You could have just thrown your support behind him."

Violet felt her features take on the same injured expression Scarlett had just worn. Once in a while she wished Harper would acknowledge that she wasn't always the smartest one in the room.

"Only family can vote the shares," she explained.

Scarlett clapped her hands in delight. "So, now you're family. That's brilliant."

"Thank you." Violet appreciated having Scarlett's support because she could see that Harper wasn't done with her objections.

"But with your eighteen percent and JT's thirty—"

Violet interrupted. "We still need three percent to control the vote." She glanced at the clock on her phone and realized JT was probably boarding his flight to Charlotte. "He's heading out to talk to some of his relatives, hoping he can persuade enough of them to either sell or throw their vote his way so he can take control of Stone Properties and get his father out."

"And you found out about this a few days ago?" Harper frowned. "Aren't you moving a little quick? I would think you'd both want to protect yourselves before getting married."

"You haven't seen the way JT looks at her," Scarlett interjected. "I don't think that man has the patience to last any longer."

To Violet's intense dismay, she felt her cheeks heating again. "It's not like that between us," she protested. "And we signed an agreement that we'd walk away with what we came into the marriage with. Really, it's just a business deal. A marriage in name only."

"How long do think that's going to last?" Scarlett's lips wore a lusty smile. "The two of you share the same house night after night. Him just down the hall? I give you a week tops before you crack. JT…" She cocked her head and considered. "Maybe three days."

"We're not going to live together," Violet explained, growing lightheaded as she remembered how hard it had been to fall asleep the previous night after kissing JT. But in the future there would be no more such kisses, passion-drenched or otherwise. They'd both agreed on that.

"You're not?" Scarlett looked scandalized at the thought.

"Lots of married couple don't," Harper said. "My parents being one of them."

And their marital separation was what had led to Ross's numerous affairs and the two daughters he'd never acknowledged. Or maybe his affairs had led to his estrangement from his wife. Violet had never asked Harper what she thought. As close as the three girls had become in the last five years, some topics remained uncomfortable.

"Are you sure you know what you're doing?" Harper continued. "I mean, how well do you know JT?"

"Not as well as she's going to get to know him," Scarlett put in slyly.

Violet shot her a repressive look. "I don't know how to explain it, but he feels like family. I know until recently that Tiberius refused to have anything to do with him, but he talked so much about his sister and what life was like for JT as a kid, I feel as if I know him." She regarded each of her sisters, trying to gauge if she was making sense.

"I get how sometimes you can feel as if you know a person even though you've never met," Harper said, a note of tension in her voice. "But often the reality is very different and you have to be careful."

Was Harper referring to JT or her own problems with celebrity chef Ashton Croft, whose latest restaurant was supposed to have opened in Harper's Fontaine Ciel hotel two weeks earlier? The charismatic executive chef-turned-television sensation was unconventional and passionate about food and adventure. Since starting negotiations with Harper for the restaurant, he'd been a thorn in her side with one outrageous demand after another.

Violet suspected her sister had been a Chef Ashton fan long before the restaurant deal. Harper's DVR was filled with Croft's television series, *The Culinary Wanderer*, in which he traveled around the world in search of the perfect meal. Why such an adventurous wanderer appealed to someone as methodical and strategic as Harper, Violet would never understand.

"I'll admit that what I know of JT is already proving incomplete." Violet considered what she'd learned over breakfast. He'd opened up to give her a glimpse into his past. A happy moment in what she suspected was a turbulent childhood. "But I don't think he has any intention of cheating me." And any heartbreak that happened would be because she'd let it.

Harper shook her head. "I just hope you know what you're doing."

"So do I," Violet muttered. "So do I."

JT should have known that letting Violet's optimism rub off on him was reckless, but he'd been seduced by her earnest smiles and luminous brown eyes. Now, with a tumbler of excellent scotch on his knee, he allowed his gaze to drift around his cousin's mahogany-paneled study and tried not to let his disappointment show.

"Sorry, JT." Brent looked as if the weight of the world rested on his shoulders. "My dad sold the shares to Preston five months ago. You're welcome to the hundred I received on my eighteenth birthday."

"Thanks for the offer, but I'd rather you remain a stockholder and help me convince the rest of the family that my dad's management isn't doing the company any favors." No wonder Tiberius hadn't created a file on Brent's father. What was the point when the shares were already lost? "Any idea why your father sold the shares to my dad? It's not as if the two of them got along."

Brent snorted. "That's an understatement. My dad hated yours. He blamed Preston for your mom's death."

Brent's father Ted was Tiberius and Fiona's first cousin. He'd been as close to them as a sibling, but Ted and Fiona's relationship had grown a bit strained over what had happened to Tiberius When Brent's dad had told Fiona her husband was out of control, she'd resolutely defended her husband. Preston became a sore spot between them, but their love remained as strong as ever.

"Then why did he sell him the shares?"

"After it happened, he felt horrible. Preston convinced him that your mom wanted more shares for you."

"Your father didn't remember that my mom's been dead for eighteen years?"

Brent grimaced. "I knew then I had to get power of attorney and take over his finances."

"He's getting worse faster than you expected, isn't he?"

"His lucid moments are fewer and fewer." Father and son had enjoyed a close connection that JT had long envied.

"Sorry," JT said. "I can't imagine how hard this is for you."

"Most people can't." Ted had been an intelligent, intuitive businessman. It had to be tearing Brent apart to lose his father this way. To watch him slip away a little more each day, knowing there was no way to ever get him back. "It's tough watching a clever, bold businessman like my father forget the dog's name or where the kitchen is in the house."

The deep throb in Brent's voice made JT's chest hurt. "Is there anything you need? Anything I can help with?" He regretted that in his preoccupation with his own troubles, he'd not kept up with his cousin the way a friend should.

Brent cleared his throat. "That's the worst of it. There's nothing anyone can do." He swallowed the last of his scotch. "But I appreciate the offer. You're not just family, you're a good friend."

A year apart in age, they'd spent time together as kids, forming bonds that made them close as adults. Fiona Stone had often traveled to Charlotte to visit her favorite cousin. JT remembered how, in this Neoclassical-style house, built more than a hundred years ago, his mother hadn't needed drugs or alcohol to cope with her life. She'd smiled all the time and given him big hugs and spoiled him with ice cream sundaes and trips to the zoo and museums. Getting his mother back had been like a miracle. But neither the trip nor his mother's happiness could last forever.

"So, why don't you tell me what's going on. Why you're suddenly buying up stock."

"I want to get control of Stone Properties."

"Seriously?" Curiosity flared in Brent's gray eyes. "And how are you planning to do that?"

"For the last six months, Tiberius had been quietly buying shares."

"That clever son of a bitch," Brent exclaimed in admiration. "So, you two were going to team up?"

JT shook his head. "I had no idea what he was planning. You know Tiberius."

"Kept his cards close to his chest. And who could blame him after what your dad did to him. How much of the company had he managed to get?"

"Eighteen percent."

"And with the thirty you came into on your last birthday, you are three percent short of control."

"It's a little more complicated than that," JT explained, thinking of Violet and her damned skinny-dipping. "Turns out, Tiberius didn't leave me the shares."

"Really?" Brent got up to refresh their drink.

"Thanks to my dad, my uncle and I weren't on the best of terms, but in the last month or so we'd started to reconnect." JT considered all the tales his father had told him about Tiberius and wished he'd been smarter about where he'd put his loyalty.

Brent frowned. "So who owns his shares?"

"Tiberius's unofficially adopted daughter." JT held up his left hand and showed off his grandfather's ring. "Last night we got married."

The number of times JT had successfully surprised his quick-witted cousin could be counted on one hand. Today marked the fifth one.

"You're married to...oh, what's her name?" Brent snapped his fingers as he searched his memory.

"Violet Fontaine."

"Tiberius took in her and her mother, didn't he?" Uncertainty fogged Brent's gaze. "But I thought her last name was Allen?"

"Turns out she's Ross Fontaine's illegitimate daughter. After he died, Violet's grandfather—Henry Fontaine, head of Fontaine Resorts and Hotels—came to Vegas to find her and make amends for his son's neglect. She's in line to succeed the old man as head of the company."

"And you married her instead of buying the stock?" Brent asked, sounding very much as if he thought JT wasn't thinking clearly. "If you're short on cash, you could have come to me."

A year ago Brent had sold the company he'd started

and had not yet found a place to invest the four billion he'd made.

"The terms of Tiberius's will don't allow her to part with the stock in any way until my dad dies."

"Good old Tiberius." Brent grinned in admiration. "And until you married her, she couldn't vote because she's not family."

JT knew he could count on his cousin to grasp the entire problem. "That sums it up."

Brent blew out a worried breath. "When your dad finds out about this, things are going to get nasty."

"That's why I need to meet with as much family as I can before he finds out."

With regret tugging his dark eyebrows together, Brent said, "I wish I could help you out."

"Me, too."

His cousin was one hell of a businessman. His father had taught him well. Again JT felt the twinge of envy. Why did bad things happen to good people while manipulative bastards like JT's father sailed through life unscathed?

"Where are you off to next?" Brent asked.

"Atlanta."

"Cousin Skip." JT's cousin rolled his eyes. "I don't envy you."

Six

At midnight, Baccarat's couches and barstools were occupied by a twenty-something clientele with palates sophisticated enough for Rick's special blends. As Violet crossed the threshold into the lounge, her pulse escalated but she immediately told herself to calm down. Even if JT was in town, it was too late for him to be at the bar. She usually swung through here at eleven-fifteen, but tonight she'd been held up by the manager of the sports book.

The only contact she'd had with JT in the last several days was a series of terse text messages, each less hopeful than the last. He was having no luck finding more shares to buy. His father had either bought up what he could or had convinced his family to vote with him.

Her phone vibrated, indicating a text message had come in. Someone at the front desk was looking for her. Violet left Baccarat without catching Rick's attention and headed for the lobby.

As she approached, she saw a tall man standing with the night manager. The stranger had his back to her, but when Violet was five feet away, he turned his head and she glimpsed his profile.

She almost stopped dead in her tracks. Preston Rhodes? What the hell was he doing here?

JT's father hadn't spotted her yet, but she was too exposed to make a run for it without drawing unwanted attention. Gathering a deep breath, Violet stiffened her spine and marched forward.

"Good evening," she said, doubting her ability to pretend she had no idea who Preston was. Although the man had never appeared in Vegas before, she recognized him from articles she'd read about him. And then there was the resemblance to JT around the man's eyes and chin. "Preston Rhodes, isn't it?"

While the night manager returned to his post, Violet held out her hand and wasn't surprised when Preston clasped it in a punishing handshake. Of course the man would choose to demonstrate his power with brute force. That he wouldn't pull any punches just because she was a woman wasn't as flattering as it might have been if he were someone else.

"Ms. Fontaine." His smooth tone did little to hide the poisonous nature of the man's character. "Or should I call you Violet since we're now family?"

She tried to keep her surprise from showing. His thin laugh let her know that she hadn't been successful. JT hadn't mentioned that he'd told his father. Irritation flared. She wished he'd warned her. Facing someone like Preston without preparation was better suited to Harper, who had a knack for staying calm no matter what the catastrophe.

"Mr. Rhodes—"

"Preston," he corrected, a viper's smile twisting his lips. "Unless you'd prefer Dad. I know you never had anyone you could call by that name."

It wasn't in her nature to call him what he deserved.

"Preston," she acceded. With that one word, she was out of polite things to say to the man who'd ruined the most important man in her life and who cared little that his son distrusted him.

"Why don't we go have a drink and get to know each other a little better."

Preston caught her by the arm and turned in the direction of Lalique, a stylish two-story bar inside a spectacular three-story crystal chandelier that was Fontaine Chic's centerpiece. Her grandfather hadn't said a word about the three million dollars she'd spent on this single item. Crystal was Violet's signature décor. Throughout the hotel and casino, multifaceted crystals sparkled above the gaming tables and from the fixtures that lined the walkways. Pillars sparkled with embedded lights made to resemble crystals and all the waitresses and dealers wore rhinestone-accented black uniforms.

Preston's firm grip left her feeling very much like a disobedient child being led to her punishment. Annoyed at being manhandled in her own hotel, Violet nonetheless went with JT's father. A scene would harm her more than him and she was certain he knew that. Preston was a master manipulator. It was how he'd gotten the best of his wife's younger brother.

Once they were seated in a quiet table near the railing on the bar's second floor, Preston signaled the waitress. "A bottle of Cristal. We must toast to becoming family."

Violet's skin itched where he'd touched her. The thought of being legally connected to this man, no matter how briefly, made her physically ill.

"I don't drink when I'm working," Violet protested.

"Nonsense. This is a special occasion."

"Then shouldn't we wait to celebrate with JT?"

"My son is running around the country visiting family." Preston's smile didn't reach his hard eyes. "Telling them his good news, I'm assuming." JT's father pinned her with merciless scrutiny. "And yet he left you—his brand-new bride—here. Why is that?"

Again Violet feared her face would betray too much. Tiberius had told her over and over that she made a lousy poker player. She couldn't bluff to save her soul.

"It wasn't a good time for me to be away from the hotel."

"No honeymoon for you then? Stone Properties has a wonderful five-star resort in the Cayman Islands. I could call and have a suite made available for you two."

"Please don't bother."

"It's no bother at all."

The waitress arrived with their champagne and a pair of flutes. Violet appreciated the momentary distraction. She needed to stop reacting and get ahead of Preston. Why had he come? Nothing he did lacked motivation. If he knew JT was traveling, he'd shown up in Vegas to catch Violet alone. Anxiety flared, but she pushed it down. No matter how vile the man, he was powerless to do more than intimidate her.

Once the champagne was poured, Preston handed her a flute. "To wedded bliss. May your life with my son be as happy as mine was with his mother."

More a curse than a blessing, Violet thought as she put the flute to her lips and wet them with the champagne. "Thank you." She set the glass down. "Now, if you'll excuse me, I really have some pressing matters to attend to." But before she could rise, Preston covered her hand with his.

"How long have you and my son been together?"

"A while."

"You must be good at keeping secrets because your wedding caught everyone by surprise."

"JT's very private." And for once she was glad. "We

run rival hotels. He wanted to maintain a low profile until we were sure of our relationship."

"You certainly managed that. No one had a clue that you and he were dating, much less falling in love." Preston leaned forward, his eyes intense. "You are in love with my son, aren't you?"

Violet hesitated before answering. Preston knew something was not on the up and up between her and JT. She saw the challenge in his gaze as if daring her to lie.

"JT is the most amazing man I know. How could I not be?"

That she didn't answer the question directly wasn't lost on Preston. His calculated smile was back.

"And I'm sure he feels the same way about you. I'm glad. I would hate for you to have married him for the wrong reasons."

"Such as?" The instant she spoke, Violet knew she should have insisted she loved JT.

"For his money."

Violet raised her eyebrow and glanced around her. "Do I look like I need money?"

"From what I understand, all this belongs to Fontaine Resorts and Hotels, not to you."

"Regardless, I don't need JT's money."

"That's good." Preston finished his glass of champagne and stood. "I'm very protective of my son. If I thought someone intended to hurt him, I would take steps to see that didn't happen."

She couldn't believe what Preston was saying. He'd done more to hurt his son than the entire rest of the world combined. "I have no plans to hurt JT. Quite the opposite."

"Good. So are you planning on giving up your suite here and moving to my son's ranch?"

Again he'd caught her unprepared. "We haven't decided yet."

"Because two people living apart isn't much of a marriage."

"We'll figure it out."

"And soon, I hope. Because if you're not living together, someone might assume that your marriage is a fake and that would lead to questions."

The entire conversation had been charged with subtext and Violet grew more concerned with each exchange. She suspected Preston had figured out she and JT weren't a love match. Not that there was anything he could do about it.

"Why would anyone care?"

"I care." Preston at last dropped all pretense of being civil. "I know why he married you. To get at the stock Tiberius bought. Well, that only gives him forty-eight percent. Not enough to challenge me."

The speed at which JT's father had figured out what they were up to startled Violet. And yet, should it? The man was devious. He would see a game being played from a mile away. How were they going to get ahead of him if he anticipated all their moves?

"You look worried, Violet."

Preston obviously enjoyed having the upper hand and rubbing his opponent's nose in the fact.

Composing her expression, Violet replied, "I have nothing to be worried about."

"Because you and JT didn't get married so he could use the stock Tiberius left you to stage a coup against me?"

Goose bumps broke out on Violet's arms, but she kept her gaze locked on Preston's cold, flat eyes. "I have no idea what you're talking about."

"Of course you do and when I prove that you two aren't married in good faith, I'm going to sue you for fraud and take back the stock in your possession."

"You can't do that."

"Maybe. Maybe not. But I can tie up the stock in a lawsuit long enough to get rid of my son the same way I got rid of my brother-in-law."

While Violet sat in stunned silence, unsure if she'd ever experienced this level of malice, Preston topped off the champagne in her glass and stood.

"Drink up, Violet. You and my son have embarked on a grand adventure. I only hope you know what you've gotten yourself into."

Preston strolled away before Violet could wrap her thoughts around his threat. Her phone buzzed and she checked the message. JT's plane had just landed at the airport. He had news.

Well…she texted back, agreeing to meet at his house in an hour…so did she.

The drive from Las Vegas to his desert ranch had never bothered JT before. But then again, he'd never had a woman like Violet to come home to either. He banished the thought the instant it entered his head. This was a business meeting. Simple as that.

Violet had used the garage door remote he'd given her and let herself in. He found her curled up on the couch in the living room, staring at the cold fireplace. He had to say her name twice before she realized she was no longer alone. There was a split second of utter delight in her eyes before she frowned.

"You look exhausted. Sit down and let me get you some tea."

"I'd rather have a beer."

"The tea will relax you and soothe your nerves."

"The beer will have the same effect, plus I prefer the way it tastes."

"Fine." When she returned, she held two bottles.

He raised his eyebrow as she handed him one, and she shrugged. "You really shouldn't drink alone."

It was on the tip of his tongue to remind her that he drank alone all the time, but decided not to push her away. Instead, he held out his free hand and pulled her down onto the couch beside him. She landed close and he slung his arm over the back of the couch above her shoulder. Her body fit nicely against his side. He sipped his beer and sighed.

"How's your week going?" he asked, resisting the urge to nuzzle his nose into her silky hair. She'd taken it down and it cascaded around her shoulders in soft waves.

"Until an hour ago, better than yours. You had no luck at all with your family?"

Her first comment snagged his attention. "What happened an hour ago?"

She tensed, and didn't immediately answer. Perplexed, JT glanced down at her. She was staring hard at the beer bottle.

"Violet?" he prompted, growing uneasy.

"We have a problem."

Keeping a sudden flare of concern from his voice, he asked, "What sort of problem?"

"Your father knows what we're doing."

JT cursed silently. "How do you know that?"

"Because he came to see me at Fontaine Chic. He basically told me if he finds out that our marriage isn't real that he'll sue us for fraud."

Fury held him immobile. How dare his father threaten Violet. This was a battle between businessmen. But JT should have been prepared for this. It wasn't the first time Preston Rhodes had intimidated someone who tried to take him on.

"I'll deal with him." JT took a healthy swallow of his beer and swallowed his irritation. No need to get Violet any more worked up than she already was. This wasn't her fight. It was his. That his father chose to confront Violet instead of him let JT know that he was feeling threatened. "It's just a threat to distract us while he shores up support amongst the other shareholders."

"But he said that it would tie up the stock until after the August stockholders' meeting. And that if he keeps control of the company he's going to do to you what he did to Tiberius."

As threats went, it lacked teeth. "There's no immediate family to turn against me," JT reminded her. "As for ejecting me from the company, I was ready to go out on my own before we found out about Tiberius buying stock." JT liked her fierce defense of him. It gave him an urgent need to pull her into his arms and offer her his ardent thanks. "Besides, if he wanted me gone, he could make that happen at any time. He hasn't. He doesn't want to risk losing the support of what shareholders he has at the moment."

"I suppose." She didn't look convinced. "But why should we risk the lawsuit and your reputation when there's a simple solution."

JT grew apprehensive when he realized she'd concocted a plan in that nimble brain of hers. "And that is?"

"We appear as if we're truly married. I'll move in here. We'll let ourselves be seen around town looking like lovebirds. Meanwhile you keep talking to your family."

A simple solution? Maybe on the surface. Definitely for her. But with Violet living here, JT knew it was only a matter of time before he trampled their bargain and made her his wife for real. And then what? He just let her go in a month? Impossible. Once he made her his, there was no going back.

"Sounds perfect," he heard himself say and wondered just how long it would remain so.

* * *

Beneath Scarlett's watchful eye, Violet packed a suitcase full of essentials and ignored most of her sister's questions.

"At least tell me this," Scarlett said. "Are you going to give the man a chance to rock your world?"

Violet sat down on the bed beside her sister. "I'm afraid that if I do that by the time we get divorced I'll be madly in love with him."

"But wouldn't it be worth discovering he's madly in love with you, too?"

"JT's right. Your happiness with Logan makes you want everyone else to find love." Violet shook her head. "It's not where JT and I are heading."

"You're just afraid. Before Logan, I was afraid, too. But trusting him—trusting myself—let me see with my heart as well as my head. All I'm suggesting is that you do the same thing."

"JT doesn't want to let me in. Trying to get to know him is like slogging through mud. Forward progress is slow and exhausting."

"But it's still progress."

"And what if I do get to know him only to discover that he's been damaged so badly he won't be able to accept love much less return it."

"If anyone can fix him, that person is you."

Scarlett's faith strengthened Violet. Was it possible that what had started out as an inspired business strategy could become a viable, satisfying and permanent merger?

"We're having a party at JT's ranch on Tuesday. I need you, Logan and Harper to come for moral support."

"Of course we'll come, but you don't really need us. You and JT will do great together. I think you make a wonderful team. I'll bet Tiberius did too. It's probably why he left the stock to you instead of to JT with the caveat that you couldn't dispose of it until far in the future."

Ever since the reading of his will, Violet had wondered about Tiberius's motivation for doing so as well. Why had he given her the stock and forced her to hold on to it knowing that she wouldn't be able to vote?

Plagued by questions she'd never know the answer to, Violet drove to JT's ranch and arrived at three in the afternoon. JT's housekeeper took charge of Violet's luggage and informed her that JT was in the barn. Curious, Violet went in search of him.

To describe JT's property as a ranch was a little misleading. What he had was a first-class training facility for show horses. The barn was a state-of-the-art structure with an impressive lobby whose walls were lined with large photos of expensive-looking horses doing dressage or jumping fences. The centerpiece of the room was a large bronze horse and female rider. Violet wondered if it had been modeled after JT's grandmother.

Off the lobby were several offices, currently empty. A door toward the back had a sign on it that indicated it led to the barn. Violet pushed her way through. She expected to be hit with heat, noise and stench, but it was a comfortable eighty degrees, and the few sounds that reached her ear were muted crunching and an occasional nose clearing. As for the smell, whatever air conditioning JT had incorporated into his design also pulled the dust from the air as well as the strongest of the horsey odors of hay, sweat and manure.

The concrete floor between the stalls was newly swept and free of dust. Violet wandered along, peering into stalls as she went. With each step she took, she found herself growing more and more calm. By the time she rounded a corner and spotted JT, down on one knee, wrapping some sort of poultice around a horse's knee, she was humming.

"Hi," she said, stopping ten feet from the large horse.

JT glanced up at her greeting and offered her a lopsided grin that made her heart jerk almost painfully. He wore camel-colored jodhpurs and knee-high boots. A navy polo shirt showed off the strong column of his throat and his powerful biceps.

"I'll be just a couple minutes more, then I can give you a tour of the place."

"Take your time."

She was enjoying the view. After not seeing JT for five days, she'd almost been able to convince herself that the way she'd melted beneath his kisses had been a symptom of her shock at learning what Tiberius had left her and reaction to her impulsive and speedy wedding. Then he'd returned and she'd proposed that they move in together. She could deny her feelings to Harper and Scarlett, but it was a lot harder to lie to herself.

She was hoping the chemistry between her and JT would combust and land them in bed together. Admitting it made her giddy. She'd disavowed the truth long enough. She wanted JT Stone in a big way and her subconscious had positioned her perfectly to act on those feelings.

"You ready?"

While she'd been coming to grips with her desires, JT had finished with the horse and a groom was leading it away.

"Sure."

JT guided her down the row of stalls, telling her a little bit about all the different horses.

"Until I stepped into the barn, I didn't realize this was a training facility," she exclaimed as he opened one of the stall doors and stepped inside. "How many horses do you have here?"

"We have fifty in training. They're all housed on this side. Across the arena is a whole other line of stalls where we keep horses for sale and the mares who are either in foal or who have babies. There's another forty over there."

"So, this is much more than a hobby for you."

"Not really. Vic manages the facility and deals with all the clients. Ralph is in charge of the training. Sid handles the sales. Bonnie keeps everyone healthy and watches over the mares. The place doesn't need me to run."

But from the way everyone they met asked his opinion or updated him on the barn's occupants, she gathered he was the heart and soul of the operation.

"This is Milo." JT laughed as they approached a stall and he had to push the horse's nose away from his pocket. "You get treats after you work, not before."

"Is he yours?"

"No. He belongs to a very talented ten-year-old girl. I've been his trainer for two years."

Keeping her gaze off her husband's handsome face—relaxed and unguarded for the first time she'd noticed—was necessary to avoid embarrassing herself with renewed pleas for his kisses. Instead, Violet stared at the horse. His back was well over five and a half feet off the ground. "A little girl rides this horse? That's a long way to fall."

"She's been riding since she was three. She has an amazing seat. The sort my grandmother had. And a real feel for the horse. She and Milo are quite a team. She'll be by for a lesson tomorrow. You can see for yourself."

"I'd like that."

JT slipped a halter over the horse's head and led him out of the stall. He held the lead rope out to her. "Can you hold him for me while I get my saddle and bridle?"

"Me?" She squeaked out the word after sizing up the enormous animal. "I've never handled a horse before."

"He's a big pussycat." JT put the rope in her hands. The horse took a step toward her, his ears forward. "Blow lightly into his nostril. He likes it and it will help you two get acquainted."

If it had been anyone but JT she might have assumed she was being pranked. Still, she felt silly following his instructions until the big horse pricked his ears and breathed back at her. On some sort of horse level they were communicating. By the time JT returned with a saddle and bridle, she had grown brave enough to pet the horse's soft nose and scratch his cheek.

"Looks like you two have hit it off," JT observed, setting the saddle carefully on the floor. He held out a brush. "Feel like giving me a hand?"

"Sure." She sounded more confident than she felt, but as she applied the brush to the animal's rich brown coat, she was overcome by a sense of peace. No wonder JT enjoyed his horses. Being with them grounded him firmly in the moment. Nothing mattered but the stroke of a brush against Milo's warm flank. It was the perfect counterpoint to the Las Vegas strip. "It's very Zen," she remarked.

"This is where I spend my days. I can handle just about any crisis after a few hours with the horses."

JT tossed the saddle onto Milo's back and fastened the cinch. While he worked, he spoke softly to the horse. Mostly nonsense, but it was his melodious tone that the horse listened and responded to. And he wasn't the only one. Violet found herself lulled as well.

"Can you hand me his bridle?"

His question snapped her out of her trance. Spending time with him like this meant she risked falling beneath JT's spell. Eventually, reality would intrude and she'd be in too deep. She just had to decide if getting hurt was worth the ride.

"Here you go."

The horse stood patiently while JT slipped off the halter and replaced it with the bridle. His actions were smooth and efficient. Remembering Scarlett's opinion about JT's hands, Violet watched as he fastened buckles, double-checked the fit of the cinch and soothed the horse with a stroke along his shoulder. By the time JT turned the horse toward the door that led into the arena, Violet was experiencing waves of heat that had nothing to do with the air temperature.

"You can watch me work Milo from there." JT pointed to the far corner where several chairs sat on a raised platform. He handed her a small towel. "We use crumb rubber as a footing to keep down the dust, but you'll probably want to wipe off the chair."

She glanced down at her flat sandals and pale blue skirt. "I guess I'm not really dressed for the barn, am I? If I'm going to visit in the future, I'd better wear jeans."

"And boots as well. Not everyone is as careful where they put their feet as Milo. I wouldn't want your pretty toes crushed."

"You think I have pretty toes?" His offhanded compliment made her grin.

His eyes glowed as he gave her a quick once-over. "I think you have pretty everything."

It was on the tip of her tongue to shoot back that he hadn't seen her everything, but then she recalled how he'd caught her skinny-dipping. At the time, he'd been so annoyed, it hadn't occurred to her to wonder how much he'd seen. Now, she suspected he'd glimpsed more than he let on.

"JT…" She had no idea how to convey what she wanted without giving away too much.

"Don't read too much into that," he told her. "You're beautiful. I find you attractive. It doesn't mean I can't control myself around you."

His words acted like an ice bath. "I'm not sure whether to be insulted or relieved."

Teeth flashing in a wry grin, JT led Milo to the center of the arena, leaving her standing in an emotional stew of her own making. When she'd set out to discover JT's true identity, the one a painful childhood had forced into hiding, she'd done so thinking that it would do him good to connect with people.

But after seeing the way he related to his barn staff and the joy he received from working with the horses, she realized he wasn't the damaged train wreck she'd assumed. He had a healthy outlet for his passion. A place of peace that benefited others. He wasn't exactly the loner she perceived him as—and felt sorry for. What else had she gotten wrong?

As Violet watched JT swing his long lean form into the saddle, she felt her perceptions shift. Her ego had fooled her into believing JT needed her when it was so obvious that he had things all figured out. He didn't need her to run to his rescue with a marriage of convenience or to draw him out of his shell for his own good. He'd been doing just fine on his own. Yet he'd accepted her help. It wasn't as if anyone could force JT to do something he didn't want to do.

Milo moved through a series of maneuvers that looked complex, but which the horse executed with ease. JT sat quietly in the saddle, appearing on first glance to be more passenger than active participant. But his concentration told a different story. Violet paid closer attention to his hands and legs. Still she couldn't discern what JT was doing to make the horse side-pass one direction for a few steps and then abruptly switch and go the other way.

JT was asking the horse to dance for him. His control over the animal was amazing. And sexy as hell.

After fifteen minutes he dropped the reins onto Milo's neck and patted the horse on both shoulders. His broad grin made Violet catch her breath. So this was what it felt like to swoon over a guy. She'd never experienced anything like it and wasn't sure how to behave now that her body had a mind of its own.

"That was amazing," Violet called, stepping off the platform.

JT dismounted and led Milo toward her. He stroked the horse's neck. "He did all the work." A slight sheen had developed on JT's forehead, contradicting his assertion.

"I don't believe that."

Their eyes connected and locked. JT's smile faded. What had been warm flesh a moment earlier became solid granite, and Violet's heart sank as she watched the doors slam shut over his thoughts. After several heartbeats, JT sucked in a deep lungful of air.

"I lied to you earlier," he said, his gaze probing hers, searching for answers, but giving nothing away.

The disappointment she'd felt seconds earlier faded slightly as her heartbeat accelerated beneath his intent expression. "About what?"

"About—"

"If you're all done with Milo, Boss, I can take him." A groom stepped into the arena. "Bonnie is in with Bullet and wonders if you can come look at the foal. She's wondering if we should call the vet."

"You're busy," Violet said, taking a half step back. "And I promised Harper I'd come in early today so we could discuss a joint promotion." As excuses went, it wasn't the best, but she needed time to regroup and figure out what she really wanted from JT before things started to happen. "We can talk after work tonight."

He caught her arm and kept her from moving away. The groom was fast approaching. Violet's heart thumped hard against her ribs as JT lowered his lips toward her ear.

"Your sister was right," he murmured, his warm breath sliding seductively over her skin. "I am hungry for you."

And then he was handing Milo off to the groom and striding away from her. Violet stared after him, her knees pressed together for stability because the strength had gone out of her muscles.

He was hungry for her?

He was hungry for her.

Well, that was good because she was hungry for him as well.

Seven

The ranch house was quiet and dark when JT let himself in at two in the morning. He'd cut his night short, unable to concentrate on business with thoughts of Violet bombarding him. He liked that she'd shown up at the barn today. Watching her overcome her anxiety about Milo had demonstrated that her interest had been genuine. Having her gaze follow his every move in the arena had been a pleasant distraction. He'd stepped up his game and showed off for her like a smitten teenage boy.

What he'd seen in her eyes made him want to throw her over his shoulder and carry her straight to his bedroom. Was she reconsidering the arrangement? He hoped so. But if she needed more convincing, he was ready for that as well.

Taking the stairs two at a time, JT headed down the hall to her bedroom. The door stood ajar, the room beyond dark. He let his eyes adjust and saw that the room was unoccupied. Reaching in, he flipped on the light. The room wasn't just empty. It showed no sign that anyone was staying there.

If JT hadn't seen Violet's car in the garage, he would've

assumed that she'd changed her mind and returned to Fontaine Chic. Perhaps she'd chosen a different room. There were four others she might prefer. But none showed signs of life. So where was she?

JT headed for the terrace outside the master suite. As soon as he stepped outside he heard the sound of splashing. She'd gone for a swim. He grabbed a set of swim trunks from a drawer and changed. It wasn't until he entered the closet to hang up his suit that he realized which bedroom she'd decided to sleep in.

His.

What had once been the empty half of the enormous his-and-hers closet was now filled with black dresses, casual daytime wear and several pairs of jeans. The shoe racks overflowed with pumps and sandals. He returned to the bedroom and discovered half his drawers filled with lacy lingerie, knit tops and scarves. The countertop in his bathroom bore perfume bottles and creams.

Holy hell.

He marched down the stairs at a deliberate pace, formulating how to approach Violet about this new development. It was one thing to perpetuate the myth of their happy marriage by living together. But sharing his room—his bed—with her was taking the playacting way too far.

JT stalked through the living room and stepped onto the pool deck. Violet stroked through the water, naked limbs breaking the surface and plunging back in again. Damn, but she was beautiful. Her movements were lazy, content. The exact opposite of the riotous emotions surging through JT.

He was standing at the edge of the pool before he even realized he'd moved. "I found all your things in my room. What's going on?"

"I got to thinking your dad might have spies in your employ. I don't want to give him any ammunition against you." She didn't meet his gaze, which made him wonder what she had to hide.

"I think you're giving him too much credit."

"Come for a swim. We can talk about it later."

He wanted to get it resolved right now. JT dove in and swam underwater toward her. With just the pool lights to see by, he didn't realize that she was naked until he was close enough to touch her.

He came up coughing.

"Are you all right?" She set her hands on his shoulders and peered at him.

"I thought we had an understanding about your skinny-dipping."

To his immense shock, she hooked her fingertips into the elastic waistband of his swim trunks and pulled it a couple inches away from his stomach. Her touch against his bare skin brought him to a swift and fierce arousal. He clenched his teeth to contain a groan.

"You should try it," she murmured, her smile come-hither. A second later he felt the snap against his belly as she let go. In a flash she was gone. Water splashed against his cheeks and blinded him as she dove sideways, swimming beyond his grasp in seconds.

Sputtering, he shook his head to clear his eyes and took off after her with a growl. It wasn't until he caught her at the edge of the pool and pinned her against the wall that he remembered she was naked. Her thighs tangled with his and she hooked one foot around his calf to anchor herself to him.

"Kiss me," she demanded, sliding her palms up the side of his neck and latching onto his hair. "Soft, slow, hard, deep. I don't care. Just make me lose myself."

His lips captured hers in a relentless assault that definitively declared that this time there would be no backpedaling, no stopping, no mercy. She accepted every stroke of his tongue, every nip of his teeth and gave him back frenzied desire and impatience. Her nails bit into his skin, her moans heightened his already explosive hunger. She writhed against him, her hips moving rhythmically against his erection, driving him wild.

He sucked the water from her neck, tasting chlorine and below that the sweetness of her skin. His breath caught as she threw her head back and offered him even more access. He wrapped his fingers around her delicate ribcage and lifted her until her perfect breasts bobbed above the water's surface. She wrapped her thighs around his waist as he locked his mouth over one hard nipple. With her wet heat pressed tight to his abdomen, he sucked and nibbled first one breast, then the other until her breath came in short, tight pants.

Her lithe body trembled in his arms as he grazed his fingertips down her spine and splayed his hands over the firm planes of her butt. She'd been working her hips in an ever-increasing rhythm. What she wanted, she wasn't getting and she unhooked her ankles from around his waist and let her feet drift to the pool bottom.

Once again he felt her tug on his trunks. This time she forced the fabric downward, freeing his erection. He hissed through his teeth as the pool water hit the sensitive head. The sound was followed a second later by his strangled moan as she closed her fingers around his hard length.

He slammed his mouth down over hers, plunging his tongue inward, all technique lost in the savage need to claim her. She matched his kiss with sweet ferocity, using her tongue and teeth to drive him wild.

"Give it all to me," she murmured, stroking him in ever more tantalizing sweeps as he sucked on her neck.

She parted her thighs and placed the tip of him at her entrance. He nudged firmly against her hot wet core, and almost cried out at the agony of holding back, but remained perfectly still.

"Protection," he garbled out the word, unsure how he was going let her go, walk all the way upstairs and fetch a condom from his nightstand.

"I'm on the pill." She arched her back and rocked her hips forward, embedding him inside her before her words fully registered.

The tightness of her encased him and nothing JT had ever dreamed of matched the reality of Violet naked and in his arms. He put his hands on her hips and settled himself deeper still, hanging onto his control for dear life so he could make the moment into something they would both find satisfying.

"You are amazing," he murmured as they rocked together in the pool, stirring the water as they kissed and caressed.

Time slowed. JT's world narrowed to the rush of air through his lungs, the surge of heat in his groin and the warm silk of Violet's skin caressing his.

"This is so much better than I imagined it would be," she whispered, her breath tickling his ear.

"You thought about it?"

He wandered his hands over her back and down her thighs as his lips drifted along her shoulder. She'd locked the soles of her feet against his calves to anchor herself in the weightlessness of the water. It gave her the leverage to add a little twisting motion to the rhythmic movements of her hips. The power of that move was close to blowing a hole in his willpower. He ground his teeth against a groan.

"Night and day since you first started showing up at Baccarat."

Her confession prompted him to offer one of his own. "Losing Rick to you was the best thing that ever happened to me."

"You don't say." Her chest vibrated with a sexy laugh, making her breasts shift tantalizingly against him. Her tight nipples were searing points of heat that quickened his breath.

"Or it was," he amended, unable to stave off the quickening of sensations any longer. "Until now."

He moved more strongly into her and felt her close tightly around him, forming a tight sheath. The friction was almost too intense to handle. But if her body brought him acute pleasure, her dreamy smile was a balm for his spirit.

And then he felt her body tighten and her focus sharpen. Using all his willpower to hold off his own release, he watched her climb higher and higher. Her eyes flew open. Her sharp gasp was followed by a shudder. Only then did JT let himself go.

His orgasm came with such speed and intensity he wondered how he'd held it off as long as he had. The pool, Violet's face, all vanished behind a wave of black. He was cast into the heavens. A thousand pinpoints of lights guided his flight. They rushed at him, through him. Each one left a mark, a permanent reminder of this perfect moment.

He came back to earth and realized that his chest hurt. The pain was caused by either his tortured lungs or the impossibly swift beat of his heart.

"Best sex ever," Violet murmured, framing his face with her hands and smiling at him. Equally winded, she seemed less shaken by their turbulent lovemaking. "I knew it would be great with you, but wow."

He couldn't match her openness. What he felt for her was too immense, too raw.

"Yes." It wasn't eloquent, but it was heartfelt. "Wow."

The corners of her eyes crinkled as her grin grew. "Am I still banned from skinny-dipping?"

Captivated by her happiness, he shook his head. "In fact, I plan to burn every bathing suit in the place."

* * *

"You're smiling a lot this morning," Harper commented, eyeing Violet over a glass of orange juice.

It was Tuesday morning and the Fontaine sisters were meeting for their weekly breakfast, this morning in Scarlett's office at Fontaine Richesse. Usually they met on Wednesdays, but Violet and JT were having their belated wedding reception at the ranch that evening and they all figured it would be a late night.

"Am I?" Violet sipped her green tea and tried to look nonchalant.

"Of course she's smiling," Scarlett put in. "She and JT have been shacked up for three days of postnuptial bliss."

"I don't think it can be called 'shacked up' if we're married," Violet corrected her.

Harper frowned in confusion. "You're living together now?"

"If you'd pay attention to something other than your hotel once in a while," Scarlett began, "you'd know that Preston showed up here and threatened to sue JT and Violet for fraud if their marriage wasn't real."

"He can't possibly have a case," Harper said.

Scarlett smirked. "Not anymore."

"What I mean," Harper continued, shooting Scarlett a look, "is there's nothing in the corporate bylaws insisting the marriage must be real, just legal."

"We were concerned that by taking us to court, he could prevent me from voting my shares at the upcoming shareholder meeting and remain CEO."

A line formed between Harper's brows. "I guess that's possible. I just don't know how likely."

"We didn't want to take the chance."

"And because of that your relationship has become physical?"

Violet resisted looking Scarlett's way for fear that her

sister's expression would make her laugh. Harper was a little too literal and that often kept her from finding the humor in a situation.

"Not exactly…"

"He's crazy about her and vice versa," Scarlett explained. "Unlike you and Ashton where you make each other crazy."

"I have every right to be crazy," Harper insisted. "The restaurant is behind schedule because he hasn't been here to make decisions. And when he does make decisions, it puts us even more behind schedule because he wants to change things."

Scarlett gave her sister a doubting look. "To say nothing of the fact that he's gorgeous and sexy and your DVR is full of his television series."

Harper's scowl would have been more intimidating if she'd been able to meet Scarlett's gaze. "It seems to me that you and Logan were in that drive-each-other-crazy place less than a month ago."

Scarlett and her security-expert fiancé were so madly in love these days it was hard to remember just how much they used to antagonize each other

"That was then. Now we just drive each other crazy with passion."

Harper's response was a rude noise. Violet chuckled. She loved her sisters. To outsiders, it sometimes appeared as if the three of them didn't get along, but in fact for three women who'd not known each other until their grandfather introduced them five years ago, they were as tight as siblings who'd grown up together. Maybe even tighter because there were no childhood battle scars.

"Putting aside all the *crazy* talk for a second," Violet said, turning to Scarlett, "you said you had something important you wanted to discuss with me."

After some meaningful eye contact with Harper, Scarlett went to her desk and brought back two files. She held one suspended in Violet's direction and said, "I know I've told you a little about the files I inherited from Tiberius. This one is about Preston Rhodes."

Curious, Violet accepted the file and quickly scanned it. The contents included old newspaper clippings about a flash flood drowning in the desert near Las Vegas as well as a grainy group photo of seven rough-looking young men. Below that was a piece of paper with a woman's name and contact information on it. Charity Rimes.

"What am I looking at?" Violet asked.

"Grady and I think the man we know as Preston Rhodes is actually a local Las Vegas kid who was supposed to have drowned during a flash flood back in 1970."

Violet glanced at Harper and saw in her sister's expression the same skepticism she was feeling. "So, the newspaper report got it wrong? It wasn't this George Barnes guy, but Preston Rhodes. How is that possible?"

"I think JT's father—whose real name I think is George Barnes—switched identities with Preston Rhodes after Preston was killed in the flash flood."

"That's a pretty wild theory," Harper interjected.

"Why would he do that?" Violet wanted to know.

"From what information Tiberius had gathered about George Barnes, he'd been a juvenile delinquent on his way to a bad end. Preston Rhodes had a bright future ahead of him. A rich kid with no family. He'd left California, where he'd grown up, to take a road trip to the East Coast where he would be attending college. Think of how easy it would have been for George to simply step into Preston's shoes."

Violet skimmed the clippings, and realized that Scarlett's explanation was sounding more reasonable by the second. And after meeting JT's father, she had no trouble believing the man was ruthless and unscrupulous enough to steal another man's identity and fortune. But what would this mean for JT? She imagined how devastating this revelation would be to him. Finding out your father had stolen someone's identity was a far cry from merely worrying that he was making poor business decisions.

With her stomach in knots, Violet set aside the file. "I don't know what you want me to do with this."

"You should talk to Charity Rimes. Tiberius tracked her down for a reason."

"Who is she?" Harper asked.

"She's the writer doing a story on a series of killings in Los Angeles back in the sixties. I don't know much about the story other than they never caught the guy. I let the whole matter drop when I realized it wasn't any of my business. But things have changed. JT married you. That makes him family." Scarlett extended a second file. "Which brings me to this. I don't know if you want to read it or not, but since you're now involved with JT, I thought I should at least give you the choice."

"Tiberius had a file on JT." Violet wondered why he hadn't kept it in his home office. "Have you read it?"

"I was tempted to when I first suspected his dad of stealing Preston Rhodes's identity, but then I decided it wasn't my place to know his secrets." She extended the file to Violet.

The amount of paper contained in the manila folder took Violet by surprise. This wasn't a simple summary of his unhappy childhood and adolescent acting out. Tiberius had spent time and energy researching his nephew. Probably in preparation for renewing their relationship.

Reading the file would be a shortcut to learning most everything that had gone into developing JT's character. No doubt she'd learn things about him he wouldn't appreciate her knowing. But maybe talking about the most painful events would help him to heal. And if he healed, perhaps he could then open himself up to love.

As soon as the thought occurred, Violet reined it in. Was she hoping that if she fixed him he'd be so grateful he'd never want their marriage to end? They'd been married less than two weeks and she was already figuring out ways to manipulate him. Better to let JT tell her what he wished her to know when he wanted her to know it.

"I shouldn't." Violet tried to hand the folder back to Scarlett, but she put up her hands.

"Keep it. Burn it. Give it to JT. I don't care, but I don't want it back in my possession." Scarlett glanced at Harper who was glaring at her smartphone. "I'm already the keeper of more secrets than I'm comfortable knowing."

Violet knew Scarlett was referring to the file she'd found on Harper's mother. The one with the potential to turn Harper's life upside down. From her calm demeanor, Violet suspected that Scarlett hadn't yet decided to share with her half sister what was in the file.

"I have to go," Harper said, getting to her feet. "I emailed Ashton another round of head chef candidates and he has fifteen minutes of free time to talk about them."

As soon as Harper left the room, Scarlett fetched another file from her desk. "I wasn't kidding when I said I'm uncomfortable with the secrets I'm keeping."

"Are you planning to tell her what you discovered about her mother?"

"I'm going to tell you what's going on and I want you to help me decide."

"Very well." When Violet had first found out about the file on Harper's mother, she'd sympathized with Scarlett's dilemma. Now she had a similar problem—what to do with the files on JT and his father. "What did Harper's mother do?"

"She had a brief affair during an extended period of time where her husband was away on business."

"Penelope?" Violet couldn't believe Harper's uptight

mother could have done anything that rash. "It's so unlike her."

Scarlett opened the file and displayed the black-and-white photos of a young Penelope Fontaine and a handsome man in a hot embrace.

"Apparently being married to our father could push even the most conservative person into reckless behavior," Scarlett remarked, sounding more tired than wry.

"I'm sure Harper will be shocked and embarrassed by her mother's actions, but it was a long time ago." Violet wanted to reject what her eyes were seeing. "But I don't understand why you think it will devastate her."

"Because she was born nine months later."

It took several seconds for Scarlett's meaning to penetrate. "You mean…?"

"Harper isn't a Fontaine."

"Are you sure?"

"Unfortunately, yes." Scarlett closed her eyes. Pain raced across her features. "How can I tell her that?"

When Harper found out the truth about her parentage, she'd be destroyed.

"I don't think you should," Violet said at last.

Harper had the education and the business savvy to run Fontaine Resorts and Hotels, not to mention the ambition and a seemingly inexhaustible store of energy, and she'd spent her whole life preparing to run the family business. In the last five years Violet had learned enough about Harper's character to guess she'd bow out of the contest to determine the next CEO.

A year ago Violet would have been excited at the prospect of moving into the lead. She had Harper's ambition and drive, but of late she'd been thinking less about her career and more about her personal life. The transition had been subtle, but she suspected it had begun around the time JT started showing up at Baccarat.

As for Scarlett, the former child star had recently decided to return part-time to acting. Splitting her time and attention between L.A. and Las Vegas meant she'd already decided not to actively compete for the CEO position. Nor was Violet convinced Scarlett had ever truly given herself props for the work she'd done to make Fontaine Richesse the standout hotel it was.

Scarlett nodded somberly and returned the photos to the file. "It's what I think, too. No good will come of telling her."

With too many secrets weighing her down, Violet left Scarlett's office and headed to her suite to find a dress to wear to her belated wedding reception. She'd been so preoccupied with the details for the party that she'd forgotten all about herself.

In the back of her closet was a pale pink chiffon dress embellished with blush and silver sequins on the bodice. Three years ago, she'd bought it to wear to a charity event that at the last minute she'd been unable to attend. Despite having spent a fortune on the dress and the matching pink slingbacks, Violet couldn't bring herself to return the ensemble. She knew eventually she'd be attending a party where she could wear it. Her wedding reception fit the bill.

As she was exiting her suite, her gaze fell on the files Scarlett had given her. She hadn't decided what to tell JT yet. He'd been through so much already. But she didn't want to go behind his back on something as serious as his father stealing another man's identity. Leaving JT's file on her home office desk, she slipped Preston's and the one containing information on Charity Rimes into her briefcase and exited the suite.

Eight

"You look gorgeous." Impatient for a last minute alone with her, JT linked his fingers with Violet's and tugged her toward the stairs. They had fifteen minutes until their guests were due to arrive.

"Is it silly that I'm nervous?" With her free hand, she smoothed her skirt and tugged at her neckline.

"Yes." He lifted her hand to his lips and kissed her knuckles. "Everyone here tonight will be a friend. And I'll be at your side the entire evening."

To his gratification, she looked reassured. "And you're sure I look okay?"

"You're perfect." He wasn't accustomed to her lack of confidence and wondered how someone as beautiful and charming as Violet could doubt herself.

"Because the dress is three years old."

"It looks brand-new."

"That's because it is. I've never worn it."

The subtleties of a woman's mind when it came to fashion were lost on JT. "Let's go have a glass of champagne. I want to make a toast."

He led her outside to the pool deck. Because of the number of guests who would be coming, they'd opted to open the living room's glass walls so people could enjoy the night air. Tiny white lights decorated the palm trees and shrubs, adding a festive air. A bottle of champagne and two flutes awaited them in the outdoor seating area.

JT popped the cork and poured the sparkling liquid. He handed one to Violet and cleared his throat.

"To you. Thank you for marrying me. It's been a long time since anyone has acted in my best interests instead of their own. Your optimism and knack for thinking outside the box have enabled me to shake loose the cobwebs and let in the sunlight. No matter what happens a month from now, I am ready for whatever the future brings."

The toast was awkward and sappy, but Violet didn't seem to notice. Her eyes remained riveted on him as he spoke. Her faith had given him wings. His father could throw every vile trick in the book his way and JT would let it all roll off him. It was impossible to convey the depth of his appreciation for all Violet had given him.

"I'm glad to hear you say that," Violet told him, clinking her glass to his. "And I hope I can continue to make good things happen for you."

"All I need is for you—"

"There's the couple of the hour," a man announced from the living room. It was Brent. He'd flown in from Charlotte earlier that day and was staying at Titanium.

Fighting back a sigh at the interruption, JT towed his wife to greet his cousin. After introductions were made, JT caught a subtle nod of approval from Brent and relaxed. His cousin's opinion mattered. Everyone else could go to hell.

Shortly after Brent's arrival, the floodgates opened and guests began to pour in. In addition to family and friends, they'd invited many business associates from Las Vegas.

Waitstaff circled with glasses of champagne and fancy

hors d'oeuvres. With the help of her catering manager, Violet had organized the party within a week and the entire evening flowed without a hitch. And with each hour that passed, JT found himself a little more enthralled with his wife.

She charmed everyone with her quick laugh and positive outlook. He was glad the evening called for them to navigate the room as a couple, because he couldn't bring himself to move more than an arm's length away.

The floral scent she wore made his head spin with shameless thoughts of what he intended to do with her later. He had a hard time keeping his hands off her bare arms.

"You've been monopolizing your wife the whole evening," Scarlett complained, tugging Violet away. "Harper and I need a couple minutes with her."

JT continued to move about the room, but what little enjoyment he'd had in the evening had been leached away the second Violet had gone. More than anything he wished everyone would just go home.

After what seemed like hours, but had been no more than fifteen minutes, Violet returned to him.

"I missed you," he murmured, after welcoming her with a quick kiss.

By the end of the night, he accepted that he was the luckiest man in the world. As they stood in the doorway and bid the last of their guests goodbye, JT became aware of a raging need to have her all to himself. The instant she closed the front door and let out an enormous sigh of relief, he lifted her onto his shoulder and headed upstairs.

At first she was too startled to protest, but she'd rediscovered her voice by the time he reached the second floor.

"Have you lost your mind? There are still things to clean up and I need to thank the caterer. Put me down."

"She left twenty minutes ago. You and I are all alone." He deposited her on the king-size bed in the master suite. "Finally."

"We've been alone these last four days," she reminded him, sliding his shirt buttons free.

He tugged the thin strap off her shoulder and buried his face in her neck. Her scent had been driving him crazy all night. It reminded him of two days ago when he'd...

JT's brain short-circuited. Her busy hands had unfastened his zipper and slipped inside his pants to cup him. He groaned, his erection growing impossibly hard beneath her clever touch.

"Slow down," he commanded, snagging her wrists and pinning them onto the pillows above her head. "We have all night."

"But I need you now." She slowly gyrated her hips in the way she knew made him crazy. "And we're both ready. Why can't you just go with it?"

Because he'd been *going with it* for four days and had yet to learn all he wanted to about pleasing her. Their chemistry was so explosive. He'd never been with anyone like her. Eager, passionate, sexy as hell. She could look at him from across the room and he'd want her. His obsession grew worse every day. It interfered with his ability to focus at work and distracted him from the purpose of their marriage in the first place: gaining the stock he needed to oust his father.

"You want me to go with it?" he asked, rolling off the bed so he could strip off his shirt, pants and underwear.

"Very much." She watched him with greedy eyes as she got to her knees and stripped off her fancy cocktail dress. Clad in a strapless bra and silk bikini underwear, she waited for him in the middle of the bed, her hands on her hips in brazen challenge.

"Very well." His smile acknowledged that if she wanted to play, he could too. "Turn and face the headboard."

Surprise and uncertainty flickered in her eyes for a

moment, but after a short hesitation she did as he asked. Peering at him over her shoulder, she asked, "Like this?"

"Just like that."

He moved onto the bed and came up behind her. Her beautiful back was a feature he'd not had much opportunity to explore these past few days and it was worth his attention. The first thing he did was pop the catch on her bra so he could appreciate her delicate spine without hindrance.

The elastic that held the bra in place had created indentations on her skin. He bent his head and kissed the marks while drawing his fingertips along her narrow shoulders. She quivered beneath his light touch and her breath hissed out in a long sigh.

Little by little she relaxed as his fingers explored the contours of her shoulder blades, lightly massaged her nape and drifted down her arms. As he sucked on the place where her neck and shoulder came together, she leaned back against him and savored the prod of his erection against her butt.

"That's nice," she murmured, arms straight at her sides, palms resting on his thighs. "But what can I do for you?"

"Enjoy this. That's all I ask."

Violet didn't ask what *this* was. She was feeling lazy and aroused. Her skin was delighted to receive all the consideration JT was lavishing on it. Despite the insistent throbbing between her thighs, she hoped he'd treat her entire body to the same attention to detail.

"You have a beautiful back. I love the dimples right here." He pointed out the particular spot with a soft caress.

"You know there's a whole 'nother side of me that would love some attention."

He kissed her neck. "Such as?"

"My breasts."

Following her command, he grazed his palms up her sides. She caught her breath as his long fingers stroked across her sensitive nipples, and exhaled as he swallowed her fullness in his hands.

"Better?"

"Much."

"Where else would you like me to touch you?"

She sucked her lower lip between her teeth and bit down as his hands moved over her abdomen and caressed the tops of her thighs. She rotated her hips as the ache built deep in her loins. Undulating waves of longing pulsed through her.

"Here."

Shaking with need, she snagged his strong hands and urged them toward her mound. He'd knelt with his knees on either side of hers. Now, he nudged her thighs apart, spreading her legs wide, opening her. She gulped at the brush of cool air against her tender flesh. Anticipation of his possession aroused her still more until she thought she'd go mad with longing.

"JT, this is not fair."

"What's not fair?"

He turned her face toward him and rubbed his lips over hers, mingling their breath, but not giving her the satisfaction of his tongue. She wanted a deep, penetrating kiss. Something to momentarily take her mind off the painful throbbing at her core.

"You aren't taking advantage of having me in this position."

"No?" He nipped at her neck. "What should I be doing?"

She wagged her hips, rubbing herself against his erection. He groaned. At last his fingers slid into the cleft between her thighs. She almost cried out at the pleasure.

"You're so hot," he muttered, his tone guttural and low. "It makes me crazy how wet you get."

"Show me." She bent forward at the waist and let her hands fall to the mattress.

From between his teeth came a savage curse. JT seized her hips and in one swift move plunged into her. The position offered Violet a whole new range of sensation and she released a soft "oh" of surprise.

JT kissed her back. "Are you okay?"

"Wonderful. Perfect." She sucked in a breath and laughed. "In fact, it's fabulous. Keep going."

Snorting his amusement, JT began rocking against her. Faster than Violet would have imagined, she felt an orgasm rising to meet her. And when JT reached between her thighs and plucked at the knot of nerves, she went off like a rocket.

"Yes!"

JT picked up his pace and continued to fondle her. To Violet's intense shock, she didn't settle to earth on a golden cloud like normal, but felt another pulse of pleasure stab her. She quaked as her second climax roared through her.

Before she had a chance to marvel at the wonder of it all, JT dove into her hard two more times and was claimed by his own release. He collapsed onto her back, his chest vibrating with laughter.

Catching her around the waist, he shifted his weight and rolled them onto the mattress. They landed in a tangle of limbs. JT pushed himself up so he could peer into her face. He had to brush her hair away from her eyes before he could meet her gaze.

"Did you just come twice?" he demanded in amazement.

She grinned. "I believe I did."

"You are the most incredible woman I've ever been with."

His words were sweet music to her ears. She'd never had a man appreciate her lovemaking the way JT did. And the feeling was mutual. He made her feel like a goddess.

It was heady stuff for a girl who'd too often been self-conscious in bed.

"It's only because you're such a wonderful lover."

He sobered. "Don't do that."

"Do what?" She couldn't imagine what she'd said to make him look so unhappy.

"Downplay how terrific you are."

She squirmed a little beneath his intense regard. "I get uncomfortable when anyone says nice things about me."

"Why is that?"

"I guess I don't always believe that I deserve it."

"That's ridiculous."

She lifted one shoulder and let it fall. "Ever since I was three, I knew my father didn't want to have anything to do with me. I thought that was my fault."

"But you know it wasn't."

It was easier to talk about her insecurities when she was staring at his chin. His outraged expression made her feel even worse. "These days, sure. But it hurt for a long time and I forged some armor that I wear when I'm feeling vulnerable."

"You don't need to wear it around me."

He kissed her with reverent gentleness, endeavoring to heal her hurts with tenderness. Violet's chest ached. Falling deep in love with him was so easy when he offered her his support like this. But she couldn't help but be saddened by the fact that he wouldn't let her help him in kind.

In the calm after their earlier passion, JT and Violet snuggled in his big bed, their hands offering comfort and connection, their lips meeting in affection. They exchanged no words. The union of their bodies was an effortless way to communicate.

Violet didn't return to the problem of how to broach the subject of his father's possible identity theft until almost five in the morning. JT lay on his stomach beside her, hands buried under the pillow, his features softened by sleep. She reclined on her side, head propped in her hand and watched him. Memories of their lovemaking moved through her nerves like a breeze through a weeping willow. Her hormones stirred lazily in response.

Too wide awake to sleep and knowing she'd be tempted to rouse JT if she kept staring at all his naked glory, Violet slipped from the bed and put on a robe. The moratorium regarding her skinny-dipping had been lifted and she padded downstairs. Earlier, their hasty retreat to the bedroom meant that the living room's glass walls had not been closed. Nor had the lights been turned off anywhere. Violet moved through the various rooms and left a trail of darkness in her wake.

The warm night air pressed against her skin as she stripped off the robe and used the stairs to enter the pool. Despite the water's comfortable temperature, she shivered. Swimming had always been both a way to exercise and a method for sorting through whatever problems she was having.

She'd been on both her high school and college swim teams. Maybe she hadn't been the fastest competitor, but driven by a fierce desire to catch her father's attention, she'd worked harder than most. All in vain, of course, because it wasn't as if he'd ever attended a meet. Eventually she'd accepted that their lack of a relationship was her father's loss not hers, and she'd learned a valuable lesson in loyalty. Never would she let anyone down. If she gave her word, she would move heaven and earth to keep it.

Which brought her to the file on Preston Rhodes. Tomorrow she would show JT what it contained. With the stockholder meeting approaching and his father still holding all the cards, if they had the chance to discredit him, they needed to take it. But was JT ready to destroy the last member of his immediate family?

Violet left the pool and grabbed a quick shower in the pool house before returning to the master suite. Dropping the damp towel on the floor, she climbed naked between the sheets. Convinced she'd left and returned without waking JT, she was surprised when his arms snaked around her waist, drawing her firmly against his side.

With his face buried in the crook of her neck, he murmured, "You smell like chlorine."

"Impossible. I showered before coming back here."

"It's barely detectible, but there." He pressed his lips against the pulse in her throat. "I wouldn't have thought you'd have enough energy for a swim. I guess I'll have to do better at wearing you out."

She laughed at the sting of his nip. "I didn't swim. I waded. It isn't always about burning off excess energy. Sometimes it just feels good to hang out and enjoy the scenery."

"Is that what you were doing tonight? Enjoying the scenery?"

"And thinking."

"About what?"

She hesitated, unsure she wanted to disrupt JT's good mood. "About the upcoming stockholders' meeting and the shares we still need."

JT stopped kissing her neck and lay very still. "I don't want you worrying about that. This is my battle to fight, you've done enough."

"This is my fight, too." Although she was certain he was merely trying to protect her, Violet bristled. "Don't shut me out. I can help."

"My father. My problem."

"We're married. Our problem."

"It's a paper marriage."

"Don't do that," she told him, an ache building in her throat. "Don't shut me out."

He heaved a sigh and rolled away from her, coming to rest on his back. She pursued him across the mattress, sitting up so she could peer down at his face. His eyes remained hard, but his hand scooped her hip, thumb moving rhythmically against her waist.

"You never stop pushing, do you?"

She set her left hand on his chest. His grandmother's ring snared the dawning light drifting in through the open window. They both stared at it.

At long last she asked, her voice scarcely rising about a whisper, "Do you want me to?"

They both knew what she wanted to know. Did she take off the ring and walk away from the marriage? Or did she stay and did they both commit to making their relationship grow and strengthen?

"What you're asking from me isn't easy."

"I know." Relief made her dizzy. He hadn't immediately challenged her bluff. "But we're a good team and we need each other."

"You need me?"

"Don't sound so surprised." Being with him she felt a part of something bigger than either of them could ever be alone. "I'm not as unselfish as you believe." She laid her cheek on his chest and snuggled against his side. "You make me feel safe and secure. I know I can count on you."

"You never seem as if you need anyone's help."

"I may be everyone's cheerleader, but once in a while, I appreciate it when someone has my back." She lifted her head and met his gaze. "I like it when you're that someone."

"You know you will always be able to call on me for anything."

She gave him a wistful smile. It wasn't a passionate declaration of love, but it was a heartfelt promise he would never betray. And she accepted at this moment it was everything he was capable of giving.

In close proximity to the kitchen, an extensive covered patio contained a barbeque pit, a seating area with fireplace and flat screen television and a table that seated eight. Unless he was entertaining, JT rarely used the space. Most often he ate a quick meal in the kitchen before heading out to the hotel or the barn. But since Violet had moved in, he'd spent a fair amount of time enjoying all the amenities.

This morning, the table was strewn with bowls of fruit, plates of bacon, eggs and waffles. More food than either of them could eat. But as soon as Violet had handed him the file on his father, he'd lost all appetite.

"This can't be real." He set the file aside and rubbed the bridge of his nose where a headache was starting.

"Maybe," Violet replied, her tone neutral. "Maybe not."

"Have you read the whole thing?"

"Twice."

"It's ridiculous. My father grew up in California. I've heard him speak about his parents and his childhood in Los Angeles. He's not some wannabe thug from Las Vegas."

"That was my exact attitude when Scarlett brought it to my attention. I thought the whole thing was crazy and told her so."

A chill formed in JT's chest. "Who else knows about this?"

Her gaze sharpened as she caught onto his irritation. "Just Harper. She was there when Scarlett gave me the file. You don't need to worry about her. She won't say anything."

"Do you have to share everything about me with your sisters?" His aggrieved tone made her flinch, but his resentment bit too deep for him to apologize. He'd barely gotten comfortable sharing bits of himself with Violet and it made him surly to think that her sisters knew a devastating secret about his father.

"They won't say anything," she said, using her fork to shred the uneaten waffle on her plate.

"I don't know that."

His logical side reminded him that behaving as if he didn't trust her would create problems between them. But he couldn't ignore his emotions as they sliced him with a double-edged sword of alarm and resentment.

"Well, I do."

Hearing the conviction in Violet's tone, JT let the matter drop, recognizing the true source of his disquiet was not Violet or her sisters. He didn't want to believe his father had stolen someone's identity.

Because if his father wasn't just greedy or ambitious, but despicable beyond belief, couldn't that badness have been passed down to his son?

Wasn't JT the reason his mother had died? He'd been acting out, defying her, and she'd died of an overdose. His adult brain could reason that she'd chosen to take the pills, but he was haunted by the question of whether she'd been so upset with him that she'd taken too many. And there was no denying if he'd come home straight after school that day, she might still be alive.

He stared at the information contained in the file about George Barnes and Preston Rhodes and wondered what the reporter from L.A. knew. "When were you planning to call this Charity Rimes person?"

"I thought it was something we should do together. Perhaps even go to Los Angeles and meet with her in person." She shrugged. "Or we could drop it entirely. Like you said, it's ridiculous that your father stole someone's identity in 1970."

Violet was too forthright to be able to hide her confusion or disappointment at his rejection of the information she'd brought him. Nor could JT point to where this surge of loyalty was coming from. What did he think he owed his father? Preston had never done anything with JT's best interests in mind.

"Let me think about it," JT muttered and Violet nodded, the gesture stiff and jerky.

Because if they discovered his father actually was George Barnes, JT would then have to decide if he should send his father to prison or simply use the information to blackmail Preston into stepping down? Neither appealed to JT. He'd much rather defeat his father the old-fashioned way: by being a better businessman.

Violet finished applying her makeup and checked her appearance in the bathroom mirror. She'd done an acceptable job of hiding the dark circles under her eyes caused by her sleepless night, but nothing could be done about the churning in her stomach.

Right after breakfast, JT had headed to the barn where he'd remained for the rest of the day. As difficult as it had been to give him space when her instincts demanded she make him feel better, she'd stayed in the house and hoped he would forgive her for delivering such a difficult message.

Her wait had been in vain. At three she'd discovered that JT had already left for Titanium. He'd gone to work without letting her know he was leaving. That meant she'd have to be patient for a little while longer and hope uncertainty wouldn't eat her alive.

Instead of heading to Fontaine Chic where she knew a hundred decisions awaited her, Violet detoured to Scarlett's hotel and tracked her sister down in the casino. Scarlett would be eager to learn how Violet's conversation with JT had gone and Violet needed a sympathetic ear.

"I was right to fear that JT wouldn't react well to Tiberius's suspicions about Preston," Violet said, as they wound their way past a hundred slot machines to a dessert bar on the second floor. "And I couldn't blame him for being upset with me."

"You did nothing wrong," Scarlett reminded her.

"I feel as if I did. He was upset because you and Harper knew what was in the file and was worried you'd tell someone. He didn't believe me when I told him you wouldn't. I wish he trusted me."

"I'm sure he does. Remember you'd just brought him shocking information about his father. No matter how strained their relationship or how badly he wants his dad to step down as CEO, Preston is still JT's father."

"Is it crazy that I'm afraid the progress we've made in our relationship has been dealt a deadly blow today?"

"Not crazy at all. But I do think you're worrying for nothing." Scarlett looped her arm through Violet's and pulled her before a glass display case loaded with absolutely scrumptious-looking treats. "We'll take one of those chocolate shells filled with white chocolate mousse and a hazelnut gelato-filled cream puff with Kahlua chocolate sauce," Scarlett said to the counter person. Catching Violet staring at her in astonishment, Scarlett grinned. "What? Heartache calls for fancy desserts."

Violet carried the tray of desserts to a table by the window that overlooked the extensive, beautifully landscaped grounds at the back of the hotel. Scarlett arrived seconds later with cups of espresso.

"I don't know why I was so caught off guard by JT's reaction." Violet dug into the white chocolate mousse. "Barely two weeks ago we were little more than casual acquaintances and today I told him his father might be a criminal."

"Do you really think you two have ever been casual?"

Scarlett asked. "You may not have been friends, but there was a strong pull between you. I saw it that night in Baccarat."

"I've been attracted to him since the first time I saw him."

"I'll bet he felt the same way. Wouldn't surprise me if Tiberius warned him off."

"I'm sure the issue never came up."

"So how did you two leave things?"

"JT is deciding if we should contact Charity Rimes."

"What do you think he'll do?"

Violet shook her head. "I think he'll want to do the right thing, but loyalty is really important to him and no matter how complicated their relationship is, JT will feel as if he's betraying his father." She finished the mousse-filled chocolate cup and began on the half of the cream puff Scarlett pushed onto her plate. "You know, I think he was almost as upset that I'm the one delivering this news about his father as he was by the thought that his dad might be a criminal."

"It makes sense," Scarlett said. "He's not a man who wears his heart on his sleeve. Watching you two last night, it was obvious you have pried the oyster out of his shell. He trusts you, but behaviors rooted in childhood trauma are difficult to overcome and the more vulnerable he feels, the more he will overreact if he something scares him." Scarlett's lips curved. "And baby, the way you make him feel terrifies him."

"I don't want him to be afraid." Doing the right thing shouldn't cause this much anxiety and hurt. "I want him to be happy."

"I know, and he'll get there."

But what if he never did? JT hadn't yet learned to make lemonade out of lemons and wasn't ready to rely on her for his wellbeing. The stockholders' meeting was less than a month away. If he refused to let her in, she was convinced he would demand the divorce they'd agreed to in the beginning. And that would be bad. He needed her. She reminded him to laugh and appreciated his romantic soul. And she needed him. He made love to her with a ferocity she'd never known before. In JT's arms, she wasn't a team player. She was a star.

Buoyed by Scarlett's assurances and a great deal of sugar, Violet went about her day with a lighter heart. It wasn't like her to worry about what hadn't happened yet. Obviously JT was rubbing off on her. If only she were having the same effect on him.

At five her cell phone rang. To her delight, JT was calling. She answered, hoping to keep her emotional state from showing up in her voice. "Hello, husband."

"Hello, wife. I'm calling to apologize."

Lightheaded, Violet leaned against a nearby pillar and squeezed her eyes shut. "No need."

"As always, you are patient and understanding, but I simply must insist on making up to you for my bad behavior this morning."

"What did you have in mind?"

"Room service. Your suite. Fifteen minutes?"

"Sounds perfect." After hanging up with him, she called her assistant and rescheduled the next three hours of meetings. Then she raced toward the elevators and jabbed impatiently at the Up button.

Ten minutes later she'd ordered a steak dinner to be served in an hour, dabbed perfume in all the places JT enjoyed exploring and was waiting for him wearing a smile and a nightie that left just enough to the imagination.

Her approach had been perfect because two seconds after he shut her door, he whisked her into his arms and made straight for the bedroom. A half an hour later she

sat astride his narrow hips, breathing heavily in the aftermath of a powerful orgasm, feeling him pulse inside her.

"I could get used to this," he said, cupping her face and
pulling her down for a long, slow kiss.

"Me on top?" She gave him a cheeky smile.

"You period."

Her heart lurched. It was the closest he'd come to mentioning the future. She drew his lower lip between her
teeth and sucked gently. Beneath her, his chest rose and
fell unsteadily.

"No reason you can't," she murmured, showing him
how much she had to offer.

"I guess it's something we should talk about."

In her head she was screaming, *Please, can we discuss
it now?* What came out of her mouth was a restrained,
"I'd like that."

When the door chimed announcing their dinner, JT
slipped on his pants and went to let in the waiter. Violet
took a second to throw on a robe and run a comb through
her disheveled hair. By the time she entered the living
room, her small table had been set for an intimate dinner
for two, complete with candles, crystal and china.

"It smells wonderful," JT commented as he held her
chair while she sat down.

Violet lifted the silver dish covers and set them aside.
By now she knew JT liked his meat rare and his vegetables
steamed seconds beyond crisp. "Sixty-day dry-aged steak
straight from Fontaine Chic's award-winning steakhouse,"
she said. "With sides of potatoes rosti and asparagus with
aged Parmesan and browned butter."

"What are these?" JT pointed to three small bowls.

"Red wine sauce, Béarnaise and a truffle sauce that I
haven't yet tried."

"Sounds wonderful."

"Only the best for you." And she meant it. "And for dessert—"

"You're all the sweet I need."

With her insides turned to mush, Violet finished, "Berries with cream."

She watched JT put a piece of steak in his mouth and chew reverently. "This is amazing. There's nothing to compare at Titanium."

He was in such a good mood she hated to spoil it with the question that had plagued her all day: what was he going to do about the information Tiberius had dug up on George Barnes?

"I was lucky Chef Baron agreed to open his third restaurant with us," Violet said, squashing her curiosity.

"I'm sure luck had nothing to do with it," JT said. "You can be quite persuasive."

The compliment warmed her faster than a July day on the strip. "When I know what I want, I go after it."

"I'm very aware of that." A lopsided grin tugged at his lips. "In fact, I'm amazed that you haven't asked if I've decided to call Charity Rimes. I imagine you're dying to know."

"I'd be lying if I said it's the furthest thing from my thoughts." She carefully phrased her next words. "But I can't imagine what a difficult choice you have to make."

"If you'd found out Tiberius had done something terrible, what would you do?"

The question was fair, but it left Violet with a terrible conundrum. She'd always had faith in Tiberius. He'd taken her in and loved her like his daughter. Her faith in his honesty had never been shaken.

"I'd like to say that I'd turn him in and never doubt myself for doing so." Violet gave JT's hand a sympathetic squeeze. "But I don't think I'd ever forgive myself for being disloyal."

JT carried her hand to his lips and kissed her palm. "After dinner, let's call Charity Rimes."

"Okay." Delighted that JT trusted her to help, Violet tucked into the meal with gusto. "I'm glad I didn't order a heavy dessert," she said as they dueled over the last berry. "I don't remember the last time I ate so much."

"Everything tasted so good, it was hard to stop."

Leaving the dishes for later, JT tugged Violet toward the couch. Together they sank into its softness. With JT's left arm around her shoulder and his right hand playing absently with the tie of her robe, Violet waited for some sign from JT that he was ready to hear what Charity Rimes had to say.

"Do you think my father belongs in jail?"

"If he stole someone's identity, yes."

JT closed his eyes and for a brief moment sadness blanketed his expression. Violet's chest tightened sympathetically at his pain. She wished she could take it away. She wanted nothing but happiness for him. But she could only offer comfort and support. JT would have to resolve his ambivalence on his own.

"Make the call," he said, his voice hard and determined.

Reluctant to budge from the circle of JT's arm, but knowing she had to act while he was still in a mood to find out what the writer knew, Violet snagged her cell off the coffee table and found Charity's number. She dialed and then held the phone so JT could listen.

"Yes?" A male voice answered.

Violet and JT exchanged a puzzled look. "Hello. I'm looking for Charity Rimes."

"Are you a friend?"

The man's question awakened Violet's anxiety. "Not exactly. My name is Violet Fontaine. She spoke with my father several months ago about a book she was writing. I was hoping to find out what she told him."

"Can't you just ask him?"

She wanted to demand he let her speak to Charity, but

some instinct stopped her. "He died." She left out the part where Tiberius had been murdered.

A long silence followed. At last the man spoke. "I'm sorry about your father, but Charity won't be able to help you right now. She was in an accident. Her car was T-boned by an SUV."

"Is she okay?"

"She has some broken ribs and a head injury that the doctors want to monitor."

JT frowned and stood. Violet's gaze followed his tense form as he paced across the room. She could only imagine his disappointment. Since this morning he'd had to assimilate potentially damning news about his father and decide whether or not to pursue the truth. No matter how damaged their relationship, inside JT was a little boy who'd once looked up to his father.

"Please tell her I hope she'll be okay. Perhaps I can call again at a later date."

"Do you want to leave your number? I can have her call you."

"That would be nice." Violet gave him the numbers for her cell and the direct line to her office phone. When she hung up a gust of air poured from her lungs. "How crazy was that?"

"It appears as if fate has once again beaten me to the punch," JT replied, his voice wearing a frustrated edge.

"We still have over three weeks until the stockholders' meeting and your cousin Phil has promised to throw his vote your way."

"That means we have forty-nine and a half percent. My father wins." He headed to the bedroom and retrieved the rest of his clothes. "I'd better get back to Titanium. There's one last relative I can call. I didn't want to reach out to her, but maybe the favor she will demand in return won't be as bad as I think."

Violet could tell this wasn't the right time to reassure JT that everything would be okay. He was obviously too disappointed in the phone call to Charity Rimes to believe that the future would work itself out for the best.

"I'll see you at home," she called before he shut the door behind him.

After a quick shower, Violet dressed and returned to her office just in time to make the first of her rescheduled meetings. Even though it was hard to concentrate, she gave it her all. JT's problems would work themselves out one way or another. All he needed to do was trust that when the time came, he'd choose the right path.

And what about her? Would he want her beside him? Violet knew she'd better brace herself in case he didn't.

Nine

"He's leaning. You want to lift his inside shoulder," JT called. "Trot him in a tight circle." The young rider did as asked, and JT nodded. "Do you feel him balance himself?"

Her bright smile was answer enough.

JT followed her progress around the area, but his attention wasn't complete. Part of him was thinking about the stockholders' meeting a week away while another portion gnawed on his relationship with Violet and what he wanted for the future.

It was relatively easy to drop his guard with her. Her lack of an agenda, coupled with her unflagging positivity, and ability to distract him from his problems made her company a balm to his troubled soul.

She seemed to understand, though not appreciate, that he possessed secrets he didn't want to share. JT knew it was unfair. She'd given him so much of herself. That he continued to hold back made their relationship uneven. He didn't know how to fix it without risking losing her. But would she eventually get frustrated with him and leave?

In the beginning, they'd agreed to divorce after the

shareholders' meeting. He hadn't yet decided how to ask her to give their marriage a little more time. He'd grown accustomed to having her around.

She'd coaxed him out of his shell. He was happy. But was she? And was it fair of him to take advantage of her generosity and give her little in return?

The question plagued him through the rest of the afternoon. He listed the pros and cons of being married to Violet, pitting logic against emotion and measuring the ratio of risk to reward. In the end, after he'd applied all his business decision-making skills, it all came down to what he needed to be truly happy.

That evening, as he waited for her to show up at Baccarat, he faced the troubling reality of his situation. No matter how many objections he'd unearthed for staying married, the biggest factor in his decision was that he was falling in love with his wife. "Good evening, husband," Violet said, sitting down beside him on the couch. "What has Rick concocted for you tonight?"

JT glanced at the drink in his hand and realized he'd consumed half of it without tasting a drop. "I have no idea."

"Let me." She plucked the glass from his grasp and sipped. "Blissful Ignorance. Plum gin, red wine syrup, egg white, lemon juice, rose water and balsamic. One of my favorites."

He blinked, a little surprised by her memory and vastly turned on by the way she licked her lips and smiled. Everything about her unleashed his desire. No sooner had he figured out one habit that aroused him than she exhibited another. To say she fascinated him would be an understatement.

"A client wants my opinion on a horse that's for sale in Kentucky," he blurt without preliminaries. "And I thought I'd take a side trip to my family's farm outside Louisville."

"I'm sure your family will be happy to see you."

"Come with me."

They could both use a change of scenery and he very much wanted to show her where he'd spent the happiest moments of his childhood.

"I'd like that. When?"

"Tomorrow."

"I'll clear my schedule." Her willingness to drop everything and run off to Kentucky said that she too felt the need to clear her head. "How long has it been since you've visited?"

"About six months. I try to get there a couple times a year." The farm was the only place he'd ever felt completely at home.

"It must be wonderful," Violet said. "I've never seen you look so happy."

"Never?" He lifted her palm to his cheek and gave her a wolfish smile. "Then you'll just have to pay close attention later tonight."

Her eyebrows rose. "I'll make sure I do."

After a night filled with lots of blissful smiles and very little sleep, they boarded the private jet JT's client had sent to take him to Kentucky.

"Nice," Violet murmured, accepting a mimosa from the flight attendant and relaxing into a butter-soft leather chair. "Fontaine owns several corporate jets, but none as nice as this one. Who's your client?"

"She's a member of the royal family of Dubai." JT smiled at Violet's wide-eyed reaction. "A princess who has a passion for horses and show jumping."

"I had no idea you were so well connected."

"We met in Miami many years ago and struck up a friendship. She knew my grandmother's reputation and likes to get my opinion when she's planning on spending six figures on a horse."

"I am impressed." Violet eyed him over the rim of her glass. "And more than a little turned on."

JT chuckled. "Then my work here is done."

The farm where JT was to evaluate the jumper was about an hour away from his family's farm, Briton Green. The plane touched down at the regional airport less than fifteen minutes away and JT's cousin Samantha was waiting to greet them. He dropped the suitcases an instant before she threw her arms around him and hugged him hard. Tall and slender, with long, dark blond hair and an infectious grin, she had always been a whirling dervish of energy.

"It's great to see you." As soon as she stopped choking JT, she turned her attention to Violet. "I'm Samantha."

"Violet. JT talked non-stop about you the whole way here. It's nice to meet you."

"Likewise." Samantha looped her arm through Violet's and drew her toward the waiting SUV.

JT followed the two women at a slower pace. Already he felt as if the weight of the world had fallen from his shoulders and they hadn't even arrived at the farm.

"How are things?" he quizzed as Samantha sped down the highway.

"Wonderful. Dancing Diva had a gorgeous colt. Mom's convinced he's the best foal we've produced in ten years."

"That's saying something." In the last decade, three national champions had been foaled at Briton Green. "I can't wait to see him. What can you tell me about the six-year-old I'm looking at over at Cal Rutledge's place?"

Samantha nodded. "Nice mover. Good legs. Athletic. I think they've had a few issues with his work ethic."

"Meaning?"

"He's lazy."

"Worth what they're asking?"

"I'd offer them thirty-five and see what happens." Samantha had always been a tough bargainer. "Is the princess open to looking at any other horses?"

"Who'd you have in mind?"

"A client of Roger Simmons has a really nice eight-year-old mare. She's done really well in the show ring, but she needs a smart rider. Roger's had trouble finding someone good enough for her."

"Never hurts to look. Any others you can suggest?"

Samantha laughed. "JT, I could keep you busy for a month looking at all the talent we have in the area."

"Unfortunately I don't have a month."

When they arrived at the farm, they were met by his mother's cousin, Phyllis, Samantha's mother. His grandmother and Phyllis's mother, Adele, had been sisters. When JT's grandmother had married and moved to Miami, Adele had stayed and taken over the running of the farm. They'd owned stock in Stone Properties, given to them by JT's grandfather in exchange for startup capital. Tiberius had bought their shares of Stone Properties stock from them months earlier.

JT hugged his aunt and introduced her to Violet. "The farm looks great," he remarked as they entered the large Greek revival house. "Samantha tells me you had a bumper crop of foals this year."

"She's dying to show them off to you." Phyllis led them into the large living room where a maid had just finished setting a pitcher of sweet tea on the sideboard. "Lunch will be served in half an hour. Would you like something to drink?"

Violet accepted a glass of tea and perched on a damask chair. The house had been built in the late 1850s and had all its original furniture. It was a vastly different from Violet's two-year-old, ultramodern hotel and she looked overwhelmed by the history embedded in every inch of the home.

"I see you're wearing my aunt's wedding ring," Phyllis remarked, her expression friendly, but slightly curious. "When JT called to tell us he was coming and bringing his new bride, we were very excited to meet you." She was too well-bred to admit her curiosity, but JT could see her eyes were bright with it.

"I was excited to meet you as well," Violet said. "I know JT spent a lot of time here as a kid."

"Where did you grow up?" Phyllis asked.

"In Las Vegas."

"What do you do there?"

"I manage a hotel and casino on the strip. Fontaine Chic. My grandfather is CEO of Fontaine Resorts and Hotels."

JT could tell Phyllis was surprised at his choice in wife. Before Violet, he'd gone for style over substance. It made it easier to remain unattached. With Violet, he had the best of both worlds. And he was in way over his head.

"That must keep you very busy," Phyllis remarked, glancing in JT's direction. "This one here has a very difficult time tearing himself away for a visit."

"Between Titanium and the ranch, he has way more on his plate than I do." Violet covered his hand with hers. "Most days I'm lucky if see him at all."

"I'm sure he understands that a wife should never be neglected," Phyllis remarked dryly.

No one in the room could have missed what Phyllis referred to. For several seconds there was complete silence. At last Violet spoke.

"It's fortunate that our work schedules are similar," she murmured.

"I'm sure." Phyllis then took pity on her and changed the subject to what was happening with JT's cousins since they'd last spoken.

After lunch, Samantha took them on a tour of the barns. There were three altogether, housing horses owned by JT's family as well as their clients. They began in the mare's barn. Violet lost track of how many horses she'd petted and how many foals she'd seen either peering out from behind their mother or boldly stepping forward to greet the newcomers. She was completely charmed by the time they headed to the training barn.

"Do you ride?" Samantha asked.

In addition to being a breeding farm, Briton Green had an outstanding reputation as a training facility.

"I'm learning." Violet glanced at JT. "He's given me a few lessons."

"She has a good seat for a beginner."

"We should all take a ride later."

JT glanced at his watch. "I don't think we'll have time. I have a four o'clock appointment with Cal to see what he's offering to Husna."

Samantha looked disappointed. "How about you, Violet?"

"I don't mind going alone to my appointment," JT said.

As much as she'd love to see more of the farm by horseback, she'd come on this trip to spend time with JT. "Maybe tomorrow before we leave?"

With that settled, they quickly toured the training barn and then JT and Violet headed out.

"It's easy to see why horses got into your blood," she remarked as they raced along the country highway in the SUV they'd borrowed from Samantha. "There's something so grounding about them."

"They keep you in the moment. A smart rider is one who anticipates that even the most well-mannered horse might react badly to something in his environment."

"I guess focusing on the present is a good thing for all of us to do from time to time." She'd been spending too much time speculating about what would happen in the aftermath of the stockholders' meeting.

"Is that comment meant for me?" he quizzed, without a trace of acidity in his tone.

"Actually, I meant it as a reminder to myself. I've been doing a lot of thinking about the future. Our future," she clarified, searching his expression for some sign that he had picked up on what was troubling her.

"I've given it some thought as well." He stopped speaking, but didn't appear as if he'd said all he intended to so Violet waited him out in silence "The shareholders' meeting is a week away. We agreed to part ways after that."

Violet held her breath, hoping he felt the same way she did. This time JT's pause was longer. She couldn't keep quiet another second.

"I don't want to divorce you."

JT took his gaze off the road and let her see the yearning that filled his eyes. "I feel the same way." He captured her hand and lifted her fingers to his lips. "Having you in my life is the best thing that has happened to me in a long time."

"Me, too." And it made her realize that if she hadn't already been falling in love with JT she never would have suggested they marry in the first place.

"Are you sure you understand what you're getting with me?" JT asked, holding their clasped hands against his chest. "I'm not the easiest man to live with."

"I know." He still had secrets locked up inside him that caused pain and made him retreat from her. She might never know everything about him, but she'd come to terms with that before she'd decided to fight for their marriage. "I also know you don't fully trust me with everything that happened in your past."

"Are you sure you can live with that?"

How could she answer him when she didn't know herself? "I'm going to try."

As if admitting their heart's desire had drained the energy available for conversation, they both lapsed into silence. Violet stared at the green landscape around the car and waited for her rapid heartbeat to return to normal.

JT wanted to stay married. She made him happy. The thought thrilled her. But Violet wasn't a hopeless romantic.

What lay between them still required work and trust in order to grow, but the fact that neither of them appeared ready to throw in the towel gave them a fighting chance.

The conversation in the SUV had cleared the subtle tension between them. To Violet's delight, JT smiled more readily than she'd ever seen and his kisses grew abundantly more plentiful and passionate.

Snuggling with JT beneath the handmade quilt in the guest room, Violet sighed in utter contentment.

"I'd love it if we could come back here and stay longer," she told him. "I've really enjoyed meeting your family and want to get to know them better."

"I think they feel the same way."

"You're lucky to have them." She pondered her own lack of extended family and sighed. "Until Scarlett and Harper came along I didn't have any family but my mom and Tiberius."

"I get why you weren't in contact with the Fontaine family, but what about your mom's relatives?"

"She lost contact with them after coming to Las Vegas. I asked about them a couple times, but it really upset her so I stopped mentioning them." Violet had gotten the feeling that her mother had been running from an unhappy place when she left home.

"I'm sorry you grew up like that."

"It was okay. At the time I didn't know any different. The lack of family didn't really bother me until after college when I was in a friend's wedding." It had been a huge affair with six bridesmaids and groomsmen. The bride had looked radiant walking down the aisle on her father's arm. "I was the only one of the wedding party that wasn't a family member."

"Does it bother you that we got married without your family there?"

Violet didn't have to think about her answer. "A little. Mostly it bothered me that Tiberius wasn't there to give me away."

"When the shareholder meeting is over we should get married again. Properly this time. With friends and family around us."

"You don't have to do this for me." But she was thrilled that he'd suggested it.

"I'm doing it for us. We should make a fresh start." He kissed her on the forehead. "A real marriage deserves a real wedding. Don't you think?"

Violet tilted her head back so she could read JT's expression. His tender smile made her heart hiccup.

"It sounds like a perfect idea."

Ten

JT was in his office reviewing a capital expenditure request for remodeling the exercise room and upgrading the machines when his assistant hailed him on his phone's intercom.

"Mr. Rhodes is on line one."

It was three days until the stockholder meeting and JT remained short of the votes he needed to oust his father as chairman of the board and strip him of his CEO position. Was Preston calling to gloat?

"Hello, Father."

"You didn't really expect to beat me, did you, son?" Preston gave the final word a disparaging twist. "I've taken on much more skilled players than you."

"I've no doubt you have."

"Then you won't be surprised when I tell you that I'm in negotiations to sell Titanium."

"Not surprised at all." JT had known that challenging his father would be a one-shot deal. He either secured the votes to get Preston voted out as chairman or went out on his own. JT wasn't afraid to do the latter. He'd been ready to abandon any hope of saving Stone Properties before Violet had inherited Tiberius's stock.

"I'm sure we can find you a hotel to manage somewhere," Preston said. "I think the general manager of Platinum Macao plans to retire later this year."

JT saw no reason to react to his father's taunt. "I'm certain you have a number of managers who would jump at the chance to take over that hotel. I have several opportunities I can explore."

"Perhaps your wife can find you a job working for Fontaine Resorts and Hotels."

"In fact we've already discussed that," JT lied. Why was his father trying so hard to get him riled up? "Fontaine is negotiating to buy the Lucky Heart. They're planning to demolish it and build a new hotel. They want someone who can oversee the entire process."

More lies. JT had no idea what would become of the Lucky Heart now that Tiberius was dead, but investigating the fabrication would distract his father for a little while.

"You were lucky to marry your heiress when you did."

"Is there anything else you'd like to discuss?" JT glanced at his watch and saw it was almost time to rendezvous with Violet. They'd taken to enjoying late dinners in her suite. "Otherwise I have a meeting I must get to."

"Nothing else. I'll see you in Miami in a few days."

"Looking forward to it." JT hung up without saying goodbye, unsure if it had been worth his effort to try and shake his father's confidence.

Before leaving his office, JT signed off on the exercise room upgrade, then made his way to the first floor and strolled through the casino. As much as he loved the hotel and was proud of all he'd done to turn the property around in the last six years, JT had always known that his time here was limited. As CEO, his father called the shots. JT could stay working for Stone Properties and do what Preston wanted or abandon the company and strike out on his own. Leaving would have been better for him financially and professionally, but he knew his grandfather would want him to stay and loyalty was deeply imbedded in his psyche.

Even at nine o'clock at night the air on the strip hung hot and thick with exhaust and the sweat of many thousands of bodies. JT sucked in a lungful. Leaving Las Vegas had just become inevitable. The investment opportunities he'd been investigating had involved properties in California, Arizona and the Caribbean. He would be traveling a great deal and setting up his corporate office here didn't seem likely.

What did that mean for him and Violet? They had agreed to stay married. Maybe that had been shortsighted of him. Or she'd gotten him so accustomed to thinking positive that he hadn't truly believed he would lose. Tonight they would have to discuss what changes the future would bring.

Violet sent him a text as he entered the suite to say she was running fifteen minutes late and that the dinner she'd ordered would arrive before she did. JT saw her dining table was littered with copies of Tiberius's files on his family. They'd been going through them the night before, talking strategy. A waste of time. It would take a miracle to topple his father's solid base of supporters.

Was it idiotic of him to ignore the possibility that his father had committed a crime? Preston Rhodes, or George Barnes if he bought into Scarlett's theory, was a ruthless bastard to those who stood in his way. He'd schemed to turn JT's grandfather against his only son. He'd psychologically abused his wife until she'd turned to drugs and alcohol and overdosed. And he'd blackmailed a Stone Properties stockholder to manipulate the annual vote in his favor.

Maybe it was time someone pushed back. And who better than the son he was determined to hurt next.

Not wanting to start their evening by talking about his father, JT gathered the files and carried them into her home office. He set the pile on her desk and was turning to go when a lone file caught his eye.

JT looked closer and went cold as he spied his name in Tiberius's handwriting on the tab.

Violet had a file on him.

If Tiberius had investigated Preston's past, didn't it make sense that he'd have looked at JT as well? And when he'd left his files to Scarlett, of course she would share his file with her sister.

Dread collecting in the pit of his stomach, JT opened the file and stared at the top sheet. It was the police report on his mother's death. They'd ruled it an accidental overdose but right there in black and white was JT's darkest secret.

How long had Violet pretended not to know what he'd done? Had she played him for a fool from the start? Acted as if it was important that he confide in her when she'd already known every agonizing truth of his childhood. Bile rose in JT's throat at her betrayal.

Below the police report was a copy of the psychiatrist's initial assessment when JT had been hospitalized for a severe concussion and broken ribs after trying to jump his bicycle over his father's yellow Ferrari convertible. He'd attempted the risky stunt a month after his mother's death. Based on the timing, the doctor had determined he was depressed and put him on medication. But no pill had been capable of taking away JT's guilt.

A knock sounded on the suite's front door startling JT. For a long black moment he'd been twelve again, hearing the news that his mother was dead. Lightheaded, he backed away from Violet's desk and those horrible childhood memories.

His heart pounded madly as he shook his head to clear it. There was a second knock on the front door. Rousing himself, JT made his way through the living room and let in the waiter. The smell of the food turned his stomach as it passed and he stood in the doorway while the man unloaded the dishes onto the dining room table. Moving on autopilot, JT signed for their dinner and was about to close the door when Violet stepped off the elevator and headed down the hallway towards him.

"It smells wonderful," she said cheerfully, lifting on tiptoe to press her lips to his.

JT stood with his hands at his sides and didn't return her kiss. She pulled back with a frown and surveyed his expression.

"What's happened?" she asked, closing the door.

"You have a file on me."

Guilt flashed across her lovely features and drove a spear into his heart. "Tiberius had a file on all of us."

"All this time you've been lying to me." A heavy note of sadness weighed down his voice.

"That's not true."

"You've known everything all along and pretended you didn't."

"Scarlett gave me the file," Violet explained. "But I've never opened it. If I've done anything wrong it was in not handing over the file to you as soon as I got it."

"You really expect me to believe that you didn't satisfy your curiosity about me by reading what my uncle dug up about my life?"

"If I had, why would I bother to ask you to share your past with me?"

"To make me believe you were the perfect woman for me. It's all in there, you know. The psychologist's report explains that before my mother's death I badly wanted her love and when she chose my father over me I retreated into belligerence and bad behavior. The more I acted out, the less likely it was that anyone would love me. And then you came along, and knowing what I most wanted was what I most feared, you did everything you could to make me trust you."

Violet looked stricken. "You don't know me at all if you believe I would ever manipulate you."

"No? You suggested we get married. You claimed my father threatened to sue us if we didn't act like a real married couple."

Now it was her turn to get angry. "I married you to help you."

"You married me to help yourself."

The part of him she'd touched with her compassion and optimism wanted very much to take her at her word, but he'd been protecting himself against being hurt for so long. It was a compulsion he couldn't resist.

"I spoke with my father tonight and he let me know he's selling Titanium. I'll be leaving Las Vegas to pursue some investment opportunities." He hadn't intended to present the situation so bluntly, but in lieu of what he'd discovered here tonight, he wasn't capable of being sensitive.

"How long will you be gone?"

"This is a permanent move. I'm going to sell the ranch and resettle elsewhere."

Violet recoiled as if he'd struck her. "Just like that without discussing it with me?"

"What would be the point? As per our original agreement as soon as the annual shareholder meeting is over, I'll be filing for divorce."

"Can't we talk about this?"

"There's really no point. Your life, your career is here. I have no reason to stay."

"You really don't get it, do you?" Violet's soft question resonated with compassion.

JT's chest ached to the point where he couldn't draw a full breath. "Get what?" he asked coldly.

"That I love you."

"I'm sorry you said that," JT told her, his voice low and flat.

Violet nodded. "I'm sure you are."

He'd torn out her heart and thrown it at her feet, but Violet wasn't about to let him think he'd won. His mask of indifference might have worked on her once upon a time, but she'd glimpsed his sensitivity. He'd rather be the most hated man on the planet than let people see his vulnerability.

Not that she was immune to what he'd told her. Stung by pain and disillusionment, he was going to isolate himself beyond anyone's ability to reach him. In her heart, she knew that was the last thing he wanted. If she'd shown him anything, it was that being alone only made him miserable.

"I don't think I'll stay for dinner." He stepped around her and put his hand on the doorknob.

"Before you go." Violet headed to her home office where she found the file that had destroyed any hope of happiness for her or JT. She straightened the pages he'd disrupted while reading and closed the cover. In less than a minute she'd returned with his file and the one on his father. "You should take these with you."

He looked ready to toss more angry words at her, but accepted the files in silence.

"If you need anything, just call," she added as he opened the door and stepped into the hallway.

His back stiffened as if she'd cursed at him. "Goodbye, Violet."

And then he was striding away, his long legs carrying him around the corner and out of sight. Only then did Violet turn into a puddle of shaking limbs and wracking sobs.

She shut the door and slid onto the floor and wrapped her arms around her knees. Drawing a complete breath was impossible so she closed her eyes and let the storm roll over her. By the time she'd calmed enough to pick herself off the floor, half an hour had passed.

She stumbled into the living room and dropped onto the couch. Greeted by silence, she immediately grabbed her phone and texted her sisters.

I messed up. In my suite, could use some sympathetic company.

Harper was the first to respond. Bringing both red and white wine.

Scarlett texted a minute later. Got chocolate.

With a shaky smile Violet rubbed tears from her cheeks. How lucky she was to have two wonderful sisters who dropped everything in order to rush over to make her feel better. Fifteen minutes later, wearing sweats and feeling marginally calmer, Violet opened her door to admit Harper.

"Which one should we start with?" she quizzed holding both bottles out for inspection.

"Definitely the red," Violet replied, knowing Scarlett would vote for that as well. She led the way into the kitchen to find the bottle opener.

"What's with the uneaten dinner?" Harper quizzed.

"JT and I ended things before we had a chance to eat."

"What?" Scarlett demanded from the living room, having come through the door to the hallway Violet had left open. "How is that possible? You two were doing great." Scarlett came into the kitchen, and both her sisters stopped what they were doing.

Harper held up her hand as she took in Scarlett's outfit. "Before we get to that, can you please tell me what you're wearing?"

Scarlett looked surprised at the question. "It's Princess Leia's harem costume from *The Empire Strikes Back*."

"Were you wearing that in the casino?" Violet quizzed, imagining the ruckus her sister must have caused among the male customers.

"Don't be ridiculous. I wore it for Logan."

Harper looked sorry she'd asked.

"I didn't mean to interrupt your evening," Violet said.

"Don't worry about it. Logan understands that a call for help from one of my sisters will never be ignored."

Tears surged in Violet's eyes once more, causing Scarlett to curse and Harper to put her arms around Violet's shoulders.

"You guys are the best," she whispered past the lump in her throat.

Harper poured the wine and the three of them moved to the couch. Snuggled between her sisters, Violet sipped at the excellent red and told them about JT finding his file and accusing her of using its contents to trick him into marriage.

"How does he not realize that if anyone benefited from you two getting together it was him?" Harper demanded hotly.

"He's used to being manipulated," Violet said. "It's made him guarded and secretive."

Harper regarded her in dismay. "You're still defending him?"

"She's in love with him," Scarlett said, patting Violet's knee. "And if anyone is to blame in all this, it's me. I never should have given you his file."

"Not true. I could have given him the file immediately or shredded the thing. He never should have discovered it sitting on my desk."

"But you aren't to blame for the way he reacted," Harper insisted.

"In a strange way, even though I never looked at what was in his file, I feel as if I betrayed him."

Scarlett shook her head. "You're acting far too reasonable. Rant. Cry. Call him terrible names. He deserves it."

That wrung a weak smile from Violet. "You know I'll never do that."

"Any chance this will just blow over?" Harper asked.

Violet exhaled shakily. "Maybe if it had happened weeks ago, but we've grown really close recently. We've talked about the future and agreed to give our marriage a chance."

"That could still happen." Scarlett looked hopeful.

"Preston is selling Titanium. JT has no reason to stay in Las Vegas."

"Bastard," Scarlett muttered. "I think for JT's sake we need to find out the truth about his father."

Before tonight Violet might have protested that it was JT's business not hers, but since he'd called it quits, she no longer had to consider his feelings in the matter. Still, guilt tweaked her. What if he didn't want his father exposed?

"I spoke with Charity Rimes earlier today," Violet admitted. "I was going to talk to JT about it tonight before…"

"What did she have to say?" Scarlett demanded, her expression alive with curiosity. "Why did Tiberius contact her?"

"Remember how she was doing research on a serial killer who was operating in Los Angeles in the sixties? He invaded homes and attacked families. The police never caught him."

"How is that related to Preston?"

"Turns out one of the families killed was named Rhodes. They left behind a ten-year-old son, Preston, who'd been spending the night with a friend."

Harper had been leaning forward, fully engaged. Now

she sank back against the couch cushions with a whoosh of exhaled air. "That's awful."

"Charity was blogging about the families who were killed and Tiberius had been running internet searching on Preston when he stumbled on her."

"So, how does this help us?" Harper persisted.

"After speaking with Tiberius, Charity got curious about Preston and tracked down his high school yearbook."

"And," Scarlet prompted.

"She promised to send me the photo."

Harper prodded. "Did she?"

"After what happened with JT I haven't thought to check."

"Where's your phone?" Harper was on her feet.

"I left it in my home office when I went to get the files for JT."

All three women raced to find Violet's phone. Sure enough, an email from Charity Rimes sat in Violet's inbox. She opened the message and held it so both her sisters could survey the image.

"That's not JT's father," Harper intoned.

Scarlett agreed. "No it's not."

Violet felt a peculiar lightness envelop her. In her hands was a way to save JT. But did he want to be saved? More importantly, would he want to be saved by her?

"We need to go to the police," Harper said.

"Which police?" Scarlett asked. "It won't do us any good to take it to the Las Vegas PD because Preston lives in Miami." She plucked the cell phone from Violet's grip and began typing. "I'm going to send this to Logan. He'll know the best way to handle it."

Twenty minutes later, Scarlett's fiancé sat on the coffee table and scowled at each of the three sisters in turn. When his gaze settled on Scarlett, he growled, "I thought I told you to drop it."

"I did." She gave him a winning smile. "Right after I gave Charity Rimes's phone number to Violet."

Logan sighed and shifted his hard gaze to Violet. "Have you spoken with JT about this?"

"We aren't on speaking terms at the moment."

That seemed to surprise Logan. "He should know what you've discovered."

She shook her head. "I doubt he'll take my call. Would you tell him?"

"You're his wife. It would be better coming from you."

"I'm the woman he married to get access to his family's stock," she corrected him. "And tonight he found out I had a file that Tiberius had put together on him. That I never looked at," she added when Logan's expression grew even grimmer.

"Every one of those files should have been burned," Logan growled, shooting his fiancée an unhappy look.

"What's done is done," Scarlett replied unapologetically. "We need to move forward. Preston Rhodes is an imposter and it's time that caught up with him."

Clad in a towel, JT stood in the enormous walk-in closet off his master suite and stared at the array of feminine fashions that occupied half the space. In addition to Violet's clothes, there were twenty pairs of shoes and assorted purses. Her jewelry was on his bureau, her lingerie in his dresser drawers. The scent of her clung to the sheets. Her cosmetics occupied the bathroom countertops. Traces of her lingered everywhere.

"Damn."

He'd been unable to sleep the night before so he'd sat in his living room, alternately staring out at his empty swimming pool and reading the file Tiberius had put together on Preston. He'd grown queasier with each page he'd turned. A dozen times he'd started to close the file, but then he'd hear Violet's voice and knew he could no long pretend that his father hadn't maliciously sabotaged his competition and blackmailed friends. He'd fled the truth for too long. His father was evil.

Sometime around dawn he'd drifted off. When he woke around six, he'd been having a dream where he chased Violet through a casino, calling her name, but she was always far out of reach. The memory of it left him with a cottony taste in his mouth and an ache in his temples. Interpreting the dream was easy. He'd lost the best woman he'd ever known because he was too closed down to give her the intimacy she deserved.

In the center of the large master suite, his empty king-size bed stood as a reminder of all the things he'd never enjoy again. Violet's body moving beneath him. Her soft moans. The bite of her nails as she climaxed. The brilliance of her smile in the aftermath of their lovemaking. The utter peace he felt with her nestled beside him.

He could burn the sheets, replace the mattress, hell, even toss out all the furniture, but he'd never be free of the mistakes that had led him to shove her away. Worse, he suspected she'd forgive him for being such an ungrateful jerk if he'd just share with her his feelings about what haunted him. But he'd clung to the secret for so long. It was impossible for him to set it free.

For a moment he was almost grateful to his father for selling Titanium. Staying in Las Vegas would have been impossible. Only with a change of scenery could he hope to adapt to life without her. Not that it was going to be easy. He'd given her access to places inside him that no one else had ever seen. Or was that true? Thanks to the file Tiberius had put together on him, didn't she already know all his secrets?

From the nightstand, his cell began to ring. Teeth locked together in irritation, JT left the closet and went to answer it.

"Yes?" he snapped.

There was a momentary pause before a man spoke. "JT? This is Logan Wolfe."

The security expert's connection to the Fontaine family immediately roused JT's suspicion. "What can I do for you, Logan?"

"I was wondering if we could meet. I have something to talk to you about and it shouldn't be done over the phone."

"If this is about Violet, you can forget it. We're done. End of story."

Another short but significant pause followed JT's declaration.

"Actually, this is about your father."

"I don't know what he's up to but he can go to hell. I'm done with him. I'm done with Stone Properties. I'm done with everything." Aware that he was working himself into a rant, JT sucked in a breath to steady his emotions. "Sorry," he muttered more calmly. "It's been a bad twenty-four hours."

"I get it," Logan said, sympathy in his voice. "I was there. And I have to tell you that the way you're feeling right now is not worth taking out on a terrific woman like Violet."

The unsolicited advice was a sucker punch to his gut. "You have no idea what I'm going through."

"Trust me, I do," Logan said, and the words were so heartfelt that JT believed him. "Scarlett and I almost didn't make it because I overreacted to something that happened. I would have been the sorriest son-of-a-bitch on the planet if she hadn't forgiven me for taking it out on her."

JT's anger faded, leaving a sick feeling in his gut. "It's too late. We're over."

"Do you really believe that or is it just fear talking?"

JT had no answer.

After a moment, Logan said, "I know you and your dad

have issues, but he is your father. Do you want to meet with me and hear what I have to say?"

"No. I don't owe him anything."

"Have it your way. Take care, JT." And then he hung up, leaving JT wondering if he was really as done with everything as he thought.

Eleven

The black town car her grandfather had sent to meet her at LaGuardia Airport stopped in front of the building that held Fontaine Resorts and Hotels' corporate headquarters in New York. Without waiting for the driver to open her door, Violet slipped from the back of the vehicle and crossed the sidewalk to the entrance.

Her heart was racing as she passed through security and ascended the elevator to the executive offices on the twentieth floor. She'd been here several times in the last five years, but those had been social visits with her grandfather. Most of her meetings with Fontaine's top executives happened in Las Vegas via video conference.

"You can go right in, Ms. Fontaine," her grandfather's assistant told her. "He's expecting you."

"Hello, Grandfather." By the time Violet crossed the enormous executive office, her grandfather had circled the desk. She walked straight into his arms and hugged him tight.

"My dear Violet." He squeezed back and released her. "You sounded upset on the phone. What's happened?"

"I've done so many things wrong I don't know where to begin."

"Start anywhere. I'll try to keep up." He drew her to the leather couch occupying one side of his office and surveyed her face for a long moment before calling to his assistant. "Jean, can you get Violet a cup of tea?" He settled her on the sofa as if she was a fine piece of porcelain and added, "Something soothing."

Three minutes later Violet cradled a china cup of herbal tea and let the warmth seep into her skin. "Thank you," she murmured. "I'm afraid I'm a bit of a mess these days."

"Why don't you tell me what happened."

"As you know, I married JT Stone so that I could vote the shares of stock Tiberius left to me." Violet could tell her grandfather was making an effort not to offer his opinion on her rash action. "It started out as a business deal."

"And then you fell in love."

Violet nodded. "He's very guarded and has a hard time trusting because of the way his father has always treated him. But I really thought in time I could get through."

"And now you don't believe you can."

"Scarlett gave me some files that she inherited from Tiberius. Apparently there was an entire storage unit filled with thousands of files dating back fifty years. He had one for each of us—" she paused "—even you."

Henry smiled wryly. "I suppose when I entered your life, Tiberius wanted to make sure I wouldn't cause you harm. I rather liked his protective streak. Made me glad that you had someone looking out for you while you were growing up."

Something his own son had failed to do. It went unspoken, but Violet sensed Henry Fontaine was deeply disappointed that Ross had behaved with so little honor.

"When Scarlett started looking through the files, she discovered one on JT and his father. As I've already told you, Tiberius was making a move to take his family's company back from Preston. I think he wanted JT as his partner, but wanted to make sure his nephew wasn't like Preston."

"And JT found out about the file?"

"Scarlett had given it to me. I should have shown it to JT right away but so much happened so fast and I forgot about it. Instead he found out I had it and accused me of using the information to trick him into getting married. Only Scarlett didn't give it to me until after JT and I got married and I never read it." The words tumbled out of her, each sentence coming faster until she ran out of breath.

"I'm sorry things are difficult between you," her grandfather said. "What can I do to help?"

"JT is losing Titanium. Preston is selling it to punish JT for going up against him. I don't think JT cares. He was planning on striking out on his own before I found out Tiberius had left me his stock. But that was before we got married. When Titanium is sold, he's going to leave Las Vegas."

"I'm still not sure how I can help," Henry said gently.

"I'd hoped you'd be able to find out who had shown an interest in Titanium and somehow interfere with the sale. I need some time. The longer JT sticks around, the more chance I have to save my marriage."

"And if he is still determined to go?"

"I belong with him. Wherever that is."

Her grandfather's expression registered surprise at her passionate declaration, but he didn't hesitate before asking, "Are you sure that's what you want to do?"

"Of course." She needed her grandfather to understand why this was important to her. "I love him and whether he believes it or not, he needs me."

"You know what's at stake if you leave Fontaine Chic."

"Any chance to run Fontaine Resorts and Hotels." Violet gave him a sad smile. "In the last year I've stopped seeing myself in the CEO job. Harper is the one you should choose. She's trained all her life to take over. You won't find anyone more dedicated or driven."

"I must say, I'm surprised."

Violet didn't pretend to wonder what he meant. "I'm not giving up because I feel I'm not capable or because I'm not performing well, but because I recognize the depth of commitment the position requires and I'm reluctant to make those sacrifices."

"I value your honesty, and you're right about the job requiring all your time and energy. Since starting the company I've lost my wife and my son and I've had to face that neither relationship was as good as I wished they'd been."

Nodding because her throat was too tight to allow words, Violet smiled at her grandfather. "Thank you for understanding. I was worried that after you gave me such an amazing opportunity, you'd be disappointed in my decision."

"You are an intelligent, compassionate woman with a creative, enthusiastic business presence. From the first you've been an asset to the Fontaine team. And I couldn't be more proud to call you my granddaughter. I've had my concerns that your heart might lie in Las Vegas and that you would eventually decide you wished to stay there, instead of coming here to assume the role of CEO. But now I see that what you truly love, you commit to, and I want you to understand that whatever happens with JT, you will always be a Fontaine."

His words were a warm embrace and Violet smiled gratefully. "Thank you."

She couldn't help but contrast JT's family experiences with her own. If she'd faced nothing but a string of ridicule and rejection from those who were supposed to love her, would she still wake up each morning feeling optimistic?

Would she be able to create a safe haven that supported her and gave her a place to hide from all the negative words and actions that came at her?

"What are your plans for the rest of the day?" her grandfather asked.

"I thought I would do a little shopping for Scarlett's bridal shower and then head back to the apartment."

"I'll make some calls to see what I can find out about Titanium and meet you there at six. I'd like to take you to dinner. There's a restaurant I'd like your opinion on. I thought perhaps we could discuss the opportunity to open a new restaurant in Fontaine Richesse with the chef."

"Grandfather, I don't know," Violet said with a laugh. "The last chef you found has made Harper's life hell. I'm not sure the food is worth the drama."

"I had no idea she was having trouble."

And maybe Violet shouldn't have spilled the truth. "It's their personalities. Ashton is creative and spontaneous. And even more of a perfectionist than Harper, if you can believe it. He's had input on everything from the font on the menu to the décor and is forever changing things in his obsessive search for better or more spectacular. I'm starting to wonder if they'll ever get the restaurant open."

"Is that why the opening has been postponed two times? She told me there was a problem with the fixtures being delayed."

"Because he changed his mind on what he wanted at the last minute and new things had to be ordered." Violet put a hand on her grandfather's arm. "Please don't tell her I mentioned this. She'd kill me if she knew I'd said anything."

"Ross's neglect made her think she had to prove her worth. Even after his death the need for acceptance drives her hard." Henry's eyes darkened with sadness. "I'll figure out a way to speak with her without letting her know you and I discussed it."

As Violet kissed her grandfather on the cheek, her phone buzzed. Her stomach in knots, she exited his office. She'd been waiting for this call for the last three weeks. What she'd put in motion might not solve her problem with JT, but it was the best way she knew to convince him she had no intention of letting him go without a fight.

JT stepped off the plane he'd chartered to Miami and headed in the direction of the Porsche 911 Cabriolet waiting by the hangar. His cousin Brent leaned his six-foot-two-inch frame against the sports car, arms crossed, looking relaxed and amused at JT's surprise.

"What the hell are you doing here?" JT demanded, enfolding his cousin in a hearty hug, shocked by the strength of his emotion.

Brent looked equally caught off guard, but recovered quickly and gave JT a toothy grin. "Thought you could use a little moral support tomorrow."

"You have no idea."

"Violet couldn't come?"

"She..." What excuse could he give for his wife not being at his side, lending her support, at such a crucial time? He owed Brent the truth. "We're over."

"No way. You two are crazy about each other." Brent's confused dismay added punch to JT's self-doubt. "What happened?"

"It's a long story and better told over drinks." JT circled the car and opened the passenger door. "I've got a suite at the Marriott."

Brent slid his long frame behind the wheel. "You're not staying at Cobalt?" It was the premier Stone Properties hotel in downtown Miami where the stockholders' meeting would take place the next day.

JT grimaced. "That's another story better told with alcohol."

"Sounds like it's going to be a long evening." Brent started the car.

The explanations began when the two men settled into a booth at the hotel's bar. JT figured he'd start with what happened with his father and work his way into the more painful story.

Brent didn't look surprised when JT recounted how Preston had informed him that Titanium was going to be sold. "It's the only property without any significant debt," Brent reflected. "He needs the capital to make the balloon payments coming due."

"Despite how hard I fought to get my father out," JT said, for the first time voicing what had dawned on him several days earlier, "I'm not really sorry to be leaving Stone Properties."

"Really? The last time we talked you were determined to take over. It's your legacy."

JT shook his head. "A tainted one. My father ruined so many lives in order to take over the company. How can I sit in the CEO's chair and not be haunted by what he did to my uncle and countless others?"

"So, you're giving up?"

"I'm moving on." JT offered his cousin a wry smile. "Feel like buying thirty percent of Stone Properties?"

"You own forty-eight percent."

"Eighteen percent of that is Violet's."

"But if you two are divorced, she can no longer vote the shares."

"True." JT's focus sharpened. "Are you telling me you're interested?"

"With restructuring, the company could be made solid once more. I thought you'd want to be the one to do that."

"And now that you know I'm not?"

"I will."

The idea that his cousin wanted to take over Stone Properties gave JT a great deal of satisfaction, but there was still the problem of not having enough shares to remove Preston as chairman of the board. He refrained from bringing it up. The mood at the table had brightened considerably and JT wasn't about to kick sand on the fire.

After several more drinks over which Brent spelled out his plan to fix Stone Properties, JT's cousin grew somber.

"Are you drunk enough to tell me what went wrong between you and Violet?"

"No." JT offered an unhappy smile. "But I'll tell you anyway."

He then explained about Tiberius's files and how Violet had been in possession of one on JT. "She played me."

"How do you figure?"

"Every dirty little secret I have was in that file." All except one. The worst one.

And no one would ever know what happened the day his mother died. How he could have been the one to save her if he hadn't disobeyed her.

"She knew exactly how to make me…" JT stopped. He'd been about to say *make me fall in love with her.* Because that's exactly what had happened. Suddenly he felt ill.

"Make you what?" Brent prompted.

"Make me trust her."

"She seemed pretty trustworthy to me," his cousin said. "Loyal, too."

"She is." JT was aware he wasn't thinking straight. "I mean she seems trustworthy." In fact she had been. Violet hadn't done a single thing to hurt him. Quite the opposite. She'd supported him.

JT dropped his head into his hands. "Oh, hell."

"I'm guessing you just realized you messed up."

So what if she'd had a file on him. So what if she'd memorized the damned thing. The fact that he refused to let her in, to open up his past so she could understand why he retreated the way he did, hadn't left her much choice. Given her open nature, it must have been stressful for her to come up against his defenses day after day. Sure, he'd let her in a little, but that could only have given her hope that he'd share more.

But how could he let her in when what lay hidden was so ugly? He was selfish and filled with bitter anger. His childhood scars made it impossible for anyone to love him, even Violet. So he'd pushed her away.

"I don't feel like drinking anymore," JT said, besieged by the need to retreat and regroup. His nerves were raw and exposed. If he went into the stockholders' meeting like this tomorrow, his father would eat him alive. "I'm heading back to my room."

"Sure." Brent regarded him with concern. "Are you sure you're okay?"

"No, but after some aspirin, a shower and a few hours' sleep, I might be able to get through tomorrow." What happened after that was anyone's guess.

Her grandfather's Gulfstream enabled Violet to arrive in Miami an hour before the shareholders' meeting was set to start. JT wasn't expecting her and she wasn't sure what sort of reception she'd receive. With each mile of road that passed beneath the town car's tires, her anxiety grew until she ran out of time to worry. She'd arrived at Cobalt.

The Stone Properties' flagship hotel was a towering thirty-story structure that overlooked the bright blue waters of Biscayne Bay. Everything about the lush landscaping bordering the circular driveway and the glassed entrance to the lobby was staged to impress. But as Violet exited the town car and headed inside, she noted a dozen tiny flaws in the way the staff conducted themselves and spied the dust lingering in the decorative moldings. At a quick glance everything appeared to be functioning, but Violet's trained eye recognized mismanagement.

Crossing the two-story foyer, Violet made her way to the conference room where the annual meeting was taking place. She picked up her pace when she saw the doors had already closed. If she'd hoped to slip in unobtrusively, she'd underestimated the number of stockholders who would be attending.

There were less than a dozen people scattered throughout the chairs that faced a raised dais with a podium in the middle. Seven pairs of eyes shifted in her direction, but she only cared about a particular pair of hard blue ones.

Simmering with ill-concealed annoyance, JT sat beside his cousin, Brent, half way up on the far side of the room. He didn't look happy to see her, but she hoped that would change when he understood why she was here. She took a seat in the back of the room while Preston ran through the day's agenda. As stockholder meetings went it was fairly routine. They would vote to accept the company's financials as well as several amendments to the bylaws. The agenda had been sent out months ago so no one really needed the review, but clearly Preston Rhodes enjoyed hearing himself speak.

While Preston spoke about the success of the company under his leadership and the direction he was taking Stone Properties in the future, Violet watched JT. He sat like a statue, his expression tight and unreadable. If things had gone differently, she'd be sitting beside him, offering him silent support. Her heart ached at the distance between them.

At long last, the explanation of what they were voting on wound down and they were invited to mark their ballots and bring them up to the ballot box. An external auditor would then count the votes while the shareholders enjoyed a specially prepared lunch. Everyone in the room knew it was all being done to satisfy the bylaws. Preston had control over the majority of the shares. What he wanted was what he would get.

Violet lingered in the back while JT voted, hoping to catch him as he left. A muscle jumped in his jaw as he approached.

"I thought maybe you'd mail in your vote." His gaze searched her face for a second before he leaned forward and kissed her cheek.

The fleeting contact caused a hiccup in Violet's pulse. She wanted so badly to wrap her arms around him and tell him everything would be all right, but he had his guard up.

"I wanted to be here for you."

"That's nice." JT's features softened for a moment, but then his father's laugh reverberated around the rapidly emptying room and JT's expression became like stone once more.

Violet watched her husband with a sinking heart. For a second she thought he might tell her he missed her. It was what she'd flown halfway across the country hoping to hear. What a fool she'd been to think their reunion would be joyful and romantic. "I'd better go vote."

"Of course."

JT's gaze clung to Violet's slender form as she walked away. He told himself to go after her. To beg her to love him. Wasn't her appearance here today proof that she wasn't ready to give up on him? But was it fair to take and take from her and give back nothing in return?

"JT, I was hoping I'd get to see you." A stocky man of average height clapped JT on his shoulder. "Sorry about not being able to swing my vote your way, but your father has been running this company successfully for a lot of years."

Clive Ringwald was the owner of a string of auto parts stores in the Midwest and married to JT's mother's cousin.

An affable man, he was firmly in Preston's camp, believing whatever half-truths or outright lies he was told.

"I understand," he told Clive, but his attention was fixed on Violet.

She'd dropped her ballot in the box and handed some paperwork to the auditor. With a last glance his way, she slipped out the room's second door.

Watching the door close behind her, JT felt his entire world shatter. What the hell was he doing standing here letting Clive prattle on? He loved Violet. He didn't care if she'd read his file and knew every shameful thing about him. She'd known who he was and married him anyway. And here he was, acting like such a stubborn fool when he should be fighting for the woman who'd transformed his life.

Cutting off Clive with a brusque apology, JT moved to intercept Violet in the hallway, but she'd already vanished. Figuring she was heading to the restaurant where lunch was being served, JT raced down the hall to the escalator that led to the ground floor. As he rode it down, he caught a glimpse of her passing through the front doors. He was so intent on catching up to her that he didn't notice Brent waiting for him at the bottom of the escalator until his cousin stepped in front of him.

"The FBI's here." Brent's gaze was troubled. "They're taking your father in. Do you know what the hell is going on?"

JT immediately thought of George Barnes and a reporter in L.A. who might have some information on a man by the name of Preston Rhodes. "I think I do. Where are they?"

Before Brent could answer, his father appeared, flanked by two men in suits. In dazed silence JT watched the trio approach. They'd handcuffed Preston, but there was no question that JT's father was not cowed by the treatment.

"Do you know who I am?" Preston snarled.

The man to the left smirked. "Actually, that's what we'd like to chat with you about."

Preston caught sight of JT and his lips curled in disdain. "I suppose this is your doing."

JT shook his head. "I wish it was." And to his surprise he meant it. "Seems as if all your bad choices have finally caught up with you."

"Tell my assistant to call my lawyer," he snapped before he was out of range.

"You're not really going to do that, are you?" Brent inquired.

"Nope." JT glanced at his cousin. "Can I get a rain check on that drink? I need to catch my wife before she leaves."

"No problem. Give me a call later."

But before taking more than a step, once again, JT was prevented from going after Violet. This time it was the auditor who stopped him.

"Excuse me, but was that Mr. Rhodes I just saw leave?"

"It was."

"But I have the results of the election."

"The stockholders are having lunch in the dining room. Perhaps you'd like to tell them what happened." JT turned to go.

"Before you leave, Mr. Stone, you should know that your father was voted off the board."

JT spun around and stared at the auditor, wondering if he'd heard correctly. Then, JT realized he was grinning like an idiot. "Explain it to him." He indicated Brent. "I have more important things to take care of."

Twelve

Violet was unpacking the last of her personal items from her suite at Fontaine Chic when her husband strode through the bedroom door. She glanced up as his presence filled the master suite and made the very air crackle with energy.

"Hello, husband," she said, her tone matter of fact. "Was your trip successful?"

"You know damned well it was." He tugged his tie loose and shrugged out of his suit jacket. When he looked as if he planned to drop both articles on a nearby chair, Violet moved to take them from him. A gentle tug-of-war ensued between them. "I don't need rescuing," he murmured a second before giving her the win.

"Not anymore," she responded, her voice equally soft.

It was going to be all right, she realized as she hung up his jacket and tie. He hadn't demanded to know what she was doing in his house. He'd simply accepted her presence. Her anxiety quieted.

She came out of the closet and found her husband had stripped off his shirt and was working on his shoes. Her mouth went dry as she took in all his chiseled perfection.

Had it only been a week since they'd last made love? The severe ache in her loins made it seem like a whole lot longer.

His socks landed in a pile next to his shirt as he commented, "The FBI hauled my father in for questioning." JT slipped off his pants. Clad only in his boxer briefs, he carried his discarded clothes into the closet. "Any idea what that was about?"

"You didn't stick around to find out?"

"I was too busy chasing after my wife to care." He reappeared in fully naked glory and stood with his arms crossed, staring at her. "Perhaps you can enlighten me."

It was difficult for her to concentrate with her husband's flawless physique artlessly displayed for her perusal. Did he really intend to stand there like that and have a serious discussion? Her blood heated as she took in the rise and dip of his muscular arms and the flawless definition of his rock hard abs.

"Perhaps you'd like to shower first and then we can talk?" Violet suggested, hoping he'd take the hint that it was a conversation better conducted without distractions.

"Actually, I'd like to hear what you have to say first."

Damn him. Well, two could play at this game. She reached behind her and took ahold of her dress's zipper. His expression didn't change as she unfastened her dress, but when it pooled at her feet, she caught a minute widening of his eyes.

"Charity Rimes finally returned our call a few days ago," she said, unfastening her bra and letting it fall to the ground. She shimmied out of her underwear before continuing. "After Tiberius had contacted her, she'd been intrigued about his theory that George Barnes had taken Preston Rhodes's identity and tracked down George's high school yearbook."

The entire time she was speaking, JT kept his gaze

fixed on hers, and off her naked form. He appeared utterly intent on what she was saying, but there was one part of his anatomy with a mind of its own. To provoke it further, Violet reached up and freed the pins holding her hair in a loose topknot. It cascaded around her shoulders, the strands tickling her sensitive nipples and turning them into hard buds. JT's Adam's apple bobbed.

"When she emailed me a copy of the photo from his graduation, it was obvious that your father is not Preston Rhodes."

"So you called the FBI?"

"No, Scarlett suggested we bring the issue to Logan. He had a buddy in the FBI."

Violet bent down and picked up her dress. As she straightened she thought she heard a strange noise emanating from JT's throat, but when she glanced his way, nothing revealed itself on his face, although his erection had surged higher.

"He called me a few days ago." JT's voice was tight and husky. "I didn't want to hear what he had to say."

"I thought you should know what we intended to do and would take it better from him."

"I was so damned mad at you."

Violet flinched at the intensity of his tone. "I know."

Needing a moment to regroup, she turned and walked to a nearby chair, putting her clothes on it. She felt more than heard JT come up behind her, and when he spoke next, he was mere feet away.

"You had a file on me. I felt betrayed."

"I know," she repeated without turning around. Rehashing their fight would not move them past her poor judgment or his interpretation of what she'd done. "I was a little surprised the FBI moved as fast as they did. I thought for certain they would investigate longer." When his hands gripped her shoulders, there was tension in his fingers.

Alarmed, Violet hurried to explain her motivation. "I know he's your father, but he certainly had no right to be in charge of your family's business."

"I don't need rescuing." JT repeated his earlier declaration and turned her to face him. "Not by you. Not by anyone."

Her temper flared. "That's your whole problem," she said, hitting him with all her pent-up frustration. "You think you're doing fine on your own, that this isolated little world you've built for yourself can keep your heart safe." She put both hands on his chest and shoved hard. He stumbled back a step, his expression reflecting surprise at her fierceness, and she stalked after him. "Well, you're wrong." She wagged her finger a scant inch from his nose and he retreated a few more steps. "You need me." She prowled after him, all her heartache and worry rising to a boiling point. "Admit it. Damn you. Admit it."

JT stopped retreating and stood staring down at her face. His fingertips brushed her cheek and came away damp. Violet didn't even realize she was crying.

"I don't just need you," JT said, bending down and lifting her onto his shoulder in a fireman's carry.

He dumped her on the bed and pounced on her. Violet gasped; his rough handling had disrupted the efficient working of her lungs. Or maybe she couldn't breathe because of the way he was staring at her: as if she was the most amazing sight he'd ever seen.

"I don't just need you," JT repeated, his tone tender. "I can't live without you. And I swear I'll do whatever it takes to make sure I never have to."

And then he was kissing her passionately, reverently, without holding back any emotion. Violet's joy knew no bounds as she realized that he'd stopped running from her. He might not have let go of the pain that kept him isolated, but he was ready to let her help him heal.

Her tongue met every greedy thrust of his, devouring just as fervently as she was devoured. With her fingers fisted in his hair, she threw back her head and moaned as his teeth nipped at her throat and he investigated the level of her arousal. Her hips bucked as he slid one finger inside her, then two.

Heat built beneath her skin as his mouth latched onto one of her nipples. The firm tug sent a spear of longing straight down to her core. She twisted beneath him, pinned to the mattress by his weight, but managing to communicate her hunger.

"Now," she commanded breathlessly. "Don't make me wait any longer."

He used his knees to spread her thighs wide, opening her for his possession. "It's been hell for me as well."

And then he was thrusting inside her in one long, measured surge that nearly made her black out, such was her pleasure.

"Yes," she murmured, smiling as his lips claimed hers once more.

He retreated at a deliberate pace, letting her savor the friction of their joining before plunging fully inside her once more. Their union couldn't be measured by the pleasure he brought her body, but by the way her heart swelled to almost bursting.

"I love you," she told him, meeting his gaze as they danced together, hips moving in ancient rhythm.

JT laced his fingers with hers and set their hands on the pillow beside her head. Without breaking his steady stroke into her body, he kissed her gently on the lips before murmuring, "You're my everything."

His confession caused her body to spasm. Her orgasm rolled over her in slow waves of ever- increasing pleasure that slowly faded. When she opened her eyes, she found JT watching her. Her lips curved at the wonder in his expression. He began to move against her powerfully, chasing his own finish. In seconds his body shuddered as his climax claimed him. He let her watch every emotion play across his face.

Breathing harshly, JT collapsed on his stomach beside her on the bed. He peered at her from beneath his long lashes, a wryness in his expression making him look younger than his thirty years. Or, Violet corrected, he looked exactly the age he was and she'd grown accustomed to how stress and unhappiness had made him seem older.

She rolled over on her side and cupped her hands beneath her cheek. "I'm here to stay."

"I assumed that when I saw all the packing boxes in the hall."

"And by here I mean wherever you are." Her lips firmed. "I fully intend to fight dirty if that's what it takes to save our marriage."

"There's nothing to save." He lifted one hand to forestall her heated rebuttal. "Let me finish. I simply mean that I was wrong to push you away and that I'm fully committed to spending the rest of my life with you."

Violet let him see her delight. "Good. I think you made a wise choice."

"So do I." JT rolled onto his side until their noses were an inch apart. His heart rate had returned to its regular resting pace, but every third beat or so it skipped a little as he realized just how happy he was.

"Feel like telling me how the shareholder vote worked out?"

Why did he get the sense that she already knew?

"Strangely enough, it came out in our favor."

"Really?" She did a lousy job of sounding surprised. "How is that possible?"

"From what Brent was able to gather after I left, Casey didn't vote his shares."

"That's odd. Any idea what happened?"

JT decided Violet's poker face was improving, but he knew her well enough to pick up on the trace of amusement in her eyes.

"I don't know if you remember but he was in the midst of a nasty divorce."

"I seem to recall something about that."

Now JT knew she'd been up to something because she'd been the one to point that out to him in the first place. "He let his wife have his four percent of Stone Properties stock in the settlement."

"You don't say." Violet looked suitably fascinated. "But if his ex-wife had the shares, she wouldn't be able to vote them because she was no longer family."

"True." JT let the rest of his explanation hang in the air, but Violet didn't press him to continue. And why would she? JT suspected she already knew how it ended. "Without Casey's four percent, my father and I controlled an equal number of shares."

"So how did we win?"

"That's an excellent question. Perhaps you'd like to explain to me."

"Me?" She sounded innocent, but a smug smile tugged at her lips. "Why would you think I had anything to do with it?"

"Because I've met the ex-Mrs. Casey Stone and she's greedy and beautiful, but not particularly bright. I don't understand why she wanted the shares at all."

"Well…" Violet drew out the word, reveling in the telling of her tale. "It seems that a year ago Casey had bought a big, beautiful love nest for his new amore and hadn't declared it as part of the divorce settlement. So, I let Brittany know and suggested that she might want to ask for the Stone Property shares and let Casey have the house."

"And he went for that? The shares had to be worth more or that was one hell of a house."

"He was in a hurry to remarry, and he stood to lose big because he hadn't disclosed the house." Violet shook her head. "Brittany was thrilled to sell me the stock. After all, I'd done her a good turn. And in the end, I think she received more than Casey intended for her to have."

"You own the four percent?"

"I do."

"This wasn't something you managed overnight, was it?" JT didn't wait for her to answer. "After I told you it wasn't worth pursuing, you went behind my back, didn't you?"

"You refused to let me help."

"And now I see I was wrong." As much as he hated admitting that, Violet's delight took the sting away.

"Good. Maybe now you'll start listening to my advice."

"Yes, oh wise one."

JT put his arms around her and softly nuzzled the side of her neck. She smelled like fresh-cut grass and summer sunshine, both favorite scents from his time on the farm in Kentucky. Lulled by the steady beat of her heart against his, JT felt the door to his most guarded secrets crack open.

"I don't know how to thank you," he told her, strangely at peace now that he was on the verge of telling her about the worst moment of his life.

"You don't have to thank me. I'm your wife. I'll always have your back."

"Then you should know what you're letting yourself in for."

"You don't think I do?" Violet's breath fell against his skin in a soothing cadence. "I didn't read your file, but I know that you're more troubled than the average person by mistakes you've made and that you carry childhood hurts that may never heal."

"I'm more troubled because the mistakes I've made aren't forgivable."

"That's impossible for me to believe."

He never stopped being astonished by her faith in him, but she needed to know everything. "The day my mother died…"

"JT." She cupped his cheek, offering comfort, and drew her thumb across his lips, silencing him. "You don't have to tell me."

"But I do. You were right about my needing to let go of the past. I can't do that if I continue to let fear hold me captive. I need you to know what happened with my mother." He pressed a kiss into her palm and closed his eyes. "I was the reason she died."

Violet's body jerked in reaction to his words, but instead of pushing him away, she moved even closer as if she wanted to slide under his skin and share the burden with him.

"That morning, she confronted me about using her credit card without asking and charging five hundred dollars' worth of video games. She didn't care that I'd bought the games, but the fact that I'd lied about it when she caught me made her angrier than I'd ever seen her. She'd found the games in my room and while I watched she threw them away. Then she told me I wasn't allowed to go on a weekend trip with my friends to Universal Studios Orlando. We were supposed to leave from school that afternoon. I don't remember ever being that mad."

JT sucked in an unsteady breath as memories of that morning washed over him. They were crystal-clear and razor-sharp as if the fight had happened yesterday, not eighteen years earlier.

"I can see why she grounded you and I understand why you were upset, but I don't see how it's your fault that she died. She overdosed. You had nothing to do with that."

"I upset her. I told her I hated her and that I understood why Dad couldn't stand to be around her."

JT shook his head, but there was no denying what he'd done. For a moment he couldn't breathe. His throat had tightened past the point of pain. He'd never told anyone the role he'd played in his mother's death. He needed to claw through years of self-loathing to let it out. It felt as if his insides were shredded.

When he continued, his voice was thick with anguish. "Then I grabbed my backpack and acted like I was leaving for school, but I snuck back to my room and packed what I would need for the weekend."

"You went anyway?"

"I figured she'd be so out of it by the middle of the afternoon, she'd never realize that I wasn't home until I was long gone. By five that evening she was dead. No one found her until the next morning when the housekeeper showed up."

"You were twelve," Violet said. "Your mother was a troubled woman who retreated into drugs and alcohol to cope with an abusive husband. How can you think you were to blame?"

"I overheard someone talking at her funeral. I realized that if I'd come home after school like I was supposed to, I could have found her still alive and called 911."

A tear slid down his cheek. Before he could lift his hand to sweep the dampness away, Violet cupped his face in a fierce grip.

"JT, your mother was an addict. She could have overdosed at any time. You were not responsible for her illness."

He heaved an unsteady breath. Part of him recognized that she was right, and he sensed her love and support would help him forgive himself.

"I love you," he told her, speaking the words out loud for the first time.

Tears filled her eyes, but her smile was brighter than the sun. She wrapped her arms around his neck and hugged him hard. "I can't tell you how much I've needed to hear you say that."

"It's taken me a long time to understand what I was feeling," he murmured into her hair. "Before you came along, the emotions I was most familiar with were dark ones."

"All that is behind us now," she said crisply, her optimism revving up. She leaned back and regarded him, her eyes determined. "Starting today, we have an abundance of new adventures awaiting us. Starting with house-hunting in Miami. I spoke with Grandfather about acquiring some property downtown and building a Fontaine property."

"About that." JT hadn't expected her to be so enthusiastic about leaving Las Vegas for Miami and was worried that his news might not be what she wanted to hear. "We're not going to Miami."

"Why not? Now that your father has lost his chairmanship and is probably going to face jail time, the company is yours."

"Here's the thing. The night before the annual meeting, Brent and I had a long chat about the future of Stone Properties. We came to the conclusion that it would be better served with him at the helm."

"But…but…" she sputtered, "it was your grandfather who started Stone Properties."

"And with Brent running things it goes back into family hands."

She cocked her head and regarded him. "What are you planning to do?"

"What I told you I was going to do before the shareholders' meeting. Get out."

"I see." But it was obvious she didn't. "So, where are we going?"

He soothed her worries with a smile and the stroke of his palm along her arm. "Nowhere. Neither one of us is leaving Las Vegas. In fact, I've decided to sell my shares of Stone Properties and buy Titanium."

Her smile was blinding. "I think that's a wonderful idea. But are you sure you want to settle for one property when you could be in charge of a dozen?"

"With Brent at the helm, Stone Properties will be in good hands. And I'm not really a sit-in-an-office-and-do-nothing-but-read-reports-and-make-policies kind of guy. I like the pulse of Las Vegas and have decided whatever else I do, here's where my headquarters will be."

Violet frowned. "That's all well and good, but what happens if I win Grandfather's contest and take over Fontaine Resorts and Hotels? I'll have to move to New York City. What becomes of us then?"

JT had never considered that possibility. It wasn't that he lacked faith in Violet's abilities to do the job or her grandfather's shortsightedness in not recognizing her talents, but she'd always seemed as much a part of Las Vegas as the strip itself.

"I guess I'll have to rethink my plans."

Her eyes softened. "You'd do that for me?"

"Did you not hear me when I said I can't live without you?"

She snuggled closer and kissed his lips. "Then you'll be happy to know that we'll be living together in Las Vegas. I spoke with Grandfather and bowed out of the CEO race."

"Why did you do that?"

"Because I made you my priority. Whatever you want to do, wherever you want to go, I intend to be by your side supporting you."

"I feel the same way."

She laughed. "Then I guess we're pretty lucky that we both love Las Vegas so much because this is where we're going to raise our children and grow old together."

Her vision of their future was so much better than any he'd ever dreamed of. Gone were the shadows that had kept him from believing he deserved to be happy. Violet's love had banished every one.

JT's arms tightened around her. "I can't imagine anything better than that."

* * * * *

A TASTE OF TEMPTATION

BY
CAT SCHIELD

To my MFW-BIAW Golden Girls:
Nan Dixon, Lizbeth Selvig and Nancy Holland.
Thanks for keeping me motivated and inspired.
You ladies rock.

One

As soon as Harper Fontaine stepped from her lively casino into her stylish new restaurant, she checked near the door for a rolling black leather duffel. Ashton Croft's *go* bag. She loathed the thing. It represented everything that drove her crazy about the celebrity chef. His tendency to show up without warning. The way he thrived on excitement, and when none could be found, his knack for either stirring it up or heading out of town on some adventure or another.

But she needed the bag to be there because it would mean that Ashton had shown up for today's head chef interview. Batouri's grand opening was two weeks away. When the original deadline for the opening of the restaurant had come and gone without it being ready, Harper had questioned the wisdom of asking an unreliable television personality to start a restaurant in her hotel.

True, the buzz about the grand opening had drawn all eyes and scads of publicity to her hotel, Fontaine Ciel, but was the attention worth the stress Ashton had heaped on those in charge of making the restaurant a success? Carlo Perrault, the restaurant's manager, wasn't sleeping and had grown irritable these past two months. Harper was grinding her teeth at night. The headaches induced by this behavior had forced to her seek medical help. She now wore a mouth guard when she went to bed. Slipping the awkward plastic device into her mouth, she would lie on the mattress and wish she had some idea what happened to Ashton's initial enthusiasm about the restaurant.

The longer the filming of *The Culinary Wanderer* had gone in Indonesia, the more difficult she'd found working with him to be. They'd had to postpone Batouri's launch date twice because of scheduling conflicts with his travels for his wildly popular television series.

Which was why Harper refused to delay again. The restaurant's black floors were polished. The chandeliers had been hung from the high cove ceiling. Their light illuminated the white napkins and crystal wine goblets on the black tables. Ten days earlier the painters had completed the metallic gold treatment on the three wide pillars down the center of the room. Near the fully stocked bar, the assistant manager was putting the waitstaff through their paces.

But for two things, Batouri was ready to open. Two key things. It lacked a head chef and a menu.

And seeing that Ashton's *go* bag wasn't in its usual place, it looked as if that menu was going to have to wait. Harper glanced at her watch. It was exactly four in the afternoon. She'd told Ashton the interview would happen at three to make certain he arrived on time. Playing these sorts of games wasn't in her nature, but she was at her wits' end in dealing with the celebrity chef.

She dialed her assistant. Mary picked up on the second ring.

Harper got straight to business. "Did Ashton Croft call to say he'd be delayed?"

"No."

"And his plane was supposed to land in Las Vegas at one?"

"Yes, I confirmed his itinerary this morning."

Damn the man. Two weeks ago Ashton had promised Harper his full attention starting today. She should have known better. "Thank you, Mary. Let me know if you hear from him."

"Sure thing." Harper was on the verge of disconnecting the call when something Mary said caught her attention. "...in your office."

Carlo Perrault emerged from the kitchen, a scowl on his handsome face. The forty-six-year-old restaurant manager was known for his composure, but even he was showing signs of stress at all the things that still needed to be done. "We have a problem."

"I'm sorry, Mary. Who did you say was in my office?"

"Your mother."

"My mother?" Surprise kept her from guarding her tone. Aware of Carlo's scrutiny, Harper turned her back on him and stepped away to give herself some semblance of privacy. "Did she say what she was doing in Vegas?"

"No, but she seems upset."

"Just upset?" Harper mused.

Penelope Fontaine wouldn't have left her elegant condo in Boca Raton to fly two thousand miles to visit Harper unless something was seriously wrong. And if it was, why had Penelope come to Harper? Usually Penelope took her problems to her father-in-law, Henry Fontaine.

"You once mentioned she smokes when she's agitated," Mary said. "She's starting her second cigarette."

"She's smoking in my office?" Harper pinched the bridge of her nose. She wanted to insist Mary tell her mother to put out the cigarette, but knew that would be asking too much of her assistant. "I'll be there in five minutes."

"You can't leave," Carlo protested. "Croft has started the interview without you."

"Great," she muttered. "How long has he been here?"

"Long enough to taste everything Chef Cole has prepared." Carlo's dour expression was enough to tell Harper that this interview was going the way the other seven had.

"Mary, looks like I am going to be a while. Get my mother settled in a suite and I'll visit her as soon as I'm done here." Harper hung up and turned to Carlo. "If he messes this interview up, I'm going to kill him."

Carlo offered her a tight nod of understanding.

The hostility in the two male voices hit her before she'd reached the food pass area.

"There's nothing wrong with the sear on these scallops," one of the men protested, his tone both arrogant and simmering with hostility. "And the sauce is not under seasoned."

"It's obvious the only thing worse than your culinary skills is your wretched palate."

Pain stabbed Harper's temple as she recognized the voice of the second speaker. Ashton Croft had been interviewing head chefs for two months, rejecting one after another for failing to live up to his exacting standards.

Harper snapped her vertebrae into a stiff line and stepped into the meticulously organized, stainless-steel kitchen. As was her habit, her gaze swung immediately to Ashton. He dominated the room with his presence. Tall and imposing in his chef whites, he stood glaring at Chef Cole, muscular arms crossed over his broad chest.

He hadn't yet noticed her, hadn't turned his Persian-blue eyes her way, hadn't noted her slight breathlessness. His passion for food sent his innate charisma soaring. She cursed the hero worship that she couldn't completely squash despite her professionalism. She was unequal parts frustrated with the restaurateur and enamored of the dashing adventurer.

His travels fascinated her. Some of the things Ashton had eaten made Harper shudder, but he boldly consumed

whatever he was offered. She'd spend her entire life knowing exactly where she was going, and the way he allowed
random opportunities to push him into unexpected and
sometimes startling discoveries both unnerved and captivated her. Watching his television shows had made her
realize just how safe her world was. And a seed of restless-
ness had sprouted inside her.

With effort Harper ripped her gaze from Ashton and
turned her attention to the other chef. Taking in the in-
terviewee's blazing eyes and clenched fists, she donned
her most diplomatic expression and entered the war zone.

"Good afternoon, gentlemen." She stepped into the middle of the clash with calm authority. She wanted Chef Dillon Cole to run Batouri's kitchen. He was an excellent chef
as well as a strong, organized leader. Harper restrained a
weary sigh. Of all the candidates, he'd been Harper's first
choice for head chef. It was why she'd saved his interview
until the last. This close to the restaurant's already delayed
grand opening, she had the leverage she needed to force
Ashton's hand. "I stopped by to see how things are going."

"Taste this," Ashton commanded, pushing the plate in
her direction without ever taking his eyes off Cole. "Tell
me if you think it's up to Batouri standards."

The first time he'd done this she'd been flattered that
he wanted her opinion. After the third candidate had been
rejected, she'd realized he was merely using her to drive
home a point. If someone with no culinary experience could
taste the inferior quality of the entrées, the chef who'd prepared the dish had failed.

Harper made no move to do as he'd asked. "May I speak
to you privately for a moment?"

"Can it wait?" Ashton never took his eyes off Chef Cole.

She fought to keep her frustration on a tight leash. How
would it play out on social media if the general manager
of Fontaine Ciel was recorded shrieking empty threats at
the famous Chef Croft?

"No."

Her conviction came through loud and clear, snagging Ashton's complete attention. His laser-sharp blue eyes scanned her expression. Sexual interest flared low in her belly. It traveled upward, leaving every nerve it touched sizzling with anticipation. She cursed silently. Her body's tendency to overreact to the man's rakish good looks and raw masculinity had distracted her all too often. She was not her professional best around him.

Once again Harper reminded herself that the flesh and blood man standing before her was unreliable and unconcerned with how his priorities impacted those around her. The dashing adventurer he portrayed on television was entertaining to watch as he charmed locals by listening attentively to their stories and sampling the regional specialties. But when it came to the routine matters necessary to start a restaurant, he easily became distracted.

Lips tightening, Ashton nodded. "Excuse us," he said to Chef Cole, and gestured for Harper to return to the dining room. "What's so important?" he demanded as soon as they'd exited the kitchen.

"The restaurant opens in two weeks."

"I'm aware of that."

"The press releases have gone out. There will be no further postponement."

"Understood."

She tamped down her irritation. "We need a head chef."

"I will take charge of the kitchen."

If only that were true. "I need someone I can rely on to be here every day."

His nod indicated he saw where she was going. "You want me to hire Cole."

"The last time I was in Chicago I ate at his restaurant. It was excellent. I was looking forward to tasting what he'd created today."

"You didn't miss much."

Harper spent a minute studying Ashton. There was something different about him today. Usually he breezed in, found something wrong with the construction or the fixtures and then stirred up everyone associated with the project before coming up with a fix for whatever he perceived wrong. Working with him had been stressful and invigorating, but in the end the restaurant was far better for his interference.

Today he seemed to be creating trouble for the sake of drama rather than because he had real issues with Chef Cole.

"Is there something going on with you?"

Her abrupt change in topic startled him into a moment of uncertainty. "Not a thing. Why?"

"Because you were on time for a change."

"I believe I was an hour early."

She gestured toward the door, making no effort to correct him. "And there's no *go* bag."

"*Go* bag?" he echoed.

"The black leather bag that you bring with you everywhere."

"You mean my rolling duffel?" He pointed toward a far corner of the restaurant where the bag sat beside a semicircular corner booth. "Why do you call it a *go* bag?"

"Because it's your crutch."

Amusement narrowed his eyes. "My crutch."

"When things get too tedious you make some excuse, grab the bag and head off in search of greater excitement."

"Leaving you behind to clean up after me?"

She let a brief silence answer his question. "You've interviewed and rejected seven head chef candidates."

He cocked an eyebrow. "What's your point?"

"I need you to hire someone. Chef Cole is that person."

"You didn't taste his entrées." When it came to food, Ashton was a creative genius. She wasn't surprised he couldn't find someone who was capable of living up to his demanding criteria. "I found them lacking."

"He has the experience and the organization to run this kitchen the way I expect it to be run—"

Ashton interrupted. "When you came to me about opening a restaurant in your hotel, I thought you understood that I had the last and final word on all creative."

"Creative, yes, but this is about the management of the kitchen." Which was why she was determined to get her way. She'd been able to control costs and manage the construction schedule, working hard to manifest Ashton's vision for the restaurant without exceeding budget.

In that respect their working relationship meshed.

"But the kitchen is where the magic happens."

"Except there's no magic happening because we don't have a menu or a head chef to work with the kitchen staff." Pain shot through her head. She winced.

"We will be ready for the opening." His absolute confidence should have shut down all her worries.

"But—"

"Trust me." His deep voice broke into her protest, his soothing cadence catching her off guard.

"I do." That's not what she'd meant to say.

But she knew it was true. They might have had completely different philosophies on how to accomplish something, but he had proven time and again he was as capable of getting things done as she. Deep down she knew he'd plan a fantastic menu and win the love of customers and critics alike.

That it would happen in the frantic last hours before the door opened was what made her crazy.

Famous dimples flashing, he countered, "No, you don't. From the minute I showed up here I've rubbed you the wrong way."

Harper stared at him in helpless fascination. This was the Ashton Croft she'd been dying to get to know. The man who charmed smiles from people who'd seen nothing but hardship and violence. The dashing adventurer who'd on occasion gamely hiked into dangerous surroundings to share a meal with locals and educate his viewers about what was unique to the area. It was always intriguing and often stuck with her long after the credits rolled.

"If you knew that, why didn't you try rubbing me the right way?" Harper regretted the words the instant they left her lips. They sounded like flirtatious banter. "What I meant was…"

Ashton shook his head, stopping her flow of words.

Not once since they'd first met nine months ago had she given him any hint that her interest in him went beyond his skills in the kitchen. Plagued by unruly flashes of lust for the überprofessional businesswoman and not wanting anything to interfere with the negotiations for the Las Vegas restaurant, he'd ignored his disobedient hormones and kept things strictly business.

But as they neared the date for the restaurant opening, he found it harder and harder to stop seeing her as an attractive—if too serious—woman.

It made him crazy that he couldn't accept that she wasn't interested and move on. This was Vegas. There were thousands of women arriving every day looking to have a good time. Perfect for a frequent flier like him. He rarely stayed in the same location for more than a few days. The time he'd spent in Vegas these past few months was the most settled he'd been since leaving New York City ten years earlier.

A low chuckle vibrated his chest. "Please don't try to explain it," he said. "I think it's the first honest thing you've ever said to me."

"That's not true." But she went no further.

"I think it is."

Ashton had watched her walking the line between frustration and diplomacy with finesse and grace these many months. He wasn't completely oblivious to how hard he'd made her life.

At the beginning of the project he'd been excited to put his creative stamp on Las Vegas. He hadn't understood until it was too late how difficult his ideas would be to communicate. He'd demanded changes that irritated the designers and caused forward progress to halt. Forced by his filming timeline to oversee the restaurant from thousands of miles away, he'd found few things that met with his approval. The layout of the kitchen wasn't to his satisfaction. Numerous shipments of lighting and furniture samples didn't meet his expectations.

Then there were the filming delays caused by the Indonesian weather. Days of rain threw off their schedule. The crew joked that their ratings would skyrocket if they captured him soaked through, his clothes plastered to his body, but no one wanted to venture out into the mud and damp.

"Why don't I tell Cole he blew the interview and then fix something delicious. You can tell me what's bothering you while we eat."

"The lack of a head chef is what's bothering me."

"There has to be something else. You're not usually so testy."

"I'm not testy. I simply don't have time to eat with you."

"Five minutes ago you were ready to sit down and taste everything Cole had prepared." He crossed his arms and regarded her solemnly. "So I have to ask, what is it about my food you don't like?"

"It's not your food. I ate at Turinos while you were executive chef and the food was brilliant. You don't seriously think I'd invite you to open a restaurant here if I didn't love your cooking."

"Then is it me you don't like?" He held up his hand to forestall her denial. "I've been told I can be difficult to work with."

She took a deep breath and let it out, releasing some of the tension. "You've been murder to work with, but I think the restaurant's going to be worth every name I've called you."

Her bluntness made the corners of his mouth twitch. "You've called me names?"

"Never where anyone could hear me."

"Of course."

"Meaning?"

"Just that you're too much of a lady to ever let loose."

"And there's something wrong with being a lady?"

In the back of his mind a rational voice warned that he was baiting her. At the beginning of their association he'd often lobbed provocative statements her way. But she'd been far too professional to react and eventually he'd stopped aggravating her. This conversation felt different. As if she'd let the mask slide and was giving him a taste of her true self.

"Only that you never seem to have any fun."

She wasn't the only one who'd done her homework. He knew about the contest she was waging against her half sisters to one day take over as CEO of the family business. She'd had a phenomenal amount of success in her career, but Harper wasn't one to rest on her past achievements. In that way, they were alike. No one could put as much pressure on Harper as she put on herself.

"I have a great deal riding on the success of my hotel." She wouldn't stop until she had everything exactly the way she wanted it. "And you aren't one to talk. You barely take any time off between filming *The Culinary Wanderer,* promoting the series and managing your other restaurants."

"I won't deny that I'm busy, but I also take time to enjoy what I'm doing." He cocked his head. "Do you?"

"I enjoy my work. I wouldn't be doing it if I didn't." But beneath her vehemence was a grain of doubt.

She'd tried to hide her weariness with a careful application of concealer and blush, but he'd watched her long hours bite deeper into her energy each time he came to check on the restaurant's progress.

"But there must be something for you besides work," he said. "What's something you've always wanted to do but haven't gotten around to yet?"

"You make it sound like I'm sacrificing everything for my career."

In fact, he hadn't been saying that at all, but that she chose to interpret his question this way told him more than she'd intended.

"Everyone has dreams of something carefree and fun they'd like to do someday."

"I agree."

"Tell me one of yours."

"I don't get the point."

Was she stalling? Trying to come up with something safe? "Humor me. What's the first thing that pops into your mind?"

With her brows drawn together in exasperation, she blurted out, "I'd like to ride a camel across the desert and sleep in a tent."

Ashton wasn't sure which of them was more surprised by her outburst. "Seriously?" He laughed. "That's not at all what I expected you to say. I thought you'd tell me you wanted to…" He trailed off. They'd worked together for nine months and he knew so little about her.

"Wanted to what?" she prompted, wary curiosity in her warm brown eyes.

"I'm not sure. You aren't the sort of woman I imagine wanting to run off to Paris on a shopping spree or lounge on a yacht." She was too driven by timetables to enjoy such frivolous pursuits. "Maybe something more serious-minded. A visit to a museum, perhaps?"

His suggestion didn't meet with her approval. "You

know, I'm a little tired of everyone criticizing me for being too serious."

Whoa, he'd definitely touched a nerve there. "Who is everyone?"

"My family. My classmates when I was in school. Friends. Life isn't all about play, you know." She glanced down at her smartphone and frowned.

"It's also not all about work."

Sharp irritation sliced through her voice. "Says the man who rarely does any."

"Well, well, well." He flashed her a big grin. "That's some hellcat you keep bottled up."

She stared at him in consternation before sputtering, "That's ridiculous. There's no hellcat here."

"You didn't see the bloodlust in your eyes just now."

Her jaw worked as if she was grinding something particularly nasty between her teeth. "I'll admit to being a little on edge. You are not the easiest man to work with."

"Maybe not work with," he agreed. "But when you're ready to have some fun, give me a call."

In the quiet of the restaurant, Harper stared at Ashton with raised brows and lips softly parted. His offer wasn't sexual in nature, but when he spied the hope that flickered in her melted-chocolate eyes, his perception of her shifted dramatically.

"I don't have time—"

"For fun." He scrutinized her expression. "Yes, so you've said."

As a teenager, he'd fallen in with some dangerous criminals. Learning to read micro expressions had helped him survive. That he'd not picked up on the passionate woman concealed beneath Harper's professional exterior pointed out just how complacent he'd become.

Time to wake up and start paying attention.

She cleared her throat. "Getting back to Chef Cole…"

"I'll hire him if you spend an evening with me." This time he was deliberately hitting on her.

She set her hands on her hips and scowled at him. "Five minutes ago you were ready to pass on him."

"Five minutes ago I didn't realize just how starved for adventure you were."

"I'm very happy right where I am."

"When the first thing on your bucket list is riding a camel in the desert and sleeping in a tent, forgive me if I don't believe your life is as satisfying as you'd have people believe."

"I don't have a bucket list," she retorted. "And if I did, that wouldn't be the first thing on it. It was just something that popped into my head. I remember you doing that in an episode of *The Culinary Wanderer.*"

"You're a fan?"

"Before I get into business with someone I do my research."

Sensible. But he hoped that hadn't been her only motivation. Swept by the urge to see her let her hair down, literally and figuratively, he decided to ignore her verbal cues and concentrate on what she was saying with her body.

"And your research involved watching my shows? I would have thought you'd be more interested in hard facts such as the financials of my four other restaurants and the uptick in advertising revenue my show brings to the network."

"All those things paint a very positive picture of you. I also spoke with a number of your employees and several of the crew who worked with you on your shows. As I said, I do my research."

Obviously she knew much more about him than he knew about her. The imbalance bothered him. "Then you know the sort of businessman I am, and when I say I'm willing to hire a chef you favor, it's not done lightly."

With her gaze firmly attached to his left shoulder, she murmured, "In exchange for a night with me."

"I proposed an evening." He couldn't help but laugh at the conclusion she'd jumped to. "You have a naughty mind if you think I'd barter hiring Cole for sex."

Hot color flared in her cheeks. "That's not what I was thinking."

"Oh, I think it was. I told you that hellcat was going to get you into trouble."

"I misspoke."

"I don't think so." Now that she was off balance, he decided to keep her that way. "I think it was a Freudian slip. You want me. You just can't admit it."

"What I want is for you to hire a chef and get him trained to your exacting standards so I don't have to worry about what happens after you leave."

She'd taken refuge in exasperation, but it wasn't fooling him.

"My offer still stands. Give me one evening and I'll hire Cole."

"Why would you want to spend an evening with me?" She looked as frazzled as he'd ever seen her.

"I thought you'd be interested in tasting the dishes I'm considering for the restaurant."

Her eyes narrowed. "And that's all there is to it?"

"Of course."

She regarded him in silence for several heartbeats before replying. "Hire Cole. You need someone accomplished to run your kitchen while you're off playing celebrity." With that, she pivoted on her conservative black pumps and strode across to his bag. Snagging the handle, she pulled it after her. "I'm taking this as collateral," she called over her shoulder.

It was a silly gesture—taking his clothes hostage wouldn't prevent him from getting on a plane—and so unlike Harper, the consummate professional. Ashton's gaze followed her, appreciating the pronounced sway of her hips. Thinking she'd put one over on him had injected a trace of strut into her stride.

"I will hire him," Ashton promised her. "And you will spend the evening with me."

"Sampling your menu." Her words floated back to him.

He'd been right about the hellcat lurking beneath her skin. It had been asleep far too long and he was the perfect guy to rouse it.

His final shot chased her out of the restaurant. "I'm going to make it a night you'll never forget."

Two

Smugness from her encounter with Ashton lasted about a second as she strode out of the restaurant and headed toward her office. What had she been thinking to walk off with his luggage? He must think she'd gone mad.

Well, hadn't she?

She'd agreed to an evening with him. Harper had no doubt she'd signed on for more than a private tasting of his menu. Which meant she was in big trouble. Already her mouth watered at the prospect of being the beneficiary of his culinary prowess. As long as that was the only prowess he plied her with, she might survive the evening without making a fool of herself. If he decided to test her level of resistance to his manly charms she wasn't going to maintain her professionalism very long.

Her skin burned as she thought of how he'd called her on her assumption that he wanted sex in exchange for hiring the chef she preferred. Not once had she suspected Ashton was the sort of man to make such a sordid offer. So why had she jumped to that conclusion? Even worse, why had she lobbed the accusation at him? Naturally, he'd presumed her misunderstanding represented her deepest desires.

And he was probably right. For the past nine months she'd been complaining that the real Ashton Croft wasn't as wonderful as the one on television. But that wasn't exactly true. His persona on TV was charismatic and amusing. He was the cool guy everyone wanted to hang out with. The flesh and blood Ashton Croft was no less appealing. It was just that the travel series didn't fully convey the masculine energy of the man. The rawness of his sex appeal.

Most of the time she focused on how frustrating he was. She was terrified of being bamboozled by his dimples and rakish grin. If he had any idea how easily he could knock her socks off, he'd probably go after a few other items of clothing, as well.

Harper shook her head at the thought. She was not going to sleep with Ashton Croft. It would be different if they'd met in some exotic locale; she could see herself being one of his random hook ups. The next morning, she would chalk up the evening as an adventure worth having. Hadn't she spent tedious hours on the treadmill imagining all sorts of spicy scenarios where she bumped into Ashton at a vineyard in Tuscany or on a walk around Dubrovnik's ancient city walls? There they would share a sunset and he'd persuade her to join him for dinner. On a private terrace overlooking the Adriatic Sea and surrounded by candles, he'd take her into his arms and…

The faint smell of cigarette smoke ripped Harper from her daydream.

Parking Ashton's *go* bag just inside the door of her office, Harper surveyed her formerly pristine sanctuary. Her mother's ostrich leather Burberry holdall sat on the sky-blue sofa, half the contents scattered around it. An empty pack of cigarettes lay crushed on the coffee table beside a crystal tumbler with a pale pink lipstick stain. The elegant lines of a cream trench coat were draped over Harper's executive chair. Her mother had definitely moved in.

Penelope Fontaine stood by the window overlooking the Las Vegas strip, her right hand resting at her throat, as if protecting the string of large black pearls she wore. A thin tendril of smoke rose from the cigarette pinched between the fingers of her other hand. In a black-and-white Chanel dress, with her long blond hair pulled away from her face in a classic chignon, she looked elegant and untouchable.

The sight stirred up memories of the day her parents had sat her down and explained that they were splitting up. Her mother needed to move to Florida for her health. Harper would remain in New York City with her father. Which basically meant she'd be alone with the staff because Ross Fontaine had spent most of his time avoiding the company's New York headquarters and his father's expectations. With Fontaine Hotels and Resorts' extensive holdings in the U.S. and abroad, Harper's father could be as irresponsible as he wanted without Henry Fontaine being the wiser.

"Mother, I would appreciate it if you didn't smoke in my office." Harper advanced toward Penelope, ready to pluck the cigarette from her mother if she didn't comply.

"I'm sorry, Harper." Crossing to the coffee table, she dropped the cigarette into the empty glass. "You know how I revert when I'm upset."

The lingering smell of smoke made Harper's nose tingle unpleasantly. "What's bothering you?" She fetched a can of air freshener from one of the cabinets that lined the east wall and sprayed the room with ocean breezes.

"I need your help." Penelope's voice warbled as she spoke the last word.

Unsure whether her mother was being theatrical or if she was truly in trouble, Harper took a quick inventory. Penelope's eyes looked like a forest after a downpour, the green enhanced by the redness that rimmed them.

"You've been crying." This was no bid for her daughter's attention. "What's wrong?"

"Something terrible has happened." Harper heard the weight of the world in Penelope's voice. "Why else do you think I came to this godforsaken city? It's not as if you'd come visit me in Florida."

"The hotel is taking all my energy right now." Harper knew better than to book passage on her mother's guilt trip, but her encounter with Ashton had stirred up her emotions. "Why didn't you go to Grandfather?"

Penelope fiddled with the ten-carat diamond she wore on her left hand despite her husband's death five years earlier. Why would she take if off now when she'd worn the ring through eighteen years of being separated from Ross Fontaine?

"Henry can't help me with this."

"But I can?" Harper struggled to get her head around this shift in her world's axis.

Never once had her mother reached out like this. Penelope was of the mindset that only men could solve the world's problems. Women were supposed to adorn their husbands' arms, looking beautiful and displaying graceful manners. They weren't supposed to run billion-dollar corporations at the expense of attracting lovers, much less suitable husbands.

"You're the only one who can."

All her life Harper had been waiting for her mother to acknowledge her as powerful and capable. That Penelope had turned to her daughter for help was as thrilling a victory as Harper had ever known. "What do you need?"

"Money."

Her mother received a sizeable allowance each month from the Fontaine family trust. What could she possibly need to buy that she couldn't turn to Harper's grandfather? "Why?"

"I'm being blackmailed."

Blackmailed? This was the last thing Harper expected to hear.

"Have you spoken to the police?" To Harper's mind, paying a blackmailer was never a good idea.

Penelope stared at Harper as if she'd suggested her mother get a job. "This is private business."

"Blackmail is illegal."

"I will not have my personal affairs become public knowledge."

Until her mother had retreated to Florida, Harper had been conditioned daily to believe that image was everything. And even though she'd subsequently found her true strength lay in being resourceful and focused, that earlier rhetoric wasn't easily ignored.

"I understand your reputation means everything to you, but what's to say the blackmailer won't leak the information even though you pay him?"

"He's promised not to." Penelope said this as if stunned that her daughter could be that stupid. "I came here thinking you'd help me."

Harper chewed on a sigh before saying, "How much do you need?"

"Three hundred and fifty thousand dollars."

The sum rendered Harper speechless for a long moment. "What did you do?"

Treating her mother with such bluntness wasn't going to win Harper any points, but the amount had caught her off guard.

Penelope gathered outrage around her like a shawl. "That's none of your concern."

"Excuse me for interrupting." Ashton strode into the room, looking far from remorseful that he'd barged in.

Too stunned by the bomb her mother had dropped to react to his intrusion, Harper sat motionless and watched him approach. His gaze shifted from her to Penelope, and Harper wondered if he was comparing mother and daughter.

Was he making the assumption that Harper and her mother were the same? Wealthy women, confident in their identity, knowing exactly how their lives were going to play out and content with the direction. Most days that's how Harper felt. Not today.

"Harper?" her mother's low warning tone prodded Harper to her feet.

"Mother, this is Chef Ashton Croft. He is the creative genius behind Batouri. Ashton, this is my mother, Penelope Fontaine."

She ignored the flash of humor in Ashton's eyes as she introduced him as a creative genius. It was true. No matter how big a pain in the ass he'd been, there was no denying the man was brilliant in the kitchen.

"Delighted to meet you," Penelope murmured, extending her hand like a queen to her subject.

Harper mentally rolled her eyes as Ashton clasped her mother's hand and flashed his charismatic celebrity grin.

"I've enjoyed working with your daughter."

Liar.

He'd tolerated her at best.

Seeing the effect his dazzling persona was having on her mother, Harper momentarily surrendered to amusement. Not normally one to be charmed by a handsome face or flirtation, Penelope appeared as if she'd forgotten all about the blackmail that had driven her more than two thousand miles to seek her daughter's help.

As much as she hated interrupting their mutual love fest, Harper wanted to return to her mother's blackmail problem and get the issue solved. "Is there something you needed from me?" she asked Ashton.

His attention swung to her. "Just my laptop. I have a video conference in ten minutes."

"It's over there." She gestured toward the black bag.

He bent to a side pocket in the duffel and took out a thin silver computer. Harper followed the smooth bunch and

flex of his muscles, and her breath hissed out in appreciation. Strong and athletic in his cargo pants, denim shirt
and hiking boots, sun-streaked shaggy hair falling into his
bright blue eyes, he represented everything that Harper was
not. Physical, unpredictable, exciting. The yang to her yin,
she realized, and felt heat rise in her cheeks.

"Leave the bag," she commanded, her voice a husky
blur. "I'm not done with you yet."

The corner of his mouth kicked up. "Of course."

She caught his smug gaze and stared him down in silence, refusing to backpedal or stumble through an explanation of what she'd actually meant. And maybe just a little
afraid to ask herself about the subtext he'd picked up on.

"Check with Mary to see which conference room is
available."

"I appreciate the accommodation."

"Come see me when you're done. I'm interested to hear
how your conversation with Chef Cole went."

"I look forward to telling you. Will you be here?"

Harper glanced at her mother. "I'm not certain where
I'll be. Ask Mary. She has a knack for finding me."

He nodded and exited her office. With his departure,
the energy level in the room plummeted. Harper's heart
pounded in her chest as if she'd done a two-minute sprint
on her treadmill.

"You're letting that scruffy man open a restaurant in
your hotel?"

Penelope's criticism would've stung if Harper hadn't
witnessed her mother batting her eyelash extensions at *that
scruffy man* only moments before. "He only recently returned from four months in Indonesia."

"I thought you said he was a chef. What was he doing
there?"

"Filming his television series, *The Culinary Wanderer*."
Harper waited for her mother to recognize the name. "He
travels all over the world, eating local cuisine and bring-

ing attention to the history or current troubles of the places where he films."

"I don't watch much television. It's too depressing."

Harper didn't bother arguing. Penelope lived in a snug bubble. She played golf in the morning and then lunched with friends. After a few hours spent shopping, the remainder of her day was taken up by something cultural or philanthropic. The only interruption to her schedule happened when she traveled to the Hamptons to visit her mother or decided a room of her condo needed updating.

"His show is very popular."

"I'm sure you know what you're doing," Penelope replied, her tone indicating that she'd dismissed a subject that no longer interested her. "How soon can you get me the money I need?"

"I'll call the bank and have them wire the funds as soon as you tell me who is blackmailing you and why."

"I'm your mother," Penelope huffed. "Don't you dare barter with me."

Before Harper could argue, Mary appeared in the doorway. "Your grandfather is on line one and Carlo called to say Chef Cole wants to talk to you as soon as you're available." Mary placed a wealth of emphasis on that last part.

She needed to do some damage control. "Tell him I'll be down as soon as I'm done talking to Grandfather. Maybe ten or fifteen minutes."

Penelope clutched her daughter's arm as Harper began to rise. "You can't say anything to Henry."

"Why don't we sort this business out over dinner later," she suggested, attempting to pacify her mother. "I need to know more details before we proceed."

"But you are going to help me," Penelope stated, anxiety shadowing her determined tone.

"Of course." Harper's gaze skittered away from the relief in her mother's eyes and fell on her assistant.

Mary had been waiting patiently through their exchange.

Seeing she'd regained Harper's attention, she switched on her headset and spoke to the caller. "She's on her way to the phone now. Okay, I'll let her know. Your grandfather has had to take another call. He'll catch up with you at four our time."

"Thank you, Mary." Harper turned to her mother. "I have some business to take care of. It shouldn't take more than twenty minutes."

Penelope glanced at her watch. "I have a manicure appointment in half an hour."

It made perfect sense to Harper that her mother would schedule a beauty treatment in the midst of a personal crisis. No matter how bad things got, she never neglected her appearance.

"Mary will get you settled in a suite. I'll order dinner to be served there at seven. We can talk then."

Ashton lounged in the Fontaine Ciel's executive conference room, tapping his fingers against the tabletop in a rhythm that called to him from the past. He had his back to the large monitor set on the wall opposite the door that led to the hall. The network suits in New York had not yet figured out the connection was live and he was gaining some useful insights into their thought processes.

He'd been in negotiations for a brand-new television series for almost five months now. The Lifestyle Network wanted him to star in a culinary show that "showcased his talent." Or at least that was the way his manager, Vince, had pitched it. Ashton agreed that it was a solid career move. Something he'd been working toward these past eight years.

It would allow him to live permanently in New York City. He'd never again have to travel under the most uncomfortable conditions to places that no one in their right mind wanted to live.

Too bad he loved all those miserable out-of-the-way places he visited. Nor was Lifestyle Network's demand that he quit *The Culinary Wanderer* if they gave him his new show sitting well with Ashton. With the sort of taping schedule he had with the travel show, there was no reason why he couldn't do both. He'd given six years to Phillips Consolidated Networks and *The Culinary Wanderer*. The show remained vital and continued to do well in the ratings. Giving it up made no sense. And then there was all the aid that the places he visited received as a result of the show.

He hadn't set.out to do a culinary series that highlighted socioeconomic and political issues around the world. He'd started out romping around the globe doing a six-part series featuring out of the way culinary adventures for the network's travel channel. At some point toward the end of the first season, he'd started to see the potential of shining the light of television on some of the places regular travelers would never go. But it wasn't until the first segments aired that he realized he was raising social awareness.

The series' high ratings caught the network executives' attention. They liked what they saw and wanted to work with him again so Ashton pitched them a show focused as much on the problems faced by the locals as it was about the regional cuisine. Six months later, *The Culinary Wanderer* was born.

By the end of the first season, his viewership had increased threefold. Inspired by the flood of emails from viewers asking how they could help, the network partnered with a world help organization to bring aid to the areas hit hardest by war and poverty. It was somewhat surreal to discover he did more good with his half-hour television series than his parents did in a year with their missionary work. And it was sad to realize no matter how much he did, they would never approve of his methods.

Still, money had been raised. People had been fed and given medicine. Sources of fresh water had been brought to villages that needed it. But no matter how much Ashton accomplished there was always another town ravaged by unrest or burdened by poverty. His gut told him he shouldn't walk away from all those who still needed help. Yet wasn't it this exact sort of arrogance—that he was somehow special and necessary for others' salvation—that made him so angry with his father?

"Chef Croft, are you ready to begin?"

Ashton swiveled around and gave the assembled group an easy smile. "Whenever you are, gentlemen."

He could see that his manager was on the call from his L.A. office. Vince's expression gave away none of the concern he'd voiced to Ashton late last night, but he wasn't looking as relaxed as usual. This show would take Ashton from celebrity chef to household name. From there the possibilities were endless.

"Chef Croft," began Steven Bell, a midlevel executive who'd been acting as the group's mouthpiece these past several months. He was the third in a line of conservatively dressed, middle-aged men with a talent for pointing out problems and little else. "We have slotted the new show to begin the end of February and would like to start taping in three weeks. Is that a problem?"

"Not at all."

Several of the men exchanged glances, and Ashton picked up on it. If he'd learned anything in the past several months, he'd discovered the path to superstardom wasn't a smooth one.

"We've been told your restaurant in the Fontaine hotel is behind schedule," said the man Ashton thought of as Executive Orange because whatever spray tan he used gave his skin a sunset glow.

"Untrue. It's set to open in two weeks."

"And your expectation is that you'll have it running smoothly immediately?"

Ashton knew what was going on. Vince had warned him that since Ashton was unwilling to give in on the matter of quitting *The Culinary Wanderer* they were looking at other chefs in an effort to force his hand.

"I will be leaving my kitchen in good hands. I offered Chef Dillon Cole the head chef position." He left out the fact that Cole hadn't agreed to take the job.

"He's out of Chicago, correct?"

Unsure which of the six executives had spoken, Ashton nodded. "A talented chef." Which was perfectly true, despite his earlier criticism. Ashton just wasn't sure he was the right man for Batouri, but he was running out of time and options. If he wanted to host the new show, he needed to be available.

"We'd like you to come to New York next week and spend a couple days working with our producers. We feel you should be on the set and run through a couple versions of the show to get some film that we could run past a couple of our current hosts for their input."

"What days did you have in mind?"

"Wednesday and Thursday. We could schedule something in the afternoon, say around two?"

Harper was going to filet him when she caught wind of this impromptu trip. "I'll be there."

"We're looking forward to seeing you."

After a few more niceties and good luck wishes for his restaurant opening, the New York executives signed off. When it was just Ashton and Vince still on the call, the manager let his true feelings show.

"Those bastards are not making this easy, are they?"

"Did you really expect them to?" Ashton countered. "This isn't a travel network with a couple hundred thousand viewers. This channel draws over a million viewers for some of its least popular primetime shows."

"What I expected is for them to be falling all over themselves to bring you in. They're looking to give their lineup more sex appeal. While the numbers have been slipping for cooking shows lately, home improvement segments are on the rise."

"Any idea why?"

"If you listen to my wife and daughter, it's all due to the hunky carpenters they've been hiring."

Ashton grinned. "So you're saying they aren't as interested in my culinary expertise as my impressive physique?"

"How does that make you feel?"

"Like we should be negotiating for more money."

"Maybe I should suggest you do the episodes shirtless."

"Don't give them any ideas." Ashton grimaced. "They'll probably turn it into a bit. Stay tuned for the next segment when Chef Croft will burn off his shirt."

"Well, you'd better get that restaurant of yours open in Vegas or you won't have to worry about what they want you to wear."

"Have you heard from the guys over at Phillips about the proposals I made regarding next season's location?"

In addition to negotiating with the Lifestyle Network, he was in talks with Phillips Consolidated Networks for his seventh season of *The Culinary Wanderer*. They were pushing him to film next season in Africa. They'd reasoned that since he was South African, he would enjoy returning to the land of his birth. The exact opposite was true, but since he'd created an elaborate backstory that had nothing to do with his true history, he couldn't provide an excuse strong enough to dissuade them.

"They rejected England immediately. Apparently your best ratings come when you are off the beaten track. The Indonesian stuff has been a huge hit with everyone who's seen it."

"What about South America? I could get six or seven episodes out of Brazil alone."

"They said they'd consider it for next year." Vince rolled a pen between his palms. "I think if you want to keep doing the show, it's going to have to be Africa. Of course, that's dependent on whether Lifestyle Network gives up on getting an exclusive on you."

Frustration with the producers of *The Culinary Wanderer* had led him to talk to Lifestyle Network. He wanted to grow his career in a big way and the new show could do that. Becoming a household name would open a lot of doors. But it wasn't where his heart lay. He'd never stop craving new adventures in exotic locations. It's why he intended to find a way to do both. Being forced to choose between his passion and his ambition wasn't an option.

"I really don't want to go to Africa."

"Come on. How bad can it be? You still have family there, don't you?"

"Sure." In fact, he had no idea if his parents were still alive. He hadn't spoken to them since he left home at fifteen. A lot of bad things could happen in twenty years, especially in the sort of places his parents took their missionary work.

He heard the door open behind him and noticed the change in Vince's demeanor. His manager sat forward in his desk chair and ran his fingers through his short sandy-blond hair. Glancing over his shoulder, Ashton noticed Harper had entered the room. She didn't look happy.

"Gotta go, Vince. Keep in touch." He ended the network connection and the monitor in the room went blank. "Thanks for letting me borrow your equipment. This is some nice stuff."

"Chef Cole tells me he's not going to be our head chef."

"I offered him the job just like you wanted."

"I wanted you to hire him."

"He turned me down." Ashton pushed his chair back from the conference table and stood up.

"So, now what?"

"You have me."

"I need someone permanent. How long before you take off again?"

Next week, but in her current state of displeasure, he wasn't going to mention that.

"Not to worry. I have someone I trust who I've been training. He arrives tomorrow."

"Who is it?"

"I met Dae Tan a few months ago. Helped him out of a jam."

"What sort of a jam?" Her skepticism came through loud and clear.

"He was arrested for something he didn't do."

"You're sure he was innocent."

"Absolutely. After that, things got a little hot for him. He's been traveling with me and I've been training him."

"Why didn't he come with you today?"

"He wanted to see L.A. He has this thing about movie stars."

Harper regarded him with suspicion. "Where has he worked? Is he capable of handling the pressure of a restaurant like Batouri?"

"It'll be fine. The kid's got talent."

"Kid?" She echoed his description and her irritation grew. "How old is he?"

"Twenty-five. Twenty-six."

"You can't be serious." Harper advanced on him. "You've passed on chefs with twenty-five *years* of experience and now you're telling me you want to hire someone who's been in the field a couple years."

"Months," Ashton corrected. "He only had the most rudimentary skills when I met him."

Harper's eyes closed while she sucked in a deep breath and let it out. When she opened them again, she looked no calmer. "You're crazy if you think I'll go for this."

"You really don't have a choice."

"We'll see about that." Harper folded her arms across her chest. "You forget we have a contract." Her tone indicated he'd stretched her goodwill as far as it would go.

"I have a great deal riding on this restaurant, as well," he reminded her.

"Then act like it."

The trouble was, he had a great deal riding on every iron he had in the fire. He was determined to leave his mark on the world and that meant going big. Would it have been smarter to not stick his neck out? Sure. He could have played it safe, kept going with the same shows he'd had success with these past eight years, but Ashton liked the rush of conquering new territory, seeing what lay beyond the horizon.

Harper continued, "Go convince Cole to take the job at Batouri."

"I thought you said he'd gone to the airport."

"I caught him before he left the hotel and convinced him to fly to Chicago tomorrow. You have reservations next door at Fontaine Chic's award-winning steakhouse at seven. You might as well sample the competition. Perhaps you will both dislike the food and find some common ground to build a relationship on."

"And our evening together?"

She shot him a cool smile. "When Cole takes the job, I'll block out two hours for you."

"Make it three and you have a deal."

Three

With the Chef Cole problem handled for the time being and her mother safely ensconced in the day spa, Harper was able to steal a few minutes to herself to take stock of the day. Thank heavens they weren't all like this.

Unable to imagine what her mother had done to open herself up to blackmail, Harper paced her hotel, trying to find comfort in achievement. The ceilings throughout had been painted to represent different aspects of the sky her hotel was named for. In the lobby, it was a pale midday blue dotted with clouds. Lighting changed from dawn to dusk to match what was happening outside. The casino ceiling was a midnight indigo sparkling with thousands of pinpoint lights configured like the star patterns above Las Vegas.

It was a simple concept, beautifully rendered. She was proud of all she'd accomplished. But today, there was no joy to be found in surveying her domain. Harper glanced at her watch. Two hours to kill. With her ability to concentrate shot and no meetings or crisis pending, she considered returning to her suite and running on her treadmill. Or she could go talk to Scarlett.

Five years ago when her grandfather had come to her with news that she had two half sisters, she'd been angry, miserable and excited. She'd been eleven when she'd first learned her father regularly cheated on his wife, but until five years ago, she'd had no idea his extramarital wandering had messed up more lives than just hers and her mother's.

A quick walk through the skyways that connected the three Fontaine hotels brought Harper to Fontaine Richesse, Scarlett's hotel. She sought out her sister in the casino. Spotting Scarlett was easy. She radiated sex appeal and charisma in her emerald-green flapper costume, her long brown hair tucked beneath a twenties-style, shingle bob wig with bangs.

The rest of the casino staff was dressed like something out of a movie from the forties and fifties: men in elegant tuxedos and suits or military uniforms from the Second World War, women in evening gowns or stylish dresses.

Harper had thought the whole idea of a Golden Age of Hollywood night was crazy. But she'd underestimated her sister's brilliance. The casino was packed. Many of those playing the machines or lining the tables were also dressed in costume. There were prizes awarded for best outfit, and casino cash was given to anyone who guessed what particular movie the dealers or waitresses were dressed from.

Scarlett wore a delighted grin as the man who'd approached her guessed her costume.

"Cyd Charrise, *Singin' In The Rain?*"

"That's right." She handed him a card he could trade in for money to gamble with. As he walked off, she spotted Harper. "What a surprise."

"You look amazing," Harper said, admiring the dress and matching green satin pumps. "Is it new?"

"First time I've worn it." She struck a pose. "I think Laurie outdid herself." Scarlett had been friends with the

Hollywood costume designer for years and used her for every costume in the casino.

"I would agree."

When she'd first met Scarlett, Harper hadn't given the former child actress much credit. She couldn't imagine what her grandfather had been thinking when he'd concocted the contest between his three granddaughters. What could someone with Scarlett's background know about running a multibillion-dollar hotel much less a corporation the size of Fontaine Hotels and Resorts? Five years later, Harper was a huge fan of Scarlett's creativity and authenticity. She knew exactly who she was and had played directly to her strengths.

"Do you have time for a drink?" Harper asked, instantly seeing her request had startled Scarlett.

Harper was the family workaholic. Rarely did she sit down in the evenings when the casino was busiest, much less take time out to eat or drink.

"For you, always." They found a table in a quiet corner of the lobby bar. Scarlett ordered two glasses of cabernet and made small talk until the drinks arrived. "What's wrong?" she asked as soon as Harper had taken a sip of wine.

"What makes you think...?" She could see Scarlett wasn't fooled. "I don't want you to assume that I'm only here because I needed help."

"I don't care why you're here." Scarlett gave her a lopsided smile. "And I'm glad Violet is out of town with JT. Otherwise, I know you'd have gone to her first."

"That's unfair." But probably true. As much as Harper loved her half sister, she wasn't always comfortable with Scarlett.

In so many ways, they were opposites. Scarlett was gorgeous, flamboyant and utterly fearless when it came to her relationships. Hadn't she tackled Logan Wolfe and turned the tetchy security expert into a big purring lion?

She'd managed to do the same thing with Harper. Wariness had become loyalty, something Harper gave rarely and not without reservation. But Scarlett had won her over for the most part.

"Okay, there is something wrong." Harper paused, knowing Scarlett deserved more. "But you aren't right about how I'd go to Violet instead of you. If she was here, I'd have come to both of you with this."

"Must be serious." Scarlett's lips curved into a wicked smile. "Do you need some advice about Ashton Croft? I heard he's back in town."

"Nothing like that."

"I suggest you sleep with him."

"What?" Harper cursed the sudden heat in her cheeks. "I'm not going to sleep with him. Our relationship is strictly professional."

"You should reconsider that. I know you have a thing for him. And he looks like he'd be a riot in bed."

Harper needed Scarlett to get off that particular subject. "My mother is being blackmailed."

All mischief went out of Scarlett. She paled. "Blackmailed? Why?"

"I don't know. She won't tell me."

"Does she know who is doing it?"

Harper shook her head. "It's all so crazy. My mother. The perfect Penelope Fontaine. I can't imagine her doing anything wrong much less anything scandalous enough to invite blackmail."

"How did you find out?"

"She came here needing to borrow money."

"How much?"

"Three hundred and fifty thousand."

Scarlett gasped. "That's a lot."

"I keep wondering what she's done. It must be something truly awful for them to be asking that much."

"From what you've told me," Scarlett began, "your

mother isn't great at considering the value of something before she spends. Is she sure what happened is worth that much money?"

"It's hard to say with my mother. She's so big on keeping her reputation unsullied, it might be something as simple as a bump and run." But Harper couldn't picture her mother having a minor accident much less fleeing the scene of one.

"Could she have cheated on her taxes?"

"Impossible. Grandfather handles all her finances." Penelope's lack of financial smarts was what had caused Grandfather to put her on an allowance and hire a money manager to pay the bills.

"I don't suppose she wants to call the police." Scarlett framed the question as if she already knew the answer.

"She won't do that," Harper said. "The blackmailer will make her secret public."

"Do you need help coming up with the cash? I have some money set aside."

Her sister's offer came so fast Harper doubted Scarlett considered the magnitude of the gesture. She was humbled by her sister's affection. "Thanks, but I didn't come here for that."

"Then why?"

"I thought talking with you would put me in a calmer frame of mind before I have dinner with my mother."

"She's here?"

"Showed up this afternoon out of the blue."

Harper had never spoken directly about how she and Penelope got along, but both her sisters knew that Harper's mother had left her daughter behind in New York City and moved to Florida. It wasn't a stretch to deduce that things between mother and daughter weren't good. But if anyone understood that family could produce the most complicated relationships, it would be Harper and Scarlett.

"Why don't I talk with Logan," Scarlett suggested. "Maybe there's something he or Lucas can do."

"I don't know if anyone can help at this point."

"Are you kidding? Logan and his brother are security experts. They should be able to figure out who's blackmailing your mom without breaking a sweat. If not before the blackmail is paid, then I know they can track where the money goes."

Harper was suddenly feeling a whole lot better. Impulsively, she hugged Scarlett. "I don't know what I would do without you and Violet."

"I'm glad to hear you say that. I wasn't always sure you liked having us in your life."

Scarlett's admission twisted Harper's stomach into knots of regret. "I'm sorry I've made you feel that way. In the beginning it wasn't easy embracing you as sisters. I'd been alone my whole life and hadn't exactly been smothered with love by my parents. I didn't really understand what it meant to be family."

"I hope that's changed."

"It has. You and Violet are the most important people in my life along with Grandfather." Seeing the tears that filled Scarlett's beautiful green eyes, Harper wished she'd made this confession long ago. "I'm sorry if I made it seem otherwise. I've been so focused on getting Fontaine Ciel built and running that I haven't been a very good sister."

Scarlett waved the apology away and dabbed at her eyes with a napkin. Delight filled her voice as she said, "You didn't need to say anything. We knew how you felt."

Harper made a resolution to be more open with her sisters going forward. It wouldn't be easy. She'd spent her whole life bottling up her feelings. Her mother wasn't demonstrative and her father's rare appearances in her life hadn't been filled with warm moments. In school she'd been a leader and her habit of ruling by persuasion and occasional ruthlessness hadn't won her the love of the majority of her classmates. But it hadn't mattered as long as they followed her. Or so she'd told herself.

"Let me call Logan and see what he suggests we do."

"I'm sure he's not going to want you to do anything," Harper said with a faint smile.

"Since when has that stopped me?"

Scarlett had given her fiancé a lot to worry about after inheriting some files from Tiberius Stone, Violet's surrogate father. The casino owner had been murdered by a local councilman who'd been embezzling campaign contributions. Tiberius had accumulated a storage unit full of people's secrets including his brother-in-law, a man who'd stolen the identity of Preston Rhodes, a wealthy orphan from California. Violet had gone to Miami intent on bringing him to justice in order to help her husband take back his family's company.

"It's rolling to voice mail," Scarlett said. After leaving Logan a brief summary of the situation, she hung up. "It won't take him long to call me back. Do you want to wait?"

About to say yes, Harper suddenly remembered she still had Ashton's *go* bag. "Can't. I have to see a man about a bag."

Scarlett cocked her head in puzzlement, but nodded. "As soon as I hear from Logan, I'll call you. In the meantime, can you stall your mother?"

"I can try."

Leaving Scarlett, Harper made her way back to the Fontaine Ciel's executive floor. Mary had gone for the day, locking Harper's office before she left. Harper half expected Ashton to have persuaded the personal assistant to give him his bag, but to her surprise, either Mary had resisted the celebrity chef's charm or Ashton had stuck to his part of the bargain.

Either way, she grabbed the bag and shot a quick text to let him know the luggage would be waiting for him at Batouri. But when she got there, she was surprised to find Ashton sitting at the corner table where his bag had sat earlier.

* * *

When the door to the restaurant opened, Ashton was
nursing a tumbler of ten-year-old Scotch. It was his third.
The first two had gone down fast and smooth. He didn't
think he should continue at that pace or his dinner with
Cole might not go the way Harper wanted.

That she spotted him so fast made him smile. She felt
it, too. This irresistible pull between them. How had he ignored it until now? Oh, she was good at hiding it. And he
hadn't exactly given her any reason to feel more than irritation toward him. He wanted to strip her layers of professionalism away and get to the firecracker below. How hot
would the fire burn? And for how long? With fireworks,
the thrill was in those seconds of exhilarating danger. The
breathtaking waterfall of light. The big boom that lingered
in the chest even after the sound faded.

Still, it might be worth sacrificing her goodwill to experience the rush.

"What brings you here?" He sipped the Scotch, felt the
burn in his chest.

"I'm returning your *go* bag."

He'd been so focused on Harper he hadn't even noticed
that she was towing his bag along.

You're slipping.

In the places he traveled, being distracted for even a
moment could be trouble.

"The deal isn't done with Cole yet," he reminded her.
"Are you sure you don't want to keep it hostage for a bit
longer?" Maybe take it back to her suite. "I could pick it
up later."

She parked the bag beside the booth. "I've lost my taste
for blackmail in the past few hours." Her gaze flicked to
the glass and then to his mouth.

His heart tapped unsteadily against his ribs. "Anything
you'd like to talk about?"

"No."

"Are you sure?"

Was it the alcohol that was making him light-headed or the way she was staring at him as if she wondered what he'd taste like? She reached for his glass, and he figured she was going to chastise him for drinking up the restaurant's stock. Instead, she lifted the tumbler to her lips and tossed back the last ounce of Scotch. He expected her to come up coughing as the strong liquor hit her throat. Instead, she licked her lips and smiled, her eyes thoughtful and distant.

"My grandfather loves Scotch." She set the glass back on the table and turned to go.

"I'm a very good listener." Ashton claimed few virtues. Giving a speaker his full attention was one. But would she trust him to share what was going on?

Harper hesitated before facing him once more. "My mother came into town unexpectedly."

Ashton relaxed, unaware until his lungs started working again that he'd been holding his breath. "I noticed the air between you two wasn't particularly cheerful."

"Do you have a good relationship with your parents?"

He shook his head, the twinge in his gut barely noticeable. "I left home at fifteen and never looked back."

"I've read everything ever written about you and I'm pretty sure that wasn't part of your history."

He knew better than to be flattered. "It's a story for another day. We're talking about you."

Her gaze was steady on his for several seconds. "My mother moved to Florida when I was eleven, leaving me in New York with my father who was rarely home. At the time I hated her for not being around, but as I grew up, I realized that being away from her criticism gave me the freedom to make mistakes and learn from them without being afraid she'd make me feel worse."

"I'm not sure many people would be as unaffected by their mother's abandonment as you are."

Harper gave him a wry smile. "Don't for a second think

I'm unaffected. I'm just realistic. My mother didn't abandon me. She fled a situation she'd didn't like. Penelope isn't someone who stands and fights when she can run away and go shopping." Harper shrugged, but she was far from sounding nonchalant. "Okay, so maybe I'm a little more bothered than I let on."

"It's nice to hear you admit that."

"Why?"

"Because I like you and I haven't been able to figure out why."

"You like me?" Her breathless laugh wasn't the reaction he'd expected.

"Very much," he admitted, more than a little disturbed by the way her delighted smile transformed her into a stunning, vivacious woman.

"After the way I've hounded you these past nine months?" She shook her head, and the career woman took over once more. "I think you're just trying to charm me. If this is your way of changing my mind about Chef Cole, you've got it all wrong."

"So suspicious," he taunted. "That's not it at all. I'm starting to come around to your opinion about Cole. As for the way you've acted these past few months, I get it. This hotel is important to you. Batouri will make a statement and depending on how it does, that statement will be good or bad. I'd be a hypocrite to criticize you for doing whatever it took to make sure Batouri is a complete success."

"That's awfully accommodating of you."

Rub me the right way and I can be very accommodating.

But that's the sort of comeback she'd expect. "Does your mother visit you in Las Vegas often?"

"Never. She hates it here."

"Must be important for her to show up then."

"She needs my help. Which is different. She usually

takes her problems to my grandfather because he's a man and taking care of women is what men do."

"That sounds very traditional minded."

"It goes against everything I believe in. I'm a modern career girl." A trace of self-mockery put a lilt in her voice. "She disapproves of my choices. Thinks I should have married a tycoon like my grandfather and dazzled New York society on his arm."

"That seems like a waste of your intelligence and drive."

"It's hard being a disappointment."

"I agree." This they shared. No matter how much either of them accomplished, they weren't living up to their parents' perception of success. "It spoils what you've achieved, doesn't it."

She looked surprised by his insight. Her gaze became keen as it rested on him. "It does."

He lifted the bottle of Scotch. "Do you want another drink?" He was dying to watch her swallow another glass. And then lick her lips again. There'd been something so decadent, so wickedly un-Harper-like about the deed.

"I should get back to work."

"See you tomorrow night."

"Text me when Chef Cole agrees to come work for you." She started to leave, but then paused. "Thanks for listening."

He suspected voicing her gratitude hadn't come easily. "Anytime. You know where to find me."

Shaking her head in exasperation, Harper spun away and headed toward the exit, her stride purposeful. Whatever sharing she'd done, it was now over. Ashton was left with an increased appreciation for Harper Fontaine.

These past few months he'd assumed her arrogance was a natural byproduct of her family's money and connections, that life was a breeze for her. He'd been as guilty of stereotyping as his critics often were. To be fair, her confidence had always been dent-free.

Now he realized there were a few pinholes in her armor. And they had more in common than he'd have ever guessed.

Harper pushed lettuce around on her plate, her appetite deadened by the smell of cigarette smoke. The suite would have to be deep cleaned before any guests could be booked in here. Over dinner, her mother had refused to speak about the blackmail. Harper's impatience was growing with each minute that ticked by. She set down her fork. It clattered on the china. The discordant sound startled her mother.

"We have to talk about why you're here."

"I don't want to."

"If you expect me to give you three hundred and fifty thousand dollars, I'm going to need to know why you're being blackmailed."

"I can't tell you."

"Did you kill someone?"

"Don't be an idiot."

"That's a relief," Harper muttered. She left the table, needing activity to think. As she crossed the room, a dozen ideas sprang into her mind. She picked the most likely one and turned to confront her mother. "You stole something."

"I'm not a thief." Penelope stubbed out her cigarette and reached for another, but Harper beat her to the package.

"No more smoking."

Her mother glared at her. "You are trying to provoke me into telling you something you're not ready to hear."

Why not? Harper mused. Her mother had been aggravating her for years. "I'm trying to figure out what could be worth three hundred and fifty thousand dollars."

"Actually it's a million."

"A mill...?" Harper crushed the cigarette package in her fist.

Penelope pouted. "It's a small price to pay compared to the consequences."

"What sort of consequences?"

"Life or death."

Now her mother had gone too far. "This is serious, Mother. You need to talk to Grandfather."

"I can't. He'd demand to know why I was being blackmailed. I can't tell him."

"Give me some idea what the blackmail is or I'm going to call him."

Penelope shot her daughter a wounded look. "There are some indelicate photos that if they got out would be very damaging."

Unsure how her conservative mother defined indelicate, Harper sought clarification. "Surely it can't be that bad."

"It could ruin us."

Us?

For a second Harper wasn't sure whom her mother was referring to. Penelope certainly hadn't worried about her daughter's welfare when she ran off to Florida.

"Who is 'us'?" she questioned, her voice scarcely audible.

Her mother looked startled. "Why you and I, of course."

Harper knelt beside Penelope. Taking her mother's hands, surprised by the icy chill in her fingers, Harper squeezed just hard enough to capture Penelope's full attention.

"If this involves me, you need to tell me what is going on."

"I had an affair," Penelope whispered, unable to maintain eye contact with Harper. Her mother was something other than mortified. She was afraid. "If that came out—" She broke off and shook her head.

Was something besides her mother's reputation at stake? "Who was it?"

"I met him at an exhibition of wildlife photography in London. His work was being honored." She released an impassioned sigh. "His photos were amazing."

"You had an affair with a photographer." Harper didn't know what to think. She had little trouble imaging her mother dallying with a duke or an Italian prince while in London, but a wildlife photographer?

"He was exciting and handsome and I couldn't get enough of his stories of Africa. He actually lived in the bush for ten months to get one particular shot of a group of lions."

Harper couldn't stop herself from drawing a parallel between her fascination with Ashton's adventures and her mother having an affair with someone who lived dangerously. Harper winced away from the comparison, dismayed to think she was more like her mother than she'd ever imagined.

"When did you have this affair?"

"Your father was out of the country a great deal."

"Before you split." Is that what had caused her mother to go to Florida? Had she been banished for being unfaithful? That seemed awfully unfair considering her husband's rampant infidelities. "Did Daddy know?"

"Not at first. I was very discreet. But in the end he figured it out."

"Why did you and father stay married when that's obviously not what either of you wanted?"

"What makes you think either of us wanted a divorce? Your father married me to cement a deal for Henry to buy my family's hotels. It was never a love match. I received security in exchange for ignoring all his affairs. It wasn't as if he intended to marry any of those women he slept with." Penelope sipped at her wine. "As for my brief indiscretion—" her mother offered an indifferent shrug "—I was out of the country and I knew I'd never see him again."

Yet thirty years later keeping the affair from being revealed was worth a million dollars. Was it just her mother's overdeveloped sense of propriety at work or was there something more going on?

"How brief an indiscretion was it?" Curiosity overpowered Harper as she tried to imagine her mother as young, impulsive and happy. All three were a stretch.

Penelope shot her a repressive frown. "What does it matter?"

How could her mother not understand how fascinating Harper found all this? Harper's whole life she'd had this image of her mother as the victim of Ross Fontaine's adulterous wandering. Suffering because her pride or a sense of honor kept her from divorcing the man who made her miserable.

"I'm just having a hard time picturing you..." Harper couldn't think of a way to say what was on her mind without it sounding like an insult.

"Engaging in a torrid affair?" Penelope spat out the words as if they tasted bad.

"I was going to say happy."

The diamond on Penelope's left hand sent out spikes of color as she waved away Harper's explanation. "Happy is overrated."

Was it? Harper considered her own life. Was she happy? Content maybe. Unless she compared herself to Violet and Scarlett and then she looked positively miserable. Being in love had certainly given her sisters a glow.

But it wasn't just being in love, for often love didn't last in a relationship. It was the fact that they'd found the other half of themselves. It wasn't something Harper had imagined for herself. Her ideal life involved a large executive office in Fontaine's New York City headquarters, rising profits, a cover article in *Forbes*. She didn't think in terms of a private life. She couldn't imagine having the energy to navigate the unpredictable waters of a serious relationship.

Once again her thoughts drifted to Ashton Croft and the awareness that spiked through her every time they occupied the same room. Regret rubbed at her. As much as he irritated her as a businessman, she was wildly attracted to the adventurous chef. If her responsibilities didn't weigh her down, she wouldn't hesitate to take those dimples of his for a spin.

"I don't see anything about this situation worth smiling over," Harper's mother stated, her voice sharp and impatient.

Harper pushed Ashton out of her mind and resumed her mask of professionalism. "You're right. There isn't."

"How soon can I get the money?"

"First thing tomorrow. What are we supposed to do? Gather the cash in a briefcase and drop it off at the bus station?"

Harper was struck with untimely amusement by the idea of her mother setting one Manolo-clad toe in such a place. But the urge to laugh vanished abruptly as she recalled Ashton's assessing gaze earlier. In all likelihood he had the same opinion about her. Worse, he'd be right. She'd never been to a bus station or ridden a bus. She'd spent her whole childhood in New York City and had only used the subway once.

"Don't be ridiculous," her mother said. "The money is to be wired. I've been given an account."

"That's safer." And she'd bet Scarlett's fiancé had a team of computer experts that could track the money to its final destination. "Give me the account number and I'll take care of everything."

Four

"Wow, boss." Dae's white grin split his tanned face as he toured Batouri's kitchen. "Nice place you got here."

The former Bali surfing instructor gazed around in admiration, taking in the pristine appliances and immaculate counters. Ashton had picked Dae up at the airport half an hour earlier and had intended to take him straight to the apartment he'd rented, but Dae had wanted to see the kitchen first. Ashton understood. He'd been discussing the project with the young Balinese man for the past four months. Naturally, he was curious.

"Glad you like it. You sure this is where you want to be? You have no idea what Chef Cole is going to be like to work with." Ashton had smoothed things over with the Chicago chef and persuaded him to accept the job at Batouri.

"Can't be worse than you."

Ashton ignored the taunt. "He'll probably start you at the bottom. I'm not sure that's the best use of your talents. I could find you something in one of my New York or London restaurants."

Dae shook his head. "I like Vegas. It's happening."

After marking the first twenty-five years of his life by island time, Dae was looking for a little excitement. Ashton understood. Hadn't he gotten out of Africa at twenty for the exact same reason?

"Just don't lose your shirt gambling."

"No worries." Dae tugged at the tails of his bright tropical shirt. "No one would give me a nickel for this thing."

"That's not what I meant," Ashton began, before seeing that his protégé was pulling his leg. "That dumb island boy stuff isn't going to get you too far."

Dae winked. "It got me here and that's pretty far."

With a rueful grin, Ashton stopped playing wise old guy. The role didn't suit him. Usually he was the one on the receiving end of advice, not the other way around. It was just that most of the time in Dae's company, the ten-year age difference seemed more like twenty.

Ever since he'd brought the young Indonesian kid under his wing, Ashton had felt responsible for him. Owner of four restaurants with over a hundred staff, he had a lot of people depending on him. But that was business. With Dae it was personal.

A chance to pay forward against a debt he could never repay.

"I found you a place to stay not far from here. It's on the bus line."

"You know I appreciate all you've done for me."

"Someone helped me out once. It changed my life." Saved it was more like it. And Dae was far more deserving of help than Ashton had ever been. "The best way to repay me is to succeed."

"You know I will."

That was the great thing about Dae. He had a limitless reserve of optimism. Even when his situation had been truly bad in Bali, he'd just grinned and said that things would get better. And they had because Ashton had traded cooking lessons for surfing lessons and discovered the kid had a natural aptitude and a fantastic palate.

"Shall we go check out your new apartment?" Ashton gestured toward the exit.

"Lead the way. How are things going with the new show?" Dae asked as Ashton got behind the wheel of the SUV he'd rented and started the engine.

"I'm not sure. They're still demanding I give up *The Culinary Wanderer*."

"You gonna?"

"The producers haven't stopped pushing Africa for next year and you know how I feel about it."

"Maybe you should forget about them. Do the show in New York."

Sound advice. Vince had been urging him in the same direction. Even his own brain was telling him to dump the travel show and move on to bigger and better things. And with the Phillips producers digging in their heels about doing next year's show in Africa, there didn't seem to be any good reason to sign a new contract.

So why was he having trouble letting go?

"That's probably what's going to end up happening," Ashton said. "I'll know more next week when I go meet with them. They want me to make a pilot for some people to look at."

"What are you going to do?"

"I have a few ideas."

None of which felt quite right. When they'd first approached him, Ashton had known exactly what he wanted to do. But as the negotiations lengthened, the more he learned about their concept for the show, the less confident he was that it was the sort of thing he wanted to do. And yet, the opportunity to take his career to the next level was a temptation he couldn't reject out of hand.

Once he'd settled Dae in his new apartment, Ashton

returned to the hotel. Dae's questions had prodded him into action.

He was beginning to wonder if they would ever see eye to eye on this project and what would happen if they didn't. After his last round of recipes had been rejected by the producers as too exotic, Ashton was finding it hard to come up with anything that excited him. Was it supposed to be this hard? Ashton didn't remember ever having to struggle like this to make anything happen in his career. Sure, he'd worked hard. Pushed himself to the limits of his energy and beyond. During his years filming *The Culinary Wanderer,* he'd been chilled to the bone, taken shelter from a tropical storm in a shallow cave, broken his arm, sprained his knee and been grazed by a ricocheting bullet. In the days before he'd landed his first television show, he'd worked for arrogant chefs who'd made his life hell but hadn't cared because it had been all about the food.

This was different. The executives of Lifestyle Network weren't thinking about good food or interesting stories— they wanted big numbers, and to them that meant doing something everyone could relate to. Ashton didn't think that would ever play to his strengths. Unless Vince was right and they were just hiring him to up their beefcake quotient.

The thought both amused and horrified him.

Ashton pushed aside the notes he'd been scribbling for the show and went to work on the more immediate problem. Figuring out Batouri's menu. Harper would expect culinary perfection and a cohesive plan for how that would happen. Impressing her should have been secondary in his thoughts. But he liked what happened when she dropped her guard and that only happened when he surprised her.

Unfortunately, an hour after sitting down with his thick notebook filled with recipes he'd gathered over the years, inspiration still eluded him. He was on the verge of picking ten at random when he heard the clink of china and looked up as Harper slid into the booth opposite him.

When Harper first entered the restaurant and spotted Ashton at the corner table he seemed to prefer, she realized they were both stuck in a rut. Him, sitting in the dim restaurant brooding. Her, tracking him down like some infatuated groupie. Which she was. But her reasons for coming here were a little more complicated than simple hero worship.

Last night, she'd left the restaurant feeling calmer and more grounded than when she'd arrived. Perhaps he wasn't the most reliable or altruistic man she'd ever met, but his brand of roguish charm had provided a much-needed distraction.

Today he was bent over a notebook, a cup of coffee at his elbow. It was the first time she'd ever seen him this utterly focused on his work. Usually he was a whirling dervish of energy. Flamboyant and passionate while interviewing chefs, directing staff in the bright stainless-steel kitchen or conveying his vision for the decor, gesturing broadly to emphasize whatever point he was trying to make.

As she studied him, some of her anxiety faded. Even sitting still, his body hummed with energy. Yet last night, he'd been an oasis of peace in her otherwise chaotic day. The experience had surprised her. She'd stayed to chat with him, looking to be distracted for a little while. With Scarlett's teasing still occupying her thoughts, was it any wonder she'd been contemplating what being with him would be like?

She'd assumed all he could offer her would be mind-blowing sex with no strings. Her perception had changed when he shared that he'd left home at fifteen and never looked back. She was certain this was something few knew. Why had he given her a glimpse of the man behind the celebrity? He was more complicated than she'd imagined and that spurred her fascination with him to new heights.

It also made tumbling into bed with him a lot riskier than she'd first thought.

Her head told her to turn around and walk out the door. Life had become complicated enough without falling for Ashton Croft. But curiosity drove her forward. She simply had to know what he was working on.

Grabbing a cup from the wait station as she passed, she slid into the booth beside Ashton. He'd been lost in thought, but looked up as the cushion shifted with her weight. Without questioning her reason for joining him, he took her cup and filled it with coffee from the stainless-steel airpot.

"Checking up on me?"

"Do I need to?"

"Probably." He flipped through the notebook, displaying pages filled with his bold handwriting. "I'm going a dozen different directions."

"I never expected you to second-guess yourself." She pulled his notebook toward her. "I always picture you jumping off the cliff without checking to see if there's a safer way down."

"Maybe you're rubbing off on me a little."

His claim made her grin. "Then my work here is done."

"Not even close. You need to help me finalize my menu."

"Me?"

"For someone who doesn't eat, you have one of the best palates I've ever known."

"I eat," she protested. "I just make sure it's healthy. And I exercise a lot. Running helps me think."

"If you ask me, you need to spend less time in your head."

"I don't remember asking you." Her mild tone kept harshness out of the retort. "But that hasn't stopped you from offering your opinion in the past."

"Stop trying to provoke me and pick a dish that appeals to you."

Resisting a grin, Harper focused on Ashton's notebook.

She'd never had a relationship where she felt comfortable being playful. In New York the men she dated were serious types whose pedigrees would satisfy her mother. Ashton didn't fit that mold. And her grandfather's opinion of him was what mattered to her. Henry Fontaine appreciated Ashton's rise from humble beginnings. Her grandfather had built his hotel empire through hard work, too.

After a while, Harper found herself unable to choose a single dish from the recipes he'd jotted down, which only caused her admiration for Ashton to grow. Each dish sounded better than the last. The man was nothing short of brilliant. She saw why he was having trouble settling on his menu. He had enough here for ten restaurants.

"Any one of these would be perfect. It's too bad you can't make them all." She slid the notebook back toward him. "You should do a cookbook. One of the things your television show didn't do was spotlight your talent."

His eyes narrowed as he studied her. "I've missed cooking. It's part of why I'm looking at doing a kitchen-based show for Lifestyle Network."

Harper sighed. Because his other restaurants were critically well received and extremely profitable, she hadn't been able to understand his lack of focus when it came to Batouri. Now she was beginning to realize it was a timing issue. He'd put his television career ahead of the restaurant at every turn. And now he was entertaining the idea of a new project. No wonder he was finding it too difficult to settle down and focus on the mundane details required to make the restaurant successful.

"We've come too far to change things now," Harper began, determined to voice her concerns. "But I have to ask if you're truly committed to making Batouri successful."

"Of course."

When she'd first approached him about the restaurant, she'd hoped they'd form a partnership. Blinded by her admiration for his talent, she hadn't realized that Ashton liked to fly solo.

"It just seems as if your attention isn't one hundred percent focused on this project."

"I'm in negotiations for the next season of my show, but most of that is being handled by my manager. I'm committed to getting the restaurant up and running."

She hoped that was true, but what was going to happen when this new show took off? He already had four other restaurants and *The Culinary Wanderer.* Now a new show?

"Will you have time to do both shows plus manage all your restaurants?"

"I'm not sure I'm going to be doing *The Culinary Wanderer* much longer."

Disappointment raced through her. "You can't stop." What could possibly provide him the same thrill as filming in a country where travel was risky due to political upheaval or in remote locations that few outsiders bothered to visit? Playing it safe wasn't Ashton's first priority. "That show is wonderful."

"I don't want to stop," he told her. "But it's a sticking point in the negotiations for the new show. They want me to be exclusive to the Lifestyle Network."

"Why exclusive?"

"They're planning on promoting the hell out of the new show and the exposure will lead to bigger things."

"And that's what's important to you?" Part of her recognized it was none of her business, but she couldn't get enough of his travel show. She'd seen every episode at least three times. "I thought you loved traveling to out-of-the-way places and meeting new people."

"I do." He rubbed his temple with his palm. "It's just that I'm looking for new challenges and this new show fits the bill."

"You're sure you can't do both?"

"You were just asking me if I was going to have time."

"That was before I realized you were going to stop doing *The Culinary Wanderer.*"

"Sorry to disappoint you."

She wished she'd kept quiet. Badgering him with her concerns wasn't constructive. He wasn't a man she could control. In the past nine months she'd learned that lesson all too well.

"It's none of my business. I just love your show."

"Thank you." Ashton put his hand over hers and squeezed gently. "I'll make several dishes I'm on the fence about including on the menu. You offer your opinion and we'll get everything finalized tonight."

Harper knew it was an unnecessary exercise. No matter what she suggested, he would select his menu based on his preferences. But she appreciated his effort to put her mind at ease.

"Sure."

"Come back at eight?"

She slid from the booth. "See you then."

As she exited the restaurant she glanced at her phone. She'd muted it before starting her conversation with Ashton, and now saw that she'd missed six calls and ten emails. Heaving a sigh, she lengthened her stride and headed for her office.

The interlude with Ashton had increased her anxiety rather than calmed her. She caught herself scowling as she rode the elevator to the administrative floor. It was just a television show, she reminded herself, unsure if that was all there was to it. For a half an hour once a week she got to escape the constant pressure of the hotel and travel with Ashton as he learned about elephant conservation in Sri Lanka or braved the Fairy Meadow Road in Pakistan.

The vicarious thrill was a secret she preferred to keep hidden because it didn't sync with the levelheaded, hard-working hotel executive she was 99 percent of the time. Her compulsive desire to protect the secret left her questioning many of the choices she'd made. And she knew nothing good would come of doubting herself.

Ashton crossed his arms over his chest, the white executive chef's jacket pulling tight against his shoulders. He had outdone himself. After Harper had left him that afternoon, he'd benefited from a creative surge that resulted in eight brand new entrées. Each one was something he thought she'd enjoy based on what had caught her attention in his notebook of recipes.

He'd gladly let her preferences define his menu. Batouri wouldn't exist without her. In the past twenty-four hours, as he'd immersed himself in planning, he'd discovered a sense of purpose he hadn't expected. It wasn't in his nature to stop and reflect. Like a shark, he needed to keep swimming in order to stay alive. Or was it to feel alive?

At precisely eight o'clock, Harper entered the kitchen. His pulse jabbed against his throat as he surveyed her. She'd changed into a sleeveless wrap dress made with layers of ethereal blue-gray material.

"What you're wearing reminds me of a fog bank I saw on a motorcycle ride in the highlands of Vietnam last year." He paused, unaccustomed to sharing his thoughts when he wasn't in front of the camera.

She tilted her head, signaling interest. "Tell me about it."

"We had a couple days off from filming so I rented a bike and headed up into the mountains. As you can imagine, the road was narrow and poorly maintained. I'd meet cars and trucks careening around hairpin turns with no guardrails between the road and the sheer cliffs."

"Sounds terrifying."

"It should have been. I'd pass villages where kids ran out into the road. I was chased by dogs." Amid all the craziness he'd felt both exhilarated and completely at peace. "At one point I glanced over my shoulder and down into the valley. A fog hung over the lush green far below."

In those hours he'd not known where he was headed and hadn't cared. The journey was everything. His time in Harper's company was the same. He wanted to live in the present, but she was a woman who needed to know what lay ahead. How far could their relationship develop before she grew frustrated with his act-first, worry-later attitude?

"You got all that from my dress?" Her brow creased. "You should write those experiences down."

"To what end?" It was one thing to put on a show for his television series; it was another to reflect on his personal experiences. "It was just a motorcycle trip."

"One that few people will have the opportunity to experience. You have a knack for drawing in your audience. It will make your cookbook that much more appealing."

"I'm not doing a cookbook."

"Why not?"

"You know why not."

"Because it would require you to sit still too long. Why don't you collaborate with someone?"

"How about I collaborate with you?"

"Me?"

"Why not? It was your idea."

"I don't know the first thing about creating a cookbook."

"But you could figure out what needed to be done."

"I'm too busy." But after a pause, she added, "We can talk about this after the restaurant opens."

He could see that she was on her way to becoming his partner. Why he'd proposed the idea to her was immediately obvious. She possessed the organization and dedication to detail he lacked. Plus, he trusted her opinion. He could count on one hand how many people fell into that category.

"Fair enough," he said, snagging her fingers with his and drawing her deeper into the kitchen. "Let's get down to why you're here."

"Your menu."

"I thought we'd start with a sea bass." He went on to explain the other seven dishes he planned to make for her.

"They all sound wonderful. Good thing I brought my appetite."

He'd prepared his sauces and assembled his ingredients through the afternoon so now it was just a matter of cooking the proteins and assembling the plates. Harper's gaze followed his every move as he shifted between burners and oven. He worked in silence, concentrating on his process, but occasionally felt the pull of her rapt attention.

"Would you mind taking these out to the dining room?" He indicated two of the plates. "I'll follow with the others in a minute."

By the time he had the last of his dishes plated, she'd returned and grabbed three more entrées, leaving the rest for him. He left the kitchen and crossed the dining room to the same table they'd sat at earlier in the day. It was his favorite in the whole restaurant. Quiet, out of the way, but with the vantage of being able to see the whole room.

Candles in crystal holders sent light flickering through the medium-bodied, golden 2006 Chenin Blanc he'd chosen to pair with the sea bass and the truffle risotto. Harper's eyes were bright with wonder as she surveyed their laden table and the assortment of wines he'd opened.

"I'm not sure how we're supposed to eat and drink all this," she said, sounding overwhelmed but delighted.

"It's a buffet. Taste a little of each. Sample the wines. I chose a selection of African vintages for tonight. We'll offer these as well as domestic and foreign."

"I love that your heritage is the backbone of Batouri. When you first told me the name, you explained that the restaurant is named after a town in Africa, but I can't remember where it was located. "

"It's in the East Province of Cameroon."

"Why did you choose it?"

He didn't think she'd like hearing the raw truth, but respected her enough to give her a doctored-up version. "I lived there for three years when I was a teenager."

"It was your home, then."

He poured her a glass of Pinotage. "Try the lamb. It's marinated in yogurt, garlic, coriander seeds, ground cumin and onion."

"Delicious," she murmured, her eyes half closing as she savored the bite.

Ashton couldn't tear his gaze from her face. Her open expression of pure sensual delight shot through him like a laser. Something came undone in his chest. He ached with the unraveling. The temptation to capture her lips with his, to share in her pleasure, swept through him. He reminded himself that a great deal of work had been involved in putting these dishes together. Work that would be for nothing if he acted on his impulse to make love to her right here and now.

He cleared his throat. "I'm glad you like it." His voice had a rough edge as if he'd been cheering on his team in a World Cup final.

"*Love* would be a better word." She sipped the wine and nodded. "This pairs very well with the lamb. What's next?"

Her eagerness made him smile. "Try the duck confit with the Chardonnay."

By the time she'd tasted the final dish, she wore a dreamy, satiated smile. He'd eaten little, preferring to watch her relish every bite. His gut took a hit every time she sighed in appreciation. It was foreplay unlike anything he'd ever known, and he was grateful for the experience.

"Everything was fantastic," she said. "Put it all on the menu. Batouri will be the most sought after reservation in Las Vegas."

He hoped she was right.

"I only have one dessert," he said, watching her take another bite of the scallop crudo with blood orange, watercress and fennel. "I hope you've left room."

"I'll make room."

He left her to fetch the dessert, bringing out only one plate since he doubted she had room for more than a bite or two. "It's a spiced chestnut cake with orange confit."

She accepted the dessert fork he handed her and dug in. "Oh, this is amazing. Are you tired of me telling you how wonderful you are?"

"That could never happen." In fact, he hadn't enjoyed her praise half as much as he'd been happy that his food had moved her to smile and laugh and groan in delight.

She shifted on the seat, turning her torso fully toward him. Taking his face between her hands, she compelled his gaze to hers. The candlelight picked out the amber flecks in her brown eyes, intensifying their compelling power. Slowly, deliberately, she leaned forward until their lips grazed in a dragonfly whisper of a kiss.

"You have an incredible gift. Thank you for sharing it with me tonight."

There was only so much a man could take. Ashton tunneled his fingers into her hair and caught her mouth with a fervent moan of surrender. Greedy for the taste of her, he licked past her lips and was greeted by no resistance, no hesitation, only the delicious slide of her tongue against his.

The layered fruitiness of Chenin Blanc and spiced chestnut danced across his taste buds as Harper tilted her head and gave him deeper access to her mouth. He hadn't realized just how ravenous he was until her arms went around his neck, and she pressed her breasts hard against his chest. Their breath combined in great heaving gasps as one kiss followed another. Drinking his fill of her soft lips seemed impossible. Each second that ticked by he wanted her more.

Dishes rattled on the table as they bumped against it. Distantly, Ashton considered the impracticality of their current location. He'd never be able to get her naked in such a confined space. And that's how he intended she be when he made love to her. Not one inch of her slender frame was going to go unexplored by him. He'd lain awake too many nights imagining her flawless skin and how it would feel to slide his palms against its softness.

He nipped lightly at her throat. Her body jerked reflexively, startling a laugh out of her. When he shifted his grip from her nape to her spine, his elbow banged the table hard. A wineglass tipped over.

"Damn it," he muttered.

"It's empty." She leaned back and surveyed the damage they'd done. "This really isn't the opportune place to get carried away like that."

"No." Desire shrieked through him, fierce and unquenched. He set his spine against the back of the booth and raked his fingers through his hair. "Damn."

"Let's clean all this up."

"There'll be a cleaning crew coming by at midnight." He didn't want to leave the intimacy of the candlelit booth for the harsh fluorescent starkness of the stainless-steel kitchen.

"Then they'll have less to do." Already she was shifting out of the booth and piling up the plates.

He paused a second before moving, taking a moment to survey her high color, mussed hair and the extra bit of skin bared by their sensual tussling. Damn but she was glorious. Graceful and romantic, confident and feminine. If her employees could see her now, would they take her seriously as a businesswoman? They would if they noticed the determination in her stare.

"Come on," she said, her tone a stern nudge.

"I suppose the faster we put everything away the sooner we can get back to the getting acquainted portion of tonight's schedule."

She gave him a *we'll see* smile and headed toward the kitchen. Ashton quickly bussed the table and followed her, unconcerned that Harper appeared to be in full retreat. He had a restaurant to open. That meant he wasn't going anywhere for now. There would be plenty of time to get better acquainted.

Once Harper had deemed the kitchen was organized enough to leave to the cleaners, they shut off the lights and exited the restaurant.

"This has been a nice night," he told her, lacing his fingers through hers. "I don't want it to end."

"If you have in mind a nightcap in your room…" She let the sentence trail off and shook her head.

He couldn't resist a wicked grin. "So, sex is a no." He tugged her close and slipped his fingers into her silky hair, captured her gaze with his and let suspense build. The way her breath hitched, she obviously expected him to push his agenda on her. "How about a walk instead?"

Five

The persistent rattle of her smartphone on the nightstand yanked Harper out of a delicious dream. She had been riding behind Ashton on a motorcycle that was speeding along a coastal highway. Each curve had offered different views of the treacherous terrain ahead, and the exhilarating danger had stolen her breath. Heart still pounding in reaction to the dream, Harper threw her arms wide and stretched, enjoying the slide of cool sheets against her bare skin. Glancing at the clock she saw it was almost nine. She should have been in the office an hour ago. No doubt Mary was frantically looking for her.

With a sigh, Harper slid out of bed and headed straight for the shower. No time to work out this morning. Breaking her routine gave Harper a guilty thrill. So did the reason why she'd turned off the alarm before falling into bed the night before. The walk that Ashton had proposed had lasted two hours. They'd meandered all over the three Fontaine hotels, taking time to tour the gardens at Richesse and have a drink at Chic's chandelier bar.

At first Harper hadn't said much. Mostly she'd asked for the stories that hadn't made it onto the show. Apparently there were hundreds of hours of footage that had gone unseen. Harper would have given a lot to view all of it. She imagined hilarious outtakes and unrehearsed moments of awkwardness. But there would also be bittersweet interviews and breathtaking scenery.

After the walk, they'd ended up at a table in Fontaine Ciel's coffee shop that overlooked the pool area. Ashton had turned the conversation away from him and gleaned a great deal of Harper's history, including her parents' difficult marriage and how she'd coped with finding out about her two half sisters. He'd known she was ambitious, but now he knew the life experiences that had molded her dreams and goals.

It was the most time she'd ever spent with him and by far the least adversarial. Ashton had proven to be an accomplished interviewer and a charming companion. Funny, perceptive and insightful, he'd turned out to be more interesting than she'd expected. And that was saying a lot.

Now a decidedly infatuated woman stared back at Harper when she cleared the steam from the bathroom mirror. Her reflection told her all she needed to know about how much trouble she was in. The last thing she should do was fall for Ashton Croft. Given his track record, he was almost guaranteed to disappoint her in the very near future.

Putting the celebrity chef out of her mind, Harper dressed and picked up her phone. She winced as she read through her emails and texts. A lot of issues needed her attention before noon when she was meeting her sisters. Because Violet hadn't returned home until late yesterday, they'd decided their weekly breakfast should change to lunch this one time.

Harper had taken advantage of this change in her schedule to spend more time with Ashton the night before. One cup of coffee had become two and then three. By the time she tumbled into bed at four in the morning, she'd been far too wired to sleep despite the fact that she'd been drinking decaf the whole time.

But the reduced amount of sleep she'd gotten didn't seem to be affecting her energy level, just her mental capacity. Harper was having a hard time concentrating on all the details competing for her attention.

Lost in daydreams featuring the lush scenery of Indonesia where Ashton had most recently been, she exited her hotel suite and headed to the executive floor. What incredible adventures he'd had. And she hadn't needed to wait another three months to learn about them on his show.

"Harper, are you okay?"

"Hmmm?" She blinked and noticed her assistant was frowning at her. Harper was standing by Mary's desk, but her mind was thousands of miles away. "Sorry. I was thinking about…" Stumped for an excuse, Harper trailed off. She couldn't admit she'd been fantasizing about Ashton Croft and the romantic beaches of Bali. "You were saying?"

"It can wait until this afternoon. Are you planning on coming back here after lunch with your sisters?"

"I think so. Unless something comes up." Rarely was she this indecisive. "I'll call you and let you know."

The walk to Scarlett's office at Fontaine Richesse through the connecting skyways took longer than her usual ten minutes of brisk walking. To maximize the all-inclusive feel of the three hotels, a variety of high-end stores lined the second floor route. The only reason Harper normally paid attention to the boutiques was to eyeball the number of customers and gauge what worked and what didn't. Today, she found herself window-shopping.

A particularly sexy black dress in a front display caught her eye, causing Harper to stop. She didn't need to glance at her watch to know she was running behind schedule, but the need to try on the dress drew her into the store. It wasn't her usual style, but Harper imagined Ashton's eyes

lighting up on Batouri's opening night and knew she had
to have it. She directed the sales clerk to send it to her office at Fontaine Ciel and made arrangements for payment.
She'd need a sexy pair of black stilettos to complete the
look, but those would have to wait until later. She was really late for lunch.

Her sisters wore matching expressions of concern as
Harper entered Scarlett's organized, roomy office.

"Sorry I'm late."

"It's fine," Violet said. "I love your hair down. You
should wear it that way more often."

Harper self-consciously brushed the fine strands away
from her face. "I was in a hurry this morning." That wasn't
exactly true. She'd been reliving the pleasure of Ashton's
fingers playing in her hair. Her skin had tingled as the ends
had swept her shoulder and caressed her cheek.

"So it has nothing to do with your canoodling with Ashton last night?" Scarlett queried, her expression knowing
and smug.

Violet's eyes went wide. "Canoodling?"

"Hardly," Harper said. "We simply went for a walk."

"Sweetie, after my night manager mentioned he'd caught
sight of you with a man last night, I watched video of that
walk," Scarlett teased. "You might not have been touching,
but that was big-time canoodling for you."

The delight fluttering in Harper's stomach was messing with her head. She tried to shoot her sister a repressive
glare, but felt the corner of her mouth tilted upward. "We
talked until almost four this morning."

"Talked?"

Harper stared Scarlett down. "Talked."

"You mean to tell me Ashton Croft didn't put the moves
on you?"

"He tried." Harper was both relieved and disappointed
that he hadn't put more effort into persuading her to have

that drink in his suite. "I'm not going to hop into bed with him that fast."

Scarlett made a disgusted noise. "That fast? You two have been flirting for nine months."

"Flirting? No. We've been politely fighting."

"For you that's flirting."

Harper threw up her hand to block any more of her sister's crazy notions. "Is there a particular reason there's a bottle of champagne chilling over there?"

"We have a lot to celebrate, starting with Violet," Scarlett explained. She poured the sparkling liquid into three flutes and motioned her sisters over.

"You were able to help JT get his company back, weren't you," Harper guessed, delighted.

The smirk on Violet's face was priceless. "And Preston has been arrested. He was dragged out of Cobalt in handcuffs."

"I would have loved to see the look on his face as he was escorted out of his hotel by the FBI," said Harper.

Violet nodded. "It was pretty satisfying."

"And things between you and JT?" Scarlett prompted.

"Perfect."

Harper's heart lifted at the joy on her sister's face. "You're not separating then."

"Not a chance." Fierce and romantic, Violet beamed. "He loves me."

"I'm happy for you," Harper said, but already she was worrying about how this would change things between the three of them. "Have you figured out what's going to happen when JT takes over Stone Properties?"

"He's not. Once his father was out of the way I thought for sure that JT would step in as CEO." The sole reason Violet had married JT was to help him take over his family's company. "Instead, he sold his shares to his cousin in order to buy Titanium." Titanium was the Stone Properties hotel and casino JT ran in Las Vegas. It was the largest and

most profitable of all the company's properties, thanks to
JT's excellent management.

Harper couldn't see the sense in his decision. "I'm surprised he would do that when he could have all of Stone
Properties to run."

"He wanted to stay in Las Vegas." Violet looked as blissful as a woman in love should. "He knew my heart was
here."

"What about Grandfather's contest?" Harper asked. The
corporate offices for Fontaine Hotels and Resorts were in
New York City.

"Last week I told Grandfather I wasn't interested in
being CEO." Violet looked at Scarlett.

Before Harper grasped what Violet's decision meant
for the future, Scarlett held her glass high and proclaimed,
"All hail the future CEO of Fontaine Hotels and Resorts."

Harper's heart twisted in her chest. Had Grandfather
made his decision? Was Scarlett his choice for a successor?

"Congratulations," Harper said to Scarlett, proud that
her voice was so bright when her heart was lost in shadow.
She'd wanted Grandfather to pick her, had spent her entire
life working toward that goal. More than that, she needed
his acceptance. To think that she wasn't good enough was
a blow she hadn't prepared herself for.

Scarlett rolled her eyes. "Not me, silly. You."

"Me?" Harper looked from Scarlett to Violet. "I don't
understand. Grandfather hasn't said anything about the
contest being over."

Scarlett piped up. "I called Grandfather this morning
and told him that the network executives loved the pilot for
my new series and picked up the show." Her starlet smile
flashed bold and brilliant. "That means you are going to
be Fontaine's next CEO."

The news should have thrilled Harper. It was why she'd
worked hard and sacrificed a social life in high school to
ensure she got into Cornell University's School of Hotel

Administration. After graduating with top honors she'd gone to work at a Fontaine property in Chicago, starting at the bottom to learn every aspect of the business. All her energy had gone into proving to her grandfather that she was not her father's daughter. She would give Fontaine Hotels and Resorts her complete attention.

But to get the job because her competition had dropped out. That wasn't her idea of winning.

"Grandfather still has the final word," she reminded her sisters, not ready to celebrate. "He might just decide that I wasn't going to be his first choice."

"Don't be ridiculous," Scarlett scoffed, clinking her crystal flute with Harper's. "You are and always have been the front-runner." She glanced at Violet. "No offense, Violet. I think if you'd hung in there you might have given Harper a run for her money."

"I'm not insulted," Violet said, a fond look in her eyes. "I love Las Vegas. And I love running my hotel. I'm not really cut out to sit in endless meetings and read reports all day." But Harper knew Violet was downplaying how serious her decision had been.

At Scarlett's urging, Harper sipped at the sparkling wine, but the effervescent liquid didn't ignite joy or even relief. As soon as Ashton's restaurant opened, she would head to New York and have a face-to-face chat with her grandfather. Until she knew his thoughts on her future with the company, she wouldn't let herself hope her dreams were coming true.

In a state of conflicting emotions, Harper ate her salad in silence and listened to Violet and Scarlett with half her attention. Both of them were madly in love with wonderful men. It was hard for Harper to contribute to the conversation. Listening to them discuss Violet's upcoming belated honeymoon and Scarlett's wedding arrangements demonstrated just how two-dimensional Harper's life was. She had her work and her sisters. Both meant everything to her, but after spending the evening with Ashton, she couldn't help feeling as if she was missing out on something important.

"I got an update from Logan a little before you showed up today," Scarlett said, catching Harper's eye. "He said his people have tracked the million your mother wired to the blackmailer." Scarlett didn't explain how this had been done and Harper refrained from asking, expecting that the methods were not official. "It went through several banks before it landed in an account belonging to some guy named Saul Eddings. The strange part is he doesn't seem to exist."

So, the blackmailer was clever. Harper had been racking her brains for days trying to figure out who could have dug up a thirty-year-old affair. Why wait until now to trade the information for money?

"What's going on?" Violet asked.

"My mother is being blackmailed."

"Your mother?" Violet shot Scarlett a worried look. "Blackmailed about what?"

"Ancient history," Harper explained, wondering what was causing Violet's escalating tension. "Apparently she had an affair thirty years ago."

Violet whirled on Scarlett. "You didn't tell her, did you?"

"No." Scarlett eyes grew hard as she stared at Violet.

"She needs to know."

"I need to know what?" Harper demanded, alarmed by the sudden animosity between her sisters.

"It won't help," Scarlett said. "Logan will find out who's doing this and he and Lucas will take care of it. So, you need to just let it go."

"Have you thought of what's best for Harper?"

"Repeatedly." Scarlett could be a force of nature when she sank her teeth into something. "Drop it."

Harper couldn't take it anymore. "Stop it, both of you.

I need to know what's going on. Who's blackmailing my mother?"

"I don't know," Scarlett admitted, as somber as Harper had ever seen her.

Harper persisted. "But you know something about it."

"I think so."

"And you weren't planning on telling me?" The room suddenly felt cold, as if the air conditioners were working at twice their normal capacity. Harper rubbed her arms. "Why?"

"Because no good will come of it," Scarlett said.

All the more reason for her to know. "It's about my mother and the affair?"

"Yes." Violet reached out and took Harper's icy fingers, rubbing them to bring back some warmth. "Tiberius had files on all of us."

"I already knew that."

"Including your mother."

"When I was attacked and the files were stolen," Scarlett explained, her voice quiet and reluctant, "the one on your mother was taken."

"That explains where the photos came from and why the blackmail began now." One question answered. But was that all there was to the sharp looks and tense exchange between Violet and Scarlett? "Is there more to it?"

"If you don't tell her, I will," Violet declared.

"It's about the timing of the affair," Scarlett said. "It happened nine months before you were born."

"That doesn't mean…" Harper wasn't sure she wanted to make the connections Scarlett was hinting at. "The affair only lasted two weeks."

"And from what we've determined about your father's travels, he was gone for almost six weeks around that same time."

Bile rose in Harper's throat. It couldn't be possible. It certainly wasn't fair.

She wasn't a Fontaine.

These two wonderful women weren't her sisters.

She had no right to run Fontaine Ciel, much less become CEO of the company.

Suddenly, Harper couldn't breathe. She put her hand to her chest. "I have to go."

She pushed back from the table so abruptly her chair crashed to the ground. Scarlett's office spun as Harper struggled to figure out where the door had gone.

"Harper, are you okay?"

Okay? Would she ever be okay again?

"Fine. I just remembered that I was going to…" She never finished the sentence. The door had come into view and Harper made for it.

"Are you sure you're all right?" Violet had pursued her from Scarlett's office into the hallway. "I know this must be a huge shock. But it doesn't matter. You know that."

"Of course it matters." Harper didn't know how to make Violet understand. Everything she'd worked for. Every sacrifice she'd made. Was it all for nothing? "I'll talk to you and Scarlett later. Right now I just need to grab some air."

Scarlett appeared on Harper's other side, her fingers biting hard into Harper's arm. "You are our sister. You will be Fontaine's next CEO. It's what you've always wanted."

"Of course." Harper patted Scarlett's hand. "I get it. This is our secret."

Violet relaxed. "Exactly."

"I love you both, but I need to get back to work. I'll check in with you later."

And before they could protest further, she briskly walked away.

Instead of retracing her steps through the skyways, she wound through the casino and emerged onto the Vegas Strip. The heat, noise and press of the crowd hit her like a rogue wave. How long had it been since she'd ventured beyond the insulation of Fontaine walls? She slept, ate and worked within a square city block, finding little need to explore the world outside. There was a drugstore attached to the hotel if she needed sundries. When she traveled, it was in a hired car that swept her to the airport and a private plane that carried her to her destination.

Always there was someone around to guide her to meetings and keep her on schedule. She'd never detoured because the mood hadn't struck her. Her activities were planned and organized. It was the way she liked it. What had made her successful.

With more vigor than necessary, Harper pushed through the ground floor door that led into Fontaine Ciel's casino. Nothing looked familiar. The persistent noise from the slot machines and the dazzling lights battered her senses. She had no idea how to get to her office. Disoriented, Harper turned in a slow circle. Confusion overwhelmed her. Harper put her arms out for balance as the edges of her vision began to darken.

"Harper, are you okay?"

She couldn't remember the name of the man who spoke. Distantly she knew she should. That she dealt with him on a daily basis. Tom something. Tim maybe.

"I'm a little dizzy all of a sudden." She shook her head, hoping to clear her vision. To her right was an open slot machine. "I just need to sit down for a second." She took a step and swayed.

"Let me help," Tom or Tim said, reaching for her arm.

She flinched away from his touch. Her skin felt as if it was on fire. "No." She reached the chair and dropped into it. "Sorry. I'll be fine in a couple seconds. Perhaps you could get me a glass of water."

"Sure."

While he headed off to intercept a waitress, Harper closed her eyes and rubbed at her temples. Her brain was coming back online, allowing her to think more clearly. What the hell had just happened? From her symptoms she guessed it had been a panic attack. Made sense. Her whole world was spinning out of control.

By the time Tim Hoffman—she'd finally recalled the name of her facilities manager—returned with her water, Harper was on her feet and feeling much steadier. But her need to run hadn't abated. For someone who always met problems head-on, she wasn't sure what to make of the impulse to flee. Work wasn't the remedy for her troubles. It was the cause of her angst. Better that she spend some time alone. To think. To sort out her emotions.

"I should have taken the skyway back from Richesse. Must have been the heat outside that made me dizzy."

The short, dark-haired man looked relieved. "It's warmer than usual, that's for sure."

"Thanks for the water." Without another word, Harper headed for the elevators. Maybe an hour on her treadmill would enable her to reach some clarity.

Six

Ashton stretched out on the couch in his suite and stared at the ceiling. Beyond the wall of windows the day was fading and the Las Vegas Strip was lighting up. As much as he loved the fascinating sights he'd seen in some of the most remote spots on the planet, enjoying the luxury of a first-class hotel was an indulgence he appreciated most of all.

Unfortunately, his current career issues weren't allowing him to put aside his worries and savor the lavender scented sheets, decadent bathroom or spectacular view. Vince had called this morning with bad news. Unless the producers of *The Culinary Wanderer* received his decision about filming in Africa three days from now they were cancelling the show.

As much as Ashton hated having anyone force his hand, he should be relieved that he would soon be free to sign with the Lifestyle Network. He and Phillips could part without bad feelings. But if everything was so great, why did he feel numb?

A knock sounded on his door. Shoving to a sitting position, Ashton ran his fingers through his hair and got to his feet. Dae had said he'd call later and see if Ashton wanted to check out the Strip. He hadn't expected the kid to show up.

But it wasn't Dae. The visitor at his door was so unexpected, he stood staring at her in dumfounded silence.

"Hi." Harper stood in the hallway wearing stretchy gray pants that highlighted her long, lean legs and an oversized pale pink sweater that she wrapped tight around her body. "I probably should have called before stopping by." Her casual attire and indecisive posture meant she hadn't come here to talk business.

"No need. I was just thinking that I could use a little company." He gestured her inside.

"That's how I felt, too." She shuffled in and gazed around the suite as if she hadn't been instrumental in overseeing every aspect of the design and decor. Sounding dreamy and vague, she continued. "I enjoyed our conversation last night."

"So did I." Catching her hand, he drew her toward the couch. "Do you want some wine?"

"Sure."

He poured glasses for both of them and sat close beside her. Content to enjoy her company, Ashton sipped his wine and watched her. She wore no makeup and that added to the aura of vulnerability that surrounded her at the moment. The scent of jasmine clung to her skin. A trace of damp lingered in the thick wave of brown hair cascading around her delicate shoulders. He guessed she'd been working out recently for a healthy glow suffused her skin.

"Did you always want to be a chef?" With her feet tucked beneath her, she took up very little space, but vibrancy had returned to her voice.

"I sort of stumbled into it."

The truth wanted to spill out of him. Last night she'd shared a great deal about her childhood and school years.

Her openness had tempted him to talk about his own past. But most of the people who knew what he'd done had either been dumped in the African jungle or buried in a shallow grave. An elegant, cultured woman like Harper would be horrified by what it had cost him to survive.

"When I was fifteen," he began, abandoning the press release version of his past, "I left home and fell in with some bad guys."

Describing Chapman's ruthless gang of smugglers as bad guys was woefully inadequate. They'd been a mean bunch of criminals brought together by the most loathsome man Ashton had ever met.

"How bad?"

He pushed back his left sleeve and showed her a pair of long, faint scars on his forearm. "They liked to play with knives."

"They did this to you? That doesn't look much like playing. Why did you stick around?"

"Because I was cocky and stubborn. I thought I could take care of myself." And he'd had nowhere else to go. Ashton brushed his sleeve down. "One of the guys did all the cooking for the gang. He took me under his wing. Kept me away from the worst of the lot. Turns out I had a knack for combining flavors." Not the whole truth, just a sterilized version of what had really happened.

"Had you planned to do anything else?"

Ashton shrugged. He'd been a stupid, rebellious teenager who'd rarely thought beyond the moment. "I only knew I wasn't going to follow in my father's footsteps."

Her lips twisted into an unhappy grimace. "What did he do?"

"He was a missionary." He hadn't planned to disclose that fact. Usually, he told people his father was a salesman. Which was pretty close to the truth. His parents spent their whole lives selling salvation to people who had no idea they were damned.

For the first time since she'd arrived on his doorstep, her eyes brightened. "A missionary? Forgive me if I say that you don't strike me as the son of a religious man."

She made no attempt to hide her curiosity. Nor did she curb the trace of laughter in her tone. This wasn't the withdrawn, mentally drained woman who'd shown up at his door. The cloud that had followed her into his suite had retreated for the moment.

"I could say I'm not and explain that there are all sorts of missionaries in Africa, but my father and mother spent a great deal of my childhood visiting villages and spreading Christian values."

His muscles grew more taut with each syllable that passed his lips. He began to notice an ache in his shoulders. The pain reminded him that he'd never set down the burden of unfinished business created by his choice to leave home and never look back.

"Wow, that was not a happy memory for you at all." She set her fingertips on his forearm, her touch light and friendly.

Too bad his heart didn't recognize the contact as casual. It gave a giant lurch like a racehorse surging from a starting gate. In seconds his breath came more quickly. Usually when desire hit him, he rolled with the blow. Why resist? Beautiful women were their own type of adventure.

But Harper Fontaine wasn't just a beautiful woman. She was intelligent and ambitious, dynamic and resourceful. When he'd first started working with her, he'd been annoyed by her bluntness and impressed by her sincerity. Last night he'd discovered she was also a warm, passionate woman and the chemistry between them was electrifying.

"What about you?" he asked, turning the topic away from himself. "Did you always want to be a hotel executive?"

"From the time I was five years old." She smiled fondly. "My father took me to the Waldorf Astoria and I fell in love. It was everything a grand hotel should be. We went at Christmas and the lobby was filled with these enormous evergreen trees covered in white lights and big red and gold balls. The railings were decorated with swags of ribbon and lights. It was magical. I knew I wanted to be a part of that someday."

He had little trouble imagining her as a wide-eyed child, holding tight to her father's hand while she soaked up the magnificence of that fine old hotel. For her, it had probably been as exciting a place to visit as FAO Schwarz would be for most other children.

"I suppose being a Fontaine, hotels are in your blood."

Her expression changed—the glow in her eyes dimmed, her mouth flattening into a somber line. "What's it like traveling all over the world like you do?"

"Exciting. Exhausting." Sometimes he longed to go home. Or at least that's what he assumed he wanted. He never really felt as if he belonged anywhere. "I crave an ever-changing landscape."

"That's so different from what I'm used to." Setting her elbow on the back of the couch, she propped her head on her hand and sipped her wine. "I've never traveled anywhere."

"I find that hard to believe. There are Fontaine hotels all over the world."

"Yes, but when I've visited the hotels I've never had time to sightsee. You said you couldn't see me shopping in Paris. You were right. I've been there three times and never once toured the city."

"That's a shame. It's a wonderful city. I spent two years there attending culinary school and working in various restaurants." It had been the first place he'd gone after leaving South Africa. At the time, it had seemed the perfect place to re-create himself.

"I spent the first eighteen years of my life in New York City and the next four in Ithaca attending Cornell University."

"You didn't want to travel?"

"My parents were separated from the time I was eleven. My mother lived in Florida, and I visited her during the holidays. My father…" She stumbled over the word and appeared distressed for a moment. "He was gone a lot, overseeing various hotels. The company expanded a great deal in the nineties."

Her childhood sounded as lonely as his had been. "Who did you stay with when your father was away?"

"Servants. Once in a while my grandfather." Her sweater had slipped off one shoulder, baring the thin strap of her gray camisole. "Is there any place you want to visit but haven't?"

The smooth line of her shoulder captivated him. Could her skin be as soft as it looked? "Niagara Falls."

She stared at him in stunned silence for a few moments and then began to laugh. "Niagara Falls? Even I've been there."

Her deep, throaty laugh made him want to kiss her. The mischief dancing in her eyes captivated him. Strong. Soft. Smart. Sexy. Was she as oblivious to her appeal as she appeared or was it all a ruse to catch him off guard?

"Then you'd be a good tour guide."

"I don't know about that. I was seven at the time." Her good mood faded. "My father took me." She blinked rapidly and pushed off the couch. "Damn it. I swore I wasn't going to cry."

Curiosity induced him to follow her. At least that's what he told himself until she was wrapped in his arms, her face pressed against his chest. Her body shuddered as she gulped in air and released an unsteady sigh.

"What's wrong?" He nuzzled the top of her head with his chin while a part of his mind wondered where this urge to comfort had come from. Selfish. Self-involved. Those were the words that described him. It balanced out the fifteen years of selflessness his parents had shoved down his throat.

"Why Niagara Falls?"

"I have a thing for waterfalls." He paused a beat. "What do you have a thing for?"

"You…" she shifted as far away from him as his arms snaked around her waist would allow "…r show."

"Nice save."

"Okay, I'll admit I'm a fan."

He leaned back and peered down at her. "That explains why you've been so nice to me."

"I've been nothing but professional to you."

"Your lips say civilized things," he taunted. "But your eyes tell me how much you'd like to lock me in the walk-in freezer."

"Be honest. Have you been easy to work with?"

"Of course not, but I'm a genius and everyone knows that geniuses are notoriously difficult to get along with."

His candor gave her pause. Head cocked, she regarded him. "Even your arrogance is charming."

"I don't get you."

She avoided his gaze. "What's there to get?"

"You have money and family connections. Anything you want could be yours."

"Is that how you see me?" She asked the question calmly enough, but below the surface he sensed tension.

"That's who you are."

"And if I lacked money and family connections, what am I then?"

The intensity with which she awaited his answer kept Ashton from spouting some flippant remark. "A beautiful, intelligent woman who is ambitious and focused enough to do anything she sets her mind to."

"What if I don't know what I want to do?"

"I don't understand. I thought you were going to take over as CEO of Fontaine Hotels and Resorts."

"I'm no longer sure that's where I belong." She pushed out of his arms and headed toward the door to the hallway. "Thanks for the wine and the shoulder to cry on. I should turn in for the night. I've got a lot to do tomorrow."

Ashton followed her to the door and caught her arm as she reached for the handle, stopping her from leaving. She turned at his touch and swayed into him. Pushing onto her toes, she kissed his cheek.

The warmth of her lips against his skin set his blood alight. His fingers slid into the small of her back and held her against him as he cupped her cheek in his palm and angled her face so he could reach her mouth.

Pliant and slightly salty from her earlier tears, her lips moved beneath his, responding to his searching kiss. It wasn't passion that consumed him. Her somber mood connected him to an emotion he believed he'd lost long ago: compassion. Something radical had happened to her today. Something related to the visit from her mother. The encounter had knocked her off her game.

Just like this kiss was throwing him.

He lifted his lips from hers, shocked by his lightheadedness. One simple kiss shouldn't have affected him so strongly. But then again, he couldn't remember wanting to kiss away someone's unhappiness, either.

"Stay," he urged, brushing his lips across her cheek.

Her muscles tensed. A flight response?

"That's not a good idea."

"You're wrong," he assured her. "It's a great idea."

"I've never jumped into bed with a man I scarcely know."

He'd divulged the truth about his parents with her. That was a huge secret from his past he hadn't shared with anyone else in his present. "Consider it an adventure into the unfamiliar territory."

"I guess I'm not ready to leave behind everything I know."

Yet another enigmatic statement. Ashton was starting to think that Harper had more weighing on her mind than she wanted to confront.

"Why would you think you have to?"

"I don't need to ask you what you'd do if you couldn't be a chef. You've already made a name for yourself as a TV personality and a restaurateur."

This would have been an excellent moment to tell her his project was taking him to New York for a few days, but he was reluctant to shatter the rapport between them.

"Have you been considering a career change?"

A faint smile found its way to her lips. "I was thinking of a television series that featured exotic hotels around the world."

"Want me to talk to my manager about pitching your idea to the network?"

Her eyes widened. "You're serious."

"You seem as if you're grappling with the status quo. Maybe you need to take some risks, challenge yourself. Do something that terrifies you."

"I've already done that." Her expression grew wry. "I came here, didn't I?"

"I terrify you?"

"Not you. Just what you represent."

"And that is?"

"Everything that I grew up avoiding."

He didn't respond to her jab. Better to give her space to assemble her thoughts, let the silence expand to an uncomfortable level until she gave up more than she intended. It was an interview technique he'd often used with great results.

"I didn't mean that as an insult," she said at last. "It's just that I like everything organized and predictable. You thrive on the unexpected."

"It's what makes life interesting. Some of my best recipes have come from putting together flavors that I've never tried before." Hell, his entire career had been framed by a combination of happenstance and his ability to capitalize on all things unconventional. "And I never would've made a career out of cooking if I hadn't run away from home at fifteen and needed to survive."

She didn't look at all surprised by what he'd told her. "I've never wanted to be in a desperate situation, so i never have been." The rest of her admission remained unspoken, but her expression was easy to read.

"And now you're wondering what you've missed?"

"I'm fully aware of what I've missed. I've made sacrifices to keep on track with my goal."

"To run the company someday."

"It was my job to win or lose."

"Has that changed?"

"You must have guessed that it has or I wouldn't have come here tonight and cried all over you." She stepped back and gathered her soft sweater tight about her slim body. "I found out something today that I'm not ready to talk about."

"Use me as a sounding board or keep everything bottled up. It's no matter to me."

"I guess I should say thank you."

"There's no need. As you probably already figured out, I'm a selfish bastard. If a beautiful woman comes to me for comfort, I'm going to enjoy every second of the time she spends in my arms."

"And if she decides to let you comfort her through the night?"

"All the better."

"How do women manage to resist you?"

"Usually they don't."

"So I'm an anomaly?"

"In a class all of your own."

She put her hand on the door handle once again, and this time Ashton didn't stop her. He'd learned to coax the flavor out of food. Forcing something to happen often led to an inferior outcome and above all else, he wanted the first time he made love to Harper to be a moment she'd never forget.

Harper couldn't make herself open the door. Her body ached for his touch. Last night when they'd kissed she'd been able to resist him—just barely. But she'd been nervous about being discovered and had no intention of being seen accompanying Ashton to his suite.

Would it be any better if she was seen exiting his suite in the morning? No, but she was on the verge of not caring.

He must have picked up on her ambivalence because he gently pried her fingers from the handle and dropped a sizzling kiss in her palm. She melted beneath the heat of his gaze and didn't protest when his fingers sought the small of her back. Nor did she resist when with a soft groan he pulled her torso up and firmly into his body.

"Ask me again to stay," she whispered, exhilarated by the leashed passion vibrating in Ashton's muscles.

She dug her fingers into his biceps as he set his open mouth on her neck. The sweep of his tongue against her skin made her moan. Her breasts felt heavy as his arm tightened around her, his chest pushing into her as his breath deepened. The burn beneath her skin made the touch of her clothes unbearable. She needed them gone. Needed to feel his naked flesh against her.

She was half out of her mind with hunger by the time he murmured, "Stay."

"Okay."

He swept her off her feet before the word faded. The air around her cooled as his long, rapid strides brought them to the bedroom. With gentleness she never imagined he possessed, he laid her on the mattress and braced his hands on either side of her head. Wondering what he was up to, she peered at his looming form from beneath her lashes. The intensity of his stare ramped up her desire to be utterly devoured by him.

Raising one hand, she traced the faint hollow of his dimple with her fingertips. The corner of his mouth lifted in response to her touch, deepening the sexy indent. He leaned over her to rub his lips over hers in a tantalizing caress. With an encouraging murmur, she slid her fingers into his hair and brought him closer, deepening the kiss.

Tongues dancing, mouths fused as the heat between them increased, Harper decided the reality of Ashton Croft's kisses was so much better than any fantasy. She wanted to savor the feel of his lips on hers forever, but already her body needed more. Working blindly, she slipped all his shirt buttons free and stroked the fabric off his shoulders. A purr of satisfaction rumbled from her as her palms coasted over the hills and valleys of muscle from his collarbone to his belt.

He seized her lip between his teeth and bit lightly before licking the tender spot. Standing up, he stripped off his shirt, shed his pants and shoes. She scrambled to her knees and peeled off her sweater, but in her haste got her arms caught. Turning the soft knit inside out, she freed herself in time to meet the rush of Ashton's lips as he rejoined her on the bed.

In a jumble of limbs, they rolled across the mattress. Somehow Harper ended up on top. Breathless and laughing, she pressed her lips against Ashton's throat. His hands coasted over her butt and down the backs of her thighs, urging her against the erection straining his boxer briefs. Her head spun as she waited to see where his fingers would explore next.

When they dipped below the waistband of her yoga pants and followed the seam between her butt cheeks to the molten core of her, she gasped. As fleeting as his touch was, it seared her through. She whimpered a protest as he retreated, palms gliding back over the same path. This time he caressed upward, riding the hem of her camisole up over her rib cage.

Almost too shaken to move, but dying to feel his hands on her breasts, Harper placed her palms on the mattress and shoved herself upward. As she'd hoped, he claimed her breasts in his large hands, sending wave after wave of acute pleasure surging through her with his firm touch. She ducked her head as he finished removing her top and emerged from the folds of fabric with a jubilant cry. The sound was cut short as Ashton rolled her beneath him and pulled her nipple into his mouth.

First he sucked, and then swirled his tongue around her nipple, the sensation heightening the lust rampaging through her. She combed her fingers into his hair and held him close. From her throat, mindless, encouraging sounds erupted. She was beyond words. Completely at his command. Whatever he wanted from her she'd give him.

Why had she denied herself this amazing experience for so long? She should have slept with him the first day they met and every time after that. Obviously she wasn't thinking straight because she'd completely forgiven him for all those months of frustration.

Ashton shifted his attention to her second breast and devoted a considerable amount of time driving her desire to alarming heights. His fingers were as busy as his mouth, tracing the skin across her belly, making her stomach muscles pitch and roll. At last he hooked her waistband and applied pressure downward. Harper lifted her hips off the bed to make his job easier. He peeled her pants down her legs, and she finished removing them with three frantic kicks.

His tongue dipped into her navel. Sensation lanced downward. He shifted his broad shoulders between her thighs and used his thumbs to part her folds. Harper clutched the sheets just as his mouth settled over her. Her body jolted, the movement wringing a murmur from her. That's all she had strength for. The rest of her energy was focused on the amazing thing he was doing with his tongue.

Sex wasn't usually on her weekly agenda. She found it

difficult to make time to indulge in a decadent spa treatment or take an afternoon and go shopping. Finding a man she was attracted to seemed far too challenging a prospect, so she went long periods of time without being intimate with anyone.

When first Scarlett and then Violet had fallen in love, Harper might never admit it out loud, but she had envied their glow, the satisfied glint in their eye. Nor had it helped that she'd just begun working with the roguishly handsome Ashton Croft. Hormones long asleep had begun to stir with ever-increasing agitation.

She'd put his ability to exasperate her down to their differing approaches, but with Ashton's mouth sending her into orbit she realized it had just been sexual chemistry and she'd been too long absorbed in her work to recognize the signs.

As pleasure rose, she planted her feet against the mattress and hung on for dear life. His fingers flexed into the soft flesh of her butt, his firm grasp the perfect catalyst to send her spinning out of control. She cried his name as her body exploded. For a second there was a burst of light behind her eyes, and then it slowly faded and she drifted in darkness.

Dimly she felt Ashton shift away from her, but she couldn't move, couldn't protest his leaving. Dimly, she heard the rustle of a condom wrapper and was glad that he'd thought to protect them both. Very few seconds passed before the mattress dipped again. Her lashes fluttered upward as he moved over her once more. His mouth stroked across her lips, tongue dipping between them to tease and arouse all over. Harper put her arms around his shoulders as he shifted his hips between her thighs.

She felt him nudge against her entrance and raised up to meet his thrust as he pushed inside her in one fluid movement. Her inner muscles shuddered in delight, and Ashton buried his face in her neck with a ragged sigh. He was not a small man, and she was a little shocked that her body was able to take him fully. But the rightness of their joining was not to be denied.

Slowly, he started to move. Finding his rhythm took her barely any time at all. Soon it was as if they'd made love a hundred times. She ran her hands over him, finding spots that excited him. He adjusted the angle of her hips and drove into her a little more forcefully. The evocative twist he gave as he plunged into her over and over quickly brought Harper back to the brink of release. As it swept up to claim her once again, she clutched Ashton's forearms and welcomed the frenzied pounding of his body into her as he, too, closed in on his orgasm.

They didn't quite climax together, but it was awfully close. Harper felt the first spasm hit her and dug her nails into Ashton's skin. He kissed her long and hard and with two deep thrusts emptied himself into her with a powerful shudder.

Stunned by the power of what had just happened between them, Harper buried her nose in Ashton's neck and held on while his body trembled. Her sparse personal life hadn't given her a lot of experience in these sorts of matters, but Harper was pretty sure Ashton was as moved as she was.

So what came next?

As if in answer to her question, Ashton shifted his lax muscles and collapsed onto the mattress beside her. They lay side by side, staring up at the ceiling. Harper listened as his breath returned to normal. Her skin was cooling fast. She needed to decide whether to put on her clothes and get out of here or to snuggle against Ashton. Before she'd made up her mind, his fingers closed over hers.

"Don't run off just yet."

Harper turned her head and realized he was watching her. "You don't know that's what I was thinking."

"Don't I?" He rolled onto his side and caught her around

the waist, pulling her beneath him. "Tell me you weren't going to make the excuse that you had to get back to work."

With his warm skin pressing against hers, she knew her opportunity to make a clean getaway had just vanished. Surrendering to the pleasure of his large body overwhelming her, she slid her hands along his muscular arms and marveled at the beauty of his broad shoulders. Already her body craved to be possessed by his once more. He was going to be a hard man to get over.

"I wasn't."

"That doesn't sound much like the Harper I know." He drew back so he could look into her face. "What's happened?"

"I'm pretty sure I'm not the Harper anyone knows."

"I don't understand."

"I found out something today." She pressed her lips together, knowing she shouldn't talk about her secret. If the truth about her paternity got out, she'd never become the CEO of Fontaine Hotels and Resorts. "Something that has changed everything I thought I ever knew about myself."

"That sounds troubling." He stroked her cheek with the tips of his fingers. "What are you going to do?"

Most people would have asked what she'd discovered. With what she'd learned about him in these past few days, Harper understood why he didn't pry. He had a past he wanted to keep private. Things he wasn't proud of.

"I don't know," she told him. "I haven't been thinking too clearly these past few hours." She gave him a wry grin. "I mean, look at me. Twenty-four hours earlier, would I have slept with you?"

"I like to think you were heading down that road."

And she probably had been. "Maybe I'm just making excuses for doing something I've wanted all along."

"Why do you have to make excuses?"

"I don't take sex lightly. For me it's something that comes out of a relationship that has the chance of lasting."

"And you don't think ours will?"

"I think our business relationship will be a lasting one."

He kissed her lightly on the mouth. "I hope so. As for the other, I think we are good for each other. Let's hold on to that for the time being."

As promises went, it wasn't much, but Harper reasoned that for Ashton it was major. She snuggled against his body and let the rhythmic thump of his heart mesmerize her into complete relaxation. The shock of earlier revelations faded as did her ambivalence about what the future held. In Ashton's arms she knew exactly who she was. More than that could wait until the next day.

Seven

Ashton was on his second cup of coffee when the sound of a knock at the door of his suite made him smile. So, after sneaking off while he slept at some point during the wee hours, she'd decided to come back for round four. Smirking, Ashton went to let her in. Only, it wasn't Harper standing in the hall, but Vince.

"What's going on?" he asked his manager, not liking the grim expression Vince wore. "How come you're here?"

"The Lifestyle people have moved up the taping date on your pilot. They want you to come to New York and do it tomorrow."

Ashton cursed, disliking that they were making him jump through hoops. "What's going on?"

"I don't know. We might have dug our heels in a little too hard. I heard they may be looking at other chefs."

And he was going to lose this fantastic opportunity if he didn't move quickly. "What can we do?"

"I'd suggest that we show them how committed we are to Lifestyle Network."

"You want me to quit *The Culinary Wanderer.*"

"You're not happy with the direction they intend to take the show next year. I think it's a good time to cut ties."

His gut told him this was the wrong thing to do, but he'd hired Vince because his gut wasn't right 100 percent of the time. Nor was Ashton convinced he could make decisions about the show he'd worked on for so many years without letting his emotions get the better of him.

"Call Phillips and tell them I'm not going to continue with *The Culinary Wanderer.*" Harper's face flashed before his eyes as he said this. She would be disappointed. And that bothered him more than it should. But this was business. In the end she'd accept that.

"I have things to do before I can head to New York." Chef Cole had not yet arrived from Chicago to take up his duties. Ashton would brief Dae on all the things that needed to be done in the next few days. The kid was smart and resourceful. "How did you get here?"

"Commercial. The network is sending their plane to pick us up tonight."

Well, at least that was one thing he didn't have to worry about. The biggest challenge was going to be telling Harper that he was leaving ten days before Batouri was due to open. That was a conversation he'd better have sooner than later.

After leaving Ashton slumbering peacefully in his bed, Harper had spent the rest of the night on her couch, burrowed beneath a cotton throw, watching one episode after another of *The Culinary Wanderer.* She'd stared at Ashton's image on the screen, unable to believe she'd fulfilled the only sexual fantasy she'd ever had.

Reality had far exceeded anything she could have dreamed up. She'd expected Ashton would be a skilled and masterful lover, but he'd demonstrated a level of caring and consideration of her pleasure that had far surpassed any intimacy she'd ever known. Even now, after several rounds of lovemaking, her body throbbed with desire for him.

But would she have made love with him last night if her defenses hadn't been crushed by the knowledge that she wasn't a Fontaine? The answer wasn't clear enough for Harper's liking. She felt lost and adrift. It's why she couldn't sleep, couldn't make her mind function the way it normally did. No patterns emerged out of the chaos of her thoughts. Her ability to plan and make things happen had left her. She was a shell, waiting to be filled with purpose.

Harper passed her hand over her dry, tired eyes before levering herself off the cushions and heading to make coffee. Her cell phone chirped. A text message. Probably Mary wondering why she hadn't picked up the report on last night's numbers.

Harper picked up the phone, intending to shut it off. For the first time in her life, she didn't feel like being responsible. But she really should call Mary. Unless Harper explicitly stated her unavailability, her assistant expected her to answer, and if she didn't, Mary would probably send security to check on her.

Heaving a sigh, Harper dialed. With Fontaine Ciel open and running smoothly, she could hand over the reins to her general manager for a while. When her assistant picked up, Harper said, "I'm going to take some time off. If anything comes up have Bob handle it."

As simple as that, she was free. She'd expected to feel lighter with the concerns of the hotel off her shoulders, but it was only a matter of time before her hours of playing hooky would end and she'd take up the reins once more.

Mug in hand, she headed off to shower. In the past ten hours she'd watched the entire season Ashton had spent in Europe. She'd chosen these particular episodes to watch because she'd visited several of the same countries. The contrast between her experiences and his could not have been more dramatic. He loved what he did. The people he met fascinated him. His culinary encounters often astonished him. Not everything was to his taste, but he was always game to try.

She'd visited and left countries without ever getting to know their cultures. Most of the time she was on a tight deadline that left little room to go exploring. She'd been proud of how hard she worked, had wallowed in her arrogance that she knew best in almost every situation.

In her own way, she was as committed to her path as Ashton was to his. She'd grown impatient with his lack of focus on the restaurant. How many people had she frustrated with her inability to relax? She drove herself hard and expected her employees to follow in her footsteps. Being a woman, she'd known she'd have to work hard to prove to her grandfather that she was executive material, worthy of someday taking her place as head of the family business.

All that work only to find out she'd wasted the past twenty-nine years of her life chasing a goal that wasn't hers to pursue. The futility of it all infuriated her. Leaving her suite, Harper headed to the parking garage where she retrieved her car and headed to the mall for a little shopping therapy.

Harper cruised store after store without buying anything while she pondered how profoundly her life had changed. She had to tell her grandfather the truth, didn't she? Neither Scarlett nor Violet thought it was a good idea. But what toll would living a lie take on her psyche?

Sick of questions that had no easy answers, Harper ducked into a bookstore, deciding what she needed was a few hours of getting lost in someone else's problems. It had been too long since she'd taken time to read something besides reports. She picked up a copy of her favorite author's latest novel and headed to the front to pay.

While she waited behind a mother with two children under the age of five, her attention drifted toward a display of coffee table books. The leopard on the cover of one caught her attention. As a child she'd spent hours flipping through a book of African wildlife photos at her grandmother's home in the Hamptons. She'd found the images riveting and realized now that it was probably what had planted the seeds of longing to travel.

The hair on Harper's arms lifted as she was struck by a sudden realization. Penelope had engaged in an affair with a wildlife photographer. Was it just a coincidence that she'd given Harper's grandmother a book of wildlife photos? Deep in her soul, Harper knew it wasn't.

She stepped out of the checkout line and headed toward the display that had caught her attention. This book wasn't the same as the one in her grandmother's library. Gripped by sudden urgency, she dialed her grandmother's Hamptons house. As expected, Tilly, her grandmother's housekeeper, answered.

"Hi, Tilly, it's Harper."

"Hello, Harper. I'm afraid your grandmother isn't here at the moment."

"Oh, that's right. She mentioned her plans to go shopping when I spoke with her last Sunday." Which was why Harper knew she could call at this time and accomplish her goal without explaining why she was so interested in a book of photographs. "Could you do me a favor?"

"Of course."

"There's a book of African wildlife photos in the library that my mother gave Grandma for her birthday a long time ago. I used to look at it when I visited, but I don't think I've see it since I was thirteen or fourteen. Could you find it for me?"

"Give me a second." If Tilly thought the request was odd, coming out of the blue like this, she gave no sign. The Hamptons house had a five-thousand-square-foot first floor so it took a few minutes before Tilly came back on the line. "I have it here."

Harper exhaled in relief. She'd been half afraid that

the book would have been lost in the past fifteen years. Her grandmother wasn't the most sentimental woman and might not have kept a birthday present from her daughter that long.

"Can you tell me who the photographer was?"

"Greg LeDay."

"Perfect. Thank you, Tilly. And don't mention to anyone that I called. I'll check in with Grandma on Sunday as usual."

"She always loves to hear from you."

Harper ended the call and felt a bit light-headed. Was Greg LeDay her father? With shaking fingers, she tapped his name into the internet browser on her phone and waited impatiently for the search results to come up. To her immense delight he had a website. She went straight to his bio page and spent a long moment staring at the black-and-white photo of a handsome, rugged man in his mid-fifties standing beside a battered jeep, a camera with an enormous lens in his hands. Five giraffes loped across the landscape behind him.

His easy posture and half grin reminded her so much of Ashton that she couldn't breathe for a second. The two men were obviously cut from the same cloth. No wonder she was so drawn to the man who starred in *The Culinary Wanderer*. She had an adventurer's blood running through her veins.

After several minutes of staring at the photo, she began exploring LeDay's website. In addition to being a photographer, he also acted as a guide for others who were interested in taking pictures of wildlife. In fact, he had several tours lined up in the coming months. One left in two days.

An idea bloomed. She emailed LeDay about joining the safari. Abandoning the book she'd come to purchase for a travel guide to South Africa, Harper headed for her car and the nearest sporting goods store. Within ten minutes, she stood before a display of travel bags and finally understood the importance of Ashton's *go* bag. Pack light and be ready to take off for the next exotic location at a moment's notice.

Isn't that what fascinated her about his television show? His lack of baggage, both physical and spiritual? He took what he could comfortably carry. Lightweight clothes that would travel well. His notebooks for when inspiration struck. Some toiletries. And most important? A camera.

Seized by a vision of what she would take on her own adventure, Harper picked out a rolling backpack system and gathered whatever accessories she would need for the next few weeks.

It wasn't until she'd paid for her purchases and lugged them out to her car that she began to question the sanity of what she intended to do. What made her think that this man who might be her father would appreciate her showing up out of the blue? She had no idea if he knew she existed. But if she didn't take the chance and meet him, she might never stop questioning who she was. Her identity secure, she would know whether or not she could stay quiet about her true parentage and spend the rest of her life living a lie. Scarlett and Violet had already promised to support whatever decision she made. She was lucky to have them in her life.

Anticipation filled her with a wild sort of joy as she returned to her hotel suite and sifted through all she'd bought. It was a ridiculous amount, she realized, staring at it scattered over her bed. Never before had she needed to mull over every ounce of what she was packing. Her trips had involved porters, bellhops and hired cars.

Harper abandoned her packing conundrum and went online to check flights to Johannesburg, South Africa. To her surprise she had several choices all leaving that evening. Why wait? Now that she'd made the decision to go, every minute that went by increased her craving to be off.

Unable to believe how easy the whole thing was, she assembled her own *go* bag. Small enough to fit in an overhead bin, it weighed thirty pounds completely loaded. By the time she'd dressed in jeans, a white T-shirt and a brown leather bomber jacket she'd found in the back of her closet, her nerves were humming with excitement.

As she turned off the lights and pulled the door of her suite shut behind her, Harper was struck by a profound sense of stepping across the threshold into a whole new state of being. It was thrilling to be rushing off into the night with no idea what to anticipate next and no way of controlling the outcome.

She was halfway down the hall when the elevator door opened and Ashton emerged pulling his own *go* bag behind him. When he spotted her, he stopped dead. His position in the doorway kept the elevator open.

"Where are you going?" he demanded as she stepped onto the elevator beside him.

"I could ask you the same thing." Disappointment hit her. She needed him in Las Vegas, focused on the soon-to-open restaurant.

"I was coming to see you."

She glanced pointedly at his luggage. "And after that?"

"I'm flying to New York for a few days. The negotiations for the new show have reached a critical point."

"How critical?"

"I may be on the verge of losing the deal."

Hope flared. If he didn't do the new show he could stay on with *The Culinary Wanderer*. She was careful to keep her voice neutral as she said, "Maybe that's not the worst that could happen."

"But doing the new show means I'll get to spend most of the year in New York City."

Where she would be if she stopped asking questions about her biological father and accepted that she belonged in charge of Fontaine Hotels and Resorts. Would her relationship with Ashton develop into something serious if they were both in New York?

"It sounds like an amazing opportunity," she told him. "I just wish you could do both the new show and *The Culinary Wanderer*."

"Sounds like you don't want me around." He said it with a wry kick of his lips, but his eyes were serious as he awaited her response.

She'd felt connected to him these past few days. He'd filled her head with his stories and inspired her to go in search of a few of her own.

"It isn't that." She paused, unsure if she should voice how much she craved his company. The man had one foot out the door on the best of days. "Are you sure you're going to be happy if you're stuck in one place for a long time? Won't you get bored?"

"If you're worried about my ability to control my need for change, don't be. Once I find something I love, I have no trouble sticking with it."

"And yet here you are leaving town a week and a half before Batouri is set to open."

His lips tightened momentarily. "Everything is handled. I've given Dae my recipes and instructions and he knows how I work. He can keep things on track until Cole gets here. And I'll be back in a few days."

"It's your restaurant. Your reputation on the line." From his expression she could tell he hadn't expected her to pass complete control of the project to him. "I'm sure you know what you're doing."

"Which brings us to you. If you're heading to New York, I can give you a ride in the network's corporate jet."

"Thank you, but I've already booked my flight."

"Wouldn't you rather travel in style? I can promise the pantry is well stocked."

"It's kind of you to offer, but we are destined for different locations."

He scrutinized her clothes and her bag. "Where are you going?"

"South Africa."

Ashton didn't know what to make of her answer. Two nights earlier they'd enjoyed a playful evening of food and wine. Last night they'd made love. She'd never once made mention of an upcoming trip much less one to Africa. Maybe he wasn't the only one keeping secrets.

The elevator doors opened, and Harper stepped forward with purpose and energy. Ashton followed. Since they were both heading to the airport, he'd have a good twenty minutes to get to the core of what was going on.

He eyed her suitcase. It was the size he'd expect a woman to take for a long weekend. "How long are you planning to be gone?"

"I don't know. A week. Maybe two. It depends." She trailed off.

Not normally one to pick up on the nuances of other people's emotional states, Ashton found that when it came to Harper, he'd become hyperaware of her moods. Something was up and he wasn't going to let her go until he knew what it was.

"I didn't realize Fontaine had expanded into Africa."

"It hasn't."

"Then you're scouting locations?"

"No."

Her short answers were creating more confusion than understanding. Harper was many things. Goal oriented, resourceful, outspoken. Never evasive.

Ashton used his height and weight advantage to herd her away from the line of taxis. She was not escaping from him until he was satisfied he knew the whole story. "I have a car waiting."

"I can take a cab."

"You can also accept a ride."

"Thank you." But there was very little gratitude in her tone. She wanted to go her own way. It made him all that much more determined to not let her.

After giving instructions to the driver where to drop Harper off, he waited until their luggage was stowed in the trunk and the town car was navigating East Flamingo Road before he continued his interrogation. "Is this trip business or pleasure?"

"Why are you so curious?"

"Because I would think with Batouri set to open in less than two weeks you might have mentioned an impending trip out of the country."

"It came up rather fast."

"How fast?"

"This afternoon."

The traffic was flowing more smoothly than usual down Paradise Road. The short ride to the airport, which usually took twenty minutes, was going to take closer to ten. Ashton was running out of time to get the answers he wanted.

"What the hell is going on with you, Harper? This isn't like you at all."

Her brown eyes were fierce as she met his gaze. "I'm not sure that's true."

"You've lost me."

"Since I was eleven I've had a plan for how my life was going to go. I set goals and achieved them, all with one target in mind."

"Running Fontaine Hotels and Resorts."

She nodded. "But what no one knows is how often I've wondered what it would be like to give it all up and run away. To pack a bag and see the world, not from the back of a taxi, but on the back of a motorcycle or in an open jeep or even on a camel."

Passion drenched her tone. Her longing made his heart contract. He recognized what it felt like to yearn, even though he'd long ago come to terms with the futility of craving what could never be. He'd promised himself to never be that weak again, but his developing connection with Harper sparked a long-buried emotion. Hope.

"What does all this have to do with your trip to South Africa?"

"I realize it's all been in vain."

Harper's hand had been hovering near the door handle since the car had entered the airport limits. As soon as the vehicle came to a complete stop, she was out the door. The driver popped the trunk, and Harper had her bag on the curb before Ashton even exited the car. Despite her haste, he moved quickly enough to block her path into the terminal.

"My flight leaves in ninety minutes. I have to get through security."

"Then you don't have a lot of time to waste. Why are you going to Africa?"

"I have something I need to take care of."

"Such as?" He crossed his arms over his chest and regarded her as if he had all the time in the world to wait for her answer.

She blew out a breath. "Some complicated family business."

"Hotel business?"

"Personal business."

"And you don't feel like sharing?"

"Maybe when I get back."

"Talk to me, Harper." Ashton was more than a little disturbed to feel her slipping away from him. "I told you things no one else knows."

Her gaze pleaded with him to let her go, but he held firm and at last she caved. "Fine. I'm going to find a man who might be my father."

"I thought your father was dead."

She paused a beat before answering. "The man I thought was my father is dead. I think my real father is a wildlife photographer who leads photography safaris throughout Africa." She sounded completely composed as if this was old news, but the tension around her mouth betrayed that all was not well.

It all came together in a heartbeat. "So you're not a Fontaine?"

"It appears I'm not."

"And finding this out has led to the questions you've been having about the decisions you've made in your career?"

"I'm not a Fontaine." Agony fractured her voice. "I have no right to be CEO."

"You have worked toward this all your life."

"My grandfather wants one of his granddaughters to take over the company."

"And you think he will reject you after twenty-nine years because you're not biologically related? Could anyone be that heartless?"

"You don't understand how important family is to my grandfather. After my father…" She grimaced. "After my father died and Grandfather discovered he had other granddaughters, he came up with his contest to determine who was best qualified to run the company." She dashed away a tear from the corner of her eye and rushed on. "It was my birthright. My dream. I'd dedicated my life to proving I deserved to be CEO one day, and he expected me to prove it all over again."

Horns honked behind him as cars jockeyed for space at the curb. Departing passengers hurried past. A police officer, directing traffic, blew his whistle. The chaos pressed against Ashton's back, but he braced himself and focused completely on Harper.

Four words summed up everything he felt for her. "How can I help?"

He put out a hand, offering comfort and support, but she backed away.

"You can't." She gave her head a vehement shake.

Despite being stung by her rejection, he persisted. "Where in South Africa are you heading?"

"Pretoria."

"Where are you staying?"

"I haven't decided." It wasn't like her to be so unprepared.

"I have a friend at the Pretoria Capital Hotel. Ask for Giles Dumas. He's the executive chef for their restaurant."

"Thank you." Gratitude softened her lips into a smile for a second. "I have to go. I can't miss my flight."

Staying put and letting her walk away from him was the hardest thing he'd done in a long time. When she disappeared through the sliding glass doors of the terminal, Ashton slid into the back of the town car and focused his attention on the traffic visible through the windshield.

She had her path to follow. He had his. If only he could shake his thoughts free of her. He had his own problems to worry about. The network folks would expect him to make a strong showing during his taping. He needed to be completely focused to impress them.

Eight

With the first and shortest leg of her long journey behind her, Harper fastened her seat belt and stared out the window with dry, scratchy eyes. By flying business class, she'd saved eight thousand dollars on her ticket, but she'd found herself incapable of sleeping sitting up during the nearly ten-hour flight to London. Nor had she been able to nod off during her five-hour layover. Pair that with her sleepless night the previous evening and Harper estimated she'd been awake around forty-eight hours.

At least on the leg between London and Johannesburg she wasn't stuck in a middle seat. She propped a pillow between her head and the wall of the cabin and let out a huge breath as a wave of exhaustion flowed over her. She fell asleep not long after the plane stopped climbing.

The popping of her ears woke her as the plane reduced altitude. She checked the seat back monitor that kept track of the distance traveled and saw that they were a little over an hour from touching down in South Africa. Her pulse jumped. She was about to land in a foreign country and go in search of a man she hadn't known existed two days earlier. The town where he lived was a forty-five minute drive from Johannesburg and she had yet to receive a response to her email requesting information on the seven-day safari he was leading the day after she arrived.

She thought it might be a good idea to get to know him a little before announcing that she'd traveled halfway around the world to see if she was his daughter.

From his bio she knew that he'd never been married. Dedicating his life to his passion for Africa, he'd won several prestigious awards and had his work published in more than two dozen magazines. For the past day and a half she'd tried to find herself in this man she shared genes with. They shared a focus on their work and a determination to achieve greatness, but when it came to their careers, Greg LeDay had more in common with Ashton than her.

Both men were creative geniuses. LeDay's photography was brilliant in the same way Ashton's culinary masterpieces won him notoriety.

By comparison, what had she done? She'd worked hard and had nothing she was proud to display as her body of work. Her passion involved planning, organizing and making things happen. She was good at telling people what to do, being ruthless. How many of her employees called her a bitch behind her back?

Harper wasn't feeling all that organized or ruthless at the moment. She was drifting on a sea of uncertainty. Impatient with herself, she pulled out her phone and logged on to the plane's Wi-Fi network. It was time to reconnect with her organized self. She hadn't yet planned her trip beyond booking her flight to Johannesburg. She needed to figure out how she was going to get to Pretoria and where she was going to stay once she got there.

To her delight, the two cities were linked by a high-speed train line that she could pick up at the airport. She would have to change trains, but after doing so she would arrive in Pretoria in less than half an hour. Harper then turned her attention to finding the hotel Ashton had suggested and booked a room for two nights. By the time the plane's doors opened to allow the passengers to disembark, she was feeling completely in charge once more.

Finding the train was easy. She'd exchanged dollars for rand along the way and arrived at the platform just as the train was pulling in. As adventures went, this trip was feeling awfully mundane. She stepped onto the train, secured her bag and settled into a clean, comfortable seat by the window. Despite getting sleep on the plane, the train's rocking motion made it difficult to keep her eyes open. She fought the pull. The distance between the stations wasn't great and she could miss her exchange if she wasn't careful.

As it was, she wasn't fully awake when the train pulled into Marlboro station. Yawning wearily, she got to her feet and waited for an opening in the crowd of exiting passengers so she could step into the aisle and collect her bag. Something hard clipped her temple, knocking her sideways. Stunned by the blow, on the verge of losing consciousness, she didn't fight the hands that shoved her into the seat and stripped away the bag that held her cash and passport.

Before her head cleared, her assailant was long gone and the last of the passengers had disembarked. Harper staggered to her feet, but before she could reach her luggage, the door closed and the train moved forward. The pain in her head made Harper's thoughts thick and sluggish. She dropped into the closest empty seat and closed her eyes. What was she supposed to do now?

Ashton stepped out of a cab on the corner of Ninth Avenue and Twenty-eighth Street in Chelsea and saw his old friend Craig Turner waiting for him by the curb. Since the Lifestyle people weren't expecting him until two that afternoon, Ashton had decided to check in with his old mentor and wasn't surprised to learn that Craig was still volunteering at Holy Apostles Soup Kitchen.

"Ashton, good to see you." The sixty-five-year-old restaurateur wrapped Ashton in a tight bear hug. "You're looking wonderful. Television suits you."

"It has its moments."

When Ashton had first come to New York before landing his first television series, he'd spent two years in Craig's kitchen learning everything there was to know about what it took to run a successful restaurant. He'd gleaned a lot. And yet, with four restaurants under his belt, Ashton knew he still had plenty of Craig's wisdom left to absorb.

"And now you're stepping into the big time with a show here in New York."

It shouldn't have astonished him that Craig knew this; little happened in New York having to do with food that Craig missed. "We'll see. Nothing's finalized yet."

"And your restaurant in Las Vegas. That's set to open next week. Things going okay?"

"I'll tell you in a couple weeks."

Craig laughed heartily. "I'm glad you could meet me here."

"No problem."

"Once a week I come down to volunteer. For two hours every day they serve a hot meal to over a thousand people. Makes me feel good to give back."

"Of course." Ashton smiled, but as soon as he entered the busy church, he felt his muscles tense as long-forgotten memories of the dinners his parents had organized for the locals resurfaced.

As a kid he'd resented the hours of free time he'd lost helping his mother fix and serve the meals while his father practiced his ministry on the captive audience. Now, as he put on an apron and rolled up his sleeves, he recalled the day when his outlook had changed—when a loathsome chore had become an opportunity to create something amazing in the kitchen. But for a long time after he'd left home and joined up with Chapman's gang, he'd equated his love for cooking with surrendering to his parents' insistence that he become more like them.

He fell into the rhythm of serving as if twenty years hadn't passed. Looking back on those days, he could recall his resentment and frustration, but lacked empathy for his younger self. Seeing the gratitude in the eyes of those who moved past him now, Ashton recalled how many people his parents had been able to help.

So maybe he'd been too hard on his mother and father all these years. But he still wasn't able to excuse his father's insistence that everyone should believe the same things he did. His disregard for any opinion that wasn't his had put father and son at odds too many times. If his father had listened to him once or twice, maybe Ashton would have felt valued and wouldn't have left. He'd never know.

Several hours later, Ashton waved off the thanks from the volunteer leaders and followed Craig outside. It might not have been how he'd chosen to spend the morning, but it had given him some fodder for thought.

"Thanks for the help. Can I drop you somewhere?"

Ashton shook his head. "I'm going to walk a bit."

"It was good seeing you. Perhaps when your new series gets rolling you can come have dinner with me."

"I'd like that."

The two men parted ways and Ashton strode down the street as if he had someplace to be, when in truth, he was just trying to escape the pressure inside himself.

He'd not yet heard anything from Giles. Given that Harper's flight time was a little over twenty-six hours and the time difference between New York and Johannesburg was seven hours, he imagined she should be arriving in Pretoria around one in the morning New York time, depending on her stops and layovers. Being out of touch with her bothered him. He craved the sound of her voice and longed to share with her his revelations while serving at the soup kitchen.

Something about her invited him to confide his secrets. He wasn't sure why he'd told her about his parents or how he'd left home. Disclosing his past wasn't something he did. He wasn't sure why he didn't want anyone to know that he was the son of missionaries or that he'd left home at an early age. Maybe it was the mess he'd been involved in when he left home that he was ashamed of. What he'd been forced to do. The darkness he'd faced in his soul.

He reflected on his decision to keep those things hidden. Who was he really protecting? If Harper had an inkling of what he held back, she would dig until she unearthed the truth. Would she turn away in disgust or understand? She'd grown up in a cocoon of wealth and polite society. Instinct told him she'd be appalled to learn what he'd done while living with Chapman's gang.

They were so different. She, all bossy businesswoman, planning every little thing to death. He, the go-getter, leaping before looking because what fun was life without a little danger? She conquered. He explored. Very different philosophies.

That they'd been able to work together these past nine months without driving each other mad continued to baffle him. Maybe it worked because they were good for each other. He needed her planning capabilities to keep him in check. And he knew his adventurous side had rubbed off on her. Why else would she have hopped on a plane to South Africa?

Harper gripped the armrest as the train sped through the flat landscape dotted with buildings. She was traveling in the wrong direction. How far out of her way had she gone? Almost as soon as the question surfaced, the train began to slow down. She was on her feet, her luggage in her hand by the time the doors opened.

No longer able to assume the people around her were innocuous fellow travelers, Harper regarded everyone who drew near her as a potential threat. When no one in her vicinity seemed at all interested in her, she took a seat on a nearby bench and took stock of her situation.

Her cash and passport were gone. She still had her rail pass and the credit card she'd used to purchase it tucked in her back pocket. Her phone had been in her hand at the time of the attack and she'd managed to keep ahold of it. And she had her luggage. All was not lost. She would get on the train to Pretoria and catch a cab to the American Embassy there.

All she needed was her birth certificate and the extra photo…which she kept in the luggage she'd left behind in Las Vegas. Anxiety swelled once more. Without identification how was she supposed to prove who she was?

Frozen and unable to function, Harper stared at her hands. She was far from home and quite alone. Not to mention her head ached and panic was jumbling her thoughts. The ebb and flow of train passengers caused her suspicion to spike.

By fits and starts her brain began to function again. She needed to figure out which train traveled north so she could get back on track. The Gautrain's schedule was still in her internet browser. She located the route map and discovered she wasn't in as bad a shape as she thought. The train to Pretoria passed through this station, as well. She just needed to find the correct track.

Fifteen minutes later, Harper collapsed into her seat on the Pretoria-bound train and patted herself on the back. With the shock of being robbed fading, she was better able to function. During the journey north she pinned the American Embassy on her map app and located the hotel, as well.

Her stomach growled, reminding her she hadn't eaten anything since her stopover in London. She would worry about that later. She had to secure a home base where Mary could send her documents. Once she had those in hand, she could go to the embassy. Ashton had told her to ask for his friend. Perhaps that would be enough to enable her to check in without her passport. She crossed her fingers and hoped.

An hour after stepping onto the platform in Pretoria station and taking a taxi to the hotel, Harper launched into her story of being mugged for the third time. Hunger and frustration were draining what few reserves she had left.

"No, I didn't file a report with the police. I didn't know where to find a police station. I just wanted to get here and register."

"But we can't do that without you having documentation," the manager in charge of the front desk explained. "Don't you have a copy of your passport page to show us?"

"As I've already told your staff, the decision to visit Pretoria was a last-minute thing and I left all my backup documentation behind. My assistant is going to overnight it to me, but I need to have a place she can send it."

"She can't send it here unless you're registered."

Harper closed her eyes and sucked in a huge breath. "Giles." She'd forgotten about him. "I was supposed to ask for Giles…" His last name eluded her. "I believe he's the executive chef here?"

The manager regarded her solemnly. "He is our executive chef."

"Would he be around? I was told to come here and to say that Ashton Croft sent me."

"We'll call the kitchen. Perhaps you should take a seat over there and we'll see if he has time to speak to you."

It wasn't the most promising offer, but at this point Harper was ready to take what she could get. "I'm quite hungry. Tell him I'll be in the restaurant."

She followed the hostess toward a table on the patio and sank into the plastic chair with a grateful sigh. A smiling waitress came almost immediately to take her order. The dinner menu had so many delicious items on it she had trouble choosing. In the end she settled on game picatta because the description made her mouth water. Tender slices of game pan fried with button mushrooms, mixed peppercorns, doused with sweet Marsala and bound with cream, served on fettuccine dusted with Parmesan cheese.

It arrived at her table, delivered by a tall, handsome man with salt-and-pepper hair and a dashing goatee. She glanced from his face to his chef whites without comprehension as he set the plate before her.

"You're Harper Fontaine?"

At his recognition tears began streaming down her face. She nodded, too overcome by relief to speak.

"My name is Giles Dumas. I understand you ran into a little trouble getting here." He smiled gently as she nodded a second time. "Our mutual friend will be very glad to hear you've arrived. Now, what can I do to help?"

Nine

Gut tight with foreboding, Ashton stood with his back to the conference table and stared out over the Manhattan skyline. Behind him two of the network guys were speaking with Vince. The taping hadn't gone as well as he would have liked. Since dropping Harper off at the airport he'd been edgy and distracted. Nor could he be certain that she'd taken his advice and booked a room at the Pretoria Capital Hotel until he heard from his buddy Giles.

He told himself just because he enjoyed venturing off the beaten track didn't mean she would be foolish enough to go somewhere she could get into trouble. But until he knew she was safe, Ashton wouldn't be able to shake the sensation that he'd made a mistake letting her go by herself halfway around the world to find a father she'd never met. Even after she shoved his offer of help back at him he couldn't get her out of his head. He was worried about her emotional state and the fact that she was a woman unused to traveling alone.

Vince came to stand beside him. His manager's lack of chatter felt as ominous as the clouds above the city.

Ashton broke the silence. "They weren't wowed by my audition tape."

"It wasn't quite what they were expecting," Vince agreed. "Some aspects of it went over great, others they'd like to work on with you."

"And?" Ashton prompted, hearing the low note in Vince's voice and guessing there was more bad news.

"It's just this little thing about your image. You've been the bad boy of travel adventures, eating exotic cuisine, meeting the natives."

The description was a little off-putting, but Ashton figured Vince was offering his own spin on what the producers had said.

"How do they want my image to change?"

"They're thinking lose the jeans and leather jacket and put you into chef whites. But mostly..." Vince hesitated. "They want you to cut your hair so that you'll look more... polished."

It wasn't an outrageous demand, but Ashton wasn't sure he wanted to look like something he wasn't. And yet, wasn't the whole point of doing this cooking show so he could change things up in his career? "Anything else?"

Vince looked relieved that Ashton's temper hadn't blown up. "They're wondering if you can stay in New York a few more days."

He needed to get back to Las Vegas and Batouri. Even though Dae was sending him frequent updates that things were running smoothly, it was a week and a half before the restaurant opened. And as Harper had repeatedly pointed out, Batouri was his responsibility.

"Ash?" Vince prompted. "What should I tell them?"

Harper had accused him of putting his television career before Batouri, but hadn't he also put it before her? So what if they barely knew each other? Ashton couldn't shake the notion that she needed him and he'd let her down.

"Tell them no."

"Have you lost your mind? You can't say no after quitting *The Culinary Wanderer*. What if they find someone else? What are you going to do then?"

Vince seemed to have forgotten that with several restaurants in various countries, Ashton wasn't dependent on the money he made doing television shows. He just enjoyed the celebrity and the experiences he'd had over the years.

"Write a cookbook." With the help of a very special woman who was at a crossroads of her own.

"A cookbook? Have you lost your mind? Lifestyle Network is going to make you famous."

"They've left me hanging for four months. Now they're demanding I drop everything at a moment's notice?" Ashton's frustration spilled over. "They're going to have to wait."

"I'm not sure they'll like that answer." Vince's eyes shifted toward the group of executives. "They could go with someone else."

Ashton mentally cursed. This was his project. They'd strung him along and now they were threatening to replace him?

"Let them," he snarled. "Whatever they do with the show, it's not going to be a success without me." His gaze collided with Vince's.

"Okay." But his manager didn't look happy. "You're the star. We walk away from this deal." Vince assessed Ashton's expression and shed his doubts with a nod. "Once word gets out you'll be hit with a dozen offers before the week's out."

Ashton wasn't sure his manager was right, but he was confident something bigger and better was just around the next curve. In the meantime he would see to Batouri's grand opening and spend some time getting to know more about Harper Fontaine.

As his thoughts returned to her, all optimism drained away. Why couldn't he shake the notion that he should travel to Africa to be with her? The thought was ridiculous. She'd insisted he focus his full attention on Batouri. He'd incur her fury if he did anything as idiotic as leave the country mere days before its opening.

"I need to get to the airport," Ashton announced. "Let me know what the outcome of the meeting is."

"Are you heading back to Las Vegas now?"

"Not yet."

"Where then?"

"Pretoria."

Vince looked utterly baffled. "Where?"

"South Africa."

Harper's second day in South Africa had gone much more smoothly than her first. Before going to bed the night before, she'd contacted Mary and arranged to have her backup documentation shipped to the hotel. Then, with nothing to do but wait, she took the opportunity to sleep late and get her bearings.

Now, bathed in early afternoon sunshine, Harper was enjoying a glass of wine in a corner of the patio. A shadow fell across her South African tour book. Thinking it was her waitress she looked up. Ashton stood beside her chair looking every inch a dashing world traveler in jeans and a pale blue button-down shirt with the sleeves rolled up to expose the long faint scars on his forearms. With one hand he held a black leather jacket over his shoulder and the other rested on the handle of his *go* bag.

Heart jumping wildly, Harper was too stunned to answer the come-and-get-me call of his lopsided grin. "What are you doing here?"

"I decided someone needed to chronicle your first adventure, so here I am." He pulled out the chair beside hers and settled into it.

"I thought you had a meeting in New York."

"It was over sooner than I expected so I hopped on a plane and here I am."

He didn't elaborate, and she wondered how things had gone.

"My trip took over twenty-six hours. How did you get here so fast?"

"Direct flights from JFK only take fifteen hours." He settled into the chair across from hers. "What are you drinking?"

"Something local. It's quite good." Her brain still wasn't functioning properly. She continued to stare at him in amazement. With his arrival, being in South Africa had taken on a whole new joy. "Shouldn't you be in Las Vegas preparing for Batouri's opening?"

"I spoke with Cole an hour ago. He arrived in Vegas and has everything running smoothly. Tell me about your visit so far."

Concern for what might be going wrong with the opening buzzed in the back of her mind, but she'd made the decision to abandon her post at this critical time and had to trust that Ashton knew what he was doing, too. "You called Giles to tell him I was coming. How did you know I would?"

"Since you usually have everything planned to the second and hadn't yet booked a hotel, I knew you'd be open to my recommendation." He paused a beat. "And you trust me."

The knowing glint in his gaze made her cross. Harper picked up her wine and took a sip. "Your meeting in New York must have gone your way for you to be here right now."

"Actually, it went rather poorly." He signaled the waitress. "They want me to cut my hair. I told them to go to hell."

While he ordered wine for himself and a melted cheese bowl appetizer, Harper narrowed her eyes and tried to picture him without his wayward, sun-streaked locks. With his dimples and sparkling blue eyes it didn't really matter what the producers did to try and make him look more civilized. In his heart, he was always going to be a reckless adventurer. That they were trying to change him was idiotic. Didn't they understand that was the basis of his charm?

"And instead of returning to Las Vegas where your restaurant is opening in a week you decided to come here?" Did he expect her to be glad to see him? Which she was.

"I didn't think you were ready to fly solo."

"You think I need a babysitter."

He radiated innocence. "Did I say that?"

"You've spoken with Giles."

"He called me before my flight left."

"He told you, didn't he?"

"Told me what?"

She didn't believe his casualness for a second. "That I was mugged on the train." When he didn't react with shock and concern, she knew her suspicions had been right. "I suppose you think I was foolish for coming here alone."

"Not at all. This is a very safe country for tourists. The same thing could have happened to you in New York or Las Vegas. I'm sorry you were attacked and I'm angry with myself for not coming with you."

His words stirred up the emotional tornado she'd been caught in all week. A tear formed in the corner of her eye. She dashed it away. "You had important things to do."

"None of them are more important than you."

It was a huge admission for her to hear, and she wondered how he'd react if she told him that she was falling in love with him. Better not. She was feeling too vulnerable and he'd already confessed that he didn't want her depending on him. If she harnessed him with the burden of her growing attachment, he might turn right around and get back on a plane. And she very badly needed him. She'd just have to keep letting him think she didn't.

"Because you aren't free to pursue another project until Batouri is opened and I'm satisfied that your end of our arrangement is complete?" It hurt to see shadows overcome the bright blue of his gaze.

His wine arrived at the same time as the food, interrupting the silence that hung between them. Harper focused on putting the goat cheese and roasted tomato bruschetta mixture on a slice of toasted baguette.

"When are you planning on going to the embassy about getting a new passport?"

"My assistant overnighted my documents. I'll go when they get here."

"And in the meantime? Have you had any luck locating the man you believe is your father?"

"His name is Greg LeDay. He left this morning for Kruger National Park. The safari he's leading was booked and I couldn't get in. He won't be back in town for ten days. I can't wait around that long." She gave him a sheepish smile. "Seems my first impulsive adventure is a complete disaster."

"Adventure is immune to disaster." Ashton pointed at her with the knife he'd been using to smooth cheese on his bread. "There may be setbacks and detours, but often those are what send you in a new and exciting direction."

His optimism was contagious. "See, this is why I'm such a fan." She couldn't help but be drawn in by his enthusiasm. "You have a knack for transforming the challenges into opportunities."

"Words to put on my tombstone."

"It's a lot better than what they'd inscribe on mine. 'She planned every second of her life to death.'"

Ashton coughed long and hard until tears ran from his eyes.

"Are you okay?" she asked him as the fit slowly abated.

"I inhaled some of my wine. That was some pretty dark humor just now," he said. "It caught me by surprise."

"Did it?" She considered what she'd said. "I guess I think that way fairly often, but it rarely comes out. It's not the sort of thing my mother appreciated hearing so I learned to bottle it up."

"There are more layers to you than anyone realizes, aren't there?"

Harper shrugged. The admiration in his gaze was both thrilling and a touch uncomfortable. She'd concentrated on doing and saying the right thing her whole life. It was liberating to let loose, but it worried her a little how unmanageable her impulses might become.

It wasn't until after a second round of wine, when Ashton glanced at his watch, that Harper realized the shadows had lengthened. Once again she noticed how in his entertaining company time seemed to fly.

"I'm going to shower and then take you out for a terrific dinner."

"Have you registered?"

"Not yet." He rose and went to where he'd stashed his *go* bag by a large planter.

"Why don't you use my shower then?"

He turned and looked at her, his eyes searching her face.

"We both know how tonight will end up. Why pay for two rooms?"

"That's rather presumptuous of you."

Despite the cooling air, her skin heated. She got to her feet, hoping to appear more confident than she felt. "I'm just being realistic."

Ashton wrapped his arm around her waist and kissed

her, his lips warm and sweetly persuasive. "Have I mentioned how much I appreciate your practical nature?"

Relaxing against his solid body, Harper gave in to a satisfied smile. "You can after dinner."

"How about a little before and a lot after?"

"That sounds quite acceptable."

A sliver of sunlight lanced through a narrow gap between the closed curtains, waking Ashton. From the angle, he surmised it was early afternoon. Jumping multiple time zones had always been a part of his life and from an early age he'd adapted to functioning on less sleep than the average person, but combine his long trip with an insatiable Harper Fontaine and it was amazing he hadn't slept until dusk.

He rolled onto his back and stretched his arm across the empty mattress. It was cool to the touch. She'd been gone some time. He couldn't blame her. From the heaviness of his limbs he'd probably been sleeping like the dead. Some fun traveling companion he was.

A tented piece of paper sat on her pillow. He read her note and grimaced. She'd gone to the embassy to see about her passport. That meant she wouldn't return anytime soon.

Ashton pushed upright and ran his fingers through his hair. He'd use the time to make some arrangements. Last night as they'd talked over dinner, it came to him that no matter how short her trip was, she really shouldn't leave South Africa without seeing a little of its natural beauty.

It took him an hour's worth of phone calls to get everything in place. When she arrived half an hour later, looking jubilant and proud of herself, he wrapped her in a warm embrace.

"How'd it go at the embassy?"

"They scolded me for not filing a police report, but I should have a temporary passport early afternoon tomorrow."

"That's good news. And I have some, as well." He drew her toward the hotel room door. "Let's get something to eat and I'll tell you all about it."

This time he took her to a restaurant with unassuming furnishings and mouthwatering aromas emanating from the long buffet. They filled their plates with authentic South African dishes and returned to their table. As they ate, Ashton did his best to explain all the things they'd chosen. It had been over ten years since he'd last visited South Africa and some of the more exotic fare wasn't familiar.

As he chewed a bite of crocodile, he wondered if maybe the producers of *The Culinary Wanderer* had been right about coming to Africa for this next season. He'd blocked out just how diverse and delicious the cuisine was.

"Tell me your news."

"I found your father."

"But I'd already done that."

"Yes, but I know where he is right now."

"How?"

"You forget how well-connected I am." He saluted himself with his wineglass before continuing. "A guy I knew knew another guy who has used your father to gather wildlife footage in the past and had his phone number. Turns out he's not far from here. I wasn't able to get us into the camp where he's staying, but there's a lodge about an hour away that a friend of mine owns."

Harper had stopped eating and was looking a little shell-shocked. "When?"

"Late tomorrow after you get your passport. I chartered a plane to take us into Nelspruit where we'll pick up a car and drive to Kruger National Park. It shouldn't take more than a couple hours. We can catch up with him before he heads out the following day."

What he really needed to do was get on a plane and go back to Las Vegas, but she couldn't bring herself to remind him that his first priority should be Batouri.

"I don't know what to say." Her voice wavered. "I'd prepared myself to leave without even meeting him. Thank you."

"No thanks required."

Her gaze locked on his face. "Well, I won't take it back."

Warmth spread from his chest through his whole body. He reached for her hand and smiled as she slipped her fingers through his. The couple sitting at the table beside them smiled. Ashton imagined the romantic picture he and Harper made. In the past while he'd never kept his personal life hidden, he hadn't indulged in public displays of affection, either. With Harper he wanted the whole world to notice that she belonged with him.

He'd even started thinking in terms of guiding her to all the places he'd visited and loved. Her ambivalence about her future was a perfect opening to present all the possibilities they could explore together.

By two the next day, Harper's temporary passport was ready to pick up. They headed straight for the airport where they were met by their flight's copilot and escorted onto a well-maintained eight-passenger plane.

As the sun was approaching the horizon almost three hours later, Ashton was braking to a halt alongside a Range Rover of similar age to their own at the Grant Tented Camp. Scattered along the river were six luxurious tents with king-size beds, en suite bathrooms and private terraces. Tucked among thick stands of mature trees and connected by a raised wooden walkway, each tent enjoyed a great deal of privacy.

"Why don't you have a look around while I get us checked in."

Harper opened her door and stepped out, a look of awe on her face. "This isn't exactly what I pictured when you told me we were going to spend a couple nights in a tent camp."

He patted the roof of the Range Rover. "It's not exactly a

camel." He gestured around them. "And it's not exactly the desert, although we are close to the end of the dry season. But at least there are tents. I hope you enjoy it."

She was touched that he'd gone to so much trouble to make her quest to South Africa such a marvelous experience. "Of course I will. How could I not?"

She accompanied him into the tented, open-air lounge and wandered toward the small pool nestled against the deck that overlooked the river. Built of local rock and surrounded by lush plants, it seemed like a completely natural addition to the landscape. Ashton went to see about their accommodations, and Harper wandered until she found the small dining room, also tented, with tables set with white cloth, china and crystal, mahogany chairs and candelabras awaiting the touch of a match.

Such elegance tucked into a wild, untamed landscape charmed Harper. Had Ashton guessed the place was so romantic? She was almost dizzy in anticipation of seeing where they would sleep as she went back to the lounge to await Ashton's return.

The dozen or so guests she noticed scattered about spoke in low voices as if not wanting to disturb the peacefulness of such a tranquil spot. Harper hadn't been here more than ten minutes and she was as relaxed as if she'd been hypnotized by a master.

"Ready?" Ashton's low voice rumbled behind her.

She turned and willingly accepted the hand he held out to her. "I love it here."

"I'm glad."

They walked down a path bordered by hanging lanterns that wound through the vegetation behind the cottages. When they reached the last one, Ashton unlocked the door and pushed it open. Harper took a few steps inside and hesitated in the dimness until Ashton located a light switch.

She gasped in delight.

The tent fabric was held up by a pole in the middle of

the large space, forming a fifteen-foot-high ceiling. There was a king-size bed with white bedding, a walnut wardrobe with glass doors and a chandelier suspended overhead, and a sitting area that held a couch flanked by two chairs and a fireplace. Golden light spilled from an assortment of lamps both attached to the olive-green walls and scattered on the various small tables. A bottle of champagne was cooling in a wine bucket on the colonial-style coffee table.

Kicking off her sandals, she curled her toes into the thick area rug that covered the tent's wood floor. After a slow spin to catalog their accommodations, she pulled Ashton toward her and dazzled him with a long, sexy kiss. "I've been in five-star hotels that weren't as nice as this," she murmured, leaning her cheek against his heaving chest. "It's the most perfect place I've ever seen."

"I'm glad you approve."

A knock sounded on the screen door. Ashton's arms tightened around her briefly before he went to answer. It was a porter. He deposited their luggage inside the door and showed them the canvas flaps they could roll down over the wall of screen windows if the night grew too chilly. When he left, Harper turned to Ashton with a predatory smile and backed him up to the couch.

He ripped his navy Henley shirt over his head while her fingers plucked his belt loose and released the button that held his waistband closed. As she unzipped his pants, she used her free hand to shove him onto the couch. He landed with a soft bounce, and she climbed onto his lap, her knees sinking into the pale gold cushions on either side of his thighs.

With her fingers tangled in his hair, she sought his mouth with hers in an open, wet kiss that left no doubt about her intentions. He gave her all the passion she demanded, groaning deep in his chest as she rocked against his swollen erection, the brief contact satisfying neither of them. Her fingers stroked over his skin in hot, frantic movements. The feel of him brushing against where she needed him the most shot a bolt of the purest frustration through her.

Her hunger communicated itself to Ashton. He stripped off her T-shirt and popped the clasp of her bra, tossing both aside with a ragged exhale. Then his fingers cupped her bare breasts, kneading evocatively until her nipples pebbled against his palms. The thrumming in her blood grew more urgent.

She sucked on his lip and let his breath fill her. A growl greeted her ears as she eased her hand between their bodies and lifted him free of his confining clothes. Smiling, she nipped his neck and at the same time grasped his erection firmly and stroked from base to tip before putting her mouth down over him. His hips bucked. He let out a startled curse, and she chuckled.

"Damn." He had no more words.

His head fell back against the cushion as she continued her slow, steady strokes. When she felt she had him completely beneath her spell, she slid his pants down his muscular thighs and tossed them aside. Naked, he lay half sprawled before her, a gorgeous powerful male who was all hers.

Quick as she could, Harper shimmied out of her pants and returned to her earlier position on the couch. Without opening his eyes, Ashton ran his hands over the curve of her hips and butt and down the back of her thighs. She gasped when his fingers dipped into the heat of her and stroked deep. Shuddering, she braced her hands against his shoulders and surrendered to the pleasure he gave.

He lifted her so he could fill his mouth with her breast. Harper wrapped her arms around his neck and gave a soft cry as he sucked hard. Pummeled by desire, she rode the waves of pleasure, each one a little stronger than the last.

"Ashton, I can't wait any longer."

He eased her down until she was poised over him. She

was so wet that he slid inside her an inch without meaning to. He intended to savor the anticipation, let the hunger build, but he underestimated Harper's passion. With a smile of sheer bliss she lowered herself onto his shaft, taking him deep. The perfection of her snug fit cradled him in a way that he'd never known before. Almost immediately, she began to move, her hips dancing in a seductive rhythm that slammed into his willpower and sent his lust into overdrive.

Digging his fingers into the soft flesh of her backside, he began to thrust in time with her movements. Her breasts swayed, hypnotically close to his face as she arched her back and surrendered to the pressure building inside her.

A soft keening escaped her parted lips as her skin flushed red. Ashton slowed his movements and deepened each thrust, watching her come apart. Her body bowed, muscles tensing as she climaxed. In this magical place he felt humbled by her vulnerability and her strength. She'd given him her all, held nothing back. She opened her eyes and locked gazes at him.

"That was incredible." She licked her lips and puffed out a breath, then murmured, "Come for me."

At her command, he renewed his drive toward orgasm. He pumped into her, distantly hearing her encouraging words. It was over faster than he would have liked. Her hands on his body, her inner muscles clenching to increase that amazing friction and her teeth on his earlobe sent him spiraling into one hell of a climax. He came for what seemed like forever. The pleasure of his release was almost painful in its intensity.

While the last spasms were fading he wrapped his arms around her slim form and buried his face in her neck. He drifted his fingertips over the bumps of her spine and waited for the hammering in his chest to slow. It hurt to breathe.

"You are amazing," he said.

"You're not so bad yourself." She kissed his neck. "How long do we have until dinner?"

"A couple hours, I think." Sucking in a lungful of her spicy scent, he closed his eyes and imprinted this moment forever on his soul. "But if I don't eat until morning, I'll be fine."

"Won't Franco wonder what happened to us?"

"Oh, he'll know. He got a look at you while you stood beside the pool. And he'll understand if my appetite this evening won't be sated by food."

She poked him in the ribs and made him grunt. "Is there a bathroom in this lovely tent or do we bathe in the river?"

"Only if you wish to meet a crocodile face-to-face." He pushed aside damp strands of her hair and drifted his lips across her cheek, tasting the saltiness of her sweat. "There's an outdoor shower."

"I'm not sure I'm ready for that much adventure."

"Then I won't recommend the fried caterpillars Franco might have on the menu."

Harper shuddered. "I'm sure you'll tell me they're delicious but I'm just going to have to take your word on that."

"There should be a bathroom behind there with a slipper tub." He pointed to the wall behind the wardrobe.

Ashton accepted the perfunctory kiss she dropped onto his lips and watched with appreciation as she padded naked to collect her bag and then head to the bathroom. The last of the afternoon sunlight played over her soft skin, highlighting the different textures of bone, sinew and muscle. She had an athletic body that she pushed hard. In fact, she had it all. Resilient body. Strong mind. Romantic heart. Idealist soul.

Was the last going to survive the meeting with her father? Ashton had a bad feeling about what was to come tomorrow. A man didn't dedicate himself completely to a lifestyle that involved being gone for several months or even a year at a time without understanding it would be difficult to maintain close relationships. A wife and family wouldn't be a top priority.

More than anything Ashton wanted to spare Harper any disappointment Greg LeDay might heap upon her, but she'd come too far to turn back now. The best he could do was be a shoulder to cry on.

Not wishing his solemn mood to put a damper on their evening, Ashton chose to use the shower outside before dressing for dinner. Slipping on a pair of khaki pants and a beige knit shirt, he toyed with his Saint Christopher medal while he waited for Harper to appear. His mother had given the medal to him on a trip back to South Africa. They were traveling by plane. He'd been six. They'd encountered a storm halfway and been tossed around. While lightning darted around the wings, his mother had removed the medal from her neck and fastened it around his, telling him that Saint Christopher, the patron saint of travelers, would protect him.

When he'd left home at fifteen, he'd taken the medal with him and had worn it every day since. Ashton wasn't sure why, whether it was superstition or faith. Whichever it was, it had kept him safe.

He'd spent more time thinking about his parents in the past week than he had in the past twenty years. Being on the front lines of Harper's identity struggle had opened doors he'd thought long locked and barred. What awaited him hadn't been as painful as he'd expected. Having someone he cared about accept him unconditionally had made the difference.

Now all he had to do was offer Harper the same unequivocal support, no matter how misguided he thought her decision to confront her biological father was. He would be there to comfort her if things went awry.

Ten

Harper's fingers bit into the passenger door armrest as the Range Rover neared the camp that Greg LeDay was using as the base for the safari he was leading. The sun was lowering toward the horizon, casting a warm glow over the landscape. This morning they'd overslept and arrived too late to catch LeDay before he took out his clients.

For the past six hours she and Ashton had been driving around Kruger National Park, hoping for a glimpse of wildlife. The roads they'd taken had been paved, and the truck had decent springs, but her stomach wasn't feeling particularly settled. She blamed it on nerves. Soon she would get to meet the man who might be her father.

How it went would determine the rest of her life. There was a great deal riding on the outcome of this meeting.

"Hang in there." Ashton's hand covered hers in a reassuring squeeze. As he'd been doing these past few days, he'd picked up on her mood and knew just what to say.

"I wish I knew how he was going to react."

"Looks like the trucks are back. You should know pretty quick."

Before Ashton threw the Range Rover into Park, she spotted Greg LeDay. He wore khaki-colored cotton pants, a short-sleeved beige shirt and a tan vest with six pockets. A wide-brimmed hat in some drab color between gray and brown shielded his face from the sun. But even with that protection, he looked older than the photo on his webpage. Years of living in the bush had etched lines around his eyes and given his skin a look of worn leather.

Heart thumping erratically, Harper approached the group he was addressing. She'd asked Ashton to hang back and give her time to introduce herself. He wasn't happy about her request, but he'd agreed.

LeDay's gaze found her lingering on the fringes of the crowd and dwelled on her for a moment before he returned his attention to his charges. "This was a great day. Tomorrow we'll go out and see if we can't find some cats."

The crowd dispersed, sidestepping Harper, who stood tongue-tied and uncertain. She'd practiced a hundred different openings and none of them seemed right.

"Can I help you?"

"My name is Harper Fontaine." She stumbled over her surname, wondering at the last second if he'd recognize it.

"Nice to meet you." No recognition flared in his eyes.

"I believe you met my mother several years ago. Penelope Fontaine?"

"Was she on one of my safaris?"

Things had just gotten awkward. "You met her in London. At an exhibition of your work."

"I'm sorry. The name just doesn't ring a bell."

"Perhaps a picture would help." Harper pulled out her smartphone and showed him an image of her mother, knowing Penelope would be quite put out that a lover—even one she'd had a brief affair with thirty years prior—could forget her so easily.

LeDay didn't look at the photo; he stared at Harper. "Why don't you tell me what this is about."

"You had an affair with my mother." Now that the words were out, Harper was struck with an awful thought. What if she'd flown halfway around the world to meet the wrong man?

"And if I did?"

"Then I'm your daughter."

Other than a brief tightening of his mouth, LeDay didn't react to her announcement. He regarded Harper in silence for a long time and she started to understand how he'd captured all those incredible moments in his photographs. He had the ability to stay very still for long periods of time. Meanwhile her heart rate was escalating and her breath had gone unsteady.

At last LeDay moved. He crossed his arms over his chest. "What do you want?"

"Nothing." Obviously that wasn't true, but Harper hadn't defined for herself what chasing him halfway around the globe was supposed to accomplish. "I only recently found out. I simply wanted to meet you." Her voice trailed off. His expression hadn't changed. He looked as welcoming as a rock pile.

"Where are you from?"

"I live in Las Vegas at the moment."

"That's a long way to come for nothing."

"I guess I was hoping that getting to know you would help answer some questions I have."

"Are you staying here?"

"No, we drove over from Grant's."

His eyebrows rose. "We?"

Harper turned in Ashton's direction and he left the car and headed toward them. "This is Ashton Croft," she said, catching his hand and drawing him to her side.

The two men shook hands, sizing each other up, like a

pair of competing alpha males. Harper sensed they came to some sort of understanding.

"I've seen your show. You've traveled extensively."

"Experiencing new cultures and cuisine is a passion of mine."

LeDay shifted his attention to Harper, but he continued to speak to Ashton. "It's hard having a career where you're gone all the time and maintaining a relationship."

"I know."

They were two of a kind, Harper realized. Adventure-loving men who didn't want to be tied down. She'd known that going in and didn't want to domesticate Ashton. He'd never be happy staying put for long. He would go wherever the wind blew next. Two questions remained. Would he ever invite her to travel with him? Would she say yes if he did?

LeDay gestured toward the cluster of buildings. "The restaurant has opened for dinner. If you'd like to eat before returning to your camp."

"Would you join us?" Harper asked, barely able to hope he'd agree.

He hesitated and then nodded. Still hand in hand, she and Ashton followed him toward the outdoor dining area. Trembling slightly in reaction to the stress of meeting the man she believed to be her father, Harper leaned her head against Ashton's shoulder.

"You okay?" he asked, his fingers brushing her cheek.

"Just a little overwhelmed."

"That's to be expected."

"I'm glad you're here," she whispered.

He squeezed her hand in response as they followed a waiter to their table. Once they sat down and Harper had a chance to survey the menu, she wasn't sure she'd be able to eat anything. She glanced to Ashton for help.

"Will you order something for me? I can't make up my mind."

"Of course."

The waiter brought beer for the men and a glass of red wine for Harper, wrote down their dinner selections and left.

Harper gathered a breath, surprised by how unsteady she felt, and plunged in. "I know you must be annoyed with me for showing up here like this, and I'm sorry that I didn't give you some warning. But I wasn't sure if you'd see me."

"I'm still not sure I'm the person you're looking for."

"Frankly, neither am I, but my mother said she met a wildlife photographer at an exhibition of his work in London and then she bought a book of your photographs for my grandmother." Hearing herself, Harper broke off. She caught Ashton's gaze and saw reassurance there. "It sounds a bit crazy when I say it out loud."

"Let me see that photo of your mother."

Harper pulled out her phone and handed it to him.

LeDay looked at the photo for a long time before speaking. "Penny."

Penny?

"A beautiful girl."

Harper clapped a hand over her mouth to smother a wild bubble of laughter. It was weird to hear someone call her formal, inflexible mother a girl. Even weirder to hear a man use a nickname in such fond tones. Penelope hated nicknames. And then Harper remembered.

"Her father used to call her that. He died when she was nine."

"We spent almost two weeks together. She was quite the mystery. Had never tasted beer before. Couldn't comprehend how to navigate the Tube. And yet she spoke effortlessly about art, history and politics."

"My mother is fascinated with current events and the background that shaped them. Sometimes I think she knows more about what's going on in Washington, D.C., than the journalists."

"Is she a politician?"

"It's just her hobby."

"What do you do in Las Vegas?"

"My family... I manage a hotel. Fontaine Ciel."

"Fontaine. That's your mother's last name?"

Harper nodded. "Did you know she was married when you were together?"

"She didn't say and wasn't wearing a ring, but I sensed that might have been the case." He paused and stared out over the valley. "What gives you the idea that I'm your father?"

"My father... I recently found out the man I believed was my father was out of town in Macao when I was conceived. My mother isn't the sort of woman to have an affair." Harper glimpsed LeDay's doubt and rushed on. "She was married to a man who cheated on her every chance he got, but I know you were the only time she broke her vows."

"You said you had questions you needed answers to. I don't know what I can tell you."

She hesitated. What had happened to the woman who had all the answers? She never entered a negotiation without a strategy for how to get what she wanted. Beneath the table, Ashton's hand closed over hers, offering support and strength.

"I don't know what to ask. I thought everything would be clear if I met you."

Harper had no choice but to fall silent. Meeting this man hadn't made her confusion disappear. If anything, she was even more lost. As Ashton drew the man out, asking questions about his life in Africa and the magnificent photos he'd taken over the years, Harper listened in fascination and growing dismay. What had she been thinking to come here and expect he would gladly welcome her into his life?

His passion for the country of his birth was all-consuming. The wildlife. The ecosystem. He devoted himself to sharing his experiences and by doing so hoped to increase people's appreciation for the animals and support for his conservation efforts.

A noble cause and one he was ideally suited for. Harper pushed food around on her plate, her appetite nonexistent, and listened with only half her attention until he said something that pulled her out of her thoughts.

"You have two sisters?"

It shocked Harper to think she had aunts she'd never known.

"And a half-dozen nieces and nephews."

"That sounds lovely."

She stopped herself from asking for further details. As much as she longed to hear about this family she'd never known, she remembered what it had been like when her grandfather had told her she had two half sisters. She'd initially viewed them as trespassers in her neatly planned life. This must be how LeDay was feeling. She'd descended into his life without warning and how he must resent her intrusion.

Never mind that Violet and Scarlett had gone from being strangers to family at their first meeting.

"Ashton," she finally said, deciding it was time to stop waiting for some sign that she and LeDay had a connection. The man had enjoyed a brief encounter with a beautiful woman. End of story. That the affair had produced a daughter wasn't going to touch his life. "We should be getting back to camp." She gave LeDay a bright smile. "Thank you for having dinner with us. I enjoyed meeting you."

"Nice meeting you, as well," he replied.

"Ready?" Ashton gave her a searching look.

"Absolutely."

There were no halfhearted offers to stay in touch. Just a simple wave goodbye and a sinking feeling in Harper's stomach that she should have stayed home.

Overwhelmed by futility, Harper trudged back to the car. Her boots felt as if they weighed ten pounds each.

She'd been uncharacteristically naive to expect that she and LeDay would have some sort of immediate connection.

"That didn't go as you'd hoped," Ashton said, stating the obvious. "I suspected he wasn't going to welcome you with open arms."

That he was right didn't make Harper feel any better about how meeting her father had gone. She was angry with herself for wondering if the reason Ross Fontaine hadn't been a loving father was because they weren't biologically related.

"A man like that isn't interested in family," Ashton continued, and Harper wasn't sure if he was trying to make her feel better or just pointing out the obvious. "He has his photography and the safaris. They're his passion. He doesn't seem to need anyone."

Weighed down by disappointment, Harper's temper got the better of her. "Like someone else I know?"

"Criticize me all you want, but I'm here for you."

As she threw herself into the Range Rover and waited for him to get behind the wheel, she wondered what he did feel about her. The way he'd made love to her left her emotions jumbled and her confidence rocky. Could a man kiss with such gut-wrenching passion and feel nothing more than uncomplicated lust? Ashton wasn't exactly the easiest person to read and she couldn't expect him to start spouting poetry.

Who was Ashton Croft? Selfish adventurer? Celebrity hound? Romantic lover?

Seeing that Ashton continued to stand where she'd left him, Harper got out of the vehicle and crossed to stand before him. Hands bracketing his hips, he was staring at the distant horizon, a scowl of absolute frustration drawing his brows together. If he'd noticed she'd reappeared, he gave no sign.

"How do I make you feel?" she asked softly, scarcely

able to believe she had the nerve to have her heart stomped all over for a second time that day.

"Dependable." He made the word sound like a curse.

It wasn't at all what she expected him to say, and the giddy relief that struck her made little sense. "You don't like being dependable?"

"I don't like living up to anyone's expectations but my own."

"I wish you could teach me your trick of living that way."

He cupped her face in his hands and kissed her hard. She met the bold thrust of his tongue with matching hunger and let herself be swept up in the rising passion of their embrace. This was easy. Surrendering to his mastery. Letting his insistent kisses and eager hands sweep away all her worries.

Breathing unevenly, Ashton placed his forehead against hers. They stayed that way for several minutes as the sun sank below the horizon and the night sounds swelled. At long last he stirred.

"We'd better get going. It's an hour back to camp."

She nodded and let him draw her back to the truck. As the ancient shocks struggled to absorb the road's dips and bumps, Harper reflected over the past few hours.

"You know it doesn't matter that LeDay disappointed me," she said, determination in her voice. "In fact, I'm glad. I can stop second-guessing who I am. I can go back to my life and my career and never look back again. It's better for everyone this way."

Ashton's features could have been carved from stone. "You're not going to tell your grandfather the truth about who your father really is."

"Why should I?"

"Because maybe if you know you'll never be Fontaine's CEO you might look around and see there's something you'd rather be doing."

"Being CEO is what I want."

"Then why did you hop on a plane at the last second and fly all this way to meet your father? You could have saved time and money by staying home and making the same decision."

He was right. "I became a businesswoman because that's what my father and grandfather did. It defined me. Then I find out I'm not a businessman's daughter, but the offspring of a brilliant photographer. I know I should take something away from that, but I don't know what."

"Who your parents are doesn't define you any more than your environment does. You are the sum of your choices."

"You're a fool to believe your parents didn't define you. You've spent your whole life rejecting their selflessness and believing you're out for no one but yourself."

"At least I admit that I'm selfish. It's my parents who are hypocrites. They were so obsessed with their mission to save every person they met that they couldn't take two minutes to recognize the person closest to them needed their help, as well."

Ashton made the accusation without heat or bitterness, as if he'd made peace with his parents' flaws long ago. By proclaiming his own selfishness he warned the world what they could expect from him.

Harper's heart constricted in sympathy.

"So you ran away and got caught up with a bad group."

"I was fifteen and my parents never tried to find me." And there was the crux of all his pain. Abandoned. Left to fend for himself. Terrorized for three years. Of course he'd developed a protective shell.

"How do you know that? The criminals you fell in with needed to stay way below the radar. They couldn't have been easy for the police to find."

"My parents never filed a report that I was missing. No one was looking for me." He took one hand off the wheel and pinched the bridge of his nose. "When I first joined the gang, Franco checked. Couldn't find anyone looking for a fifteen-year-old white kid. He told me to go home, offered to help me get out."

"Why didn't you?"

"Go home to what? I'd left because my parents didn't give a damn about me. Nothing had changed. They went on with their work. That's what was important to them."

The unfairness of it burned like acid in Harper's stomach. She knew loneliness. Hadn't she been an afterthought in her parents' lives? Ross Fontaine had taken to fatherhood with less enthusiasm than he'd put into being a husband. But her situation hadn't been unique among her classmates. Many of them had successful, driven parents who worked eighty hours a week and traveled extensively.

But she couldn't imagine any of them losing a child and going on as if nothing had happened.

"Do you ever wonder what happened to them?"

For a moment Ashton regretted sharing his past with Harper. She wasn't good at leaving things alone. That her journey to self-discovery hadn't ended well wasn't going to diminish her confidence for long. He was certain by the time they got on the plane tomorrow that she would have the plan for her future all documented with bullet points and colorful graphs.

"I don't wonder." Or he hadn't until she'd raised the question. Franco had offered to track down his parents on several occasions, but Ashton had turned him down each time. If they hadn't looked for him, why should he make sure they were doing all right? "They were committed to their ministry. Whatever happened to them, they will not regret the sacrifices they made."

And for that he couldn't condemn them. They'd chosen a path that gave them satisfaction. He'd done the same. He accepted that they wouldn't be proud that he'd made a great deal of money and become famous. Nothing about what he did fell into their value system.

"I envy your ability to put your past behind you like that."

He wasn't completely sure he'd attained the sort of peace of mind she believed he had. Returning to Africa had raised too many old ghosts. He might have left his life here behind fifteen years ago, but it had shaped him into the man he was. That wasn't something he could completely escape.

They were silent for the rest of the drive back to the camp, the barrier between them created by his stubbornness and her disappointment. Ashton was aware of a sharp ache in his chest. It was a sensation he hadn't felt in a long time. Harper's questions about his parents had unlocked the door on regret. Wanting to know if his mother and father were all right meant he cared. By caring about them he betrayed himself, and the choice he'd made to put his needs first because they never had.

Being selfish at thirty-five wasn't the same as acting out when he was fifteen. In the years since he'd left home, he'd learned to feel compassion for others the way his parents hoped he would. Even if he hated to admit it and seemed to live his life as if it wasn't the case, they'd had a powerful influence on him. Maybe it was past time he surrendered to it.

The walkways and outdoor areas of the tent camp were lit with softly glowing oil lamps by the time the Range Rover rolled into a parking space. Ashton glanced at Harper and saw her gaze was fixed on the fanciful beauty of the camp nestled among thousands of acres of wild African countryside.

He took her hand as they traversed the raised walkway to their tent. Although she neither looked his way, nor offered any inkling of her thoughts, she spread her fingers and welcomed the connection.

To Ashton's great surprise, she began stripping out of her clothes as soon as they entered the tent. Given her difficult day, he expected her to want distance and space. But as she came to stand naked before him and attacked his buttons with single-minded intensity, he decided not to question her motivation.

They tumbled into the big soft bed in a tangle of tongues and limbs. Ashton made love to her with demanding passion, offering no tenderness. She seemed to need none. Her movements beneath him were feverish. Fingernails bit into his skin. Teeth found sensitive areas and left marks.

At last he settled between her thighs, spreading them wide so she would feel a tiny spark of helplessness. Her head thrashed on the pillow as his size and weight pinned her to the mattress, but he hesitated before joining their bodies. He wanted her to recognize his strength, wanted to demonstrate what it felt like to be at his mercy. His power, his determination would protect her from anything, but she had to let him.

As she reached out to touch him, he grasped her wrists and pinned them above her head. She fought his hold, glaring at him the whole time. It wasn't until her lashes fell and her muscles relaxed that he shifted his hips forward and slid his entire length into her.

Almost immediately her body began to shake with release. He pushed deeper, and she began to cry out. He released her wrists and meshed their fingers, withdrawing so he could drive into her a second time. The strength and swiftness of her climax stirred an uproar in his own body and he followed her over the edge in a matter of seconds.

They lay panting in the aftermath. Ashton shifted to lie on his back and drew her snugly against his side. She fit against him with such blissful perfection that he closed his eyes to savor the moment. For a long time the only sound in the room was their breathing and the muted tick of the clock on the nightstand. Before long, however, as their bodies settled into normal rhythms, he realized the buzzing in his ears wasn't the pounding of his blood through his veins, but the nighttime chorus of cicadas and frogs.

"Hear that?" Ashton whispered.

Beside him, Harper held her breath and listened. From far off came the sound of someone trying to get a chainsaw going with short quick pulls of the start cord. "Yes."

"That's a leopard call."

A thrill of excitement raced down her arms. "It sounds close."

"Probably a half mile away."

Safe in Ashton's embrace, she snuggled her face into the crook of his neck and smiled. No one could be in better hands than her right now. Absently she traced the scar crisscrossing his abdomen. When she'd touched it before, he'd seemed to withdraw from her. Despite her curiosity, she hadn't asked him to expand on his days with the gang. This time, he might be more open to her inquisitiveness.

"More knife play?"

His answer took a long time coming. "Yes."

Hearing the tightness in his voice, she held silent. They were old scars. From a lifetime ago. Long healed, but permanent reminders of what…?

Beneath her hand his torso rose and fell on a deep breath. The force of it ruffled the hair scattered across her shoulder and tickled her skin.

"Chapman didn't hire weaklings." His voice sounded ghostly in the dim room. "Everyone had to prove they could fight. Even a fifteen-year-old boy whose only knife experience had come from slicing vegetables." His short laugh held no amusement. "He was a sadistic bastard. Once a week he pitted one of his crew against another in sporting matches. Some sport. Whoever drew first blood won. Three losses and you were out." Ashton threw his forearm over his eyes. "Throat slit, dumped in the jungle for the scavengers to feast on."

Harper couldn't imagine what this had been like for a teenager. "Why'd anyone stay working for him?"

"He made them rich. How do you think Franco could open this place?"

"Why did you stay?"

"I was proving a point to my parents."

"At the risk of your life?"

"Who doesn't think they're invincible at fifteen? I was big for my age. I'd gotten into a lot of trouble fighting the neighborhood kids. What I lacked was the technique to fight with a knife. Franco took me under his wing right away, but I didn't learn fast enough and lost two weeks in a row."

"So Chapman wanted you dead?"

Ashton shook his head. "I don't think so. The pairings were random. It was bad luck is all. My second bout I almost took the guy out. His reach was longer, but he was bulky and I was fast." He caught her fingers and drew them to a spot on his left side just below the ribs. "A wild swing caught me here. It took twenty stitches to sew me up."

"You're lucky you didn't die from infection."

"My luck turned when Chapman didn't pull my name for two months. I spent a lot of time with Franco after that. Never lost again."

The strain in Ashton's voice betrayed the toll that had taken on him. He might not have killed anyone directly, but he had to know that by saving himself he was signing someone else's death warrant. From missionaries' son to criminal to world-renowned chef.

"You can't forgive yourself."

"Should I?"

"What happened wasn't your fault. Chapman's game went on whether you were there or not. Those men made a choice just as you did. And you got out."

"But I never turned him in. When the opportunity presented itself I ran."

And pursued by guilt he'd been running ever since.

"Do you really want the cooking show in New York?"

she asked. "I can't help but feel you'll be turning your back on what made you successful."

"And what is that?"

"You thrived in situations that would terrify most people. Every episode contained an edge of danger that kept me glued to the TV."

"As much as I enjoyed doing the show, I'm looking to change my image. Go more mainstream." He rolled away from her and sat with his legs hanging off the side of the bed, his back toward her. "The network is going to push it hard. My popularity will skyrocket. It's what I've been working for."

"And all this time I thought it was the joy of food that motivated you." If he hoped to find legitimacy in success, how high did his star have to rise before he could be at peace with what he'd done to survive?

"More viewers means my culinary point of view reaches more people."

With their earlier rapport slipping away, Harper left the bed and slipped into a pair of leggings and a sweater. She handed Ashton his clothes and waited in silence while he put them on. Then she drew him out onto the deck and stood beside him near the rail, looking out over the river.

Surrounded by the night sounds it was easy to feel one with the bush. For several minutes they listened without speaking. One call was repeated several times, causing Harper to break the quiet.

"What is that?"

"A baboon sounding an alarm. Probably because of the leopard we heard earlier."

"You were right when you said we're the sum of our experiences. The things that you've been through had a profound effect on the man you've become. If you'd stayed with your parents you wouldn't resent them any less, but your strength of will might never have been tested and you might never have discovered the heights of your courage."

Harper paused to let her words sink in. "But I'm right, too. You inherited their generosity of spirit and desire to help those less fortunate. How many thousands of people have been helped through the foundations you promote?"

"I'm nothing more than a spokesman. I don't tangibly help anyone."

"What about Dae? You saved him from going to prison for something he didn't do and taught him how to cook. Someday he'll run one of your restaurants. How far is that from where he started?"

Ashton bumped his shoulder against her, forcing her to step to the side in order to maintain her balance. His fingers snaked around her waist and pulled her against his side. "This was supposed to be your journey to self-discovery, not mine."

"Ironic, isn't it?" Suddenly she felt a weight lift off her shoulders. "You know what? I don't care about the man who impregnated my mother. He doesn't want to be anyone's father. Why should I take that personally and cry about it?" She gripped the railing hard. "I need to worry about me."

"So, you've decided what to do when you get home?"

"I'm going to do what everyone expects of me and keep my mother's secret. I came to South Africa in search of who I am. Now I know. I'm Harper Fontaine. Future CEO of Fontaine Hotels and Resorts. I've worked my whole life to run the company. I don't know who else to be."

"And that's all you need to make you happy in the long run?"

"It's been my goal since I was five, so, achieving it will bring me great satisfaction."

"I hope you're right."

Eleven

Harper woke to an empty bed and a heavy heart. From the light outside she gathered it was a few hours after sunrise. She sat up and glanced around the tent, but from the room's low energy level, she could tell Ashton wasn't nearby. Flopping back onto the pillows, she closed her eyes and willed herself to stop feeling so vulnerable and out of sorts. It wasn't as if she hadn't endured setbacks in her life before. Failure was a necessary part of growing. But one emotional blow after the other had weakened her ability to recover swiftly.

Still, she did recover and an hour after waking, she was showered, dressed, packed and on her way to breakfast. That Ashton still hadn't made an appearance didn't bother her. He and Franco hadn't spent much time together since they'd arrived. Ashton was probably with his old friend. Or maybe taking a walk along the river. There were several trails around the camp.

Harper was accustomed to spending a great deal of time

alone. Being surrounded by staff wasn't like sharing a bathroom and a bed with someone. The intimacy she'd enjoyed with Ashton these past few days had been pretty all-consuming. She wouldn't blame him if he needed a break.

And she needed to get used to being without him. She had no illusions about their relationship. It was an interlude, similar to what her mother had enjoyed with LeDay. A break from routine. A wonderful adventure. Harper recognized that she couldn't hold on to Ashton. His career took him all over the world. Hers kept her grounded in one place.

Except he was on the verge of doing a show that would keep him in New York for an extended period of time. They could be together if she accepted the job of Fontaine's CEO. Unfortunately, he'd made her question if that was the best choice for her.

As she was finishing up her breakfast, Ashton found her. She didn't ask him where he'd been and he didn't volunteer the information. His mouth was set in a grim line as he sat down across from her and poured himself a cup of coffee from the silver pot on the table.

"Are you okay?" she asked, unable to shake the feeling that their magical trip was over.

"Fine."

"Have you eaten?"

"I had a little something earlier." He sipped his coffee and stared past her. "I saw that you're packed."

"I wasn't sure what time the plane would be returning us to Johannesburg so I thought I'd be ready to leave."

"I told them noon."

Harper checked her watch. If they left in the next fifteen minutes, they would be right on time. She reached out her hand and placed it over his, calling his attention back to her.

"Thank you for coming to Africa to help me. I've really appreciated having you here."

"No need to thank me."

His short replies were starting to irritate her. She needed

to get to the bottom of it before they started the long journey home.

"So this is it then?"

"What do you mean?"

"The end of the road for us. It was a fun week, but now it's over."

"Is that what you want?"

"No." Her throat tightened, but she'd taken too many emotional risks to let fear dominate her now. "I want for us to be together." For the first time she understood Violet's decision to put her marriage before her ambition. "It would be nice to hear that you feel the same."

"Are you sure you really know what you want? A few days ago you couldn't wait to run off to Africa to meet your biological father. What would you have done if he'd wanted to have a relationship with you? Would you have stayed in Africa? Made a new life here?"

"I don't know. I hadn't thought that far ahead."

"Then last night you decided you weren't going to let anything stand in the way of your becoming CEO. You claim you want to know who you are, yet instead of pushing forward and doing what you want for a change, you fall back into old patterns."

Was Ashton asking her to quit the hotel business and spend the rest of her life…doing what?

She still didn't know her true passion. Damn him for being right. And for being the practical one for a change. She needed the old Ashton, the impulsive one, to sweep her into adventure. She was sick of planning her future. She'd come to Africa because she wanted to be bold and daring. But obviously that wasn't her nature. It had taken less than a week before she regressed to comfortable patterns. What she needed to do was take a risk and keep taking them until she felt completely free.

"I love you," she said, captured by a yearning that grew

stronger the more time she spent with Ashton. "I can't imagine my days without you. I'm ready to give up everything and be with you. Just tell me you want me."

Ashton closed his eyes. "I don't want you to give up anything."

"Then what do you want?"

"Don't use me as an excuse to avoid admitting who you are and what you truly want."

"I already told you, I want you."

"Because it's easier to explain to your grandfather that you want to be with the man you love than disappoint him by revealing you're not actually his granddaughter?"

"That's unfair."

"Is it?"

She couldn't answer him truthfully so she traded him question for question. "What about you?"

"What about me?"

"Would you give up the new show and go back to doing *The Culinary Wanderer* again?" It wasn't fair to ask him to set aside his goals. So what if she didn't think he would be happy. They'd been lovers for little more than a week. Who was she to judge what was best for him?

"I already quit and I don't want to go backward."

Her heart sank. "Then you're going to do whatever it takes to make the new network want you."

"That's the plan."

"Then I guess we're destined to disappoint each other, aren't we?"

"I don't believe that's true."

Was his faith so much greater than hers? She wished she could do as he asked and start over, but she'd tried that when she'd come here to meet her father and look how poorly that had turned out.

Her phone chimed. A text message from Violet had come in.

Grandfather has had a mild stroke. He's going to be okay. Wants to see you.

A sound in her ears swelled as if every insect in the entire bush had chosen that moment to sing. Disoriented, she shook her head to clear it. Ashton grabbed her hand and said something that she couldn't catch, but she guessed he was asking her what was wrong.

With her voice unable to escape her tight throat, she showed him the message.

"You should call and let them know we're coming."

"We?" she whispered. "You're coming with me?"

"Whatever you need from me. I'll be there."

Ashton didn't expect to be heading to Las Vegas mere hours after completing the transatlantic flight from Johannesburg. While the charter jet he'd hired cruised over the heartland of the U.S., he fidgeted with his phone, restlessly checking for updated emails and new texts, knowing if anything came in he would be notified with a tone.

That he'd left Harper behind wasn't sitting well, but she'd insisted. An hour before they'd touched down at JFK, she'd sat straighter in her seat and gathered herself. He'd gotten used to taking care of her these past few days. Discovered he liked that she needed him. But with their return to the States, her independent nature had reasserted itself.

And she'd been right when she'd insisted the restaurant was days away from opening. He needed to be at Batouri overseeing the last-minute details. He should have been there these past five days instead of traveling to South Africa. But Dae's updates had reassured him that the staff was working well together. Chef Cole had proven to be a good choice. He was organized and a good leader. Harper had been right about that.

When his phone chimed, it wasn't the person he'd been hoping to hear from. Vince had sent him a terse text.

Call me.

The brevity of the message could only mean the network had decided to take the cooking show in a different direction and not use him. Ashton had been expecting this ever since he'd walked out and was surprised how little he cared. In the past few days he'd had a lot of time to think. Conversations with Harper regarding her ambivalence toward her career left him debating what he wanted to do versus what he thought he should do.

"Vince," he said as soon as his manager picked up. "What's the word?"

"Lifestyle Network wants you."

Ashton didn't feel the rush of satisfaction he'd expected. "That's not the impression I got from the last meeting."

"They took another look at the tape and saw what I see. You're a star. Soon every household in America is going to know it. They sent me a contract. I've looked it over and everything we asked for is in there."

"I need a few days to think about it."

Silence greeted his response. Ashton imagined his manager was pretty pissed at him right now.

"I've put in a lot of time on this deal," Vince said. "They're giving us everything we want except for the whole *Culinary Wanderer* thing, but you've already quit, so that's a nonfactor."

"Frankly, Vince, when I left the conference room last Monday I was under the impression they wanted to go a different way."

"But they don't."

With nothing standing in the way of signing onto the new show, Ashton had to tackle the doubts raised by his conversation with Harper. "I'm questioning whether staying put in New York is the best thing for me."

Vince's disappointment came through the phone seconds before he spoke. "I wish I'd known that three days ago."

"Why don't we table this for a while. I need to focus on the restaurant right now. Send me the contract and give me a few days to sort through everything."

"Sending it now. Don't leave them hanging too long about this."

"I won't."

When he received Vince's email a minute later, Ashton scanned through the contract with only half his mind on the words. He could really use Harper's input on this. But the last thing he wanted to do right now was disturb her. She had enough on her plate.

Maybe he could talk to her when she returned to Las Vegas for the opening. If she returned. It occurred to him with her grandfather out of commission, it was a perfect time for her to step into the role she'd been training for. She'd decided to follow her head not her heart. He wasn't convinced that was the right decision. And now he had the project that would allow him to be with her. If only it all felt right.

Harper entered her grandfather's New York apartment and was immediately embraced by Violet. The warmth of her greeting was a delightful contrast to the indifference Harper had felt from LeDay. Biology didn't make a family. Caring did.

"How's grandfather?"

"Much better," Violet said, reaching her hand back to her husband for support. JT Stone put his arm around his wife and hugged gently. "He's already protesting the doctor's order to rest."

"Did the stroke cause any permanent damage?"

"From what Dr. Amhull told us, it was a very minor stroke so there shouldn't be any lasting effects. It was a warning that worse could come. He prescribed medication and wants Grandfather to slow down."

"Can I go see him?"

"Of course. And afterward, I think we should talk. Scarlett and Logan went for a walk. They should be back shortly. The six of us should sit down before dinner. There are some things we think you should know."

"The six of us?"

"Isn't Ashton in New York with you?"

"The restaurant is opening in a few days." Harper's stomach turned over as she pictured his tight expression when she told him to go on to Las Vegas without her. "He needs to be in Vegas for that."

Violet stared at her a long moment before nodding. "Of course."

Further explanations would have to wait until later. The most important thing was seeing her grandfather. "Is Grandfather in his room?"

"No. He's in his study. We confiscated his cell phone to keep him from working, but nothing can convince him to stay in bed."

Harper shook her head as she walked down the hallway toward her grandfather's favorite room in the apartment. His work ethic had inspired her own. They were so much alike. Maybe that's why it had been such a shock to discover they weren't related.

She found him sitting in one of a pair of leather chairs that flanked the fireplace. He had a stack of magazines on the table beside him eight inches high. Pausing in the doorway, she scrutinized him. His color was better than she'd expected, and he was scowling at the article he was perusing. Temper was a positive sign.

"Grandfather?"

He looked up from his reading and waved her over. "This is nothing but a fluff piece." The page he showed her had a photo of Gil Kurtz, one of her grandfather's classmates from Harvard and a Connecticut state senator. They'd been rivals since they were twenty years old, and

Henry rarely had anything but disparaging things to say about Gil's political career.

"How are you feeling?"

"I'm fine. Your sisters won't let me leave the house. Don't they understand I have a business to run?"

"They're just concerned about you."

"Violet said you were in Africa. Feel like telling me what you were doing there?"

"I just needed a little break."

Her grandfather grunted. "Bob tried not to give me the impression you'd cracked up, but wasn't able to mask his concern."

"Cracked up?" She laughed a little at the thought. "Why?"

"Because you dropped the entire running of the hotel on him and disappeared."

"I took a vacation."

"When was the last time you took any substantial time off?"

"I don't know." She thought back over the past few years and couldn't recall a span of more than three days where she'd been unavailable to her staff. "Which should make it even more evident I needed a vacation."

"The last time was when I told you about Scarlett and Violet."

"Was it?" She had a vague recollection of going to her grandmother's Hamptons house for a few days.

"You were gone almost two weeks."

"Sorry, but I don't recall that. And I'm sure I had the time coming."

"You did. And much more besides. You're more like me than your father." He was staring out the window at the park across the street. "But occasionally you remind me that you're also your mother's daughter. She's an emotional woman who has difficulty handling any sort of turmoil in her life. Which leads me to wonder what is going on with you. Is that Croft fellow causing problems?"

"Ashton?" Harper was more than a little stunned by her grandfather's analysis of her. He never appeared to notice anything that didn't pertain to his business, but now she wondered if he saw everything and just kept it to himself. "No, he and I have reached a place where we're working well together."

"How about your personal relationship? Everything okay there, too?"

"Ah…" What was he asking? "We work well together."

Her grandfather blew out an impatient breath. "I'm not dense. I know you went to Africa with him."

"Technically, I went to Africa and he followed."

"Why?"

What was her grandfather asking? "Why did he follow me to Africa?"

"Yes. And why did you go in the first place?"

"I wanted an adventure, and Ashton thought I was acting recklessly by traveling alone. Turns out he was a little right."

"More than a little. You were mugged on the train. Had your passport stolen."

How was she going to keep the truth about her biological father hidden when her grandfather was so good at keeping tabs on her?

"Who told you?"

"When I heard you were traveling to South Africa I called a buddy of mine in the State Department and had him keep an eye out for you."

Harper was both touched and annoyed. Didn't anyone think she could take care of herself? "Is that why I was able to get a temporary passport so fast?"

"Partially." Her grandfather's eyes narrowed. "Anything else you'd like to tell me about your time in South Africa?"

"Ashton took me on safari where I was fortunate enough

to see three of the big five. Elephants, cape buffalo and lions." She paused. "Although one night we heard a leopard, as well."

"And that's all?"

"It's a beautiful country. We should consider putting a hotel there."

"Maybe when you become CEO of Fontaine Hotels and Resorts you can do that."

The walls of her grandfather's study seemed to close in. Ashton's warning sounded in her mind. She wanted to silence it, but couldn't. He was right. Becoming CEO under false pretenses would never make her happy. "When that happens, I'll definitely look into it."

They chatted about her impression of Africa until Scarlett appeared in the doorway.

"Can I tear you away for a bit?" she asked Harper, giving Henry a fond smile.

"Sure."

"Are you staying for dinner?" he asked. Despite his protests that he was feeling fine, he looked pale.

"Of course," Harper said. She kissed his cheek and followed Scarlett from the room.

"He looks better than I expected."

Scarlett linked her arm through Harper's and guided her toward the den. "You probably thought he'd be in bed."

"I did."

Inside the comfortable room, Violet, JT and Logan awaited her. Feeling very much like a fifth wheel, Harper sat down in a chair and waited until everyone else had been seated before she broke the silence.

"You all look so grim. What's going on?"

"How did your trip to South Africa turn out?" Violet began.

Sensing they were warming up to the difficult topic, Harper decided to play along. "It's a lovely country. I told Grandfather we should look at putting a hotel there."

"And what did he think of that?" Again Violet.

Scarlett rolled her eyes. "Stop dancing around what we want to know." Her tone was exasperated. "Did you meet your father?"

"Yes."

"How did it go?"

"No worse than you'd imagine. Being confronted by a twenty-nine-year-old daughter he never knew caught him by surprise."

"Was he courteous?" Violet asked.

"He invited Ashton and me to dinner."

Scarlet piped up. "Where is Ashton?"

"On his way to Las Vegas. The restaurant is opening in two days. I have no idea if it will go well."

"I'm sure it will be fine," Violet said. She glanced at Scarlett and then at JT, who nodded. "Logan was able to figure out who blackmailed your mother."

In the craziness of the past week, Harper had forgotten that little tidbit. "Who?"

JT spoke. "My father. He needed money for a top-notch defense lawyer."

"How did he come by the files?"

"It's my fault," Scarlett said. "If I hadn't brought them home, I wouldn't have lost them."

"You didn't lose them," Logan reminded her, a muscle popping in his jaw. "Someone broke into your suite, knocked you out and stole them."

"Technically," she countered, "I opened the door thinking it was you."

Violet stepped in. "I blame Tiberius. If he hadn't poked his nose in where it didn't belong there wouldn't have been any files in the first place."

"It was my father who went after the information my uncle had gathered on him and hired the guy who hurt Scarlett. He's the one who blackmailed Harper's mother," JT chimed in.

Harper shut her eyes and let the voices wash over her. She floated in darkness until someone touched her arm and brought her back.

Logan knelt before her, his dark brown gaze confident and reassuring. "We retrieved both the information and the money."

She sandwiched Logan's hand between hers, leaned forward and kissed him on the cheek. "Thank you."

"No need to thank me."

She gazed from him to her sisters and finally to JT. This was her family, she realized. Not some stranger in South Africa who wanted nothing to do with her.

"I'm so lucky to have all of you," she told them.

"So, now that your secret is safe," Violet began, "are you going to take the CEO job?"

This was important to all of them, she realized. It meant that Scarlett could continue pursuing her acting and Violet could stay in Las Vegas with JT. They expected her to do the job she was trained for.

"Whenever grandfather wants me to take over, I will."

Twelve

Two hours before the restaurant opened for the first time, Batouri's kitchen was operating more smoothly than Ashton had a right to expect. After being gone during the week before their grand opening, he'd half feared he was coming back to absolute chaos. Thanks to Cole, this was not the case.

Without any major crisis to deal with, Ashton had too much space to think. He tried to focus on the food, but bits of conversations with Harper kept intruding. He second-guessed how he'd handled things when she'd told him she loved him. Had it been a mistake to question her sudden change of heart? He'd been on the verge of sweeping her into his arms and agreeing to make all her dreams come true when the message about her grandfather's stroke had come to her phone.

Carlo approached him. "Harper is here. She's asking for you."

Ashton followed Carlo from the kitchen, struggling to

keep from rushing past the restaurant manager in his excitement to see Harper. She stood by the hostess stand, tense and uncertain in a white dress that draped her slim form in wispy layers of lace. Her hair had been pulled back from her face and loosely clipped in a romantic style. The impact of her appearance stole his breath.

He crossed to her and gave her a kiss on the cheek. From her surprised expression, she'd obviously expected something different.

"I haven't heard from you," he said, making no attempt to hide his unhappiness. "How is your grandfather?"

"The stroke was minor and he's stubborn. Keeping him at home for the past few days has been a challenge when he already feels strong enough to go back to work."

"I'm glad to hear it. What did you tell him about South Africa?"

"That it's a lovely country."

Her answer disappointed him. "That's not what I meant. Did you tell your grandfather the truth about LeDay and your mother?"

"He's just had a stroke. It would be cruel of me to burden him with such a shock." She looked down at her hands. "And thanks to Logan, my mother's blackmailer has been stopped."

"You don't ever plan to tell him." He saw the truth in the way she was avoiding meeting his gaze. "You don't think he'll love you anymore if you're not his flesh and blood."

"Five years ago he went looking for Violet and Scarlett simply because they were his granddaughters. He loves them. What's to say he wouldn't stop loving me when he finds out we're not related?"

"You don't really believe he would do that."

"I don't." Her voice didn't rise above a whisper. "But I can't take the chance. And they're all counting on me."

"Who?"

"My sisters. JT and Logan. They're happy. Their lives

are perfect exactly as they are. If I don't take over as CEO either Scarlett or Violet will have to and neither one wants the job."

In a flash, he saw the future unfold. She would take the CEO job and live in New York City. He would move on to bigger and better things with the new show. The network was ready to get behind him and push him into superstar range. There would be more shows, more opportunities to expand his career. Most important, he and Harper could start a life together.

But was it the life either of them wanted?

"Can we talk about this later?" he asked.

"There's no need. I think you've told me everything you need to."

"Not by a long shot." But he could tell she wasn't listening. "Meet me after the restaurant closes tonight."

"I have too much hotel business to take care of before I fly back to New York tomorrow afternoon. I promised Grandfather that I would step into his shoes for a while. It was the only way I could get him to rest and not worry about the company."

"When will you be back?"

She shook her head. "I'm not sure. It might be a permanent move."

Ashton's heart sank. She would spend the rest of her life living a lie. He wanted what was best for her and this wasn't it. But there was a bright spot to her decision.

"Then I guess we'll be seeing a lot of each other. Lifestyle Network agreed to most of my demands."

"Not all?" Her half-smile was wry.

Ashton gave a one-shoulder shrug. "Those I didn't get aren't all that important."

"You're going to do the show?"

"It means we can be together in New York."

She avoided his gaze. "You know you'll hate being stuck in the city."

"I don't know that." Her lack of enthusiasm for their up-coming proximity left him questioning whether she wanted him in her life. "New York has a lot to offer in terms of culinary experiences."

"Did you agree to cut your hair?"

"It's part of the rebranding."

"Don't do it." She reached up and swept her fingers into his hair, tugging his head down. "Promise me."

"I can't. They're right. In order to appeal to a wider au-dience, I need a different look."

"You won't look like you."

"It's just hair."

"It's not. It's part of your image. You are the daring ad-venturer. The guy that charges into dangerous locales and bravely eats whatever exotic fare the population consid-ers typical."

"I can't be that guy the rest of my life."

"Why not?" She stared at him intently. "That's the man I fell in love with."

Her words hit him square in the breastbone. Living with-out her these past few days had been hell. He couldn't face a future apart from her. But telling her that he loved her wasn't going to make the problem between them go away.

"Because I realized after meeting your father that the traveling I do keeps me apart from people I care about. I don't want to be alone the rest of my life. I want you."

"You can have me and all the adventures you could ever want."

"A part-time relationship with you isn't what I had in mind."

Then her lips were on his and his arms went around her slim body. The kiss was frantic and tasted like goodbye. Ashton's heart was a bowling ball in his chest by the time her lips peeled away from his.

"We're good together," she said.

"The key word is *together*." He cupped her face and

kissed her lightly on the lips. "Tell your grandfather the truth and we can go adventuring together."

"I thought you wanted the Lifestyle Network show."

"I'd rather have you happy and whole."

"Then you understand how I feel about you." She grabbed his hands and pulled them away from her face. "Do the show. It's what's right for your career."

"In the past few weeks I've decided I'm more than my career. What about you?"

She wouldn't meet his gaze. "It's getting late. Shouldn't you be in the kitchen inspiring your staff?"

Ashton eyed her set expression and wondered what would change her mind about permanently taking over as Fontaine's CEO. With a tight nod, he gently kissed her forehead.

"I'll see you in the restaurant later."

"Good luck tonight." With those parting words, she was gone.

With the opening of Batouri mere hours away, Ashton should have been completely consumed by what was happening in his kitchen. He wasn't. Reporters and food critics as well as celebrities and other assorted VIPs would be among the evening's guests. They were expecting a masterful culinary performance tonight. He needed to score big.

That would be easier if Harper hadn't shown up in his kitchen this afternoon. Telling himself that keeping her feet to the fire was for her own good didn't unravel the knot of misery in his chest.

It wasn't until service was well underway that he had a chance to step out of the kitchen and circulate through the room. Before he'd ever stepped in front of a camera, he'd been a successful executive chef and restaurant owner. He recognized a satisfied crowd when he saw one.

As he schmoozed those who could make or break Batouri with a single negative review, he tried not to make it obvious that there was only one table in the room that held his complete attention. And it was the last one he visited.

"Absolutely fabulous," Scarlett said, the first to speak up. The vivacious, stunningly beautiful brunette glanced away from Ashton and nudged Harper's arm. "My sister's idea to have you open a restaurant in her hotel was nothing short of brilliant."

"Wonderful," Violet agreed, a note of concern beneath her upbeat tone. "I think you two make a terrific team."

"That's nice of you to say, but I'm sure your sister would disagree." Ashton had no idea why he felt like baiting Harper on a night where he needed her complete support. Maybe it was the fact that she was looking through him rather than at him. "In fact, the success of the restaurant should be placed squarely at her feet. She smoothed every feather I ruffled in the construction process and probably had to stop the chefs I interviewed from adding arsenic to the food they served me."

Scarlett laughed in delight.

Violet looked appalled.

Harper glared at him. "It's your food everyone loves."

"You were the one who inspired me." The room fell away as he captured her gaze and held it. For a second he saw past her unhappiness and glimpsed the passion she'd demonstrated in Africa. His heart stopped. Maybe there was hope for them yet. He shifted his attention to her sisters and offered them a smile. "Thank you for coming to support Harper."

Not waiting for a response, he moved off.

Behind him, Scarlett spoke up. "Do whatever you have to, but don't let that man get away."

Harper said something in reply, but it was too faint for him to catch. Still, he was feeling better than he had in days as he reentered the kitchen. Nothing was a done deal. Persuading her to be true to herself would be a lot easier if he showed her how to do it.

* * *

At a little after six in the afternoon the day after Batouri's successful opening, Harper entered her grandfather's apartment and found him in the living room, his cell phone in one hand, a glass of Scotch in the other. This is how she imagined he'd go out: running his business while relaxing at home. Working was as much a part of him as breathing. Is this what she wanted for her own life?

Spotting her, he gestured her in. "Sam, I have to go. My granddaughter just arrived, and we're going to have dinner together."

As soon as he hung up, she came forward and hugged him. What she'd come here tonight to say wasn't going to be easy. The urge to blurt it out nearly overpowered her, but that sort of shock couldn't be good for a man who'd suffered a stroke a little over a week ago.

"I heard the opening of your restaurant was a resounding success," he said as they sat down at the large dining table.

Only two places had been set. To Harper's relief, they weren't at opposite ends of the twenty-foot table. Her mother would be horrified if she discovered that Harper had shouted the tale of her infidelity from one end of the dining room to the other.

"It went very well. The reviews had nothing but wonderful things to say. You were right to suggest I approach Ashton."

"I had a feeling you two would be good for each other."

Unexpectedly, Harper flashed back to their two nights at the tent camp and felt heat rise in her cheeks. "How come?"

"He's a hugely talented chef and the adventurous sort. You've always been an armchair globetrotter too focused on the future to have fun in the present. I thought he might benefit from your knack of focusing on the finish line and you might give him an opportunity to surprise you."

Her grandfather had nailed what had happened between her and Ashton. "How did you know?"

"You don't think I'm this successful in business because I'm a lucky devil, do you?" Her grandfather offered her a crafty smile. "Did you ever wonder why, after you worked so hard to learn the business, I still went ahead and created the contest between you, Violet and Scarlett?"

Since her grandfather was laying his cards on the table, she might as well play hers, as well. "Because you weren't sure I was the best choice?"

"I knew you were the best choice. I just wasn't sure you knew it."

Harper had little trouble following his logic. "I never really believed I was going to be CEO. I wanted it very badly and worked hard to make sure you approved of me."

"I more than approve of you, Harper. I want you to succeed me."

She had to state the obvious even though it exemplified the lack of confidence her grandfather had just criticized about her. "I'm the only one left standing as far as the contest goes. Scarlett has returned to acting part-time. Violet intends to stay in Las Vegas with JT."

"And what do you want?"

His question surprised her. "To be CEO." But she was not as confident as she'd been a month earlier.

"Do you?"

A better lead-in to what she had to confess wasn't going to present itself. "A week ago you asked me what I was doing in Africa." She gathered a steadying breath and tried to calm her agitated pulse. "The truth is, I went looking for my father. My biological father."

Now that she'd made her shocking revelation, she braced herself for her grandfather's outrage. When he continued to eat his steak without reacting, she frowned.

"Why aren't you asking me anything?"

"Did you find him?"

"Yes."

"And?"

"What do you mean, and?"

"I'm assuming you didn't travel that far without some idea of what you expected out of the encounter." He gave her more credit than was due. "Was he pleased to meet you?"

"Not really." She set her fork down and picked up her wine. "He had no idea I existed."

"Your mother never contacted him." A statement. Not a question.

"Why are you so calm about this?" And then it dawned on her. "You knew about my mother's affair and the fact that I wasn't your biological granddaughter."

"Yes."

"You never told me."

"Why should I? You're my granddaughter."

"Not by blood."

"I love you, Harper. You have been my joy for every single one of your twenty-nine years."

"I had no idea you'd feel that way. You went to such lengths to find Violet and Scarlett and make them part of the business. I worried that you didn't have faith in my ability to succeed you."

"Scarlett was unhappy in Los Angeles and her career was sinking fast. What she lacked in business experience she made up for in intelligence and people savvy. Violet deserved better than Tiberius Stone's small-time casino. She knows Las Vegas inside and out and it shows. Her hotel is the most profitable of all three." He grinned. "You're surprised."

She really wasn't. "Would you have picked her if she hadn't taken herself out of the running?"

"No. She might know Vegas, but you understand our entire organization. I need you as CEO." When she didn't immediately speak, he regarded her solemnly. "Unless you decide you no longer want the job."

"In truth, I'm not sure. One of the reasons I went to Africa was because when I learned I wasn't a Fontaine, a part of me was relieved."

"I can understand that. You've put a lot of pressure on yourself."

"Then I met Greg LeDay and I didn't have an aha moment. He wasn't happy to meet me. He had no interest in starting any sort of relationship. There are a whole bunch of people I'm related to that I'll never get to know."

"Give him some time to think about it. He may change his mind."

"I doubt it."

The epiphany she'd expected upon meeting her biological father hadn't happened. She'd been no closer to discovering who she really was. What had changed her was the time she'd spent with Ashton, seeing Africa through his eyes. Those days had given her a deeper understanding of what made her happy.

"All my life I've wanted you to be proud of me," she said. "It's why I worked so hard."

"And I am."

"From things my father said, I knew you wanted a Fontaine to be at the company's helm."

"Now you're thinking that if you take over one won't be?"

"Actually, I'm not sure I'm as ready to be in charge as I thought."

"You want to stay in Las Vegas?"

"No, I think Violet should take over Fontaine Ciel." That would surprise her very capable sister. "I'd like to spend several years consulting in the area of development."

"Let me guess. Traveling the world to determine the best places to expand?"

"Something like that."

"And you think I should stay on in the meantime?"

She smiled. "You and I both know you're not ready to

stop working. Maybe you could try slowing down a bit. Let your staff handle more."

"You're asking a lot of an old man."

"I trust that you have it in you."

At eight in the morning, Batouri's kitchen was a peaceful place. Surrounded by stainless steel, alone with his thoughts, Ashton did the one thing that had saved him for the past twenty years. He cooked.

The five days since Batouri had opened had been hectic ones. He'd been tweaking the menu daily, using the specials to experiment, finding the perfect blend of traditional and unexpected.

He hadn't seen Harper since the night Batouri had opened. She'd gone to New York City and hadn't yet returned. Each day Ashton grew less confident that he'd made the right decision. He'd turned down the Lifestyle Network show, deciding if he wanted to prove how committed he was to her happiness, he'd have to demonstrate it in a big way. Now his hopes that she'd choose traveling with him over living a lie were dwindling.

Despite how things turned out, he was glad he hadn't pressed her to join him. She'd wanted him to. But for him to make such an important decision for her would have brought her back full circle to her current dilemma. What was it Harper wanted for herself?

Almost as if thinking about her had compelled her to find him, Harper stepped into his kitchen.

"I thought I might find you here."

"Where else?"

She looked exactly the same as the first day he'd met her. The unflappable executive with her hair smoothed back into an elegant French roll. Expensive but understated jewelry adorned her slim neck and delicate earlobes. The hem of her designer power suit sliced her kneecaps in half and showed off her toned calves.

Polished. Professional. Perfect.

His heart sank. She'd obviously chosen her future.

"I spoke to my grandfather about taking over as CEO."

"You didn't tell him the truth then."

"No, I told him." She shook her head in bemusement. "Turns out he's known all along."

"Smart man, your grandfather. But I don't know why that surprises me. Look how you turned out."

"I hope you're going to be okay with my decision."

"I will get behind whatever you choose."

"You're going to take the job with the network then?" She looked disappointed.

He decided not to leave her feeling that way for long. "No. I turned them down."

She brightened. "You're going back to *The Culinary Wanderer*. That's wonderful."

"No to that, as well."

"What? I don't understand."

"You were determined to take the CEO job, which meant I couldn't continue traveling with *The Culinary Wanderer* if we were going to be together. But at the same time, you were right about going with the network. They wanted me to become something I'm not."

"What are you planning to do?"

"You suggested that I work on a cookbook. With the success of Batouri, I was considering opening another restaurant in New York, and Vince is exploring opportunities with other networks."

"You've given up your television career to be with me?" She regarded him in confusion. "But why?"

"I realized something these past few days. I no longer feel invincible. Before I met you I had nothing to lose. That's changed."

Harper stood perfectly still while her mind raced. "I don't understand. You had a great deal at stake. *The Culinary Wanderer*. A brand-new cooking show. Batouri."

"Television shows and restaurants will come and go. The only irreplaceable thing in my life is you."

"Me?"

"The woman I love."

"You love me?"

"Hadn't you guessed?"

"When it comes to love, I'm not too well versed on the ins and outs of romance."

"You haven't had much experience." He took her left hand and placed her palm over his heart. "Neither have I, so you'll have to excuse me if I've bungled a few things."

"I suppose it's something we could work on together."

"I'm glad you said that." He reached into his pocket. "Because I want to spend the rest of my life working on it with you. Marry me?"

His eyes were the most brilliant blue she'd ever seen as he gazed down at her. Harper's mouth went dry. Spinning through her head were all the reasons why it would never work between them.

Like her father, he wouldn't be able to stay put for long. He had restaurants in several countries. Traveling for business meant temptation would lurk around every corner. Would they end up like her parents?

Their opposite approaches to decisions—he would be rash and impulsive while she would study and plan—guaranteed they would fight endlessly.

Her tendency to work too much would cause him to get impatient and bored.

"Yes." Not one of her doubts could stand up against the love she felt for this man. "Oh, yes. Scarlett told me make sure you didn't get away and I wholeheartedly agree."

As metal touched her skin, she looked down. Ashton was sliding a large ring onto the third finger of her left hand. Two circles of diamonds, one white, one pale pink, surrounded a pink diamond. It was a unique take on a traditional halo style engagement ring and absolutely...

"Beautiful," she murmured.

"Not nearly as beautiful as the woman who will wear it." He kissed her long and deep. "I love you."

"I hope you still feel that way when I tell you that I'm not taking over as Fontaine's CEO."

"Why not?"

"Because I'm going to travel to cities that don't have a Fontaine hotel to scout locations. Good thing you're going to be free to travel with me because I don't much like the idea of leaving you home alone."

"Interesting that you should bring this up. Remember that idea you had for a travel series on romantic hotel destinations?"

"Did I say romantic?" she teased. "Actually, romantic is probably a great idea."

"Phillips Consolidated Networks agrees with you and they want us to come up with a list of hotels. The more exotic, the better."

"I thought you were done with them."

"Not completely."

"Were you going to run off and do another travel show without me?"

"Of course not. You don't seriously expect that the producers are going to send me to romantic destinations by myself, do you?"

Dismay made her frown. "If you think I'm going to stand by and let you travel to the world's most beautiful places with some gorgeous, charming female version of you…"

His mouth settled over hers, effectively cutting off her tirade. She wasn't quite done fighting and it took several minutes of kissing for her to become sufficiently limp in his arms. When he thought he could get a word in edgewise, he relinquished her lips.

"My darling, I know you perfectly well. There is no gorgeous, charming female version of me as my costar.

There is only the gorgeous, charming female better half of me that is you."

"Me? Starring on television?"

"What do you say?"

"I'm absolutely terrified." She paused, and a broad grin bloomed. "So yes."

"This is going to be a fantastic project." Sweeping her off her feet, he carried her out into the restaurant's dining area. "You. Me. Exotic destinations. Think of all the amazing places we'll make love."

She laughed. "It all sounds very exciting."

And perfect. Because with Ashton's help she'd discovered her passion and the best version of herself. Most days she might still work too hard, but Ashton would be there to remind her to play, as well. Together they would accomplish anything they set their minds to.

When it looked like Ashton intended to carry her out of the restaurant, Harper stopped him. "Wait, I need my *go* bag."

Ashton paused near the door. "You have a *go* bag?"

"Over there by our booth." She pointed over his shoulder.

"Why do you have it with you?"

"So I'll be ready to leave at a moment's notice."

With a disgusted noise, Ashton exited the restaurant, leaving her bag behind.

"Wait, I need that."

"Not right now." With long strides, he carried her past the casino floor and straight to the elevators. "Because the only place you're going is your suite. With me."

And that sounded just right because the biggest adventure of her life was being with the man she loved.

* * * * *

MILLS & BOON®
By Request

RELIVE THE ROMANCE WITH THE BEST OF THE BEST

A sneak peek at next month's titles...

In stores from 15th December 2016:

- **Unbiddable Attraction** – Kathie DeNosky, Robyn Grady & Barbara Dunlop

In stores from 29th December 2016:

- **Matched to Mr Right** – Kat Cantrell

- **His Ultimate Demand** – Maya Blake, Dani Collins & Victoria Parker

- **Capturing Her Heart** – Leanne Banks & Cindy Kirk

Just can't wait?
Buy our books online a month before they hit the shops!
www.millsandboon.co.uk

Also available as eBooks.

Give a 12 month subscription to a friend today!

Call Customer Services
0844 844 1358[*]

or visit
millsandboon.co.uk/subscription

MILLS & BOON®

Why shop at millsandboon.co.uk?

Each year, thousands of romance readers find their perfect read at millsandboon.co.uk. That's because we're passionate about bringing you the very best romantic fiction. Here are some of the advantages of shopping at www.millsandboon.co.uk:

✳ **Get new books first**—you'll be able to buy your favourite books one month before they hit the shops

✳ **Get exclusive discounts**—you'll also be able to buy our specially created monthly collections, with up to 50% off the RRP

✳ **Find your favourite authors**—latest news, interviews and new releases for all your favourite authors and series on our website, plus ideas for what to try next

✳ **Join in**—once you've bought your favourite books, don't forget to register with us to rate, review and join in the discussions

Visit **www.millsandboon.co.uk**
for all this and more today!